THE NOVELS AND TALES OF
HENRY JAMES

New York Edition

VOLUME XVIII

DAISY MILLER

PANDORA

THE PATAGONIA

AND OTHER TALES

HENRY JAMES

NEW YORK

CHARLES SCRIBNER'S SONS

PREFACE

IT was in Rome during the autumn of 1877; a friend then living there but settled now in a South less weighted with appeals and memories happened to mention — which she might perfectly not have done — some simple and uninformed American lady of the previous winter, whose young daughter, a child of nature and of freedom, accompanying her from hotel to hotel, had " picked up " by the wayside, with the best conscience in the world, a good-looking Roman, of vague identity, astonished at his luck, yet (so far as might be, by the pair) all innocently, all serenely exhibited and introduced: this at least till the occurrence of some small social check, some interrupting incident, of no great gravity or dignity, and which I forget. I had never heard, save on this showing, of the amiable but not otherwise eminent ladies, who weren't in fact named, I think, and whose case had merely served to point a familiar moral; and it must have been just their want of salience that left a margin for the small pencil-mark inveterately signifying, in such connexions, " Dramatise, dramatise! " The result of my recognising a few months later the sense of my pencil-mark was the short chronicle of " Daisy Miller," which I indited in London the following spring and then addressed, with no conditions attached, as I remember, to the editor of a magazine that had its seat of publication at Philadelphia and had lately appeared to appreciate my contributions. That gentleman however (an historian of some repute) promptly returned me my missive, and with an absence of comment that struck me at the time as rather grim — as, given the circumstances, requiring indeed some explanation: till a friend to whom I appealed for light, giving him the thing to read, declared it could only have passed with the Philadelphian critic for "an outrage on American girlhood."

v

PREFACE

This was verily a light, and of bewildering intensity; though I was presently to read into the matter a further helpful inference. To the fault of being outrageous this little composition added that of being essentially and pre-eminently a *nouvelle;* a signal example in fact of that type, foredoomed at the best, in more cases than not, to editorial disfavour. If accordingly I was afterwards to be cradled, almost blissfully, in the conception that " Daisy " at least, among my productions, might approach "success," such success for example, on her eventual appearance, as the state of being promptly pirated in Boston — a sweet tribute I had n't yet received and was never again to know — the irony of things yet claimed its rights, I could n't but long continue to feel, in the circumstance that quite a special reprobation had waited on the first appearance in the world of the ultimately most prosperous child of my invention. So doubly discredited, at all events, this bantling met indulgence, with no great delay, in the eyes of my admirable friend the late Leslie Stephen and was published in two numbers of *The Cornhill Magazine* (1878).

It qualified itself in that publication and afterwards as " a Study "; for reasons which I confess I fail to recapture unless they may have taken account simply of a certain flatness in my poor little heroine's literal denomination. Flatness indeed, one must have felt, was the very sum of her story; so that perhaps after all the attached epithet was meant but as a deprecation, addressed to the reader, of any great critical hope of stirring scenes. It provided for mere concentration, and on an object scant and superficially vulgar — from which, however, a sufficiently brooding tenderness might eventually extract a shy incongruous charm. I suppress at all events here the appended qualification — in view of the simple truth, which ought from the first to have been apparent to me, that my little exhibition is made to no degree whatever in critical but, quite inordinately and extravagantly, in poetical terms. It comes back to me that I was at a certain hour long afterwards to have reflected, in this connexion, on the characteristic free play of the whirligig of time. It was in Italy again — in Venice and in the prized society of an interesting friend, now dead, with whom I happened to wait, on the Grand Canal, at the animated water-steps of one of the hotels. The considerable little terrace there was so disposed as to make a salient stage for certain demonstrations on the part of two young girls, children *they*, if ever, of nature and of freedom, whose use of those resources, in the general public eye, and under our own as we sat in the gondola, drew from the lips of a second companion, sociably afloat with us, the remark that there before us, with no sign absent, were a couple of attesting Daisy Millers. Then it was that, in my charming hostess's prompt protest, the whirligig, as I have called it, at once betrayed itself. " How can you liken *those* creatures to a figure of which the only fault is touchingly to have transmuted so sorry a type and to have, by a poetic artifice, not only led our judgement of it astray, but made *any* judgement quite impossible ? " With which this gentle lady and admirable critic turned on the author himself. " You *know* you quite falsified, by the turn you gave it, the thing you had begun with having in mind, the thing you had had, to satiety, the chance of ' observing ' : your pretty perversion of it, or your unprincipled mystification of our sense of it, does it really too much honour — in spite of which, none the less, as anything charming or touching always to that extent justifies itself, we after a fashion forgive and understand you. But why *waste* your romance ? There are cases, too many, in which you 've done it again ; in which, provoked by a spirit of observation at first no doubt sufficiently sincere, and with the measured and felt truth fairly twitching your sleeve, you have yielded to your incurable prejudice in favour of grace — to whatever it is in you that makes so inordinately for form and prettiness and pathos ; not to say sometimes for misplaced drolling. Is it that you 've after all too much imagination ? Those awful young women capering at the hotel-door, *they* are the real little Daisy Millers that were ; whereas yours in the tale is such a one, more 's the pity, as — for pitch of the ingenuous, for quality of the

PREFACE

artless — could n't possibly have been at all." My answer to all which bristled of course with more professions than I can or need report here; the chief of them inevitably to the effect that my supposedly typical little figure was of course pure poetry, and had never been anything else; since this is what helpful imagination, in however slight a dose, ever directly makes for. As for the original grossness of readers, I dare say I added, that was another matter — but one which at any rate had then quite ceased to signify.

A good deal of the same element has doubtless sneaked into " Pandora," which I also reprint here for congruity's sake, and even while the circumstances attending the birth of this anecdote, given to the light in a New York news-paper (1884), pretty well lose themselves for me in the mists of time. I do nevertheless connect " Pandora " with one of the scantest of memoranda, twenty words jotted down in New York during a few weeks spent there a year or two before. I had put a question to a friend about a young lady present at a certain pleasure-party, but present in rather perceptibly unsupported and unguaranteed fash-ion, as without other connexions, without more operative " backers," than a proposer possibly half-hearted and a slightly sceptical seconder; and had been answered to the effect that she was an interesting representative of a new social and local variety, the " self-made," or at least self-making, girl, whose sign was that — given some measur-ably amusing appeal in her to more or less ironic curiosity or to a certain complacency of patronage — she was any-where made welcome enough if she only came, like one of the dismembered charges of Little Bo-Peep, leaving her " tail " behind her. Docked of all natural appendages and having enjoyed, as was supposed, no natural advantages; with the " line drawn," that is, at her father and her mother, her sisters and her brothers, at everything that was hers, and with the presumption crushing as against these adjuncts, she was yet held free to prove her case and sail her boat her-self; even quite quaintly or quite touchingly free, as might be — working out thus on her own lines her social salvation.

PREFACE

This was but five-and-twenty years ago; yet what to-day most strikes me in the connexion, and quite with surprise, is that at a period so recent there should have been novelty for me in a situation so little formed by more contemporary lights to startle or waylay. The evolution of varieties moves fast; the Pandora Days can no longer, I fear, pass for quaint or fresh or for exclusively native to any one tract of Anglo-Saxon soil. Little Bo-Peep's charges may, as manners have developed, leave their tails behind them for the season, but quite knowing what they have done with them and where they shall find them again — as is proved for the most part by the promptest disavowal of any apparent ground for ruefulness. To "dramatise" the hint thus gathered was of course, rudimentarily, to see the self-made girl apply her very first independent measure to the renovation of her house, founding its fortunes, introducing her parents, placing her brothers, marrying her sisters (this care on her own behalf being — a high note of superiority — quite secondary), in fine floating the heavy mass on the flood she had learned to breast. Something of that sort must have proposed itself to me at that time as the latent "drama" of the case; very little of which, however, I am obliged to recognise, was to struggle to the surface. What is more to the point is the moral I at present find myself drawing from the fact that, then turning over my American impressions, those proceeding from a brief but profusely peopled stay in New York, I should have fished up that none so very precious particle as one of the pearls of the collection. Such a circumstance comes back, for me, to that fact of my insuperably restricted experience and my various missing American clues — or rather at least to my felt lack of the most important of them all — on which the current of these remarks has already led me to dilate. There had been indubitably and multitudinously, for me, in my native city, the world "down-town" — since how otherwise should the sense of "going" down, the sense of hovering at the narrow gates and skirting the so violently overscored outer face of the monstrous labyrinth

ix

that stretches from Canal Street to the Battery, have taken on, to me, the intensity of a worrying, a tormenting impression ? Yet it was an impression any attempt at the active cultivation of which, one had been almost violently admonished, could but find one in the last degree unprepared and uneducated. It was essentially New York, and New York was, for force and accent, nothing else worth speaking of ; but without the special lights it remained impenetrable and inconceivable ; so that one but mooned about superficially, circumferentially, taking in, through the pores of whatever wistfulness, no good material at all. I had had to retire, accordingly, with my yearning presumptions all unverified — presumptions, I mean, as to the privilege of the imaginative initiation, as to the hived stuff of drama, at the service there of the literary adventurer really informed enough and bold enough ; and with my one drop of comfort the observation already made — that at least I descried, for my own early humiliation and exposure, no semblance of such a competitor slipping in at any door or perched, for raking the scene, on any coign of vantage. *That* invidious attestation of my own appointed and incurable deafness to the major key I frankly surmise I could scarce have borne. For there it was ; not only that the major key was " down-town " but that down-town was, all itself, the major key — absolutely, exclusively ; with the inevitable consequence that if the minor was " up-town," and (by a parity of reasoning) up-town the minor, so the field was meagre and the inspiration thin for any unfortunate practically banished from the true pasture. Such an unfortunate, even at the time I speak of, had still to confess to the memory of a not inconsiderably earlier season when, seated for several months at the very moderate altitude of Twenty-Fifth Street, he felt himself day by day alone in that scale of the balance ; alone, I mean, with the music-masters and French pastry-cooks, the ladies and children — immensely present and immensely numerous these, but testifying with a collective voice to the extraordinary absence (save as pieced together through a thousand gaps and indirectnesses) of a serious male interest. One had

heard and seen novels and plays appraised as lacking, detri-
mentally, a serious female; but the higher walks in that
community might at the period I speak of have formed a
picture bright and animated, no doubt, but marked with the
very opposite defect.

Here it was accordingly that loomed into view more than
ever the anomaly, in various ways dissimulated to a first impression, rendering one of the biggest and loudest of cities one
of the very least of Capitals; together with the immediate reminder, on the scene, that an adequate muster of Capital characteristics would have remedied half my complaint. To have
lived in capitals, even in some of the smaller, was to be sure of
that and to know why — and all the more was this a consequence of having happened to live in some of the greater.
Neither scale of the balance, in these, had ever struck one as
so monstrously heaped-up at the expense of the other; there
had been manners and customs enough, so to speak, there had
been features and functions, elements, appearances, social
material, enough to go round. The question was to have
appeared, however, and the question was to remain, this
interrogated mystery of what American town-life had left to
entertain the observer withal when nineteen twentieths of it,
or in other words the huge organised mystery of the consummately, the supremely applied money-passion, were inexor-
ably closed to him. My own practical answer figures here
perforce in the terms, and in them only, of such propositions
as are constituted by the four or five longest tales comprised
in this series. What it came to was that up-town would do
for me simply what up-town could — and seemed in a manner apologetically conscious that this might n't be described
as much. The kind of appeal to interest embodied in these
portrayals and in several of their like companions was the
measure of the whole minor exhibition, which affected me
as virtually saying: " Yes I 'm either *that* — that range and
order of things, or I 'm nothing at all; therefore make the
most of me ! " Whether " Daisy Miller," " Pandora," " The
Patagonia," " Miss Gunton," " Julia Bride " and *tutti
quanti* do in fact conform to any such admonition would be

PREFACE

an issue by itself and which must n't overcome my shyness;
all the more that the point of interest is really but this —
that I was on the basis of the loved *nouvelle* form, with the
best will in the world and the best conscience, almost helplessly cornered. To ride the *nouvelle* down-town, to prance
and curvet and caracole with it there — that would have been
the true ecstasy. But a single "spill" — such as I so easily
might have had in Wall Street or wherever — would have
forbidden me, for very shame, in the eyes of the expert and
the knowing, ever to mount again; so that in short it was n't
to be risked on any terms.

There were meanwhile the alternatives of course — that
I might renounce the *nouvelle*, or else might abjure that
"American life" the characteristic towniness of which was
lighted for me, even though so imperfectly, by New York
and Boston — by those centres only. Such extremities,
however, I simply could n't afford — artistically, sentiment-
ally, financially, or by any other sacrifice — to face; and
if the fact nevertheless remains that an adjustment, under
both the heads in question, had eventually to take place,
every inch of my doubtless meagre ground was yet first
contested, every turn and twist of my scant material eco-
nomically used. Add to this that if the other constituents
of the volume, the intermediate ones, serve to specify what
I was then thrown back on, I need n't perhaps even at the
worst have found within my limits a thinness of interest
to resent: seeing that still after years the common appeal
remained sharp enough to flower again into such a composition as "Julia Bride" (which independently of its appearance here has seen the light but in *Harper's Magazine*,
1908). As I wind up with this companion-study to " Daisy
Miller " the considerable assortment of my shorter tales I
seem to see it symbolise my sense of my having waited
with something of a subtle patience, my having still hoped
as against hope that the so ebbing and obliging seasons
would somehow strike for me some small flash of what I
have called the major light — would suffer, I mean, to glim-
mer out, through however odd a crevice or however vouch-

PREFACE

safed a contact, just enough of a wandering air from the down-town penetralia as might embolden, as might inform, as might, straining a point, even conceivably inspire (always where the *nouvelle*, and the *nouvelle* only, should be concerned); all to the advantage of my extension of view and my variation of theme. A whole passage of intellectual history, if the term be not too pompous, occupies in fact, to my present sense, the waiting, the so fondly speculative interval: in which I seem to see myself rather a high and dry, yet irrepressibly hopeful artistic Micawber, cocking an ostensibly confident hat and practising an almost passionate system of " bluff " ; insisting, in fine, that something (out of the just-named penetralia) *would* turn up if only the right imaginative hanging-about on the chance, if only the true intelligent attention, were piously persisted in.

I forget exactly what Micawber, who had hung about so on the chance, I forget exactly what *he*, at the climax of his exquisite consciousness, found himself in fact reverting to ; but I feel that my analogy loses nothing from the circumstance that so recently as on the publication of " Fordham Castle " (1904), for which I refer my reader to Volume XVI, the miracle, after all, alas, had n't happened, the stray emitted gleam had n't fallen across my page, the particular supreme " something " those who live by their wits finally and *most* yearningly look for had n't, in fine, turned up. What better proof of this than that, with the call of the " four or five thousand words" of " Fordham Castle " for instance to meet, or even with the easier allowance of space for its successor to rise to, I was but to feel myself fumble again in the old limp pocket of the minor exhibition, was but to know myself reduced to finger once more, not a little ruefully, a chord perhaps now at last too warped and rusty for complicated music at short order ? I trace myself, for that matter, in " Fordham Castle " positively " squirming " with the ingenuity of my effort to create for my scrap of an up-town subject — *such* a scrap as I at the same time felt myself admonished to keep it down to ! — a certain larger connexion ; I may also add that of the exceedingly close complexus of

PREFACE

intentions represented by the packed density of those few pages it would take some ampler glance here to give an account. My point is that my pair of little up-town identities, the respectively typical objects of parental and conjugal interest, the more or less mitigated, more or less embellished or disfigured, intensified or modernised Daisy Millers, Pandora Days, Julia Brides, Miss Guntons or whatever, of the anxious pair, the ignored husband and relegated mother, brought together in the Swiss lakeside pension — my point is that these irrepressible agents yet betrayed the conscious need of tricking-out their time-honoured case. To this we owe it that the elder couple bear the brunt of immediate appearance and are charged with the function of adorning at least the foreground of the general scene; they convey, by implication, the moral of the tale, at least its æsthetic one, if there be such a thing : they fairly hint, and from the very centre of the familiar field, at positive deprecation (should an imagined critic care not to neglect such a shade) of too unbroken an eternity of mere international young ladies. It's as if the international young ladies, felt by me as once more, as verily once too much, my appointed thematic doom, had inspired me with the fond thought of attacking them at an angle and from a quarter by which the peril and discredit of their rash inveteracy might be a bit conjured away.

These in fact are the saving sanities of the dramatic poet's always rather mad undertaking — the rigour of his artistic need to cultivate almost at any price variety of appearance and experiment, to dissimulate likenesses, samenesses, stalenesses, by the infinite play of a form pretending to a life of its own. There are not so many quite distinct things in his field, I think, as there are sides by which the main masses may be approached ; and he is after all but a nimble besieger or nocturnal sneaking adventurer who perpetually plans, watches, circles for penetrable places. I offer " Fordham Castle," positively for a rare little memento of that truth : once I had to be, for the light wind of it in my sails, " internationally " American, what amount of truth my subject

xiv

PREFACE

might n't aspire to was urgently enough indicated — which condition straightway placed it in the time-honoured category; but the range of choice as to treatment, by which I mean as to my pressing the clear liquor of amusement and refreshment from the golden apple of composition, *that* blest freedom, with its infinite power of renewal, was still my resource, and I felt myself invoke it not in vain. There was always the difficulty — I have in the course of these so numerous preliminary observations repeatedly referred to it, but the point is so interesting that it can scarce be made too often — that the simplest truth about a human entity, a situation, a relation, an aspect of life, however small, on behalf of which the claim to charmed attention is made, strains ever, under one's hand, more intensely, *most* intensely, to justify that claim; strains ever, as it were, toward the uttermost end or aim of one's meaning or of its own numerous connexions; struggles at each step, and in defiance of one's raised admonitory finger, fully and completely to express itself. Any real art of representation is, I make out, a controlled and guarded acceptance, in fact a perfect economic mastery, of that conflict : the general sense of the expansive, the explosive principle in one's material thoroughly noted, adroitly allowed to flush and colour and animate the disputed value, but with its other appetites and treacheries, its characteristic space-hunger and space-cunning, kept down. The fair flower of this artful compromise is to my sense the secret of " foreshortening " — the particular economic device for which one must have a name and which has in its single blessedness and its determined pitch, I think, a higher price than twenty other clustered loosenesses; and just because full-fed statement, just because the picture of as many of the conditions as possible made and kept proportionate, just because the surface iridescent, even in the short piece, by what is beneath it and what throbs and gleams through, are things all conducive to the only compactness that has a charm, to the only spareness that has a force, to the only simplicity that has a grace — those, in each order, that produce the *rich* effect.

PREFACE

Let me say, however, that such reflexions had never helped to close my eyes, at any moment, to all that had come and gone, over the rest of the field, in the fictive world of adventure more complacently so called — the American world, I particularly mean, that might have put me so completely out of countenance by having drawn its inspiration, that of thousands of celebrated works, neither from up-town nor from down-town nor from my lady's chamber, but from the vast wild garden of " unconventional" life in no matter what part of our country. I grant in fact that this demonstration of how consummately my own meagrely-conceived sources were to be dispensed with by the more initiated minds would but for a single circumstance, grasped at in recovery of self-respect, have thrown me back in absolute dejection on the poverty of my own categories. Why had n't so quickened a vision of the great neglected native quarry *at large* more troubled my dreams, instead of leaving my imagination on the whole so resigned? Well, with many reasons I could count over, there was one that all exhaustively covered the ground and all completely answered the question: the reflexion, namely, that the common sign of the productions " unconventionally" prompted (and this positively without exception) was nothing less than the birthmark of Dialect, general or special — dialect with the literary rein loose on its agitated back and with its shambling power of traction, not to say, more analytically, of *at*traction, trusted for all such a magic might be worth. Distinctly that was the odd case: the key to the *whole* of the treasure of romance independently garnered was the riot of the vulgar tongue. One might state it more freely still and the truth would be as evident: the plural number, the vulgar tongues, each with its intensest note, but pointed the moral more luridly. Grand generalised continental riot or particular pedantic, particular discriminated and " sectional " and self-conscious riot — to feel the thick breath, to catch the ugly snarl, of all or of either, was to be reminded afresh of the only conditions that guard the grace, the only origins that save the honour, or even the life, of dialect: those preced-

xvi

ent to the invasion, to the sophistication, of schools and unconscious of the smartness of echoes and the taint of slang. The thousands of celebrated productions raised their monument but to the bastard vernacular of communities disinherited of the felt difference between the speech of the soil and the speech of the newspaper, and capable thereby, accordingly, of taking slang for simplicity, the composite for the quaint and the vulgar for the natural. These were unutterable depths, and, as they yawned about one, *what* appreciable coherent sound did they seem most to give out? Well, to my ear surely, at the worst, none that determined even a tardy compunction. The monument was there, if one would, but was one to regret one's own failure to have contributed a stone? Perish, and all ignobly, the thought!

Each of the other pieces of which this volume is composed would have its small history; but they have above all in common that they mark my escape from the predicament, as I have called it, just glanced at; my at least partial way out of the dilemma formed by the respective discouragements of down-town, of up-town and of the great dialectic tracts. Various up-town figures flit, I allow, across these pages; but they too, as it were, have for the time dodged the dilemma; I meet them, I exhibit them, in an air of different and, I think, more numerous alternatives. Such is the case with the young American subject in " Flickerbridge " (1902) and with the old American subject, as my signally mature heroine may here be pronounced, in " The Beldonald Holbein " (1901). In these two cases the idea is but a stray spark of the old " international " flame; of course, however, it was quite internationally that I from far back sought my salvation. Let such matters as those I have named represent accordingly so many renewed, and perhaps at moments even rather desperate, clutches of that useful torch. We may put it in this way that the scale of variety had, by the facts of one's situation, been rather oddly predetermined — with Europe so constantly in requisition as the more salient American stage or more effective *repoussoir*, and yet with any particular *action* on this great lighted and decorated scene depending for half its sense on one of my outland importations. Comparatively few those of my productions in which I appear to have felt, and with confidence, that source of credit freely negligible; "The Princess Casamassima," "The Tragic Muse," "The Spoils of Poynton," "The Other House," "What Maisie Knew," "The Sacred Fount," practically, among the more or less sustained things, exhausting the list — in which moreover I have set down two compositions not included in the present series. Against these longer and shorter novels stand many of the other category; though when it comes to the array of mere brevities — as in "The Marriages" (1891) and four of its companions here — the balance is more evenly struck : a proof, doubtless, that confidence in what he may call the *indirect* initiation, in the comparatively hampered saturation, may even after long years often fail an earnest worker in these fields. Conclusive that, in turn, as to the innumerable parts of the huge machine, a thing of a myriad parts, about which the intending painter of even a few aspects of the life of a great old complex society must either be right or be ridiculous. He has to be, for authority — and on all such ground authority is everything — but continuously and confidently right; to which end, in many a case, if he happens to be but a civil alien, he had best be simply born again — I mean born differently.

Only then, as he's quite liable to say to himself, what would perhaps become, under the dead collective weight of those knowledges that he may, as the case stands for him, often separately miss, what would become of the free intensity of the perceptions which serve him in their stead, in which he never hesitates to rejoice, and to which, in a hundred connexions, he just impudently trusts ? The question is too beguiling, alas, now to be gone into; though the mere putting of it fairly *describes* the racked consciousness of the unfortunate who has incurred the dread heritage of easy comparisons. His wealth, in this possession, is supposed to be his freedom of choice, but there are too many days when he asks himself if the artist may n't easily

PREFACE

know an excess of that freedom. Those of the smaller sort never use all the freedom they have — which is the sign, exactly, by which we know them; but those of the greater have never had too much immediately to use — which is the sovereign mark of their felicity. From which range of speculation let me narrow down none the less a little ruefully; since I confess to no great provision of " history " on behalf of " The Marriages." The embodied notion, for this matter, sufficiently tells its story; one has never to go far afield to speculate on the possible pangs of filial piety in face of the successor, in the given instance, to either lost parent, but perhaps more particularly to the lost mother, often inflicted on it by the parent surviving. As in the classic case of Mrs. Glasse's receipt, it's but a question of " first catching " the example of piety intense enough. Granted that, the drama is all there — all in the consciousness, the fond imagination, the possibly poisoned and inflamed judgement, of the suffering subject; where, exactly, " The Marriages " was to find it.

As to the " The Real Thing " (1890) and " Brooksmith " (1891) my recollection is sharp; the subject of each of these tales was suggested to me by a briefly-reported case. To begin with the second-named of them, the appreciative daughter of a friend some time dead had mentioned to me a visit received by her from a servant of the late distinguished lady, a devoted maid whom I remembered well to have repeatedly seen at the latter's side and who had come to discharge herself so far as she might of a sorry burden. She had lived in her mistress's delightful society and in that of the many so interesting friends of the house; she had been formed by nature, as unluckily happened, to enjoy this privilege to the utmost, and the deprivation of everything was now bitterness in her cup. She had had her choice, and had made her trial, of common situations or of a return to her own people, and had found these ordeals alike too cruel. She had in her years of service tasted of conversation and been spoiled for life; she had, in recall of Stendhal's inveterate motto, caught a glimpse, all un-

PREFACE

timely, of " la beauté parfaite," and should never find again what she had lost — so that nothing was left her but to languish to her end. *There* was a touched spring, of course, to make " Dramatise, dramatise ! " ring out ; only my little derived drama, in the event, seemed to require, to be ample enough, a hero rather than a heroine. I desired for my poor lost spirit the measured maximum of the fatal experience : the thing became, in a word, to my imagination, the obscure tragedy of the " intelligent " butler present at rare table-talk, rather than that of the more effaced tirewoman ; with which of course was involved a corresponding change from mistress to master.

In like manner my much-loved friend George du Maurier had spoken to me of a call from a strange and striking couple desirous to propose themselves as artist's models for his weekly " social " illustrations to *Punch*, and the acceptance of whose services would have entailed the dismissal of an undistinguished but highly expert pair, also husband and wife, who had come to him from far back on the irregular day and whom, thanks to a happy, and to that extent lucrative, appearance of " type " on the part of each, he had reproduced, to the best effect, in a thousand drawing-room attitudes and combinations. Exceedingly modest members of society, they earned their bread by looking and, with the aid of supplied toggery, dressing, greater favourites of fortune to the life ; or, otherwise expressed, by skilfully feigning a virtue not in the least native to them. Here meanwhile were their so handsome proposed, so anxious, so almost haggard competitors, originally, by every sign, of the best condition and estate, but overtaken by reverses even while conforming impeccably to the standard of superficial " smartness " and pleading with well-bred ease and the right light tone, not to say with feverish gaiety, that (as in the interest of art itself) *they* at least should n't have to " make believe." The question thus thrown up by the two friendly critics of the rather lurid little passage was of whether their not having to make believe *would* in fact serve them, and above all serve their interpreter as well as the borrowed graces of the comparatively sordid professionals who had had, for dear life, to *know how* (which was to have learnt how) to do something. The question, I recall, struck me as exquisite, and out of a momentary fond consideration of it "The Real Thing" sprang at a bound.

"Flickerbridge" indeed I verily give up: so thoroughly does this highly-finished little anecdote cover its tracks; looking at me, over the few years and out of its bland neatness, with the fine inscrutability, in fact the positive coquetry, of the refusal to answer free-and-easy questions, the mere cold smile for their impertinence, characteristic of any complete artistic thing. "Dramatise, dramatise!"—there had of course been that preliminary, there could n't not have been; but how represent here clearly enough the small succession of steps by which such a case as the admonition is applied to in my picture of Frank Granger's visit to Miss Wenham came to issue from the whole thick-looming cloud of the noted appearances, the dark and dismal consequences, involved more and more to-day in our celebration, our commemoration, our unguardedly-uttered appreciation, of any charming impression? Living as we do under permanent visitation of the deadly epidemic of publicity, any rash word, any light thought that chances to escape us, may instantly, by that accident, find itself propagated and perverted, multiplied and diffused, after a fashion poisonous, practically, and speedily fatal, to its subject — that is to our idea, our sentiment, our figured interest, our too foolishly blabbed secret. Fine old leisure, in George Eliot's phrase, was long ago extinct, but rarity, precious rarity, its twin-sister, lingered on a while only to begin, in like manner, to perish by inches — to learn, in other words, that to be so much as breathed about is to be handed over to the big drum and the brazen blare, with all the effects of the vulgarised, trampled, desecrated state after the cyclone of sound and fury has spent itself. To have observed that, in turn, is to learn to dread reverberation, mere mechanical ventilation, more than the Black Death; which lesson the hero of my little apologue is represented as, all by himself and with anguish at his heart, spelling out the rudiments of. Of course it was a far cry, over intervals of thought, artistically speaking, from the dire truth I here glance at to my small projected example, looking so all unconscious of any such portentous burden of sense; but through that wilderness I shall not attempt to guide my reader. Let the accomplishment of the march figure for him, on the author's part, the arduous sport, in such a waste, of "dramatising."

Intervals of thought and a desolation of missing links strike me, not less, as marking the approach to any simple expression of my "original hint" for "The Story In It." What I definitely recall of the history of this tolerably recent production is that, even after I had exerted a ferocious and far from fruitless ingenuity to keep it from becoming a *nouvelle* — for it is in fact one of the briefest of my compositions — it still haunted, a graceless beggar, for a couple of years, the cold avenues of publicity; till finally an old acquaintance, about to "start a magazine," begged it in turn of me and published it (1903) at no cost to himself but the cost of his confidence, in that first number which was in the event, if I mistake not, to prove only one of a pair. I like perhaps "morbidly" to think that the Story in it may have been more than the magazine could carry. There at any rate — *for* the "story," that is for the pure pearl of my idea — I had to take, in the name of the particular instance, no less deep and straight a dive into the deep sea of a certain general truth than I had taken in quest of "Flickerbridge." The general truth had been positively phrased for me by a distinguished friend, a novelist not to *our* manner either born or bred, on the occasion of his having made such answer as he could to an interlocutor (he, oh distinctly, indigenous and glib!) bent on learning from him why the adventures he imputed to his heroines were so perversely and persistently but of a type impossible to ladies respecting themselves. My friend's reply had been, not unnaturally, and above all not incongruously, that ladies who respected themselves took particular care never to *have* adventures; not the least little adventure that would be worth (worth any self-respecting

PREFACE

novelist's) speaking of. There were certainly, it was to be hoped, ladies who practised that reserve — which, however beneficial to themselves, was yet fatally detrimental to literature, in the sense of promptly making any artistic harmony pitched in the same low key trivial and empty. A picture of life founded on the mere reserves and omissions and suppressions of life, what sort of a performance — for beauty, for interest, for tone — could *that* hope to be? The enquiry was n't answered in any hearing of mine, and of course indeed, on all such ground, discussion, to be really luminous, would have to rest on some such perfect definition of terms as is not of this muddled world. It is, not surprisingly, one of the rudiments of criticism that a human, a personal "adventure" is no *a priori*, no positive and absolute and inelastic thing, but just a matter of relation and appreciation — a name we conveniently give, after the fact, to any passage, to any situation, that has added the sharp taste of uncertainty to a quickened sense of life. Therefore the thing is, all beautifully, a matter of interpretation and of the particular conditions; without a view of which latter some of the most prodigious adventures, as one has often had occasion to say, may vulgarly show for nothing. However that may be, I hasten to add, the mere stir of the air round the question reflected in the brief but earnest interchange I have just reported was to cause a " subject," to my sense, immediately to bloom there. So it suddenly, on its small scale, seemed to stand erect — or at least quite intelligently to lift its head; just *a* subject, clearly, though I could n't immediately tell which or what. To find out I had to get a little closer to it, and " The Story In It " precisely represents that undertaking.

As for " The Beldonald Holbein," about which I have said nothing, *that* story — by which I mean the story *of* it — would take us much too far. " Mrs. Medwin," published in *Punch* (1902) and in " The Better Sort " (1903), I have also accommodated here for convenience. There is a note or two I would fain add to this; but I check myself with the sense of having, as it is, to all probability, vin-

PREFACE

dicated with a due zeal, not to say a due extravagance, the most general truth of many a story-teller's case : the truth, already more than once elsewhere glanced at, that what longest lives to his backward vision, in the whole business, is not the variable question of the " success," but the inveterate romance of the labour.

HENRY JAMES.

CONTENTS

DAISY MILLER

DAISY MILLER

I

AT the little town of Vevey, in Switzerland, there is a particularly comfortable hotel; there are indeed many hotels, since the entertainment of tourists is the business of the place, which, as many travellers will remember, is seated upon the edge of a remarkably blue lake — a lake that it behoves every tourist to visit. The shore of the lake presents an unbroken array of establishments of this order, of every category, from the "grand hotel" of the newest fashion, with a chalk-white front, a hundred balconies, and a dozen flags flying from its roof, to the small Swiss pension of an elder day, with its name inscribed in German-looking lettering upon a pink or yellow wall and an awkward summer-house in the angle of the garden. One of the hotels at Vevey, however, is famous, even classical, being distinguished from many of its upstart neighbours by an air both of luxury and of maturity. In this region, through the month of June, American travellers are extremely numerous; it may be said indeed that Vevey assumes at that time some of the characteristics of an American watering-place. There are sights and sounds that evoke a vision, an echo, of Newport and Saratoga. There is a flitting hither and thither of "stylish" young girls, a rustling of muslin

3

flounces, a rattle of dance-music in the morning hours, a sound of high-pitched voices at all times. You receive an impression of these things at the excellent inn of the "Trois Couronnes," and are transported in fancy to the Ocean House or to Congress Hall. But at the "Trois Couronnes," it must be added, there are other features much at variance with these suggestions: neat German waiters who look like secretaries of legation; Russian princesses sitting in the garden; little Polish boys walking about, held by the hand, with their governors; a view of the snowy crest of the Dent du Midi and the picturesque towers of the Castle of Chillon.

I hardly know whether it was the analogies or the differences that were uppermost in the mind of a young American, who, two or three years ago, sat in the garden of the "Trois Couronnes," looking about him rather idly at some of the graceful objects I have mentioned. It was a beautiful summer morning, and in whatever fashion the young American looked at things they must have seemed to him charming. He had come from Geneva the day before, by the little steamer, to see his aunt, who was staying at the hotel — Geneva having been for a long time his place of residence. But his aunt had a headache — his aunt had almost always a headache — and she was now shut up in her room smelling camphor, so that he was at liberty to wander about. He was some seven-and-twenty years of age; when his friends spoke of him they usually said that he was at Geneva "studying." When his enemies spoke of him they said — but after all he had no enemies: he was extremely amiable and

4

generally liked. What I should say is simply that when certain persons spoke of him they conveyed that the reason of his spending so much time at Geneva was that he was extremely devoted to a lady who lived there — a foreign lady, a person older than himself. Very few Americans — truly I think none — had ever seen this lady, about whom there were some singular stories. But Winterbourne had an old attachment for the little capital of Calvinism; he had been put to school there as a boy and had afterwards even gone, on trial — trial of the grey old "Academy" on the steep and stony hillside — to college there; circumstances which had led to his forming a great many youthful friendships. Many of these he had kept, and they were a source of great satisfaction to him.

After knocking at his aunt's door and learning that she was indisposed he had taken a walk about the town and then he had come in to his breakfast. He had now finished that repast, but was enjoying a small cup of coffee which had been served him on a little table in the garden by one of the waiters who looked like *attachés*. At last he finished his coffee and lit a cigarette. Presently a small boy came walking along the path — an urchin of nine or ten. The child, who was diminutive for his years, had an aged expression of countenance, a pale complexion and sharp little features. He was dressed in knickerbockers and had red stockings that displayed his poor little spindle-shanks; he also wore a brilliant red cravat. He carried in his hand a long alpenstock, the sharp point of which he thrust into everything he approached — the flower-beds, the garden-benches, the trains of the

5

ladies' dresses. In front of Winterbourne he paused, looking at him with a pair of bright and penetrating little eyes.

"Will you give me a lump of sugar?" he asked in a small sharp hard voice — a voice immature and yet somehow not young.

Winterbourne glanced at the light table near him, on which his coffee-service rested, and saw that several morsels of sugar remained. "Yes, you may take one," he answered; "but I don't think too much sugar good for little boys."

This little boy stepped forward and carefully selected three of the coveted fragments, two of which he buried in the pocket of his knickerbockers, depositing the other as promptly in another place. He poked his alpenstock, lance-fashion, into Winterbourne's bench and tried to crack the lump of sugar with his teeth.

"Oh blazes; it's har-r-d!" he exclaimed, divesting vowel and consonants, pertinently enough, of any taint of softness.

Winterbourne had immediately gathered that he might have the honour of claiming him as a countryman. "Take care you don't hurt your teeth," he said paternally.

"I have n't got any teeth to hurt. They've all come out. I've only got seven teeth. Mother counted them last night, and one came out right afterwards. She said she'd slap me if any more came out. I can't help it. It's this old Europe. It's the climate that makes them come out. In America they did n't come out. It's these hotels."

6

Winterbourne was much amused. "If you eat three lumps of sugar your mother will certainly slap you," he ventured.

"She's got to give me some candy then," rejoined his young interlocutor. "I can't get any candy here — any American candy. American candy's the best candy."

"And are American little boys the best little boys?" Winterbourne asked.

"I don't know. I'm an American boy," said the child.

"I see you're one of the best!" the young man laughed.

"Are you an American man?" pursued this vivacious infant. And then on his friend's affirmative reply, "American men are the best," he declared with assurance.

His companion thanked him for the compliment, and the child, who had now got astride of his alpenstock, stood looking about him while he attacked another lump of sugar. Winterbourne wondered if he himself had been like this in his infancy, for he had been brought to Europe at about the same age.

"Here comes my sister!" cried his young compatriot. "She's an American girl, you bet!"

Winterbourne looked along the path and saw a beautiful young lady advancing. "American girls are the best girls," he thereupon cheerfully remarked to his visitor.

"My sister ain't the best!" the child promptly returned. "She's always blowing at me."

"I imagine that's your fault, not hers," said Win-

7

terbourne. The young lady meanwhile had drawn near. She was dressed in white muslin, with a hundred frills and flounces and knots of pale-coloured ribbon. Bareheaded, she balanced in her hand a large parasol with a deep border of embroidery; and she was strikingly, admirably pretty. "How pretty they are!" thought our friend, who straightened himself in his seat as if he were ready to rise.

The young lady paused in front of his bench, near the parapet of the garden, which overlooked the lake. The small boy had now converted his alpenstock into a vaulting-pole, by the aid of which he was springing about in the gravel and kicking it up not a little. "Why Randolph," she freely began, "what *are* you doing?"

"I'm going up the Alps!" cried Randolph. "This is the way!" And he gave another extravagant jump, scattering the pebbles about Winterbourne's ears.

"That's the way they come down," said Winterbourne.

"He's an American man!" proclaimed Randolph in his harsh little voice.

The young lady gave no heed to this circumstance, but looked straight at her brother. "Well, I guess you'd better be quiet," she simply observed.

It seemed to Winterbourne that he had been in a manner presented. He got up and stepped slowly toward the charming creature, throwing away his cigarette. "This little boy and I have made acquaintance," he said with great civility. In Geneva, as he had been perfectly aware, a young man wasn't at lib-

8

erty to speak to a young unmarried lady save under
certain rarely-occurring conditions; but here at Vevey
what conditions could be better than these? — a
pretty American girl coming to stand in front of you
in a garden with all the confidence in life. This pretty
American girl, whatever that might prove, on hearing
Winterbourne's observation simply glanced at him;
she then turned her head and looked over the parapet,
at the lake and the opposite mountains. He wondered
whether he had gone too far, but decided that he must
gallantly advance rather than retreat. While he was
thinking of something else to say the young lady
turned again to the little boy, whom she addressed
quite as if they were alone together. "I should like to
know where you got that pole."

"I bought it!" Randolph shouted.

"You don't mean to say you're going to take it to
Italy!"

"Yes, I'm going to take it t' Italy!" the child rang
out.

She glanced over the front of her dress and smoothed
out a knot or two of ribbon. Then she gave her sweet
eyes to the prospect again. "Well, I guess you'd
better leave it somewhere," she dropped after a moment.

"Are you going to Italy?" Winterbourne now decided very respectfully to enquire.

She glanced at him with lovely remoteness. "Yes,
sir," she then replied. And she said nothing more.

"And are you — a — thinking of the Simplon?"
he pursued with a slight drop of assurance.

"I don't know," she said. "I suppose it's some

mountain. Randolph, what mountain are we thinking of?"

"Thinking of?" — the boy stared.

"Why going right over."

"Going to where?" he demanded.

"Why right down to Italy" — Winterbourne felt vague emulations.

"I don't know," said Randolph. "I don't want to go t' Italy. I want to go to America."

"Oh Italy's a beautiful place!" the young man laughed.

"Can you get candy there?" Randolph asked of all the echoes.

"I hope not," said his sister. "I guess you've had enough candy, and mother thinks so too."

"I haven't had any for ever so long — for a hundred weeks!" cried the boy, still jumping about.

The young lady inspected her flounces and smoothed her ribbons again; and Winterbourne presently risked an observation on the beauty of the view. He was ceasing to be in doubt, for he had begun to perceive that she was really not in the least embarrassed. She might be cold, she might be austere, she might even be prim; for that was apparently — he had already so generalised — what the most "distant" American girls did: they came and planted themselves straight in front of you to show how rigidly unapproachable they were. There hadn't been the slightest flush in her fresh fairness however; so that she was clearly neither offended nor fluttered. Only she was composed — he had seen that before too — of charming little parts that didn't match and that made no

10

ensemble; and if she looked another way when he spoke to her, and seemed not particularly to hear him, this was simply her habit, her manner, the result of her having no idea whatever of "form" (with such a tell-tale appendage as Randolph where in the world would she have got it?) in any such connexion. As he talked a little more and pointed out some of the objects of interest in the view, with which she appeared wholly unacquainted, she gradually, none the less, gave him more of the benefit of her attention; and then he saw that act unqualified by the faintest shadow of reserve. It was n't however what would have been called a "bold" front that she presented, for her expression was as decently limpid as the very cleanest water. Her eyes were the very prettiest conceivable, and indeed Winterbourne had n't for a long time seen anything prettier than his fair countrywoman's various features—her complexion, her nose, her ears, her teeth. He took a great interest generally in that range of effects and was addicted to noting and, as it were, recording them; so that in regard to this young lady's face he made several observations. It was n't at all insipid, yet at the same time was n't pointedly — what point, on earth, could she ever make? — expressive; and hough it offered such a collection of small finenesses and neatnesses he mentally accused it — very forgivingly — of a want of finish. He thought nothing more likely than that its wearer would have had her own experience of the action of her charms, as she would certainly have acquired a resulting confidence; but even should she depend on this for her main amusement her bright sweet superficial little visage gave out neither mockery nor irony. Before long it became clear that, however these things might be, she was much disposed to conversation. She remarked to Winterbourne that they were going to Rome for the winter — she and her mother and Randolph. She asked him if he was a "real American"; she would n't have taken him for one; he seemed more like a German — this flower was gathered as from a large field of comparison — especially when he spoke. Winterbourne, laughing, answered that he had met Germans who spoke like Americans, but not, so far as he remembered, any American with the resemblance she noted. Then he asked her if she might n't be more at ease should she occupy the bench he had just quitted. She answered that she liked hanging round, but she none the less resignedly, after a little, dropped to the bench. She told him she was from New York State — "if you know where that is"; but our friend really quickened this current by catching hold of her small slippery brother and making him stand a few minutes by his side.

"Tell me your honest name, my boy." So he artfully proceeded.

In response to which the child was indeed unvarnished truth. "Randolph C. Miller. And I'll tell you hers." With which he levelled his alpenstock at his sister.

"You had better wait till you're asked!" said this young lady quite at her leisure.

"I should like very much to know *your* name," Winterbourne made free to reply.

"Her name's Daisy Miller!" cried the urchin.

12

"But that ain't her real name; that ain't her name on her cards."

"It's a pity you have n't got one of my cards!" Miss Miller quite as naturally remarked.

"Her real name's Annie P. Miller," the boy went on.

It seemed, all amazingly, to do her good. "Ask him *his* now " — and she indicated their friend.

But to this point Randolph seemed perfectly indifferent; he continued to supply information with regard to his own family. "My father's name is Ezra B. Miller. My father ain't in Europe — he's in a better place than Europe." Winterbourne for a moment supposed this the manner in which the child had been taught to intimate that Mr. Miller had been removed to the sphere of celestial rewards. But Randolph immediately added: "My father's in Schenectady. He's got a big business. My father's rich, you bet."

"Well!" ejaculated Miss Miller, lowering her parasol and looking at the embroidered border. Winterbourne presently released the child, who departed, dragging his alpenstock along the path. "He don't like Europe," said the girl as with an artless instinct for historic truth. "He wants to go back."

"To Schenectady, you mean?"

"Yes, he wants to go right home. He has n't got any boys here. There's one boy here, but he always goes round with a teacher. They won't let him play."

"And your brother has n't any teacher?" Winterbourne enquired.

It tapped, at a touch, the spring of confidence. "Mother thought of getting him one — to travel

13

round with us. There was a lady told her of a very good teacher; an American lady — perhaps you know her — Mrs. Sanders. I think she came from Boston. She told her of this teacher, and we thought of getting him to travel round with us. But Randolph said he did n't want a teacher travelling round with us. He said he would n't have lessons when he was in the cars. And we *are* in the cars about half the time. There was an English lady we met in the cars — I think her name was Miss Featherstone; perhaps you know her. She wanted to know why I did n't give Randolph lessons — give him 'instruction,' she called it. I guess he could give me more instruction than I could give him. He's very smart."

"Yes," said Winterbourne; "he seems very smart."

"Mother's going to get a teacher for him as soon as we get t' Italy. Can you get good teachers in Italy?"

"Very good, I should think," Winterbourne hastened to reply.

"Or else she's going to find some school. He ought to learn some more. He's only nine. He's going to college." And in this way Miss Miller continued to converse upon the affairs of her family and upon other topics. She sat there with her extremely pretty hands, ornamented with very brilliant rings, folded in her lap, and with her pretty eyes now resting upon those of Winterbourne, now wandering over the garden, the people who passed before her and the beautiful view. She addressed her new acquaintance as if she had known him a long time. He found it very pleasant. It was many years since he had heard a young girl talk so much. It might have been said of this wandering maiden who had come and sat down beside him upon a bench that she chattered. She was very quiet, she sat in a charming tranquil attitude; but her lips and her eyes were constantly moving. She had a soft slender agreeable voice, and her tone was distinctly sociable. She gave Winterbourne a report of her movements and intentions, and those of her mother and brother, in Europe, and enumerated in particular the various hotels at which they had stopped. "That English lady in the cars," she said — "Miss Featherstone — asked me if we did n't all live in hotels in America. I told her I had never been in so many hotels in my life as since I came to Europe. I 've never seen so many — it 's nothing but hotels." But Miss Miller made this remark with no querulous accent; she appeared to be in the best humour with everything. She declared that the hotels were very good when once you got used to their ways and that Europe was perfectly entrancing. She was n't disappointed — not a bit. Perhaps it was because she had heard so much about it before. She had ever so many intimate friends who had been there ever so many times, and that way she had got thoroughly posted. And then she had had ever so many dresses and things from Paris. Whenever she put on a Paris dress she felt as if she were in Europe.

"It was a kind of a wishing-cap," Winterbourne smiled.

"Yes," said Miss Miller at once and without examining this analogy; "it always made me wish I was here. But I need n't have done that for dresses. I 'm

15

sure they send all the pretty ones to America; you see the most frightful things here. The only thing I don't like," she proceeded, "is the society. There ain't any society — or if there is I don't know where it keeps itself. Do you? I suppose there's some society somewhere, but I haven't seen anything of it. I'm very fond of society and I've always had plenty of it. I don't mean only in Schenectady, but in New York. I used to go to New York every winter. In New York I had lots of society. Last winter I had seventeen dinners given me, and three of them were by gentlemen," added Daisy Miller. "I've more friends in New York than in Schenectady — more gentlemen friends; and more young lady friends too," she resumed in a moment. She paused again for an instant; she was looking at Winterbourne with all her prettiness in her frank gay eyes and in her clear rather uniform smile. "I've always had," she said, "a great deal of gentlemen's society."

Poor Winterbourne was amused and perplexed — above all he was charmed. He had never yet heard a young girl express herself in just this fashion; never at least save in cases where to say such things was to have at the same time some rather complicated consciousness about them. And yet was he to accuse Miss Daisy Miller of an actual or a potential *arrière-pensée*, as they said at Geneva? He felt he had lived at Geneva so long as to have got morally muddled; he had lost the right sense for the young American tone. Never indeed since he had grown old enough to appreciate things had he encountered a young compatriot of so "strong" a type as this. Certainly she was very

charming, but how extraordinarily communicative
and how tremendously easy! Was she simply a pretty
girl from New York State — were they all like that,
the pretty girls who had had a good deal of gentlemen's society? Or was she also a designing, an auda-
cious, in short an expert young person? Yes, his instinct for such a question had ceased to serve him, and
his reason could but mislead. Miss Daisy Miller
looked extremely innocent. Some people had told him
that after all American girls *were* exceedingly innocent, and others had told him that after all they
were n't. He must on the whole take Miss Daisy
Miller for a flirt — a pretty American flirt. He had
never as yet had relations with representatives of that
class. He had known here in Europe two or three women — persons older than Miss Daisy Miller and provided, for respectability's sake, with husbands — who
were great coquettes; dangerous terrible women with
whom one's light commerce might indeed take a serious turn. But this charming apparition was n't a
coquette in that sense; she was very unsophisticated;
she was only a pretty American flirt. Winterbourne
was almost grateful for having found the formula that
applied to Miss Daisy Miller. He leaned back in his
seat; he remarked to himself that she had the finest
little nose he had ever seen; he wondered what were
the regular conditions and limitations of one's intercourse with a pretty American flirt. It presently
became apparent that he was on the way to learn.

"Have you been to that old castle?" the girl soon
asked, pointing with her parasol to the far-shining
walls of the Château de Chillon.

"Yes, formerly, more than once," said Winterbourne. "You too, I suppose, have seen it?"

"No, we have n't been there. I want to go there dreadfully. Of course I mean to go there. I would n't go away from here without having seen that old castle."

"It's a very pretty excursion," the young man returned, "and very easy to make. You can drive, you know, or you can go by the little steamer."

"You can go in the cars," said Miss Miller.

"Yes, you can go in the cars," Winterbourne assented.

"Our courier says they take you right up to the castle," she continued. "We were going last week, but mother gave out. She suffers dreadfully from dyspepsia. She said she could n't any more go —!" But this sketch of Mrs. Miller's plea remained unfinished. "Randolph would n't go either; he says he don't think much of old castles. But I guess we'll go this week if we can get Randolph."

"Your brother is n't interested in ancient monuments?" Winterbourne indulgently asked.

He now drew her, as he guessed she would herself have said, every time. "Why no, he says he don't care much about old castles. He's only nine. He wants to stay at the hotel. Mother's afraid to leave him alone, and the courier won't stay with him; so we have n't been to many places. But it will be too bad if we don't go up there." And Miss Miller pointed again at the Château de Chillon.

"I should think it might be arranged," Winterbourne was thus emboldened to reply. "Could n't you

DAISY MILLER

get some one to stay — for the afternoon — with Randolph?"

Miss Miller looked at him a moment, and then with all serenity, "I wish *you'd* stay with him!" she said.

He pretended to consider it. "I'd much rather go to Chillon with you."

"With me?" she asked without a shadow of emotion.

She didn't rise blushing, as a young person at Geneva would have done; and yet, conscious that he had gone very far, he thought it possible she had drawn back. "And with your mother," he answered very respectfully.

But it seemed that both his audacity and his respect were lost on Miss Daisy Miller. "I guess mother would n't go — for *you*," she smiled. "And she ain't much *bent* on going, anyway. She don't like to ride round in the afternoon." After which she familiarly proceeded: "But did you really mean what you said just now — that you'd like to go up there?"

"Most earnestly I meant it," Winterbourne declared.

"Then we may arrange it. If mother will stay with Randolph I guess Eugenio will."

"Eugenio?" the young man echoed.

"Eugenio's our courier. He does n't like to stay with Randolph — he's the most fastidious man I ever saw. But he's a splendid courier. I guess he'll stay at home with Randolph if mother does, and then we can go to the castle."

Winterbourne reflected for an instant as lucidly as possible: "we" could only mean Miss Miller and

19

himself. This prospect seemed almost too good to
believe; he felt as if he ought to kiss the young lady's
hand. Possibly he would have done so, — and quite
spoiled his chance; but at this moment another person
— presumably Eugenio — appeared. A tall handsome man, with superb whiskers and wearing a velvet
morning-coat and a voluminous watch-guard, approached the young lady, looking sharply at her companion. "Oh Eugenio!" she said with the friendliest
accent.

Eugenio had eyed Winterbourne from head to foot;
he now bowed gravely to Miss Miller. "I have the
honour to inform Mademoiselle that luncheon's on
table."

Mademoiselle slowly rose. "See here, Eugenio, I'm
going to that old castle anyway."

"To the Château de Chillon, Mademoiselle?" the
courier enquired. "Mademoiselle has made arrangements?" he added in a tone that struck Winterbourne
as impertinent.

Eugenio's tone apparently threw, even to Miss
Miller's own apprehension, a slightly ironical light on
her position. She turned to Winterbourne with the
slightest blush. "You won't back out?"

"I shall not be happy till we go!" he protested.

"And you're staying in this hotel?" she went on.
"And you're really American?"

The courier still stood there with an effect of
offence for the young man so far as the latter saw in it
a tacit reflexion on Miss Miller's behaviour and an
insinuation that she "picked up" acquaintances. "I
shall have the honour of presenting to you a person

who'll tell you all about me," he said, smiling, and referring to his aunt.

"Oh well, we'll go some day," she beautifully answered; with which she gave him a smile and turned away. She put up her parasol and walked back to the inn beside Eugenio. Winterbourne stood watching her, and as she moved away, drawing her muslin furbelows over the walk, he spoke to himself of her natural elegance.

II

HE had, however, engaged to do more than proved feasible in promising to present his aunt, Mrs. Costello, to Miss Daisy Miller. As soon as that lady had got better of her headache he waited on her in her apartment and, after a show of the proper solicitude about her health, asked if she had noticed in the hotel an American family — a mamma, a daughter and an obstreperous little boy.

"An obstreperous little boy and a preposterous big courier?" said Mrs. Costello. "Oh yes, I've noticed them. Seen them, heard them and kept out of their way." Mrs. Costello was a widow of fortune, a person of much distinction and who frequently intimated that if she had n't been so dreadfully liable to sick-headaches she would probably have left a deeper impress on her time. She had a long pale face, a high nose and a great deal of very striking white hair, which she wore in large puffs and over the top of her head. She had two sons married in New York and another who was now in Europe. This young man was amusing himself at Homburg and, though guided by his taste, was rarely observed to visit any particular city at the moment selected by his mother for her appearance there. Her nephew, who had come to Vevey expressly to see her, was therefore more attentive than, as she said, her very own. He had imbibed at Geneva the idea that one must be irreproachable in all such forms. Mrs.

Costello had n't seen him for many years and was now greatly pleased with him, manifesting her approbation by initiating him into many of the secrets of that social sway which, as he could see she would like him to think, she exerted from her stronghold in Forty-Second Street. She admitted that she was very exclusive, but if he had been better acquainted with New York he would see that one had to be. And her picture of the minutely hierarchical constitution of the society of that city, which she presented to him in many different lights, was, to Winterbourne's imagination, almost oppressively striking.

He at once recognised from her tone that Miss Daisy Miller's place in the social scale was low. "I'm afraid you don't approve of them," he pursued in reference to his new friends.

"They 're horribly common" — it was perfectly simple. "They 're the sort of Americans that one does one's duty by just ignoring."

"Ah you just ignore them ?" — the young man took it in.

"I can't *not*, my dear Frederick. I would n't if I had n't to, but I have to."

"The little girl 's very pretty," he went on in a moment.

"Of course she 's very pretty. But she 's of the last crudity."

"I see what you mean of course," he allowed after another pause.

"She has that charming look they all have," his aunt resumed. "I can't think where they pick it up; and she dresses in perfection — no, you don't know how well she dresses. I can't think where they get their taste."

"But, my dear aunt, she's not, after all, a Comanche savage."

"She is a young lady," said Mrs. Costello, "who has an intimacy with her mamma's courier?"

"An 'intimacy' with him?" Ah there it was!

"There's no other name for such a relation. But the skinny little mother's just as bad! They treat the courier as a familiar friend — as a gentleman and a scholar. I should n't wonder if he dines with them. Very likely they've never seen a man with such good manners, such fine clothes, so *like* a gentleman — or a scholar. He probably corresponds to the young lady's idea of a count. He sits with them in the garden of an evening. I think he smokes in their faces."

Winterbourne listened with interest to these disclosures; they helped him to make up his mind about Miss Daisy. Evidently she was rather wild. "Well," he said, "I'm not a courier and I did n't smoke in her face, and yet she was very charming to me."

"You had better have mentioned at first," Mrs. Costello returned with dignity, "that you had made her valuable acquaintance."

"We simply met in the garden and talked a bit."

"By appointment — no? Ah that's still to come! Pray what did you say?"

"I said I should take the liberty of introducing her to my admirable aunt."

"Your admirable aunt's a thousand times obliged to you."

"It was to guarantee my respectability."

DAISY MILLER

"And pray who's to guarantee hers?"

"Ah you're cruel!" said the young man. "She's a very innocent girl."

"You don't say that as if you believed it," Mrs. Costello returned.

"She's completely uneducated," Winterbourne acknowledged, "but she's wonderfully pretty, and in short she's very nice. To prove I believe it I'm going to take her to the Château de Chillon."

Mrs. Costello made a wondrous face. "You two are going off there together? I should say it proved just the contrary. How long had you known her, may I ask, when this interesting project was formed? You haven't been twenty-four hours in the house."

"I had known her half an hour!" Winterbourne smiled.

"Then she's just what I supposed."

"And what do you suppose?"

"Why that she's a horror."

Our youth was silent for some moments. "You really think then," he presently began, and with a desire for trustworthy information, "you really think that—" But he paused again while his aunt waited.

"Think what, sir?"

"That she's the sort of young lady who expects a man sooner or later to—well, we'll call it carry her off?"

"I haven't the least idea what such young ladies expect a man to do. But I really consider you had better not meddle with little American girls who are uneducated, as you mildly put it. You've lived too

25

15261

long out of the country. You'll be sure to make some great mistake. You're too innocent."

"My dear aunt, not so much as that comes to!" he protested with a laugh and a curl of his moustache.

"You're too guilty then!"

He continued all thoughtfully to finger the ornament in question. "You won't let the poor girl know you then?" he asked at last.

"Is it literally true that she's going to the Château de Chillon with you?"

"I've no doubt she fully intends it."

"Then, my dear Frederick," said Mrs. Costello, "I must decline the honour of her acquaintance. I'm an old woman, but I'm not too old — thank heaven — to be honestly shocked!"

"But don't they all do these things — the little American girls at home?" Winterbourne enquired.

Mrs. Costello stared a moment. "I should like to see my granddaughters do them!" she then grimly returned.

This seemed to throw some light on the matter, for Winterbourne remembered to have heard his pretty cousins in New York, the daughters of this lady's two daughters, called "tremendous flirts." If therefore Miss Daisy Miller exceeded the liberal licence allowed to these young women it was probable she did go even by the American allowance rather far. Winterbourne was impatient to see her again, and it vexed, it even a little humiliated him, that he should n't by instinct appreciate her justly.

Though so impatient to see her again he hardly knew what ground he should give for his aunt's refusal to become acquainted with her; but he discovered promptly enough that with Miss Daisy Miller there was no great need of walking on tiptoe. He found her that evening in the garden, wandering about in the warm starlight after the manner of an indolent sylph and swinging to and fro the largest fan he had ever beheld. It was ten o'clock. He had dined with his aunt, had been sitting with her since dinner, and had just taken leave of her till the morrow. His young friend frankly rejoiced to renew their intercourse; she pronounced it the stupidest evening she had ever passed.

"Have you been all alone?" he asked with no intention of an epigram and no effect of her perceiving one.

"I've been walking round with mother. But mother gets tired walking round," Miss Miller explained.

"Has she gone to bed?"

"No, she does n't like to go to bed. She does n't sleep scarcely any — not three hours. She says she does n't know how she lives. She's dreadfully nervous. I guess she sleeps more than she thinks. She's gone somewhere after Randolph; she wants to try to get him to go to bed. He does n't like to go to bed."

The soft impartiality of her *constatations*, as Winterbourne would have termed them, was a thing by itself — exquisite little fatalist as they seemed to make her. "Let us hope she'll persuade him," he encouragingly said.

"Well, she'll talk to him all she can — but he does n't like her to talk to him": with which Miss Daisy opened and closed her fan. "She's going to try

27

to get Eugenio to talk to him. But Randolph ain't afraid of Eugenio. Eugenio's a splendid courier, but he can't make much impression on Randolph! I don't believe he'll go to bed before eleven." Her detachment from any invidious judgement of this was, to her companion's sense, inimitable; and it appeared that Randolph's vigil was in fact triumphantly prolonged, for Winterbourne attended her in her stroll for some time without meeting her mother. "I've been looking round for that lady you want to introduce me to," she resumed — "I guess she's your aunt." Then on his admitting the fact and expressing some curiosity as to how she had learned it, she said she had heard all about Mrs. Costello from the chambermaid. She was very quiet and very *comme il faut;* she wore white puffs; she spoke to no one and she never dined at the common table. Every two days she had a headache. "I think that's a lovely description, headache and all!" said Miss Daisy, chattering along in her thin gay voice. "I want to know her ever so much. I know just what *your* aunt would be; I know I'd like her. She'd be very exclusive. I like a lady to be exclusive; I'm dying to be exclusive myself. Well, I guess we *are* exclusive, mother and I. We don't speak to any one — or they don't speak to us. I suppose it's about the same thing. Anyway, I shall be ever so glad to meet your aunt."

Winterbourne was embarrassed — he could but trump up some evasion. "She'd be most happy, but I'm afraid those tiresome headaches are always to be reckoned with."

The girl looked at him through the fine dusk.

"Well, I suppose she does n't have a headache every day."

He had to make the best of it. "She tells me she wonderfully does." He did n't know what else to say.

Miss Miller stopped and stood looking at him. Her prettiness was still visible in the darkness; she kept flapping to and fro her enormous fan. "She does n't want to know me!" she then lightly broke out. "Why don't you say so? You need n't be afraid. *I'm* not afraid!" And she quite crowed for the fun of it.

Winterbourne distinguished however a wee false note in this: he was touched, shocked, mortified by it. "My dear young lady, she knows no one. She goes through life immured. It's her wretched health."

The young girl walked on a few steps in the glee of the thing. "You need n't be afraid," she repeated. "Why should she want to know me?" Then she paused again; she was close to the parapet of the garden, and in front of her was the starlit lake. There was a vague sheen on its surface, and in the distance were dimly-seen mountain forms. Daisy Miller looked out at these great lights and shades and again proclaimed a gay indifference — "Gracious! she *is* exclusive!" Winterbourne wondered if she were seriously wounded and for a moment almost wished her sense of injury might be such as to make it becoming in him to reassure and comfort her. He had a pleasant sense that she would be all accessible to a respectful tenderness at that moment. He felt quite ready to sacrifice his aunt — conversationally; to acknowledge she was a proud rude woman and to make the point that they need n't mind her. But before he had time to commit himself to this questionable mixture of gallantry and impiety, the young lady, resuming her walk, gave an exclamation in quite another tone. "Well, here's mother! I guess she *has n't* got Randolph to go to bed." The figure of a lady appeared, at a distance, very indistinct in the darkness; it advanced with a slow and wavering step and then suddenly seemed to pause.

"Are you sure it's your mother? Can you make her out in this thick dusk?" Winterbourne asked.

"Well," the girl laughed, "I guess I know my own mother! And when she has got on my shawl too. She's always wearing my things."

The lady in question, ceasing now to approach, hovered vaguely about the spot at which she had checked her steps.

"I'm afraid your mother does n't see you," said Winterbourne. "Or perhaps," he added — thinking, with Miss Miller, the joke permissible — "perhaps she feels guilty about your shawl."

"Oh it's a fearful old thing!" his companion placidly answered. "I told her she could wear it if she did n't mind looking like a fright. She won't come here because she sees you."

"Ah then," said Winterbourne, "I had better leave you."

"Oh no — come on!" the girl insisted.

"I'm afraid your mother does n't approve of my walking with you."

She gave him, he thought, the oddest glance. "It is n't for me; it's for you — that is it's for *her*. Well, I don't know who it's for! But mother does n't like

30

DAISY MILLER

any of my gentlemen friends. She's right down timid.
She always makes a fuss if I introduce a gentleman.
But I *do* introduce them — almost always. If I
did n't introduce my gentlemen friends to mother,"
Miss Miller added, in her small flat monotone, "I
should n't think I was natural."

"Well, to introduce me," Winterbourne remarked,
"you must know my name." And he proceeded to
pronounce it.

"Oh my — I can't say all that!" cried his companion, much amused. But by this time they had
come up to Mrs. Miller, who, as they drew near,
walked to the parapet of the garden and leaned on it,
looking intently at the lake and presenting her back to
them. "Mother!" said the girl in a tone of decision —
upon which the elder lady turned round. "Mr.
Frederick Forsyth Winterbourne," said the latter's
young friend, repeating his lesson of a moment before
and introducing him very frankly and prettily. "Common" she might be, as Mrs. Costello had pronounced her; yet what provision was made by that
epithet for her queer little native grace?

Her mother was a small spare light person, with a
wandering eye, a scarce perceptible nose, and, as to
make up for it, an unmistakeable forehead, decorated
— but too far back, as Winterbourne mentally described it — with thin much-frizzled hair. Like her
daughter Mrs. Miller was dressed with extreme
elegance; she had enormous diamonds in her ears.
So far as the young man could observe, she gave
him no greeting — she certainly was n't looking
at him. Daisy was near her, pulling her shawl

31

straight. "What are you doing, poking round here?"
this young lady enquired — yet by no means with
the harshness of accent her choice of words might
have implied.

"Well, I don't know" — and the new-comer
turned to the lake again.

"I should n't think you'd want that shawl!" Daisy
familiarly proceeded.

"Well — I do!" her mother answered with a sound
that partook for Winterbourne of an odd strain between mirth and woe.

"Did you get Randolph to go to bed?" Daisy
asked.

"No, I could n't induce him" — and Mrs. Miller
seemed to confess to the same mild fatalism as her
daughter. "He wants to talk to the waiter. He *likes*
to talk to that waiter."

"I was just telling Mr. Winterbourne," the girl
went on; and to the young man's ear her tone might
have indicated that she had been uttering his name all
her life.

"Oh yes!" he concurred — "I've the pleasure of
knowing your son."

Randolph's mamma was silent; she kept her attention on the lake. But at last a sigh broke from her.
"Well, I don't see how he lives!"

"Anyhow, it is n't so bad as it was at Dover," Daisy
at least opined.

"And what occurred at Dover?" Winterbourne
desired to know.

"He would n't go to bed at all. I guess he sat up
all night — in the public parlour. He was n't in

DAISY MILLER

bed at twelve o'clock: it seemed as if he could n't
budge."

"It was half-past twelve when *I* gave up," Mrs.
Miller recorded with passionless accuracy.

It was of great interest to Winterbourne. "Does he
sleep much during the day?"

"I guess he does n't sleep *very* much," Daisy
rejoined.

"I wish he just *would!*" said her mother. "It seems
as if he *must* make it up somehow."

"Well, I guess it 's we that make it up. I think he 's
real tiresome," Daisy pursued.

After which, for some moments, there was silence.
"Well, Daisy Miller," the elder lady then unexpectedly broke out, "I should n't think you 'd want to talk
against your own brother!"

"Well, he *is* tiresome, mother," said the girl, but
with no sharpness of insistence.

"Well, he 's only nine," Mrs. Miller lucidly urged.

"Well, he would n't go up to that castle, anyway,"
her daughter replied as for accommodation. "I 'm
going up there with Mr. Winterbourne."

To this announcement, very placidly made, Daisy's
parent offered no response. Winterbourne took for
granted on this that she opposed such a course; but
he said to himself at the same time that she was a
simple easily-managed person and that a few deferential protestations would modify her attitude. "Yes,"
he therefore interposed, "your daughter has kindly
allowed me the honour of being her guide."

Mrs. Miller's wandering eyes attached themselves
with an appealing air to her other companion, who,

33

however, strolled a few steps further, gently humming to herself. "I presume you'll go in the cars," she then quite colourlessly remarked.

"Yes, or in the boat," said Winterbourne.

"Well, of course I don't know," Mrs. Miller returned. "I've never been up to that castle."

"It is a pity you should n't go," he observed, beginning to feel reassured as to her opposition. And yet he was quite prepared to find that as a matter of course she meant to accompany her daughter.

It was on this view accordingly that light was projected for him. "We've been thinking ever so much about going, but it seems as if we could n't. Of course Daisy — she wants to go round everywhere. But there's a lady here — I don't know her name — she says she should n't think we'd want to go to see castles *here;* she should think we'd want to wait till we got t' Italy. It seems as if there would be so many there," continued Mrs. Miller with an air of increasing confidence. "Of course we only want to see the principal ones. We visited several in England," she presently added.

"Ah yes, in England there are beautiful castles," said Winterbourne. "But Chillon here is very well worth seeing."

"Well, if Daisy feels up to it —" said Mrs. Miller in a tone that seemed to break under the burden of such conceptions. "It seems as if there's nothing she won't undertake."

"Oh I'm pretty sure she'll enjoy it!" Winterbourne declared. And he desired more and more to make it a certainty that he was to have the privilege of a *tête-à-tête* with the young lady who was still strolling along in front of them and softly vocalising. "You're not disposed, madam," he enquired, "to make the so interesting excursion yourself?"

So addressed Daisy's mother looked at him an instant with a certain scared obliquity and then walked forward in silence. Then, "I guess she had better go alone," she said simply.

It gave him occasion to note that this was a very different type of maternity from that of the vigilant matrons who massed themselves in the forefront of social intercourse in the dark old city at the other end of the lake. But his meditations were interrupted by hearing his name very distinctly pronounced by Mrs. Miller's unprotected daughter. "Mr. Winterbourne!" she piped from a considerable distance.

"Mademoiselle!" said the young man.

"Don't you want to take me out in a boat?"

"At present?" he asked.

"Why of course!" she gaily returned.

"Well, Annie Miller!" exclaimed her mother.

"I beg you, madam, to let her go," he hereupon eagerly pleaded; so instantly had he been struck with the romantic side of this chance to guide through the summer starlight a skiff freighted with a fresh and beautiful young girl.

"I shouldn't think she'd want to," said her mother. "I should think she'd rather go indoors."

"I'm sure Mr. Winterbourne wants to *take* me," Daisy declared. "He's so awfully devoted!"

"I'll row you over to Chillon under the stars."

"I don't believe it!" Daisy laughed.

DAISY MILLER

"Well!" the elder lady again gasped, as in rebuke of this freedom.

"You haven't spoken to me for half an hour," her daughter went on.

"I've been having some very pleasant conversation with your mother," Winterbourne replied.

"Oh pshaw! I want you to take me out in a boat!" Daisy went on as if nothing else had been said. They had all stopped and she had turned round and was looking at her friend. Her face wore a charming smile, her pretty eyes gleamed in the darkness, she swung her great fan about. No, he felt, it was impossible to be prettier than that.

"There are half a dozen boats moored at that landing-place," and he pointed to a range of steps that descended from the garden to the lake. "If you'll do me the honour to accept my arm we'll go and select one of them."

She stood there smiling; she threw back her head; she laughed as for the drollery of this. "I like a gentleman to be formal!"

"I assure you it's a formal offer."

"I was bound I'd make you say something," Daisy agreeably mocked.

"You see it's not very difficult," said Winterbourne. "But I'm afraid you're chaffing me."

"I think not, sir," Mrs. Miller shyly pleaded.

"Do then let me give you a row," he persisted to Daisy.

"It's quite lovely, the way you say that!" she cried in reward

"It will be still more lovely to do it."

36

DAISY MILLER

"Yes, it would be lovely!" But she made no movement to accompany him; she only remained an elegant image of free light irony.

"I guess you'd better find out what time it is," her mother impartially contributed.

"It's eleven o'clock, Madam," said a voice with a foreign accent out of the neighbouring darkness; and Winterbourne, turning, recognised the florid personage he had already seen in attendance. He had apparently just approached.

"Oh Eugenio," said Daisy, "I'm going out with Mr. Winterbourne in a boat!"

Eugenio bowed. "At this hour of the night, Mademoiselle?"

"I'm going with Mr. Winterbourne," she repeated with her shining smile. "I'm going this very minute."

"Do tell her she can't, Eugenio," Mrs. Miller said to the courier.

"I think you had better not go out in a boat, Mademoiselle," the man declared.

Winterbourne wished to goodness this pretty girl were not on such familiar terms with her courier; but he said nothing, and she meanwhile added to his ground. "I suppose you don't think it's proper! My!" she wailed; "Eugenio does n't think anything's proper."

"I'm nevertheless quite at your service," Winterbourne hastened to remark.

"Does Mademoiselle propose to go alone?" Eugenio asked of Mrs. Miller.

"Oh no, with this gentleman!" cried Daisy's mamma for reassurance.

37

DAISY MILLER

"I *meant* alone with the gentleman." The courier
looked for a moment at Winterbourne — the latter
seemed to make out in his face a vague presumptuous
intelligence as at the expense of their companions —
and then solemnly and with a bow, "As Mademoiselle
pleases!" he said.

But Daisy broke off at this. "Oh I hoped you'd
make a fuss! I don't care to go now."

"Ah but I myself shall make a fuss if you don't go,"
Winterbourne declared with spirit.

"That's all I want — a little fuss!" With which
she began to laugh again.

"Mr. Randolph has retired for the night!" the
courier hereupon importantly announced.

"Oh Daisy, now we can go then!" cried Mrs.
Miller.

Her daughter turned away from their friend, all
lighted with her odd perversity. "Good-night — I
hope you're disappointed or disgusted or something!"

He looked at her gravely, taking her by the hand she
offered. "I'm puzzled, if you want to know!" he answered.

"Well, I hope it won't keep you awake!" she said
very smartly; and, under the escort of the privileged
Eugenio, the two ladies passed toward the house.

Winterbourne's eyes followed them; he was indeed
quite mystified. He lingered beside the lake a quarter
of an hour, baffled by the question of the girl's sudden
familiarities and caprices. But the only very definite
conclusion he came to was that he should enjoy
deucedly "going off" with her somewhere.

DAISY MILLER

Two days later he went off with her to the Castle of Chillon. He waited for her in the large hall of the hotel, where the couriers, the servants, the foreign tourists were lounging about and staring. It was n't the place he would have chosen for a tryst, but she had placidly appointed it. She came tripping downstairs, buttoning her long gloves, squeezing her folded parasol against her pretty figure, dressed exactly in the way that consorted best, to his fancy, with their adventure. He was a man of imagination and, as our ancestors used to say, of sensibility; as he took in her charming air and caught from the great staircase her impatient confiding step the note of some small sweet strain of romance, not intense but clear and sweet, seemed to sound for their start. He could have believed he was *really* going "off" with her. He led her out through all the idle people assembled — they all looked at her straight and hard: she had begun to chatter as soon as she joined him. His preference had been that they should be conveyed to Chillon in a carriage, but she expressed a lively wish to go in the little steamer — there would be such a lovely breeze upon the water and they should see such lots of people. The sail was n't long, but Winterbourne's companion found time for many characteristic remarks and other demonstrations, not a few of which were, from the extremity of their candour, slightly disconcerting. To the young man himself their small excursion showed so for delightfully irregular and incongruously intimate that, even allowing for her habitual sense of freedom, he had some expectation of seeing her appear to find in it the same savour. But it must be confessed

39

that he was in this particular rather disappointed. Miss Miller was highly animated, she was in the brightest spirits; but she was clearly not at all in a nervous flutter — as she should have been to match *his* tension; she avoided neither his eyes nor those of any one else; she neither coloured from an awkward consciousness when she looked at him nor when she saw that people were looking at herself. People continued to look at her a great deal, and Winterbourne could at least take pleasure in his pretty companion's distinguished air. He had been privately afraid she would talk loud, laugh overmuch, and even perhaps desire to move extravagantly about the boat. But he quite forgot his fears; he sat smiling with his eyes on her face while, without stirring from her place, she delivered herself of a great number of original reflexions. It was the most charming innocent prattle he had ever heard, for, by his own experience hitherto, when young persons were so ingenuous they were less articulate and when they were so confident were more sophisticated. If he had assented to the idea that she was "common," at any rate, *was* she proving so, after all, or was he simply getting used to her commonness? Her discourse was for the most part of what immediately and superficially surrounded them, but there were moments when it threw out a longer look or took a sudden straight plunge.

"What on *earth* are you so solemn about?" she suddenly demanded, fixing her agreeable eyes on her friend's.

"*Am* I solemn?" he asked. "I had an idea I was grinning from ear to ear."

"You look as if you were taking me to a prayer-meeting or a funeral. If that's a grin your ears are very near together."

"Should you like me to dance a hornpipe on the deck?"

"Pray do, and I'll carry round your hat. It will pay the expenses of our journey."

"I never was better pleased in my life," Winterbourne returned.

She looked at him a moment, then let it renew her amusement. "I like to make you say those things. You're a queer mixture!"

In the castle, after they had landed, nothing could exceed the light independence of her humour. She tripped about the vaulted chambers, rustled her skirts in the corkscrew staircases, flirted back with a pretty little cry and a shudder from the edge of the oubliettes and turned a singularly well-shaped ear to everything Winterbourne told her about the place. But he saw she cared little for mediæval history and that the grim ghosts of Chillon loomed but faintly before her. They had the good fortune to have been able to wander without other society than that of their guide; and Winterbourne arranged with this companion that they should n't be hurried — that they should linger and pause wherever they chose. He interpreted the bargain generously — Winterbourne on his side had been generous — and ended by leaving them quite to themselves. Miss Miller's observations were marked by no logical consistency; for anything she wanted to say she was sure to find a pretext. She found a great many, in the tortuous passages and rugged embrasures

41

of the place, for asking her young man sudden questions about himself, his family, his previous history, his tastes, his habits, his designs, and for supplying information on corresponding points in her own situation. Of her own tastes, habits and designs the charming creature was prepared to give the most definite and indeed the most favourable account.

"Well, I hope you know enough!" she exclaimed after Winterbourne had sketched for her something of the story of the unhappy Bonnivard. "I never saw a man that knew so much!" The history of Bonnivard had evidently, as they say, gone into one ear and out of the other. But this easy erudition struck her none the less as wonderful, and she was soon quite sure she wished Winterbourne would travel with them and "go round" with them: they too in that case might learn something about something. "Don't you want to come and teach Randolph?" she asked; "I guess he'd improve with a gentleman teacher." Winterbourne was certain that nothing could possibly please him so much, but that he had unfortunately other occupations. "Other occupations? I don't believe a speck of it!" she protested. "What do you mean now? You're not in business." The young man allowed that he was not in business, but he had engagements which even within a day or two would necessitate his return to Geneva. "Oh bother!" she panted, "I don't believe it!" and she began to talk about something else. But a few moments later, when he was pointing out to her the interesting design of an antique fireplace, she broke out irrelevantly: "You don't mean to say you're going back to Geneva?"

"It is a melancholy fact that I shall have to report myself there to-morrow."

She met it with a vivacity that could only flatter him. "Well, Mr. Winterbourne, I think you're horrid!"

"Oh don't say such dreadful things!" he quite sincerely pleaded — "just at the last."

"The last?" the girl cried; "I call it the very first! I've half a mind to leave you here and go straight back to the hotel alone." And for the next ten minutes she did nothing but call him horrid. Poor Winterbourne was fairly bewildered; no young lady had as yet done him the honour to be so agitated by the mention of his personal plans. His companion, after this, ceased to pay any attention to the curiosities of Chillon or the beauties of the lake; she opened fire on the special charmer in Geneva whom she appeared to have instantly taken it for granted that he was hurrying back to see. How did Miss Daisy Miller know of that agent of his fate in Geneva? Winterbourne, who denied the existence of such a person, was quite unable to discover; and he was divided between amazement at the rapidity of her induction and amusement at the directness of her criticism. She struck him afresh, in all this, as an extraordinary mixture of innocence and crudity. "Does she never allow you more than three days at a time?" Miss Miller wished ironically to know. "Doesn't she give you a vacation in summer? there's no one so hard-worked but they can get leave to go off somewhere at this season. I suppose if you stay another day she'll come right after you in the boat. Do wait over till Friday and I'll go

43

down to the landing to see her arrive!" He began at last even to feel he had been wrong to be disappointed in the temper in which his young lady had embarked. If he had missed the personal accent, the personal accent was now making its appearance. It sounded very distinctly, toward the end, in her telling him she'd stop "teasing" him if he'd promise her solemnly to come down to Rome that winter.

"That's not a difficult promise to make," he hastened to acknowledge. "My aunt has taken an apartment in Rome from January and has already asked me to come and see her."

"I don't want you to come for your aunt," said Daisy; "I want you just to come for me." And this was the only allusion he was ever to hear her make again to his invidious kinswoman. He promised her that at any rate he would certainly come, and after this she forbore from teasing. Winterbourne took a carriage and they drove back to Vevey in the dusk; the girl at his side, her animation a little spent, was now quite distractingly passive.

In the evening he mentioned to Mrs. Costello that he had spent the afternoon at Chillon with Miss Daisy Miller.

"The Americans — of the courier?" asked this lady.

"Ah happily the courier stayed at home."

"She went with you all alone?"

"All alone."

Mrs. Costello sniffed a little at her smelling-bottle. "And that," she exclaimed, "is the little abomination you wanted me to know!"

III

WINTERBOURNE, who had returned to Geneva the day after his excursion to Chillon, went to Rome toward the end of January. His aunt had been established there a considerable time and he had received from her a couple of characteristic letters. "Those people you were so devoted to last summer at Vevey have turned up here, courier and all," she wrote. "They seem to have made several acquaintances, but the courier continues to be the most *intime*. The young lady, however, is also very intimate with various third-rate Italians, with whom she rackets about in a way that makes much talk. Bring me that pretty novel of Cherbuliez's —'Paule Méré'—and don't come later than the 23d."

Our friend would in the natural course of events, on arriving in Rome, have presently ascertained Mrs. Miller's address at the American banker's and gone to pay his compliments to Miss Daisy. "After what happened at Vevey I certainly think I may call upon them," he said to Mrs. Costello.

"If after what happens — at Vevey and everywhere — you desire to keep up the acquaintance, you're very welcome. Of course you're not squeamish — a man may know every one. Men are welcome to the privilege!"

"Pray what is it then that 'happens' — here for instance ?" Winterbourne asked.

"Well, the girl tears about alone with her unmis-

45

takeably low foreigners. As to what happens further you must apply elsewhere for information. She has picked up half a dozen of the regular Roman fortune-hunters of the inferior sort and she takes them about to such houses as she may put *her* nose into. When she comes to a party — such a party as she can come to — she brings with her a gentleman with a good deal of manner and a wonderful moustache."

"And where's the mother?"

"I have n't the least idea. They 're very dreadful people."

Winterbourne thought them over in these new lights. "They 're very ignorant — very innocent only, and utterly uncivilised. Depend on it they 're not 'bad.'"

"They 're hopelessly vulgar," said Mrs. Costello. "Whether or no being hopelessly vulgar is being 'bad' is a question for the metaphysicians. They 're bad enough to blush for, at any rate; and for this short life that 's quite enough."

The news that his little friend the child of nature of the Swiss lakeside was now surrounded by half a dozen wonderful moustaches checked Winterbourne's impulse to go straightway to see her. He had perhaps not definitely flattered himself that he had made an ineffaceable impression upon her heart, but he was annoyed at hearing of a state of affairs so little in harmony with an image that had lately flitted in and out of his own meditations; the image of a very pretty girl looking out of an old Roman window and asking herself urgently when Mr. Winterbourne would arrive. If, however, he determined to wait a little before reminding this young lady of his claim to her faithful remembrance, he called with more promptitude on two or three other friends. One of these friends was an American lady who had spent several winters at Geneva, where she had placed her children at school. She was a very accomplished woman and she lived in Via Gregoriana. Winterbourne found her in a little crimson drawing-room on a third floor; the room was filled with southern sunshine. He had n't been there ten minutes when the servant, appearing in the doorway, announced complacently "Madame Mila!" This announcement was presently followed by the entrance of little Randolph Miller, who stopped in the middle of the room and stood staring at Winterbourne. An instant later his pretty sister crossed the threshold; and then, after a considerable interval, the parent of the pair slowly advanced.

"I guess I know you!" Randolph broke ground without delay.

"I'm sure you know a great many things" — and his old friend clutched him all interestedly by the arm. "How's your education coming on?"

Daisy was engaged in some pretty babble with her hostess, but when she heard Winterbourne's voice she quickly turned her head with a "Well, I declare!" which he met smiling. "I told you I should come, you know."

"Well, I did n't believe it," she answered.

"I'm much obliged to you for that," laughed the young man.

"You might have come to see me then," Daisy went on as if they had parted the week before.

"I arrived only yesterday."

"I don't believe any such thing!" the girl declared afresh.

Winterbourne turned with a protesting smile to her mother, but this lady evaded his glance and, seating herself, fixed her eyes on her son. "We've got a bigger place than this," Randolph hereupon broke out. "It's all gold on the walls."

Mrs. Miller, more of a fatalist apparently than ever, turned uneasily in her chair. "I told you if I was to bring you you'd say something!" she stated as for the benefit of such of the company as might hear it.

"I told *you!*" Randolph retorted. "I tell *you*, sir!" he added jocosely, giving Winterbourne a thump on the knee. "It *is* bigger too!"

As Daisy's conversation with her hostess still occupied her Winterbourne judged it becoming to address a few words to her mother — such as "I hope you've been well since we parted at Vevey."

Mrs. Miller now certainly looked at him — at his chin. "Not very well, sir," she answered.

"She's got the dyspepsia," said Randolph. "I've got it too. Father's got it bad. But I've got it worst!"

This proclamation, instead of embarrassing Mrs. Miller, seemed to soothe her by reconstituting the environment to which she was most accustomed. "I suffer from the liver," she amiably whined to Winterbourne. "I think it's this climate; it's less bracing than Schenectady, especially in the winter season. I don't know whether you know we reside at Schenectady. I was saying to Daisy that I certainly hadn't found any one like Dr. Davis and I didn't believe I *would.* Oh up in Schenectady, he stands first; they think everything of Dr. Davis. He has so much to do, and yet there was nothing he would n't do for *me*. He said he never saw anything like my dyspepsia, but he was bound to get at it. I 'm sure there was nothing he would n't try, and I did n't care what he did to me if he only brought me relief. He was just going to try something new, and I just longed for it, when we came right off. Mr. Miller felt as if he wanted Daisy to see Europe for herself. But I could n't help writing the other day that I supposed it was all right for Daisy, but that I did n't know as I *could* get on much longer without Dr. Davis. At Schenectady he stands at the very top; and there 's a great deal of sickness there too. It affects my sleep."

Winterbourne had a good deal of pathological gossip with Dr. Davis's patient, during which Daisy chattered unremittingly to her own companion. The young man asked Mrs. Miller how she was pleased with Rome. "Well, I must say I 'm disappointed," she confessed. "We had heard so much about it — I suppose we had heard too much. But we could n't help that. We had been led to expect something different."

Winterbourne, however, abounded in reassurance. "Ah wait a little, and you 'll grow very fond of it."

"I hate it worse and worse every day!" cried Randolph.

"You 're like the infant Hannibal," his friend laughed.

"No I ain't—like any infant!" Randolph declared at a venture.

"Well, that 's so — and you never *were!*" his

49

mother concurred. "But we've seen places," she resumed, "that I'd put a long way ahead of Rome." And in reply to Winterbourne's interrogation, "There's Zürich — up there in the mountains," she instanced; "I think Zürich's real lovely, and we had n't heard half so much about it."

"The best place we've seen's the *City of Richmond!*" said Randolph.

"He means the ship," Mrs. Miller explained. "We crossed in that ship. Randolph had a good time on the *City of Richmond.*"

"It's the best place *I've* struck," the child repeated. "Only it was turned the wrong way."

"Well, we've got to turn the right way sometime," said Mrs. Miller with strained but weak optimism. Winterbourne expressed the hope that her daughter at least appreciated the so various interest of Rome, and she declared with some spirit that Daisy was quite carried away. "It's on account of the society — the society's splendid. She goes round everywhere; she has made a great number of acquaintances. Of course she goes round more than I do. I must say they've all been very sweet — they've taken her right in. And then she knows a great many gentlemen. Oh she thinks there's nothing like Rome. Of course it's a great deal pleasanter for a young lady if she knows plenty of gentlemen."

By this time Daisy had turned her attention again to Winterbourne, but in quite the same free form. "I've been telling Mrs. Walker how mean you were!"

"And what's the evidence you've offered?" he asked, a trifle disconcerted, for all his superior gallantry, by her inadequate measure of the zeal of an admirer who on his way down to Rome had stopped neither at Bologna nor at Florence, simply because of a certain sweet appeal to his fond fancy, not to say to his finest curiosity. He remembered how a cynical compatriot had once told him that American women — the pretty ones, and this gave a largeness to the axiom — were at once the most exacting in the world and the least endowed with a sense of indebtedness.

"Why you were awfully mean up at Vevey," Daisy said. "You would n't do most anything. You would n't stay there when I asked you."

"Dearest young lady," cried Winterbourne, with generous passion, "have I come all the way to Rome only to be riddled by your silver shafts?"

" Just hear him say that!" — and she gave an affectionate twist to a bow on her hostess's dress. "Did you ever hear anything so quaint?"

"So 'quaint,' my dear?" echoed Mrs. Walker more critically — quite in the tone of a partisan of Winterbourne.

"Well, I don't know" — and the girl continued to finger her ribbons. "Mrs. Walker, I want to tell you something."

"Say, mother-r," broke in Randolph with his rough ends to his words, "I tell you you 've got to go. Eugenio 'll raise something!"

"I 'm not afraid of Eugenio," said Daisy with a toss of her head. "Look here, Mrs. Walker," she went on, "you know I 'm coming to your party."

"I 'm delighted to hear it."

"I 've got a lovely dress."

DAISY MILLER

"I'm very sure of that."

"But I want to ask a favour — permission to bring a friend."

"I shall be happy to see any of your friends," said Mrs. Walker, who turned with a smile to Mrs. Miller.

"Oh they're not my friends," cried that lady, squirming in shy repudiation. "It seems as if they did n't take to *me*—I never spoke to one of them!"

"It's an intimate friend of mine, Mr. Giovanelli," Daisy pursued without a tremor in her young clearness or a shadow on her shining bloom.

Mrs. Walker had a pause and gave a rapid glance at Winterbourne. "I shall be glad to see Mr. Giovanelli," she then returned.

"He's just the finest kind of Italian," Daisy pursued with the prettiest serenity. "He's a great friend of mine and the handsomest man in the world — except Mr. Winterbourne! He knows plenty of Italians, but he wants to know some Americans. It seems as if he was crazy about Americans. He's tremendously bright. He's perfectly lovely!"

It was settled that this paragon should be brought to Mrs. Walker's party, and then Mrs. Miller prepared to take her leave. "I guess we'll go right back to the hotel," she remarked with a confessed failure of the larger imagination.

"You may go back to the hotel, mother," Daisy replied, "but I'm just going to walk round."

"She's going to go it with Mr. Giovanelli," Randolph unscrupulously commented.

"I'm going to go it on the Pincio," Daisy peace-

52

ably smiled, while the way that she "condoned" these things almost melted Winterbourne's heart.

"Alone, my dear — at this hour?" Mrs. Walker asked. The afternoon was drawing to a close — it was the hour for the throng of carriages and of contemplative pedestrians. "I don't consider it's safe, Daisy," her hostess firmly asserted.

"Neither do I then," Mrs. Miller thus borrowed confidence to add. "You'll catch the fever as sure as you live. Remember what Dr. Davis told you!"

"Give her some of that medicine before she starts in," Randolph suggested.

The company had risen to its feet; Daisy, still showing her pretty teeth, bent over and kissed her hostess. "Mrs. Walker, you're too perfect," she simply said. "I'm not going alone; I'm going to meet a friend."

"Your friend won't keep you from catching the fever even if it *is* his own second nature," Mrs. Miller observed.

"Is it Mr. Giovanelli that's the dangerous attraction?" Mrs. Walker asked without mercy.

Winterbourne was watching the challenged girl; at this question his attention quickened. She stood there smiling and smoothing her bonnet-ribbons; she glanced at Winterbourne. Then, while she glanced and smiled, she brought out all affirmatively and without a shade of hesitation: "Mr. Giovanelli — the beautiful Giovanelli."

"My dear young friend" — and, taking her hand, Mrs. Walker turned to pleading — "don't prowl off to the Pincio at this hour to meet a beautiful Italian."

53

DAISY MILLER

"Well, he speaks first-rate English," Mrs. Miller incoherently mentioned.

"Gracious me," Daisy piped up, "I don't want to do anything that's going to affect my health — or my character either! There's an easy way to settle it." Her eyes continued to play over Winterbourne. "The Pincio's only a hundred yards off, and if Mr. Winterbourne were as polite as he pretends he'd offer to walk right in with me!"

Winterbourne's politeness hastened to proclaim itself, and the girl gave him gracious leave to accompany her. They passed downstairs before her mother, and at the door he saw Mrs. Miller's carriage drawn up, with the ornamental courier whose acquaintance he had made at Vevey seated within. "Good-bye, Eugenio," cried Daisy; "I'm going to take a walk!" The distance from Via Gregoriana to the beautiful garden at the other end of the Pincian Hill is in fact rapidly traversed. As the day was splendid, however, and the concourse of vehicles, walkers and loungers numerous, the young Americans found their progress much delayed. This fact was highly agreeable to Winterbourne, in spite of his consciousness of his singular situation. The slow-moving, idly-gazing Roman crowd bestowed much attention on the extremely pretty young woman of English race who passed through it, with some difficulty, on his arm; and he wondered what on earth had been in Daisy's mind when she proposed to exhibit herself unattended to its appreciation. His own mission, to her sense, was apparently to consign her to the hands of Mr. Giovanelli; but, at once annoyed and gratified, he resolved that he would do no such thing.

"Why have n't you been to see me?" she meanwhile asked. "You can't get out of that."

"I 've had the honour of telling you that I 've only just stepped out of the train."

"You must have stayed in the train a good while after it stopped!" she derisively cried. "I suppose you were asleep. You 've had time to go to see Mrs. Walker."

"I knew Mrs. Walker —" Winterbourne began to explain.

"I know where you knew her. You knew her at Geneva. She told me so. Well, you knew me at Vevey. That 's just as good. So you ought to have come." She asked him no other question than this; she began to prattle about her own affairs. "We 've got splendid rooms at the hotel; Eugenio says they 're the best rooms in Rome. We 're going to stay all winter — if we don't die of the fever; and I guess we 'll stay then! It 's a great deal nicer than I thought; I thought it would be fearfully quiet — in fact I was sure it would be deadly pokey. I foresaw we should be going round all the time with one of those dreadful old men who explain about the pictures and things. But we only had about a week of that, and now I 'm enjoying myself. I know ever so many people, and they 're all so charming. The society 's extremely select. There are all kinds — English and Germans and Italians. I think I like the English best. I like their style of conversaticn. But there are some lovely Americans. I never saw anything so hospitable.

There's something or other every day. There's not much dancing — but I must say I never thought dancing was everything. I was always fond of conversation. I guess I'll have plenty at Mrs. Walker's — her rooms are so small." When they had passed the gate of the Pincian Gardens Miss Miller began to wonder where Mr. Giovanelli might be. "We had better go straight to that place in front, where you look at the view."

Winterbourne at this took a stand. "I certainly shan't help you to find him."

"Then I shall find him without you," Daisy said with spirit.

"You certainly won't leave me!" he protested.

She burst into her familiar little laugh. "Are you afraid you'll get lost — or run over? But there's Giovanelli leaning against that tree. He's staring at the women in the carriages: did you ever see anything so cool?"

Winterbourne descried hereupon at some distance a little figure that stood with folded arms and nursing its cane. It had a handsome face, a hat artfully poised, a glass in one eye and a nosegay in its buttonhole. Daisy's friend looked at it a moment and then said: "Do you mean to speak to that thing?"

"Do I mean to speak to him? Why you don't suppose I mean to communicate by signs!"

"Pray understand then," the young man returned, "that I intend to remain with you."

Daisy stopped and looked at him without a sign of troubled consciousness, with nothing in her face but

56

DAISY MILLER

her charming eyes, her charming teeth and her happy dimples. "Well, she's a cool one!" he thought.

"I don't like the way you say that," she declared. "It's too imperious."

"I beg your pardon if I say it wrong. The main point's to give you an idea of my meaning."

The girl looked at him more gravely, but with eyes that were prettier than ever. "I've never allowed a gentleman to dictate to me or to interfere with anything I do."

"I think that's just where your mistake has come in," he retorted. "You should sometimes listen to a gentleman — the right one."

At this she began to laugh again. "I do nothing but listen to gentlemen! Tell me if Mr. Giovanelli is the right one."

The gentleman with the nosegay in his bosom had now made out our two friends and was approaching Miss Miller with obsequious rapidity. He bowed to Winterbourne as well as to the latter's compatriot; he seemed to shine, in his coxcombical way, with the desire to please and the fact of his own intelligent joy, though Winterbourne thought him not a bad-looking fellow. But he nevertheless said to Daisy: "No, he's not the right one."

She had clearly a natural turn for free introductions; she mentioned with the easiest grace the name of each of her companions to the other. She strolled forward with one of them on either hand; Mr. Giovanelli, who spoke English very cleverly — Winterbourne afterwards learned that he had practised the idiom upon a great many American heiresses — ad-

57

dressed her a great deal of very polite nonsense. He had the best possible manners, and the young American, who said nothing, reflected on that depth of Italian subtlety, so strangely opposed to Anglo-Saxon simplicity, which enables people to show a smoother surface in proportion as they're more acutely displeased. Giovanelli of course had counted upon something more intimate — he had not bargained for a party of three; but he kept his temper in a manner that suggested far-stretching intentions. Winterbourne flattered himself he had taken his measure. "He's anything but a gentleman," said the young American; "he isn't even a very plausible imitation of one. He's a music-master or a penny-a-liner or a third-rate artist. He's awfully on his good behaviour, but damn his fine eyes!" Mr. Giovanelli had indeed great advantages; but it was deeply disgusting to Daisy's other friend that something in her should n't have instinctively discriminated against such a type. Giovanelli chattered and jested and made himself agreeable according to his honest Roman lights. It was true that if he was an imitation the imitation was studied. "Nevertheless," Winterbourne said to himself, "a nice girl ought to know!" And then he came back to the dreadful question of whether this *was* in fact a nice girl. Would a nice girl — even allowing for her being a little American flirt — make a rendezvous with a presumably low-lived foreigner? The rendezvous in this case indeed had been in broad daylight and in the most crowded corner of Rome; but was n't it possible to regard the choice of these very circumstances as a proof more of vulgarity than of anything else ? Singular though it may seem, Winterbourne was vexed that the girl, in joining her *amoroso*, should n't appear more impatient of his own company, and he was vexed precisely because of his inclination. It was impossible to regard her as a wholly unspotted flower — she lacked a certain indispensable fineness; and it would therefore much simplify the situation to be able to treat her as the subject of one of the visitations known to romancers as "lawless passions." That she should seem to wish to get rid of him would have helped him to think more lightly of her, just as to be able to think more lightly of her would have made her less perplexing. Daisy at any rate continued on this occasion to present herself as an inscrutable combination of audacity and innocence.

She had been walking some quarter of an hour, attended by her two cavaliers and responding in a tone of very childish gaiety, as it after all struck one of them, to the pretty speeches of the other, when a carriage that had detached itself from the revolving train drew up beside the path. At the same moment Winterbourne noticed that his friend Mrs. Walker — the lady whose house he had lately left — was seated in the vehicle and was beckoning to him. Leaving Miss Miller's side, he hastened to obey her summons — and all to find her flushed, excited, scandalised. "It's really too dreadful" — she earnestly appealed to him. "That crazy girl must n't do this sort of thing. She must n't walk here with you two men. Fifty people have remarked her."

Winterbourne — suddenly and rather oddly rubbed the wrong way by this — raised his grave eyebrows.

"I think it's a pity to make too much fuss about it."

"It's a pity to let the girl ruin herself!"

"She's very innocent," he reasoned in his own troubled interest.

"She's very reckless," cried Mrs. Walker, "and goodness knows how far — left to itself — it may go. Did you ever," she proceeded to enquire, "see anything so blatantly imbecile as the mother? After you had all left me just now I couldn't sit still for thinking of it. It seemed too pitiful not even to attempt to save them. I ordered the carriage and put on my bonnet and came here as quickly as possible. Thank heaven I've found you!"

"What do you propose to do with us?" Winterbourne uncomfortably smiled.

"To ask her to get in, to drive her about here for half an hour — so that the world may see she's not running absolutely wild — and then take her safely home."

"I don't think it's a very happy thought," he said after reflexion, "but you're at liberty to try."

Mrs. Walker accordingly tried. The young man went in pursuit of their young lady who had simply nodded and smiled, from her distance, at her recent patroness in the carriage and then had gone her way with her own companion. On learning, in the event, that Mrs. Walker had followed her, she retraced her steps, however, with a perfect good grace and with Mr. Giovanelli at her side. She professed herself "enchanted" to have a chance to present this gentleman to her good friend, and immediately achieved the introduction; declaring with it, and as if it were of as little importance, that she had never in her life seen anything so lovely as that lady's carriage-rug.

"I'm glad you admire it," said her poor pursuer, smiling sweetly. "Will you get in and let me put it over you?"

"Oh no, thank you!" — Daisy knew her mind. "I'll admire it ever so much more as I see you driving round with it."

"Do get in and drive round *with* me," Mrs. Walker pleaded.

"That would be charming, but it's so fascinating just as I am!" — with which the girl radiantly took in the gentlemen on either side of her.

"It may be fascinating, dear child, but it's not the custom here," urged the lady of the victoria, leaning forward in this vehicle with her hands devoutly clasped.

"Well, it ought to be then!" Daisy imperturbably laughed. "If I didn't walk I'd expire."

"You should walk with your mother, dear," cried Mrs. Walker with a loss of patience.

"With my mother dear?" the girl amusedly echoed. Winterbourne saw she scented interference. "My mother never walked ten steps in her life. And then, you know," she blandly added, "I'm more than five years old."

"You're old enough to be more reasonable. You're old enough, dear Miss Miller, to be talked about."

Daisy wondered to extravagance. "Talked about? What do you mean?"

"Come into my carriage and I'll tell you."

Daisy turned shining eyes again from one of the gentlemen beside her to the other. Mr. Giovanelli was bowing to and fro, rubbing down his gloves and laughing irresponsibly; Winterbourne thought the scene the most unpleasant possible. "I don't think I want to know what you mean," the girl presently said. "I don't think I should like it."

Winterbourne only wished Mrs. Walker would tuck up her carriage-rug and drive away; but this lady, as she afterwards told him, did n't feel she could "rest there." "Should you prefer being thought a very reckless girl?" she accordingly asked.

"Gracious me!" exclaimed Daisy. She looked again at Mr. Giovanelli, then she turned to her other companion. There was a small pink flush in her cheek; she was tremendously pretty. "Does Mr. Winterbourne think," she put to him with a wonderful bright intensity of appeal, "that — to save my reputation — I ought to get into the carriage?"

It really embarrassed him; for an instant he cast about — so strange was it to hear her speak that way of her "reputation." But he himself in fact had to speak in accordance with gallantry. The finest gallantry here was surely just to tell her the truth; and the truth, for our young man, as the few indications I have been able to give have made him known to the reader, was that his charming friend should listen to the voice of civilised society. He took in again her exquisite prettiness and then said the more distinctly: "I think you should get into the carriage."

Daisy gave the rein to her amusement. "I never heard anything so stiff! If this is improper, Mrs.

Walker," she pursued, "then I'm *all* improper, and you had better give me right up. Good-bye; I hope you'll have a lovely ride!" — and with Mr. Giovanelli, who made a triumphantly obsequious salute, she turned away.

Mrs. Walker sat looking after her, and there were tears in Mrs. Walker's eyes. "Get in here, sir," she said to Winterbourne, indicating the place beside her. The young man answered that he felt bound to accompany Miss Miller; whereupon the lady of the victoria declared that if he refused her this favour she would never speak to him again. She was evidently wound up. He accordingly hastened to overtake Daisy and her more faithful ally, and, offering her his hand, told her that Mrs. Walker had made a stringent claim on his presence. He had expected her to answer with something rather free, something still more significant of the perversity from which the voice of society, through the lips of their distressed friend, had so earnestly endeavoured to dissuade her. But she only let her hand slip, as she scarce looked at him, through his slightly awkward grasp; while Mr. Giovanelli, to make it worse, bade him farewell with too emphatic a flourish of the hat.

Winterbourne was not in the best possible humour as he took his seat beside the author of his sacrifice. "That was not clever of you," he said candidly, as the vehicle mingled again with the throng of carriages.

"In such a case," his companion answered, "I don't want to be clever — I only want to be *true!*"

"Well, your truth has only offended the strange little creature — it has only put her off."

"It has happened very well" — Mrs. Walker accepted her work. "If she's so perfectly determined to compromise herself the sooner one knows it the better — one can act accordingly."

"I suspect she meant no great harm, you know," Winterbourne maturely opined.

"So I thought a month ago. But she has been going too far."

"What has she been doing?"

"Everything that's not done here. Flirting with any man she can pick up; sitting in corners with mysterious Italians; dancing all the evening with the same partners; receiving visits at eleven o'clock at night. Her mother melts away when the visitors come."

"But her brother," laughed Winterbourne, "sits up till two in the morning."

"He must be edified by what he sees. I'm told that at their hotel every one's talking about her and that a smile goes round among the servants when a gentleman comes and asks for Miss Miller."

"Ah we needn't mind the servants!" Winterbourne compassionately signified. "The poor girl's only fault," he presently added, "is her complete lack of education."

"She's naturally indelicate," Mrs. Walker, on her side, reasoned. "Take that example this morning. How long had you known her at Vevey?"

"A couple of days."

"Imagine then the taste of her making it a personal matter that you should have left the place!"

He agreed that taste wasn't the strong point of the Millers — after which he was silent for some moments; but only at last to add: "I suspect, Mrs. Walker, that you and I have lived too long at Geneva!" And he further noted that he should be glad to learn with what particular design she had made him enter her carriage.

"I wanted to enjoin on you the importance of your ceasing your relations with Miss Miller; that of your not appearing to flirt with her; that of your giving her no further opportunity to expose herself; that of your in short letting her alone."

"I'm afraid I can't do anything quite so enlightened as *that*," he returned. "I like her awfully, you know."

"All the more reason you should n't help her to make a scandal."

"Well, there shall be nothing scandalous in my attentions to her," he was willing to promise.

"There certainly will be in the way she takes them. But I 've said what I had on my conscience," Mrs. Walker pursued. "If you wish to rejoin the young lady I 'll put you down. Here, by the way, you have a chance."

The carriage was engaged in that part of the Pincian drive which overhangs the wall of Rome and overlooks the beautiful Villa Borghese. It is bordered by a large parapet, near which are several seats. One of these, at a distance, was occupied by a gentleman and a lady, toward whom Mrs. Walker gave a toss of her head. At the same moment these persons rose and walked to the parapet. Winterbourne had asked the coachman to stop; he now descended from the carriage. His companion looked at him a moment in

65

silence and then, while he raised his hat, drove majestically away. He stood where he had alighted; he had turned his eyes toward Daisy and her cavalier. They evidently saw no one; they were too deeply occupied with each other. When they reached the low garden-wall they remained a little looking off at the great flat-topped pine-clusters of Villa Borghese; then the girl's attendant admirer seated himself familiarly on the broad ledge of the wall. The western sun in the opposite sky sent out a brilliant shaft through a couple of cloud-bars; whereupon the gallant Giovanelli took her parasol out of her hands and opened it. She came a little nearer and he held the parasol over her; then, still holding it, he let it so rest on her shoulder that both of their heads were hidden from Winterbourne. This young man stayed but a moment longer; then he began to walk. But he walked — not toward the couple united beneath the parasol, rather toward the residence of his aunt Mrs. Costello.

IV

HE flattered himself on the following day that there was no smiling among the servants when he at least asked for Mrs. Miller at her hotel. This lady and her daughter, however, were not at home; and on the next day after, repeating his visit, Winterbourne again was met by a denial. Mrs. Walker's party took place on the evening of the third day, and in spite of the final reserves that had marked his last interview with that social critic our young man was among the guests. Mrs. Walker was one of those pilgrims from the younger world who, while in contact with the elder, make a point, in their own phrase, of studying European society; and she had on this occasion collected several specimens of diversely-born humanity to serve, as might be, for text-books. When Winterbourne arrived the little person he desired most to find was n't there; but in a few moments he saw Mrs. Miller come in alone, very shyly and ruefully. This lady's hair, above the dead waste of her temples, was more frizzled than ever. As she approached their hostess Winterbourne also drew near.

"You see I've come all alone," said Daisy's unsupported parent. "I'm so frightened I don't know what to do; it's the first time I've ever been to a party alone — especially in this country. I wanted to bring Randolph or Eugenio or some one, but Daisy just pushed me off by myself. I ain't used to going round alone."

67

"And does n't your daughter intend to favour us with her society?" Mrs. Walker impressively enquired.

"Well, Daisy's all dressed," Mrs. Miller testified with that accent of the dispassionate, if not of the philosophic, historian with which she always recorded the current incidents of her daughter's career. "She got dressed on purpose before dinner. But she has a friend of hers there; that gentleman — the handsomest of the Italians — that she wanted to bring. They've got going at the piano — it seems as if they could n't leave off. Mr. Giovanelli does sing splendidly. But I guess they'll come before very long," Mrs. Miller hopefully concluded.

"I'm sorry she should come — in that particular way," Mrs. Walker permitted herself to observe.

"Well, I told her there was no use in her getting dressed before dinner if she was going to wait three hours," returned Daisy's mamma. "I did n't see the use of her putting on such a dress as that to sit round with Mr. Giovanelli."

"This is most horrible!" said Mrs. Walker, turning away and addressing herself to Winterbourne. "*Elle s'affiche, la malheureuse.* It's her revenge for my having ventured to remonstrate with her. When she comes I shan't speak to her."

Daisy came after eleven o'clock, but she was n't, on such an occasion, a young lady to wait to be spoken to. She rustled forward in radiant loveliness, smiling and chattering, carrying a large bouquet and attended by Mr. Giovanelli. Every one stopped talking and turned and looked at her while she floated up to Mrs.

68

Walker. "I'm afraid you thought I never was coming, so I sent mother off to tell you. I wanted to make Mr. Giovanelli practise some things before he came; you know he sings beautifully, and I want you to ask him to sing. This is Mr. Giovanelli; you know I introduced him to you; he's got the most lovely voice and he knows the most charming set of songs. I made him go over them this evening on purpose; we had the greatest time at the hotel." Of all this Daisy delivered herself with the sweetest brightest loudest confidence, looking now at her hostess and now at all the room, while she gave a series of little pats, round her very white shoulders, to the edges of her dress. "Is there any one I know?" she as undiscourageably asked.

"I think every one knows you!" said Mrs. Walker as with a grand intention; and she gave a very cursory greeting to Mr. Giovanelli. This gentleman bore himself gallantly; he smiled and bowed and showed his white teeth, he curled his moustaches and rolled his eyes and performed all the proper functions of a handsome Italian at an evening party. He sang, very prettily, half a dozen songs, though Mrs. Walker afterwards declared that she had been quite unable to find out who asked him. It was apparently not Daisy who had set him in motion — this young lady being seated a distance from the piano and though she had publicly, as it were, professed herself his musical patroness or guarantor, giving herself to gay and audible discourse while he warbled.

"It's a pity these rooms are so small; we can't dance," she remarked to Winterbourne as if she had seen him five minutes before.

DAISY MILLER

"I'm not sorry we can't dance," he candidly returned. "I'm incapable of a step."

"Of course you're incapable of a step," the girl assented. "I should think your legs *would* be stiff cooped in there so much of the time in that victoria."

"Well, they were very restless there three days ago," he amicably laughed; "all they really wanted was to dance attendance on you."

"Oh my other friend — my friend in need — stuck to me; he seems more at one with his limbs than you are — I'll say that for him. But did you ever hear anything so cool," Daisy demanded, "as Mrs. Walker's wanting me to get into her carriage and drop poor Mr. Giovanelli, and under the pretext that it was proper? People have different ideas! It would have been most unkind; he had been talking about that walk for ten days."

"He shouldn't have talked about it at all," Winterbourne decided to make answer on this: "he would never have proposed to a young lady of this country to walk about the streets of Rome with him."

"About the streets?" she cried with her pretty stare. "Where then would he have proposed to her to walk? The Pincio ain't the streets either, I guess; and I besides, thank goodness, am not a young lady of this country. The young ladies of this country have a dreadfully pokey time of it, by what I can discover; I don't see why I should change my habits for *such* stupids."

"I'm afraid your habits are those of a ruthless flirt," said Winterbourne with studied severity.

"Of course they are!" — and she hoped, evidently,

70

by the manner of it, to take his breath away. "I'm a fearful frightful flirt! Did you ever hear of a nice girl that was n't? But I suppose you 'll tell me now I'm not a nice girl."

He remained grave indeed under the shock of her cynical profession. "You're a very nice girl, but I wish you'd flirt with me, and me only."

"Ah thank you, thank you very much: you're the last man I should think of flirting with. As I've had the pleasure of informing you, you're too stiff."

"You say that too often," he resentfully remarked.

Daisy gave a delighted laugh. "If I could have the sweet hope of making you angry I'd say it again."

"Don't do that — when I'm angry I'm stiffer than ever. But if you won't flirt with me do cease at least to flirt with your friend at the piano. They don't," he declared as in full sympathy with "them," "understand that sort of thing here."

"I thought they understood nothing else!" Daisy cried with startling world-knowledge.

"Not in young unmarried women."

"It seems to me much more proper in young unmarried than in old married ones," she retorted.

"Well," said Winterbourne, "when you deal with natives you must go by the custom of the country. American flirting is a purely American silliness; it has — in its ineptitude of innocence — no place in *this* system. So when you show yourself in public with Mr. Giovanelli and without your mother —"

"Gracious, poor mother!" — and she made it beautifully unspeakable.

Winterbourne had a touched sense for this, but it

did n't alter his attitude. "Though *you* may be flirting Mr. Giovanelli is n't — he means something else."

"He is n't preaching at any rate," she returned. "And if you want very much to know, we 're neither of us flirting — not a little speck. We 're too good friends for that. We 're real intimate friends."

He was to continue to find her thus at moments inimitable. "Ah," he then judged, "if you 're in love with each other it 's another affair altogether!"

She had allowed him up to this point to speak so frankly that he had no thought of shocking her by the force of his logic; yet she now none the less immediately rose, blushing visibly and leaving him mentally to exclaim· that the name of little American flirts was incoherence. "Mr. Giovanelli at least," she answered, sparing but a single small queer glance for it, a queerer small glance, he felt, than he had ever yet had from her — "Mr. Giovanelli never says to me such very disagreeable things."

It had an effect on him — he stood staring. The subject of their contention had finished singing; he left the piano, and his recognition of what — a little awkwardly — did n't take place in celebration of this might nevertheless have been an acclaimed operatic tenor's series of repeated ducks before the curtain. So he bowed himself over to Daisy. "Won't you come to the other room and have some tea?" he asked — offering Mrs. Walker's slightly thin refreshment as he might have done all the kingdoms of the earth.

Daisy at last turned on Winterbourne a more natural and calculable light. He was but the more muddled by it, however, since so inconsequent a smile made nothing clear — it seemed at the most to prove in her a sweetness and softness that reverted instinctively to the pardon of offences. "It has never occurred to Mr. Winterbourne to offer me any tea," she said with her finest little intention of torment and triumph.

"I 've offered you excellent advice," the young man permitted himself to growl.

"I prefer weak tea!" cried Daisy, and she went off with the brilliant Giovanelli. She sat with him in the adjoining room, in the embrasure of the window, for the rest of the evening. There was an interesting performance at the piano, but neither of these conversers gave heed to it. When Daisy came to take leave of Mrs. Walker this lady conscientiously repaired the weakness of which she had been guilty at the moment of the girl's arrival — she turned her back straight on Miss Miller and left her to depart with what grace she might. Winterbourne happened to be near the door; he saw it all. Daisy turned very pale and looked at her mother, but Mrs. Miller was humbly unconscious of any rupture of any law or of any deviation from any custom. She appeared indeed to have felt an incongruous impulse to draw attention to her own striking conformity. "Good-night, Mrs. Walker," she said; "we 've had a beautiful evening. You see if I let Daisy come to parties without me I don't want her to go away without me." Daisy turned away, looking with a small white prettiness, a blighted grace, at the circle near the door: Winterbourne saw that for the first moment she was too much shocked and puzzled even for indignation. He on his side was greatly touched.

"That was very cruel," he promptly remarked to Mrs. Walker.

But this lady's face was also as a stone. "She never enters my drawing-room again."

Since Winterbourne then, hereupon, was not to meet her in Mrs. Walker's drawing-room he went as often as possible to Mrs. Miller's hotel. The ladies were rarely at home, but when he found them the devoted Giovanelli was always present. Very often the glossy little Roman, serene in success, but not unduly presumptuous, occupied with Daisy alone the florid salon enjoyed by Eugenio's care, Mrs. Miller being apparently ever of the opinion that discretion is the better part of solicitude. Winterbourne noted, at first with surprise, that Daisy on these occasions was neither embarrassed nor annoyed by his own entrance; but he presently began to feel that she had no more surprises for him and that he really liked, after all, not making out what she was "up to." She showed no displeasure for the interruption of her *tête-à-tête* with Giovanelli; she could chatter as freshly and freely with two gentlemen as with one, and this easy flow had ever the same anomaly for her earlier friend that it was so free without availing itself of its freedom. Winterbourne reflected that if she was seriously interested in the Italian it was odd she should n't take more trouble to preserve the sanctity of their interviews, and he liked her the better for her innocent-looking indifference and her inexhaustible gaiety. He could hardly have said why, but she struck him as a young person not formed for a troublesome jealousy. Smile at such a betrayal though the reader may, it was a fact with regard to the women who had hitherto interested him that, given certain contingencies, Winterbourne could see himself afraid — literally afraid — of these ladies. It pleased him to believe that even were twenty other things different and Daisy should love him and he should know it and like it, he would still never be afraid of Daisy. It must be added that this conviction was not altogether flattering to her: it represented that she was nothing every way if not light.

But she was evidently very much interested in Giovanelli. She looked at him whenever he spoke; she was perpetually telling him to do this and to do that; she was constantly chaffing and abusing him. She appeared completely to have forgotten that her other friend had said anything to displease her at Mrs. Walker's entertainment. One Sunday afternoon, having gone to Saint Peter's with his aunt, Winterbourne became aware that the young woman held in horror by that lady was strolling about the great church under escort of her coxcomb of the Corso. It amused him, after a debate, to point out the exemplary pair — even at the cost, as it proved, of Mrs. Costello's saying when she had taken them in through her eye-glass: "That's what makes you so pensive in these days, eh?"

"I had n't the least idea I was pensive," he pleaded.

"You're very much preoccupied; you're always thinking of something."

75

"And what is it," he asked, "that you accuse me of thinking of?"

"Of that young lady's, Miss Baker's, Miss Chandler's — what's her name? — Miss Miller's intrigue with that little barber's block."

"Do you call it an intrigue," he asked — "an affair that goes on with such peculiar publicity?"

"That's their folly," said Mrs. Costello, "it's not their merit."

"No," he insisted with a hint perhaps of the preoccupation to which his aunt had alluded — "I don't believe there's anything to be called an intrigue."

"Well" — and Mrs. Costello dropped her glass — "I've heard a dozen people speak of it: they say she's quite carried away by him."

"They're certainly as thick as thieves," our embarrassed young man allowed.

Mrs. Costello came back to them, however, after a little; and Winterbourne recognised in this a further illustration — than that supplied by his own condition — of the spell projected by the case. "He's certainly very handsome. One easily sees how it is. She thinks him the most elegant man in the world, the finest gentleman possible. She has never seen anything like him — he's better even than the courier. It was the courier probably who introduced him, and if he succeeds in marrying the young lady the courier will come in for a magnificent commission."

"I don't believe she thinks of marrying him," Winterbourne reasoned, "and I don't believe he hopes to marry her."

76

"You may be very sure she thinks of nothing at all. She romps on from day to day, from hour to hour, as they did in the Golden Age. I can imagine nothing more vulgar," said Mrs. Costello, whose figure of speech scarcely went on all fours. "And at the same time," she added, "depend upon it she may tell you any moment that she is 'engaged.'"

"I think that's more than Giovanelli really expects," said Winterbourne.

"And who is Giovanelli?"

"The shiny — but, to do him justice, not greasy — little Roman. I've asked questions about him and learned something. He's apparently a perfectly respectable little man. I believe he's in a small way a *cavaliere avvocato*. But he doesn't move in what are called the first circles. I think it really not absolutely impossible the courier introduced him. He's evidently immensely charmed with Miss Miller. If she thinks him the finest gentleman in the world, he, on his side, has never found himself in personal contact with such splendour, such opulence, such personal daintiness, as this young lady's. And then she must seem to him wonderfully pretty and interesting. Yes, he can't really hope to pull it off. That must appear to him too impossible a piece of luck. He has nothing but his handsome face to offer, and there's a substantial, a possibly explosive Mr. Miller in that mysterious land of dollars and six-shooters. Giovanelli's but too conscious that he hasn't a title to offer. If he were only a count or a *marchese!* What on earth can he make of the way they've taken him up?"

"He accounts for it by his handsome face and

thinks Miss Miller a young lady *qui se passe ses fantaisies!*"

"It's very true," Winterbourne pursued, "that Daisy and her mamma have n't yet risen to that stage of — what shall I call it? — of culture, at which the idea of catching a count or a *marchese* begins. I believe them intellectually incapable of that conception."

"Ah but the *cavaliere avvocato* does n't believe them!" cried Mrs. Costello.

Of the observation excited by Daisy's "intrigue" Winterbourne gathered that day at Saint Peter's sufficient evidence. A dozen of the American colonists in Rome came to talk with his relative, who sat on a small portable stool at the base of one of the great pilasters. The vesper-service was going forward in splendid chants and organ-tones in the adjacent choir, and meanwhile, between Mrs. Costello and her friends, much was said about poor little Miss Miller's going really "too far." Winterbourne was not pleased with what he heard; but when, coming out upon the great steps of the church, he saw Daisy, who had emerged before him, get into an open cab with her accomplice and roll away through the cynical streets of Rome, the measure of her course struck him as simply there to take. He felt very sorry for her — not exactly that he believed she had completely lost her wits, but because it was painful to see so much that was pretty and undefended and natural sink so low in human estimation. He made an attempt after this to give a hint to Mrs. Miller. He met one day in the Corso a friend — a tourist like himself — who had just come out of the Doria Palace, where he had been walking through the beautiful gallery. His friend "went on" for some moments about the great portrait of Innocent X, by Velasquez, suspended in one of the cabinets of the palace, and then said: "And in the same cabinet, by the way, I enjoyed sight of an image of a different kind; that little American who's so much more a work of nature than of art and whom you pointed out to me last week." In answer to Winterbourne's enquiries his friend narrated that the little American—prettier now than ever—was seated with a companion in the secluded nook in which the papal presence is enshrined.

"All alone?" the young man heard himself disingenuously ask.

"Alone with a little Italian who sports in his button-hole a stack of flowers. The girl's a charming beauty, but I thought I understood from you the other day that she's a young lady *du meilleur monde*."

"So she is!" said Winterbourne; and having assured himself that his informant had seen the interesting pair but ten minutes before, he jumped into a cab and went to call on Mrs. Miller. She was at home, but she apologised for receiving him in Daisy's absence.

"She's gone out somewhere with Mr. Giovanelli. She's always going round with Mr. Giovanelli."

"I've noticed they're intimate indeed," Winterbourne concurred.

"Oh it seems as if they could n't live without each other!" said Mrs. Miller. "Well, he's a real gentleman anyhow. I guess I have the joke on Daisy — that she *must* be engaged!"

"And how does your daughter *take* the joke?"

"Oh she just says she ain't. But she might as *well* be!" this philosophic parent resumed. "She goes on as if she was. But I've made Mr. Giovanelli promise to tell me if Daisy don't. I'd want to write to Mr. Miller about it — would n't you?"

Winterbourne replied that he certainly should; and the state of mind of Daisy's mamma struck him as so unprecedented in the annals of parental vigilance that he recoiled before the attempt to educate at a single interview either her conscience or her wit.

After this Daisy was never at home and he ceased to meet her at the houses of their common acquaintance, because, as he perceived, these shrewd people had quite made up their minds as to the length she must have gone. They ceased to invite her, intimating that they wished to make, and make strongly, for the benefit of observant Europeans, the point that though Miss Daisy Miller was a pretty American girl all right, her behaviour was n't pretty at all — was in fact regarded by her compatriots as quite monstrous. Winterbourne wondered how she felt about all the cold shoulders that were turned upon her, and sometimes found himself suspecting with impatience that she simply did n't feel and did n't know. He set her down as hopelessly childish and shallow, as such mere giddiness and ignorance incarnate as was powerless either to heed or to suffer. Then at other moments he could n't doubt that she carried about in her elegant and irresponsible little organism a defiant, passionate, perfectly observant consciousness of the impression she produced. He asked himself whether the defiance would come from the consciousness of innocence or from her being essentially a young person of the reckless class. Then it had to be admitted, he felt, that holding fast to a belief in her "innocence" was more and more but a matter of gallantry too fine-spun for use. As I have already had occasion to relate, he was reduced without pleasure to this chopping of logic and vexed at his poor fallibility, his want of instinctive certitude as to how far her extravagance was generic and national and how far it was crudely personal. Whatever it was he had helplessly missed her, and now it was too late. She was "carried away" by Mr. Giovanelli.

A few days after his brief interview with her mother he came across her at that supreme seat of flowering desolation known as the Palace of the Cæsars. The early Roman spring had filled the air with bloom and perfume, and the rugged surface of the Palatine was muffled with tender verdure. Daisy moved at her ease over the great mounds of ruin that are embanked with mossy marble and paved with monumental inscriptions. It seemed to him he had never known Rome so lovely as just then. He looked off at the enchanting harmony of line and colour that remotely encircles the city — he inhaled the softly humid odours and felt the freshness of the year and the antiquity of the place reaffirm themselves in deep interfusion. It struck him also that Daisy had never showed to the eye for so utterly charming; but this had been his conviction on every occasion of their meeting. Giovanelli was of course at her side, and

Giovanelli too glowed as never before with something of the glory of his race.

"Well," she broke out upon the friend it would have been such mockery to designate as the latter's rival, "I should think you'd be quite lonesome!"

"Lonesome?" Winterbourne resignedly echoed.

"You're always going round by yourself. Can't you get any one to walk with you?"

"I'm not so fortunate," he answered, "as your gallant companion."

Giovanelli had from the first treated him with distinguished politeness; he listened with a deferential air to his remarks; he laughed punctiliously at his pleasantries; he attached such importance as he could find terms for to Miss Miller's cold compatriot. He carried himself in no degree like a jealous wooer; he had obviously a great deal of tact; he had no objection to any one's expecting a little humility of him. It even struck Winterbourne that he almost yearned at times for some private communication in the interest of his character for common sense; a chance to remark to him as another intelligent man that, bless him, *he* knew how extraordinary was their young lady and did n't flatter himself with confident — at least *too* confident and too delusive — hopes of matrimony and dollars. On this occasion he strolled away from his charming charge to pluck a sprig of almond-blossom which he carefully arranged in his button-hole.

"I know why you say that," Daisy meanwhile observed. "Because you think I go round too much with *him!*" And she nodded at her discreet attendant.

82

"Every one thinks so — if you care to know," was all Winterbourne found to reply.

"Of course I care to know!" — she made this point with much expression. "But I don't believe a word of it. They're only pretending to be shocked. They don't really care a straw what I do. Besides, I don't go round so much."

"I think you'll find they do care. They'll show it — disagreeably," he took on himself to state.

Daisy weighed the importance of that idea. "How — disagreeably?"

"Have n't you noticed anything?" he compassionately asked.

"I 've noticed *you*. But I noticed you 've no more 'give' than a ramrod the first time ever I saw you."

"You'll find at least that I 've more 'give' than several others," he patiently smiled.

"How shall I find it?"

"By going to see the others."

"What will they do to me?"

"They'll show you the cold shoulder. Do you know what that means?"

Daisy was looking at him intently; she began to colour. "Do you mean as Mrs. Walker did the other night?"

"Exactly as Mrs. Walker did the other night."

She looked away at Giovanelli, still titivating with his almond-blossom. Then with her attention again on the important subject: "I should n't think you 'd let people be so unkind!"

"How can I help it?"

"I should think you 'd want to say something."

83

"I do want to say something"—and Winterbourne paused a moment. "I want to say that your mother tells me she believes you engaged."

"Well, I guess she does," said Daisy very simply.

The young man began to laugh. "And does Randolph believe it?"

"I guess Randolph doesn't believe anything." This testimony to Randolph's scepticism excited Winterbourne to further mirth, and he noticed that Giovanelli was coming back to them. Daisy, observing it as well, addressed herself again to her countryman. "Since you've mentioned it," she said, "I *am* engaged." He looked at her hard—he had stopped laughing. "You don't believe it!" she added.

He asked himself, and it was for a moment like testing a heart-beat; after which, "Yes, I believe it!" he said.

"Oh no, you don't," she answered. "But *if* you possibly do," she still more perversely pursued— "well, I ain't!"

Miss Miller and her constant guide were on their way to the gate of the enclosure, so that Winterbourne, who had but lately entered, presently took leave of them. A week later on he went to dine at a beautiful villa on the Cælian Hill, and, on arriving, dismissed his hired vehicle. The evening was perfect and he promised himself the satisfaction of walking home beneath the Arch of Constantine and past the vaguely-lighted monuments of the Forum. Above was a moon half-developed, whose radiance was not brilliant but veiled in a thin cloud-curtain that seemed to diffuse and equalise it. When on his return from the villa at eleven o'clock he approached the dusky circle of the Colosseum the sense of the romantic in him easily suggested that the interior, in such an atmosphere, would well repay a glance. He turned aside and walked to one of the empty arches, near which, as he observed, an open carriage — one of the little Roman street-cabs — was stationed. Then he passed in among the cavernous shadows of the great structure and emerged upon the clear and silent arena. The place had never seemed to him more impressive. One half of the gigantic circus was in deep shade while the other slept in the luminous dusk. As he stood there he began to murmur Byron's famous lines out of "Manfred"; but before he had finished his quotation he remembered that if nocturnal meditation thereabouts was the fruit of a rich literary culture it was none the less deprecated by medical science. The air of other ages surrounded one; but the air of other ages, coldly analysed, was no better than a villainous miasma. Winterbourne sought, however, toward the middle of the arena, a further reach of vision, intending the next moment a hasty retreat. The great cross in the centre was almost obscured; only as he drew near did he make it out distinctly. He thus also distinguished two persons stationed on the low steps that formed its base. One of these was a woman seated; her companion hovered before her.

Presently the sound of the woman's voice came to him distinctly in the warm night-air. "Well, he looks at us as one of the old lions or tigers may have looked at the Christian martyrs!" These words were winged with their accent, so that they fluttered and settled about him in the darkness like vague white doves. It was Miss Daisy Miller who had released them for flight.

"Let us hope he's not very hungry" — the bland Giovanelli fell in with her humour. "He'll have to take *me* first; you'll serve for dessert."

Winterbourne felt himself pulled up with final horror now — and, it must be added, with final relief. It was as if a sudden clearance had taken place in the ambiguity of the poor girl's appearances and the whole riddle of her contradictions had grown easy to read. She was a young lady about the *shades* of whose perversity a foolish puzzled gentleman need no longer trouble his head or his heart. That once questionable quantity *had* no shades — it was a mere black little blot. He stood there looking at her, looking at her companion too, and not reflecting that though he saw them vaguely he himself must have been more brightly presented. He felt angry at all his shiftings of view — he felt ashamed of all his tender little scruples and all his witless little mercies. He was about to advance again, and then again checked himself; not from the fear of doing her injustice, but from a sense of the danger of showing undue exhilaration for this disburdenment of cautious criticism. He turned away toward the entrance of the place; but as he did so he heard Daisy speak again.

"Why it was Mr. Winterbourne! He saw me and he cuts me dead!"

What a clever little reprobate she was, he was amply able to reflect at this, and how smartly she feigned, how promptly she sought to play off on him, a surprised and injured innocence! But nothing would induce him to cut her either "dead" or to within any measurable distance even of the famous "inch" of her life. He came forward again and went toward the great cross. Daisy had got up and Giovanelli lifted his hat. Winterbourne had now begun to think simply of the madness, on the ground of exposure and infection, of a frail young creature's lounging away such hours in a nest of malaria. What if she *were* the most plausible of little reprobates? That was no reason for her dying of the *perniciosa*. "How long have you been 'fooling round' here?" he asked with conscious roughness.

Daisy, lovely in the sinister silver radiance, appraised him a moment, roughness and all. "Well, I guess all the evening." She answered with spirit and, he could see even then, with exaggeration. "I never saw anything so quaint."

"I'm afraid," he returned, "you'll not think a bad attack of Roman fever very quaint. This is the way people catch it. I wonder," he added to Giovanelli, "that you, a native Roman, should countenance such extraordinary rashness."

"Ah," said this seasoned subject, "for myself I have no fear."

"Neither have I — for you!" Winterbourne retorted in French. "I'm speaking for this young lady."

Giovanelli raised his well-shaped eyebrows and showed his shining teeth, but took his critic's rebuke with docility. "I assured Mademoiselle it was a grave indiscretion, but when was Mademoiselle ever prudent?"

87

"I never was sick, and I don't mean to be!" Mademoiselle declared. "I don't look like much, but I'm healthy! I was bound to see the Colosseum by moonlight — I would n't have wanted to go home without *that;* and we've had the most beautiful time, have n't we, Mr. Giovanelli? If there has been any danger Eugenio can give me some pills. Eugenio has got some splendid pills."

"*I* should advise you then," said Winterbourne, "to drive home as fast as possible and take one!"

Giovanelli smiled as for the striking happy thought. "What you say is very wise. I'll go and make sure the carriage is at hand." And he went forward rapidly.

Daisy followed with Winterbourne. He tried to deny himself the small fine anguish of looking at her, but his eyes themselves refused to spare him, and she seemed moreover not in the least embarrassed. He spoke no word; Daisy chattered over the beauty of the place: "Well, I *have* seen the Colosseum by moonlight — that's one thing I can rave about!" Then noticing her companion's silence she asked him why he was so stiff — it had always been her great word. He made no answer, but he felt his laugh an immense negation of stiffness. They passed under one of the dark archways; Giovanelli was in front with the carriage. Here Daisy stopped a moment, looking at her compatriot. "*Did* you believe I was engaged the other day?"

"It does n't matter now what I believed the other day!" he replied with infinite point.

It was a wonder how she did n't wince for it. "Well, what do you believe now?"

"I believe it makes very little difference whether you're engaged or not!"

He felt her lighted eyes fairly penetrate the thick gloom of the vaulted passage — as if to seek some access to him she hadn't yet compassed. But Giovanelli, with a graceful inconsequence, was at present all for retreat. "Quick, quick; if we get in by midnight we're quite safe!"

Daisy took her seat in the carriage and the fortunate Italian placed himself beside her. "Don't forget Eugenio's pills!" said Winterbourne as he lifted his hat.

"I don't care," she unexpectedly cried out for this, "whether I have Roman fever or not!" On which the cab-driver cracked his whip and they rolled across the desultory patches of antique pavement.

Winterbourne — to do him justice, as it were — mentioned to no one that he had encountered Miss Miller at midnight in the Colosseum with a gentleman; in spite of which deep discretion, however, the fact of the scandalous adventure was known a couple of days later, with a dozen vivid details, to every member of the little American circle, and was commented accordingly. Winterbourne judged thus that the people about the hotel had been thoroughly empowered to testify, and that after Daisy's return there would have been an exchange of jokes between the porter and the cab-driver. But the young man became aware at the same moment of how thoroughly it had ceased to ruffle him that the little American flirt should be "talked about" by low-minded menials. These sources of current criticism a day or two later abounded still further: the little American flirt was alarmingly ill and the doctors now in possession of the scene. Winterbourne, when the rumour came to him, immediately went to the hotel for more news. He found that two or three charitable friends had preceded him and that they were being entertained in Mrs. Miller's salon by the all-efficient Randolph.

"It's going round at night that way, you bet — that's what has made her so sick. She's always going round at night. I shouldn't think she'd want to — it's so plaguey dark over here. You can't see anything over here without the moon's right up. In America they don't go round by the moon!" Mrs. Miller meanwhile wholly surrendered to her genius for unapparent uses; her salon knew her less than ever, and she was presumably now at least giving her daughter the advantage of her society. It was clear that Daisy was dangerously ill.

Winterbourne constantly attended for news from the sick-room, which reached him, however, but with worrying indirectness, though he once had speech, for a moment, of the poor girl's physician and once saw Mrs. Miller, who, sharply alarmed, struck him as thereby more happily inspired than he could have conceived and indeed as the most noiseless and light-handed of nurses. She invoked a good deal the remote shade of Dr. Davis, but Winterbourne paid her the compliment of taking her after all for less monstrous a goose. To this indulgence indeed something she further said perhaps even more insidiously disposed him. "Daisy spoke of you the other day quite pleasantly. Half the time she doesn't know what

90

she's saying, but that time I think she did. She gave me a message — she told me to tell you. She wanted you to know she never was engaged to that handsome Italian who was always round. I'm sure I'm very glad; Mr. Giovanelli hasn't been near us since she was taken ill. I thought he was so much of a gentleman, but I don't call that very polite! A lady told me he was afraid I hadn't approved of his being round with her so much evenings. Of course it ain't as if their evenings were as pleasant as ours — since *we* don't seem to feel that way about the poison. I guess I *don't* see the point now; but I suppose he knows I'm a lady and I'd scorn to raise a fuss. Anyway, she wants you to realise she ain't engaged. I don't know why she makes so much of it, but she said to me three times 'Mind you tell Mr. Winterbourne.' And then she told me to ask if you remembered the time you went up to that castle in Switzerland. But I said I wouldn't give any such messages as *that*. Only if she ain't engaged I guess I'm glad to realise it too."

But, as Winterbourne had originally judged, the truth on this question had small actual relevance. A week after this the poor girl died; it had been indeed a terrible case of the *perniciosa*. A grave was found for her in the little Protestant cemetery, by an angle of the wall of imperial Rome, beneath the cypresses and the thick spring-flowers. Winterbourne stood there beside it with a number of other mourners; a number larger than the scandal excited by the young lady's career might have made probable. Near him stood Giovanelli, who came nearer still before Winter-

bourne turned away. Giovanelli, in decorous mourning, showed but a whiter face; his button-hole lacked
its nosegay and he had visibly something urgent —
and even to distress — to say, which he scarce knew
how to "place." He decided at last to confide it with
a pale convulsion to Winterbourne. "She was the
most beautiful young lady I ever saw, and the most
amiable." To which he added in a moment: "Also
— naturally! — the most innocent."

Winterbourne sounded him with hard dry eyes,
but presently repeated his words, "The most innocent?"

"The most innocent!"

It came somehow so much too late that our friend
could only glare at its having come at all. "Why the
devil," he asked, "did you take her to that fatal
place?"

Giovanelli raised his neat shoulders and eyebrows
to within suspicion of a shrug. "For myself I had no
fear; and *she* — she did what she liked."

Winterbourne's eyes attached themselves to the
ground. "She did what she liked!"

It determined on the part of poor Giovanelli a further pious, a further candid, confidence. "If she
had lived I should have got nothing. She never would
have married me."

It had been spoken as if to attest, in all sincerity,
his disinterestedness, but Winterbourne scarce knew
what welcome to give it. He said, however, with a
grace inferior to his friend's: "I dare say not."

The latter was even by this not discouraged. "For
a moment I hoped so. But no. I'm convinced."

Winterbourne took it in; he stood staring at the raw protuberance among the April daisies. When he turned round again his fellow mourner had stepped back.

He almost immediately left Rome, but the following summer he again met his aunt Mrs. Costello at Vevey. Mrs. Costello extracted from the charming old hotel there a value that the Miller family had n't mastered the secret of. In the interval Winterbourne had often thought of the most interesting member of that trio — of her mystifying manners and her queer adventure. One day he spoke of her to his aunt — said it was on his conscience he had done her injustice.

"I 'm sure I don't know" — that lady showed caution. "How did your injustice affect her?"

"She sent me a message before her death which I did n't understand at the time. But I 've understood it since. She would have appreciated one's esteem."

"She took an odd way to gain it! But do you mean by what you say," Mrs. Costello asked, "that she would have reciprocated one's affection?"

As he made no answer to this she after a little looked round at him — he had n't been directly within sight; but the effect of that was n't to make her repeat her question. He spoke, however, after a while. "You were right in that remark that you made last summer. I was booked to make a mistake. I 've lived too long in foreign parts." And this time she herself said nothing.

Nevertheless he soon went back to live at Geneva,

whence there continue to come the most contradictory accounts of his motives of sojourn : a report that he's "studying" hard — an intimation that he's much interested in a very clever foreign lady.

PANDORA

PANDORA

I

It has long been the custom of the North German Lloyd steamers, which convey passengers from Bremen to New York, to anchor for several hours in the pleasant port of Southampton, where their human cargo receives many additions. An intelligent young German, Count Otto Vogelstein, hardly knew a few years ago whether to condemn this custom or approve it. He leaned over the bulwarks of the *Donau* as the American passengers crossed the plank — the travellers who embark at Southampton are mainly of that nationality — and curiously, indifferently, vaguely, through the smoke of his cigar, saw them absorbed in the huge capacity of the ship, where he had the agreeable consciousness that his own nest was comfortably made. To watch from such a point of vantage the struggles of those less fortunate than ourselves — of the uninformed, the unprovided, the belated, the bewildered — is an occupation not devoid of sweetness, and there was nothing to mitigate the complacency with which our young friend gave himself up to it; nothing, that is, save a natural benevolence which had not yet been extinguished by the consciousness of official greatness. For Count Vogelstein was official, as I think you would have seen from the straightness of his back, the lustre of his light elegant spectacles, and something discreet and diplomatic in the curve of his moustache, which looked as if it might well contribute to the principal function, as cynics say, of the lips — the active concealment of thought. He had been appointed to the secretaryship of the German legation at Washington and in these first days of the autumn was about to take possession of his post. He was a model character for such a purpose — serious civil ceremonious curious stiff, stuffed with knowledge and convinced that, as lately rearranged, the German Empire places in the most striking light the highest of all the possibilities of the greatest of all the peoples. He was quite aware, however, of the claims to economic and other consideration of the United States, and that this quarter of the globe offered a vast field for study.

The process of enquiry had already begun for him, in spite of his having as yet spoken to none of his fellow passengers; the case being that Vogelstein enquired not only with his tongue, but with his eyes — that is with his spectacles — with his ears, with his nose, with his palate, with all his senses and organs. He was a highly upright young man, whose only fault was that his sense of comedy, or of the humour of things, had never been specifically disengaged from his several other senses. He vaguely felt that something should be done about this, and in a general manner proposed to do it, for he was on his way to explore a society abounding in comic aspects. This consciousness of a missing measure gave him a certain mistrust of what might be said of him; and if circumspection is the essence of diplomacy our young aspirant promised well. His mind contained several millions of facts, packed too closely together for the light breeze of the imagination to draw through the mass. He was impatient to report himself to his superior in Washington, and the loss of time in an English port could only incommode him, inasmuch as the study of English institutions was no part of his mission. On the other hand the day was charming; the blue sea, in Southampton Water, pricked all over with light, had no movement but that of its infinite shimmer. Moreover he was by no means sure that he should be happy in the United States, where doubtless he should find himself soon enough disembarked. He knew that this was not an important question and that happiness was an unscientific term, such as a man of his education should be ashamed to use even in the silence of his thoughts. Lost none the less in the inconsiderate crowd and feeling himself neither in his own country nor in that to which he was in a manner accredited, he was reduced to his mere personality; so that during the hour, to save his importance, he cultivated such ground as lay in sight for a judgement of this delay to which the German steamer was subjected in English waters. Might n't it be proved, facts, figures and documents — or at least watch — in hand, considerably greater than the occasion demanded?

Count Vogelstein was still young enough in diplomacy to think it necessary to have opinions. He had a good many indeed which had been formed without difficulty; they had been received ready-made from a line of ancestors who knew what they liked. This was of course — and under pressure, being candid, he would have admitted it — an unscientific way of furn-

ishing one's mind. Our young man was a stiff con-
servative, a Junker of Junkers; he thought modern
democracy a temporary phase and expected to find
many arguments against it in the great Republic. In
regard to these things it was a pleasure to him to feel
that, with his complete training, he had been taught
thoroughly to appreciate the nature of evidence. The
ship was heavily laden with German emigrants, whose
mission in the United States differed considerably
from Count Otto's. They hung over the bulwarks,
densely grouped; they leaned forward on their elbows
for hours, their shoulders kept on a level with their
ears; the men in furred caps, smoking long-bowled
pipes, the women with babies hidden in remarkably
ugly shawls. Some were yellow Germans and some
were black, and all looked greasy and matted with the
sea-damp. They were destined to swell still further
the huge current of the Western democracy; and
Count Vogelstein doubtless said to himself that they
would n't improve its quality. Their numbers, however, were striking, and I know not what he thought of
the nature of this particular evidence.

The passengers who came on board at Southampton
were not of the greasy class; they were for the most
part American families who had been spending the
summer, or a longer period, in Europe. They had a
great deal of luggage, innumerable bags and rugs and
hampers and sea-chairs, and were composed largely of
ladies of various ages, a little pale with anticipation,
wrapped also in striped shawls, though in prettier ones
than the nursing mothers of the steerage, and crowned
with very high hats and feathers. They darted to and

fro across the gangway, looking for each other and for their scattered parcels; they separated and reunited, they exclaimed and declared, they eyed with dismay the occupants of the forward quarter, who seemed numerous enough to sink the vessel, and their voices sounded faint and far as they rose to Vogelstein's ear over the latter's great tarred sides. He noticed that in the new contingent there were many young girls, and he remembered what a lady in Dresden had once said to him — that America was the country of the Mädchen. He wondered whether he should like that, and reflected that it would be an aspect to study, like everything else. He had known in Dresden an American family in which there were three daughters who used to skate with the officers, and some of the ladies now coming on board struck him as of that same habit, except that in the Dresden days feathers were n't worn quite so high.

At last the ship began to creak and slowly budge, and the delay at Southampton came to an end. The gangway was removed and the vessel indulged in the awkward evolutions that were to detach her from the land. Count Vogelstein had finished his cigar, and he spent a long time in walking up and down the upper deck. The charming English coast passed before him, and he felt this to be the last of the old world. The American coast also might be pretty — he hardly knew what one would expect of an American coast; but he was sure it would be different. Differences, however, were notoriously half the charm of travel, and perhaps even most when they could n't be expressed in figures, numbers, diagrams or the other merely useful symbols. As yet indeed there were very few among the objects presented to sight on the steamer. Most of his fellow passengers appeared of one and the same persuasion, and that persuasion the least to be mistaken. They were Jews and commercial to a man. And by this time they had lighted their cigars and put on all manner of seafaring caps, some of them with big ear-lappets which somehow had the effect of bringing out their peculiar facial type. At last the new voyagers began to emerge from below and to look about them, vaguely, with that suspicious expression of face always to be noted in the newly embarked and which, as directed to the receding land, resembles that of a person who begins to perceive himself the victim of a trick. Earth and ocean, in such glances, are made the subject of a sweeping objection, and many travellers, in the general plight, have an air at once duped and superior, which seems to say that they could easily go ashore if they would.

It still wanted two hours of dinner, and by the time Vogelstein's long legs had measured three or four miles on the deck he was ready to settle himself in his sea-chair and draw from his pocket a Tauchnitz novel by an American author whose pages, he had been assured, would help to prepare him for some of the oddities. On the back of his chair his name was painted in rather large letters, this being a precaution taken at the recommendation of a friend who had told him that on the American steamers the passengers — especially the ladies — thought nothing of pilfering one's little comforts. His friend had even hinted at the correct reproduction of his coronet. This marked man of the world had added that the Americans are greatly impressed by a coronet. I know not whether it was scepticism or modesty, but Count Vogelstein had omitted every pictured plea for his rank; there were others of which he might have made use. The precious piece of furniture which on the Atlantic voyage is trusted never to flinch among universal concussions was emblazoned simply with his title and name. It happened, however, that the blazonry was huge; the back of the chair was covered with enormous German characters. This time there can be no doubt: it was modesty that caused the secretary of legation, in placing himself, to turn this portion of his seat outward, away from the eyes of his companions — to present it to the balustrade of the deck. The ship was passing the Needles — the beautiful uttermost point of the Isle of Wight. Certain tall white cones of rock rose out of the purple sea; they flushed in the afternoon light and their vague rosiness gave them a human expression in face of the cold expanse toward which the prow was turned; they seemed to say farewell, to be the last note of a peopled world. Vogelstein saw them very comfortably from his place and after a while turned his eyes to the other quarter, where the elements of air and water managed to make between them so comparatively poor an opposition. Even his American novelist was more amusing than that, and he prepared to return to this author. In the great curve which it described, however, his glance was arrested by the figure of a young lady who had just ascended to the deck and who paused at the mouth of the companionway.

This was not in itself an extraordinary phenomenon; but what attracted Vogelstein's attention was the fact that the young person appeared to have fixed her eyes on him. She was slim, brightly dressed, rather pretty; Vogelstein remembered in a moment that he had noticed her among the people on the wharf at Southampton. She was soon aware he had observed her; whereupon she began to move along the deck with a step that seemed to indicate a purpose of approaching him. Vogelstein had time to wonder whether she could be one of the girls he had known at Dresden; but he presently reflected that they would now be much older than that. It was true they were apt to advance, like this one, straight upon their victim. Yet the present specimen was no longer looking at him, and though she passed near him it was now tolerably clear she had come above but to take a general survey. She was a quick handsome competent girl, and she simply wanted to see what one could think of the ship, of the weather, of the appearance of England, from such a position as that; possibly even of one's fellow passengers. She satisfied herself promptly on these points, and then she looked about, while she walked, as if in keen search of a missing object; so that Vogelstein finally arrived at a conviction of her real motive. She passed near him again and this time almost stopped, her eyes bent upon him attentively. He thought her conduct remarkable even after he had gathered that it was not at his face, with its yellow moustache, she was looking, but at the chair on which he was seated. Then those words of his friend came back to him — the speech about the tendency of the people, especially of the ladies, on the American steamers to take to themselves one's little belongings. Especially the ladies, he might well say; for here was one who apparently wished to pull from under him the very chair he was sitting on. He was afraid she would ask him for it, so he pretended to read, systematically avoiding her eye. He was conscious she hovered near him, and was moreover curious to see what she would do. It seemed to him strange that such a nice-looking girl — for her appearance was really charming — should endeavour by arts so flagrant to work upon the quiet dignity of a secretary of legation. At last it stood out that she was trying to look round a corner, as it were — trying to see what was written on the back of his chair. "She wants to find out my name; she wants to see who I am!" This reflexion passed through his mind and caused him to raise his eyes. They rested on her own — which for an appreciable moment she did n't withdraw. The latter were brilliant and expressive, and surmounted a delicate aquiline nose, which, though pretty, was perhaps just a trifle too hawk-like. It was the oddest coincidence in the world; the story Vogelstein had taken up treated of a flighty forward little American girl who plants herself in front of a young man in the garden of an hotel. Was n't the conduct of this young lady a testimony to the truthfulness of the tale, and was n't Vogelstein himself in the position of the young man in the garden? That young man — though with more, in such connexions in general, to go upon — ended by addressing himself to his aggressor, as she might be called, and after a very short hesitation Vogelstein followed his example. "If she wants to know who I am she's welcome," he said to himself; and he got out of the chair, seized it by the back and, turning it round, exhibited the superscription to the girl. She coloured slightly, but smiled and read his name, while Vogelstein raised his hat.

"I'm much obliged to you. That's all right," she remarked as if the discovery had made her very happy.

It affected him indeed as all right that he should be Count Otto Vogelstein; this appeared even rather a flippant mode of disposing of the fact. By way of rejoinder he asked her if she desired of him the surrender of his seat.

"I'm much obliged to you; of course not. I thought you had one of our chairs, and I did n't like to ask you. It looks exactly like one of ours; not so much now as when you sit in it. Please sit down again. I don't want to trouble you. We've lost one of ours, and I've been looking for it everywhere. They look so much alike; you can't tell till you see the back. Of course I see there will be no mistake about yours," the young lady went on with a smile of which the serenity matched her other abundance. "But we've got such a small name — you can scarcely see it," she added with the same friendly intention. "Our name's just Day — you might n't think it *was* a name, might you? if we did n't make the most of it. If you see that on anything, I'd be so obliged if you'd tell me. It is n't for myself, it's for my mother; she's so dependent on her chair, and that one I'm looking for pulls out so beautifully. Now that you sit down again and hide the lower part it does look just like ours. Well, it must be somewhere. You must excuse me; I would n't disturb you."

This was a long and even confidential speech for a young woman, presumably unmarried, to make to a perfect stranger; but Miss Day acquitted herself of it with perfect simplicity and self-possession. She held up her head and stepped away, and Vogelstein could see that the foot she pressed upon the clean smooth deck was slender and shapely. He watched her disappear through the trap by which she had ascended, and he felt more than ever like the young man in his American tale. The girl in the present case was older and not so pretty, as he could easily judge, for the image of her smiling eyes and speaking lips still hovered before him. He went back to his book with the feeling that it would give him some information about her. This was rather illogical, but it indicated a certain amount of curiosity on the part of Count Vogelstein. The girl in the book had a mother, it appeared, and so had this young lady; the former had also a brother, and he now remembered that he had noticed a young man on the wharf — a young man in a high hat and a white overcoat — who seemed united to Miss Day by this natural tie. And there was some one else too, as he gradually recollected, an older man, also in a high hat, but in a black overcoat — in black altogether — who completed the group and who was presumably the head of the family. These reflexions would indicate that Count Vogelstein read his volume of Tauchnitz rather interruptedly. Moreover they represented but the loosest economy of consciousness; for was n't he to be afloat in an oblong box for ten days with such people, and could it be doubted he should see at least enough of them?

It may as well be written without delay that he saw a great deal of them. I have sketched in some detail the conditions in which he made the acquaintance of Miss Day, because the event had a certain importance for this fair square Teuton; but I must pass briefly over the incidents that immediately followed it. He wondered what it was open to him, after such an introduction, to do in relation to her, and he determined he would push through his American tale and discover what the hero did. But he satisfied himself in a very short time that Miss Day had nothing in common with the heroine of that work save certain signs of habitat and climate — and save, further, the fact that the male sex was n't terrible to her. The local stamp sharply, as he gathered, impressed upon her he estimated indeed rather in a borrowed than in a natural light, for if she was native to a small town in the interior of the American continent one of their fellow passengers, a lady from New York with whom he had a good deal of conversation, pronounced her "atrociously" provincial. How the lady arrived at this certitude did n't appear, for Vogelstein observed that she held no communication with the girl. It was true she gave it the support of her laying down that certain Americans could tell immediately who other Americans were, leaving him to judge whether or no she herself belonged to the critical or only to the criticised half of the nation. Mrs. Dangerfield was a handsome confidential insinuating woman, with whom Vogelstein felt his talk take a very wide range indeed. She convinced him rather effectually that even in a great democracy there are human differences, and that American life was full of social distinctions, of delicate shades, which foreigners often lack the intelligence to perceive. Did he suppose every one knew every one else in the biggest country in the world, and that one was n't as free to choose one's company there as in the most monarchical and most exclusive societies? She laughed such delusions to scorn as Vogelstein tucked her beautiful furred coverlet — they reclined together a great deal in their elongated chairs — well over her feet. How free an American lady was to choose her company she abundantly proved by not knowing any one on the steamer but Count Otto.

He could see for himself that Mr. and Mrs. Day had not at all her grand air. They were fat plain serious people who sat side by side on the deck for hours and looked straight before them. Mrs. Day had a white face, large cheeks and small eyes; her forehead was surrounded with a multitude of little tight black curls; her lips moved as if she had always a lozenge in her mouth. She wore entwined about her head an article which Mrs. Dangerfield spoke of as a "nuby," a knitted pink scarf concealing her hair, encircling her neck and having among its convolutions a hole for her perfectly expressionless face. Her hands were folded on her stomach, and in her still, swathed figure her little bead-like eyes, which occasionally changed their direction, alone represented life. Her husband had a stiff grey beard on his chin and a bare spacious upper lip, to which constant shaving had imparted a hard glaze. His eyebrows were thick and his nostrils wide, and when he was uncovered, in the saloon, it was visible that his grizzled hair was dense and perpendicular. He might have looked rather grim and truculent had n't it been for the mild familiar accommodating gaze with which his large light-coloured pupils — the leisurely eyes of a silent man — appeared to consider surrounding objects. He was evidently more friendly than fierce, but he was more diffident than friendly. He liked to have you in sight, but would n't have pretended to understand you much or to classify you, and would have been sorry it should put you under an obligation. He and his wife spoke sometimes, but seldom talked, and there was something vague and patient in them, as if they had become victims of a wrought spell. The spell however was of no sinister cast; it was the fascination of prosperity, the confidence of security, which sometimes makes people arrogant, but which had had such a different effect on this simple satisfied pair, in whom further development of every kind appeared to have been happily arrested.

Mrs. Dangerfield made it known to Count Otto that every morning after breakfast, the hour at which he wrote his journal in his cabin, the old couple were guided upstairs and installed in their customary corner by Pandora. This she had learned to be the name of their elder daughter, and she was immensely amused by her discovery. "Pandora" — that was in the highest degree typical; it placed them in the social scale if other evidence had been wanting; you could tell that a girl was from the interior, the mysterious interior about which Vogelstein's imagination was now quite excited, when she had such a name as that. This young lady managed the whole family, even a little the small beflounced sister, who, with bold pretty innocent eyes, a torrent of fair silky hair, a crimson fez, such as is worn by male Turks, very much askew on top of it, and a way of galloping and straddling about the ship in any company she could pick up — she had long thin legs, very short skirts and stockings of every tint — was going home, in elegant French clothes, to resume an interrupted education. Pandora overlooked and directed her relatives; Vogelstein could see this for himself, could see she was very active and decided, that she had in a high degree the sentiment of responsibility, settling on the spot most of the questions that could come up for a family from the interior.

The voyage was remarkably fine, and day after day it was possible to sit there under the salt sky and feel one's self rounding the great curves of the globe. The long deck made a white spot in the sharp black circle of the ocean and in the intense sea-light, while the shadow of the smoke-streamers trembled on the familiar floor, the shoes of fellow passengers, distinctive now, and in some cases irritating, passed and repassed, accompanied, in the air so tremendously "open," that rendered all voices weak and most remarks rather flat, by fragments of opinion on the run of the ship. Vogelstein by this time had finished his little American story and now definitely judged that Pandora Day was not at all like the heroine. She was of quite another type; much more serious and strenuous, and not at all keen, as he had supposed, about making the acquaintance of gentlemen. Her speaking to him that first afternoon had been, he was bound to believe, an incident without importance for herself; in spite of her having followed it up the next day by the remark, thrown at him as she passed, with a smile that was almost fraternal: "It's all right, sir! I've found that old chair." After this she had n't spoken to him again and had scarcely looked at him. She read a great deal, and almost always French books, in fresh yellow paper; not the lighter forms of that literature, but a volume of Sainte-Beuve, of Renan or at the most, in the way of dissipation, of Alfred de Musset. She took frequent exercise and almost always walked alone, apparently not having made many friends on the ship and being without the resource of her parents, who, as has been related, never budged out of the cosey corner in which she planted them for the day.

Her brother was always in the smoking-room, where Vogelstein observed him, in very tight clothes, his neck encircled with a collar like a palisade. He had a sharp little face, which was not disagreeable; he smoked enormous cigars and began his drinking early in the day: but his appearance gave no sign of these excesses. As regards euchre and poker and the other distractions of the place he was guilty of none. He evidently understood such games in perfection, for he used to watch the players and even at moments impartially advise them; but Vogelstein never saw the cards in his hand. He was referred to as regards disputed points, and his opinion carried the day. He took little part in the conversation, usually much relaxed, that prevailed in the smoking-room, but from time to time he made, in his soft flat youthful voice, a remark which every one paused to listen to and which was greeted with roars of laughter. Vogelstein, well as he knew English, could rarely catch the joke; but he could see at least that these must be choice specimens of that American humour admired and practised by a whole continent and yet to be rendered accessible to a trained diplomatist, clearly, but by some special and incalculable revelation. The young man, in his way, was very remarkable, for, as Vogelstein heard some one say once after the laughter had subsided, he was only nineteen. If his sister did n't resemble the dreadful little girl in the tale already mentioned, there was for Vogelstein at least an analogy between young Mr. Day and a certain small brother — a candy-loving Madison, Hamilton or Jefferson — who was, in the Tauchnitz volume, attributed to that unfortunate maid. This was what the little Madison would have grown up to at nineteen, and the improvement was greater than might have been expected.

The days were long, but the voyage was short, and it had almost come to an end before Count Otto yielded to an attraction peculiar in its nature and finally irresistible and, in spite of Mrs. Dangerfield's emphatic warning, sought occasion for a little continuous talk with Miss Pandora. To mention that this impulse took effect without mentioning sundry other of his current impressions with which it had nothing to do is perhaps to violate proportion and give a false idea; but to pass it by would be still more unjust. The Germans, as we know, are a transcendental people,

and there was at last an irresistible appeal for Vogelstein in this quick bright silent girl who could smile
and turn vocal in an instant, who imparted a rare
originality to the filial character and whose profile
was delicate as she bent it over a volume which she
cut as she read, or presented it in musing attitudes,
at the side of the ship, to the horizon they had left
behind. But he felt it to be a pity, as regards a possible acquaintance with her, that her parents should
be heavy little burghers, that her brother should not
correspond to his conception of a young man of the
upper class and that her sister should be a Daisy
Miller *en herbe*. Repeatedly admonished by Mrs.
Dangerfield, the young diplomatist was doubly careful as to the relations he might form at the beginning
of his sojourn in the United States. That lady reminded him, and he had himself made the observation in other capitals, that the first year, and even the
second, is the time for prudence. One was ignorant of
proportions and values; one was exposed to mistakes
and thankful for attention, and one might give one's
self away to people who would afterwards be as a
millstone round one's neck: Mrs. Dangerfield struck
and sustained that note, which resounded in the young
man's imagination. She assured him that if he did n't
"look out" he would be committing himself to some
American girl with an impossible family. In America,
when one committed one's self there was nothing to do
but march to the altar, and what should he say for
instance to finding himself a near relation of Mr. and
Mrs. P. W. Day? — since such were the initials inscribed on the back of the two chairs of that couple.

PANDORA

Count Otto felt the peril, for he could immediately think of a dozen men he knew who had married American girls. There appeared now to be a constant danger of marrying the American girl; it was something one had to reckon with, like the railway, the telegraph, the discovery of dynamite, the Chassepôt rifle, the Socialistic spirit: it was one of the complications of modern life.

It would doubtless be too much to say that he feared being carried away by a passion for a young woman who was not strikingly beautiful and with whom he had talked, in all, but ten minutes. But, as we recognise, he went so far as to wish that the human belongings of a person whose high spirit appeared to have no taint either of fastness, as they said in England, or of subversive opinion, and whose mouth had charming lines, should not be a little more distinguished. There was an effect of drollery in her behaviour to these subjects of her zeal, whom she seemed to regard as a care, but not as an interest; it was as if they had been entrusted to her honour and she had engaged to convey them safe to a certain point; she was detached and inadvertent, and then suddenly remembered, repented and came back to tuck them into their blankets, to alter the position of her mother's umbrella, to tell them something about the run of the ship. These little offices were usually performed deftly, rapidly, with the minimum of words, and when their daughter drew near them Mr. and Mrs. Day closed their eyes after the fashion of a pair of household dogs who expect to be scratched.

One morning she brought up the Captain of the

ship to present to them; she appeared to have a private and independent acquaintance with this officer, and the introduction to her parents had the air of a sudden happy thought. It was n't so much an introduction as an exhibition, as if she were saying to him: "This is what they look like; see how comfortable I make them. Are n't they rather queer and rather dear little people? But they leave me perfectly free. Oh I can assure you of that. Besides, you must see it for yourself." Mr. and Mrs. Day looked up at the high functionary who thus unbent to them with very little change of countenance; then looked at each other in the same way. He saluted, he inclined himself a moment; but Pandora shook her head, she seemed to be answering for them; she made little gestures as if in explanation to the good Captain of some of their peculiarities, as for instance that he need n't expect them to speak. They closed their eyes at last; she appeared to have a kind of mesmeric influence on them, and Miss Day walked away with the important friend, who treated her with evident consideration, bowing very low, for all his importance, when the two presently after separated. Vogelstein could see she was capable of making an impression; and the moral of our little matter is that in spite of Mrs. Dangerfield, in spite of the resolutions of his prudence, in spite of the limits of such acquaintance as he had momentarily made with her, in spite of Mr. and Mrs. Day and the young man in the smoking-room, she had fixed his attention.

It was in the course of the evening after the scene with the Captain that he joined her, awkwardly, abruptly, irresistibly, on the deck, where she was pacing to and fro alone, the hour being auspiciously mild and the stars remarkably fine. There were scattered talkers and smokers and couples, unrecogniseable, that moved quickly through the gloom. The vessel dipped with long regular pulsations; vague and spectral under the low stars, its swaying pinnacles spotted here and there with lights, it seemed to rush through the darkness faster than by day. Count Otto had come up to walk, and as the girl brushed past him he distinguished Pandora's face — with Mrs. Dangerfield he always spoke of her as Pandora — under the veil worn to protect it from the sea-damp. He stopped, turned, hurried after her, threw away his cigar — then asked her if she would do him the honour to accept his arm. She declined his arm but accepted his company, and he allowed her to enjoy it for an hour. They had a great deal of talk, and he was to remember afterwards some of the things she had said. There was now a certainty of the ship's getting into dock the next morning but one, and this prospect afforded an obvious topic. Some of Miss Day's expressions struck him as singular, but of course, as he was aware, his knowledge of English was not nice enough to give him a perfect measure.

"I'm not in a hurry to arrive; I'm very happy here," she said. "I'm afraid I shall have such a time putting my people through."

"Putting them through?"

"Through the Custom-House. We've made so many purchases. Well, I've written to a friend to come down, and perhaps he can help us. He's very well acquainted with the head. Once I'm chalked I don't care. I feel like a kind of blackboard by this time anyway. We found them awful in Germany."

Count Otto wondered if the friend she had written to were her lover and if they had plighted their troth, especially when she alluded to him again as "that gentleman who's coming down." He asked her about her travels, her impressions, whether she had been long in Europe and what she liked best, and she put it to him that they had gone abroad, she and her family, for a little fresh experience. Though he found her very intelligent he suspected she gave this as a reason because he was a German and she had heard the Germans were rich in culture. He wondered what form of culture Mr. and Mrs. Day had brought back from Italy, Greece and Palestine — they had travelled for two years and been everywhere — especially when their daughter said: "I wanted father and mother to see the best things. I kept them three hours on the Acropolis. I guess they won't forget that!" Perhaps it was of Phidias and Pericles they were thinking, Vogelstein reflected, as they sat ruminating in their rugs. Pandora remarked also that she wanted to show her little sister everything while she was comparatively unformed ("comparatively!" he mutely gasped); remarkable sights made so much more impression when the mind was fresh: she had read something of that sort somewhere in Goethe. She had wanted to come herself when she was her sister's age; but her father was in business then and they could n't leave Utica. The young man thought of the little sister frisking over the Parthenon and the

Mount of Olives and sharing for two years, the years of the school-room, this extraordinary pilgrimage of her parents; he wondered whether Goethe's dictum had been justified in this case. He asked Pandora if Utica were the seat of her family, if it were an important or typical place, if it would be an interesting city for him, as a stranger, to see. His companion replied frankly that this was a big question, but added that all the same she would ask him to "come and visit us at our home," if it were n't that they should probably soon leave it.

"Ah you 're going to live elsewhere?" Vogelstein asked as if that fact too would be typical.

"Well, I 'm working for New York. I flatter myself I 've loosened them while we 've been away," the girl went on. "They won't find in Utica the same charm; that was my idea. I want a big place, and of course Utica —!" She broke off as before a complex statement.

"I suppose Utica is inferior —?" Vogelstein seemed to see his way to suggest.

"Well no, I guess I can't have you call Utica inferior. It is n't supreme — that's what's the matter with it, and I hate anything middling," said Pandora Day. She gave a light dry laugh, tossing back her head a little as she made this declaration. And looking at her askance in the dusk, as she trod the deck that vaguely swayed, he recognised something in her air and port that matched such a pronouncement.

"What 's her social position?" he enquired of Mrs. Dangerfield the next day. "I can't make it out at all — it's so contradictory. She strikes me as having much cultivation and much spirit. Her appearance, too, is very neat. Yet her parents are complete little burghers. That's easily seen."

"Oh social position," and Mrs. Dangerfield nodded two or three times portentously. "What big expressions you use! Do you think everybody in the world has a social position? That's reserved for an infinitely small majority of mankind. You can't have a social position at Utica any more than you can have an opera-box. Pandora has n't got one; where, if you please, should she have got it? Poor girl, it is n't fair of you to make her the subject of such questions as that."

"Well," said Vogelstein, "if she's of the lower class it seems to me very — very —" And he paused a moment, as he often paused in speaking English, looking for his word.

"Very what, dear Count?"

"Very significant, very representative."

"Oh dear, she is n't of the lower class," Mrs. Dangerfield returned with an irritated sense of wasted wisdom. She liked to explain her country, but that somehow always required two persons.

"What is she then?"

"Well, I'm bound to admit that since I was at home last she's a novelty. A girl like that with such people — it *is* a new type."

"I like novelties" — and Count Otto smiled with an air of considerable resolution. He could n't however be satisfied with a demonstration that only begged the question; and when they disembarked in New York he felt, even amid the confusion of the wharf and the heaps of disembowelled baggage, a certain acuteness of regret at the idea that Pandora and her family were about to vanish into the unknown. He had a consolation however : it was apparent that for some reason or other — illness or absence from town — the gentleman to whom she had written had not, as she said, come down. Vogelstein was glad — he could n't have told you why — that this sympathetic person had failed her; even though without him Pandora had to engage single-handed with the United States Custom-House. Our young man's first impression of the Western world was received on the landing-place of the German steamers at Jersey City — a huge wooden shed covering a wooden wharf which resounded under the feet, an expanse palisaded with rough-hewn piles that leaned this way and that, and bestrewn with masses of heterogeneous luggage. At one end, toward the town, was a row of tall painted palings, behind which he could distinguish a press of hackney-coachmen, who brandished their whips and awaited their victims, while their voices rose, incessant, with a sharp strange sound, a challenge at once fierce and familiar. The whole place, behind the fence, appeared to bristle and resound. Out there was America, Count Otto said to himself, and he looked toward it with a sense that he should have to muster resolution. On the wharf people were rushing about amid their trunks, pulling their things together, trying to unite their scattered parcels. They were heated and angry, or else quite bewildered and discouraged. The few that had succeeded in collecting their battered boxes had an air of flushed indifference to the efforts of their neighbours, not even looking at people with whom they had been fondly intimate on the steamer. A detachment of the officers of the Customs was in attendance, and energetic passengers were engaged in attempts to drag them toward their luggage or to drag heavy pieces toward them. These functionaries were good-natured and taciturn, except when occasionally they remarked to a passenger whose open trunk stared up at them, eloquent, imploring, that they were afraid the voyage had been "rather glassy." They had a friendly leisurely speculative way of discharging their duty, and if they perceived a victim's name written on the portmanteau they addressed him by it in a tone of old acquaintance. Vogelstein found however that if they were familiar they were n't indiscreet. He had heard that in America all public functionaries were the same, that there was n't a different *tenue*, as they said in France, for different positions, and he wondered whether at Washington the President and ministers, whom he expected to see — to *have* to see — a good deal of, would be like that.

He was diverted from these speculations by the sight of Mr. and Mrs. Day seated side by side upon a trunk and encompassed apparently by the accumulations of their tour. Their faces expressed more consciousness of surrounding objects than he had hitherto recognised, and there was an air of placid expansion in the mysterious couple which suggested that this consciousness was agreeable. Mr. and Mrs. Day were, as they would have said, real glad to get back. At a little distance, on the edge of the dock, our observer remarked their son, who had found a place where,

between the sides of two big ships, he could see the
ferry-boats pass; the large pyramidal low-laden ferry-
boats of American waters. He stood there, patient
and considering, with his small neat foot on a coil of
rope, his back to everything that had been disembarked, his neck elongated in its polished cylinder,
while the fragrance of his big cigar mingled with the
odour of the rotting piles and his little sister, beside
him, hugged a huge post and tried to see how far she
could crane over the water without falling in. Vogelstein's servant was off in search of an examiner;
Count Otto himself had got his things together and
was waiting to be released, fully expecting that for a
person of his importance the ceremony would be brief.
Before it began he said a word to young Mr. Day,
raising his hat at the same time to the little girl, whom
he had not yet greeted and who dodged his salute by
swinging herself boldly outward to the dangerous side
of the pier. She was indeed still unformed, but was
evidently as light as a feather.

"I see you're kept waiting like me. It's very tiresome," Count Otto said.

The young American answered without looking behind him. "As soon as we're started we'll go all right.
My sister has written to a gentleman to come down."

"I've looked for Miss Day to bid her good-bye,"
Vogelstein went on; "but I don't see her."

"I guess she has gone to meet that gentleman; he's
a great friend of hers."

"I guess he's her lover!" the little girl broke out.
"She was always writing to him in Europe."

Her brother puffed his cigar in silence a moment.

"That was only for this. I'll tell on you, sis," he presently added.

But the younger Miss Day gave no heed to his menace; she addressed herself only, though with all freedom, to Vogelstein. "This is New York; I like it better than Utica."

He had no time to reply, for his servant had arrived with one of the dispensers of fortune; but as he turned away he wondered, in the light of the child's preference, about the towns of the interior. He was naturally exempt from the common doom. The officer who took him in hand and who had a large straw hat and a diamond breastpin, was quite a man of the world and in reply to the Count's formal declarations only said "Well, I guess it's all right; I guess I'll just pass you"; distributing chalk-marks as if they had been so many love-pats. The servant had done some superfluous unlocking and unbuckling, and while he closed the pieces the officer stood there wiping his forehead and conversing with Vogelstein. "First visit to our country, sir? — quite alone — no ladies? Of course the ladies are what we're most after." It was in this manner he expressed himself while the young diplomatist wondered what he was waiting for and whether he ought to slip something into his palm. But this representative of order left our friend only a moment in suspense; he presently turned away with the remark, quite paternally uttered, that he hoped the Count would make quite a stay; upon which the young man saw how wrong he should have been to offer a tip. It was simply the American manner, which had a finish of its own after all. Vogelstein's servant had secured a porter with a truck, and he was about to leave the place when he saw Pandora Day dart out of the crowd and address herself with much eagerness to the functionary who had just liberated him. She had an open letter in her hand which she gave him to read and over which he cast his eyes, thoughtfully stroking his beard. Then she led him away to where her parents sat on their luggage. Count Otto sent off his servant with the porter and followed Pandora, to whom he really wished to address a word of farewell. The last thing they had said to each other on the ship was that they should meet again on shore. It seemed improbable however that the meeting would occur anywhere but just here on the dock; inasmuch as Pandora was decidedly not in society, where Vogelstein would be of course, and as, if Utica — he had her sharp little sister's word for it — was worse than what was about him there, he'd be hanged if he'd go to Utica. He overtook Pandora quickly; she was in the act of introducing the representative of order to her parents, quite in the same manner in which she had introduced the Captain of the ship. Mr. and Mrs. Day got up and shook hands with him and they evidently all prepared to have a little talk. "I should like to introduce you to my brother and sister," he heard the girl say, and he saw her look about for these appendages. He caught her eye as she did so, and advanced with his hand outstretched, reflecting the while that evidently the Americans, whom he had always heard described as silent and practical, rejoiced to extravagance in the social graces. They dawdled and chattered like so many Neapolitans.

"Good-bye, Count Vogelstein," said Pandora, who was a little flushed with her various exertions but did n't look the worse for it. "I hope you 'll have a splendid time and appreciate our country."

"I hope you 'll get through all right," Vogelstein answered, smiling and feeling himself already more idiomatic.

"That gentleman's sick that I wrote to," she rejoined; "is n't it too bad ? But he sent me down a letter to a friend of his — one of the examiners — and I guess we won't have any trouble. Mr. Lansing, let me make you acquainted with Count Vogelstein," she went on, presenting to her fellow passenger the wearer of the straw hat and the breastpin, who shook hands with the young German as if he had never seen him before. Vogelstein's heart rose for an instant to his throat; he thanked his stars he had n't offered a tip to the friend of a gentleman who had often been mentioned to him and who had also been described by a member of Pandora's family as Pandora's lover.

"It's a case of ladies this time," Mr. Lansing remarked to him with a smile which seemed to confess surreptitiously, and as if neither party could be eager, to recognition.

"Well, Mr. Bellamy says you 'll do anything for *him*," Pandora said, smiling very sweetly at Mr. Lansing. "We have n't got much; we 've been gone only two years."

Mr. Lansing scratched his head a little behind, with a movement that sent his straw hat forward in the direction of his nose. "I don't know as I 'd do anything for him that I would n't do for you," he responded with an equal geniality. "I guess you'd better open that one" — and he gave a little affectionate kick to one of the trunks.

"Oh mother, is n't he lovely? It's only your sea-things," Pandora cried, stooping over the coffer with the key in her hand.

"I don't know as I like showing them," Mrs. Day modestly murmured.

Vogelstein made his German salutation to the company in general, and to Pandora he offered an audible good-bye, which she returned in a bright friendly voice, but without looking round as she fumbled at the lock of her trunk.

"We'll try another, if you like," said Mr. Lansing good-humouredly.

"Oh no, it has got to be this one! Good-bye, Count Vogelstein. I hope you'll judge us correctly!"

The young man went his way and passed the barrier of the dock. Here he was met by his English valet with a face of consternation which led him to ask if a cab were n't forthcoming.

"'They call 'em 'acks 'ere, sir," said the man, "and they're beyond everything. He wants thirty shillings to take you to the inn."

Vogelstein hesitated a moment. "Could n't you find a German?"

"By the way he talks he *is* a German!" said the man; and in a moment Count Otto began his career in America by discussing the tariff of hackney-coaches in the language of the fatherland.

II

HE went wherever he was asked, on principle, partly
to study American society and partly because in
Washington pastimes seemed to him not so numerous
that one could afford to neglect occasions. At the end
of two winters he had naturally had a good many of
various kinds — his study of American society had
yielded considerable fruit. When, however, in April,
during the second year of his residence, he presented
himself at a large party given by Mrs. Bonnycastle
and of which it was believed that it would be the last
serious affair of the season, his being there (and still
more his looking very fresh and talkative) was not the
consequence of a rule of conduct. He went to Mrs.
Bonnycastle's simply because he liked the lady, whose
receptions were the pleasantest in Washington, and
because if he did n't go there he did n't know what he
should do; that absence of alternatives having become
familiar to him by the waters of the Potomac. There
were a great many things he did because if he did n't
do them he did n't know what he should do. It must
be added that in this case even if there had been an
alternative he would still have decided to go to Mrs.
Bonnycastle's. If her house was n't the pleasantest
there it was at least difficult to say which was pleasanter; and the complaint sometimes made of it that it
was too limited, that it left out, on the whole, more
people than it took in, applied with much less force
when it was thrown open for a general party. Toward

the end of the social year, in those soft scented days
of the Washington spring when the air began to show
a southern glow and the Squares and Circles (to
which the wide empty avenues converged according
to a plan so ingenious, yet so bewildering) to flush with
pink blossom and to make one wish to sit on benches
— under this magic of expansion and condonation
Mrs. Bonnycastle, who during the winter had been
a good deal on the defensive, relaxed her vigilance a
little, became whimsically wilful, vernally reckless, as
it were, and ceased to calculate the consequences of
an hospitality which a reference to the back files or
even to the morning's issue of the newspapers might
easily prove a mistake. But Washington life, to Count
Otto's apprehension, was paved with mistakes; he
felt himself in a society founded on fundamental
fallacies and triumphant blunders. Little addicted as
he was to the sportive view of existence, he had said
to himself at an early stage of his sojourn that the only
way to enjoy the great Republic would be to burn
one's standards and warm one's self at the blaze.
Such were the reflexions of a theoretic Teuton who
now walked for the most part amid the ashes of his
prejudices.

Mrs. Bonnycastle had endeavoured more than once
to explain to him the principles on which she received
certain people and ignored certain others; but it was
with difficulty that he entered into her discrimina-
tions. American promiscuity, goodness knew, had
been strange to him, but it was nothing to the queerness of American criticism. This lady would discourse
to him à perte de vue on differences where he only saw

resemblances, and both the merits and the defects of a good many members of Washington society, as this society was interpreted to him by Mrs. Bonnycastle, he was often at a loss to understand. Fortunately she had a fund of good humour which, as I have intimated, was apt to come uppermost with the April blossoms and which made the people she did n't invite to her house almost as amusing to her as those she did. Her husband was not in politics, though politics were much in him; but the couple had taken upon themselves the responsibilities of an active patriotism; they thought it right to live in America, differing therein from many of their acquaintances who only, with some grimness, thought it inevitable. They had that burdensome heritage of foreign reminiscence with which so many Americans were saddled; but they carried it more easily than most of their country-people, and one knew they had lived in Europe only by their present exultation, never in the least by their regrets. Their regrets, that is, were only for their ever having lived there, as Mrs. Bonnycastle once told the wife of a foreign minister. They solved all their problems successfully, including those of knowing none of the people they did n't wish to, and of finding plenty of occupation in a society supposed to be meagrely provided with resources for that body which Vogelstein was to hear invoked, again and again, with the mixture of desire and of deprecation that might have attended the mention of a secret vice, under the name of a leisure-class. When as the warm weather approached they opened both the wings of their house-door, it was because they thought it would entertain

them and not because they were conscious of a pressure. Alfred Bonnycastle all winter indeed chafed
a little at the definiteness of some of his wife's reserves;
it struck him that for Washington their society was
really a little too good. Vogelstein still remembered
the puzzled feeling — it had cleared up somewhat
now — with which, more than a year before, he had
heard Mr. Bonnycastle exclaim one evening, after a
dinner in his own house, when every guest but the
German secretary (who often sat late with the pair)
had departed: "Hang it, there's only a month left; let
us be vulgar and have some fun — let us invite the
President."

This was Mrs. Bonnycastle's carnival, and on the
occasion to which I began my chapter by referring
the President had not only been invited but had
signified his intention of being present. I hasten to
add that this was not the same august ruler to whom
Alfred Bonnycastle's irreverent allusion had been
made. The White House had received a new tenant
— the old one was then just leaving it — and Count
Otto had had the advantage, during the first eighteen
months of his stay in America, of seeing an electoral
campaign, a presidential inauguration and a distribu-
tion of spoils. He had been bewildered during those
first weeks by finding that at the national capital, in
the houses he supposed to be the best, the head of the
State was not a coveted guest; for this could be the
only explanation of Mr. Bonnycastle's whimsical suggestion of their inviting him, as it were, in carnival.
His successor went out a good deal for a President.

The legislative session was over, but this made little

difference in the aspect of Mrs. Bonnycastle's rooms, which even at the height of the congressional season could scarce be said to overflow with the representatives of the people. They were garnished with an occasional Senator, whose movements and utterances often appeared to be regarded with a mixture of alarm and indulgence, as if they would be disappointing if they were n't rather odd and yet might be dangerous if not carefully watched. Our young man had come to entertain a kindness for these conscript fathers of invisible families, who had something of the toga in the voluminous folds of their conversation, but were otherwise rather bare and bald, with stony wrinkles in their faces, like busts and statues of ancient lawgivers. There seemed to him something chill and exposed in their being at once so exalted and so naked; there were frequent lonesome glances in their eyes, as if in the social world their legislative consciousness longed for the warmth of a few comfortable laws ready-made. Members of the House were very rare, and when Washington was new to the enquiring secretary he used sometimes to mistake them, in the halls and on the staircases where he met them, for the functionaries engaged, under stress, to usher in guests and wait at supper. It was only a little later that he perceived these latter public characters almost always to be impressive and of that rich racial hue which of itself served as a livery. At present, however, such confounding figures were much less to be met than during the months of winter, and indeed they were never frequent at Mrs. Bonnycastle's. At present the social vistas of Washington, like the vast fresh flatness of the lettered and numbered streets, which at this season seemed to Vogelstein more spacious and vague than ever, suggested but a paucity of political phenomena. Count Otto that evening knew every one or almost every one. There were often enquiring strangers, expecting great things, from New York and Boston, and to them, in the friendly Washington way, the young German was promptly introduced. It was a society in which familiarity reigned and in which people were liable to meet three times a day, so that their ultimate essence really became a matter of importance.

"I 've got three new girls," Mrs. Bonnycastle said. "You must talk to them all."

"All at once?" Vogelstein asked, reversing in fancy a position not at all unknown to him. He had so repeatedly heard himself addressed in even more than triple simultaneity.

"Oh no; you must have something different for each; you can't get off that way. Have n't you discovered that the American girl expects something especially adapted to herself? It 's very well for Europe to have a few phrases that will do for any girl. The American girl is n't *any* girl; she 's a remarkable specimen in a remarkable species. But you must keep the best this evening for Miss Day."

"For Miss Day!" — and Vogelstein had a stare of intelligence. "Do you mean for Pandora?"

Mrs. Bonnycastle broke on her side into free amusement. "One would think you had been looking for her over the globe! So you know her already — and you call her by her pet name?"

"Oh no, I don't know her; that is I have n't seen her or thought of her from that day to this. We came to America in the same ship."

"Is n't she an American then?"

"Oh yes; she lives at Utica — in the interior."

"In the interior of Utica? You can't mean my young woman then, who lives in New York, where she's a great beauty and a great belle and has been immensely admired this winter."

"After all," said Count Otto, considering and a little disappointed, "the name's not so uncommon; it's perhaps another. But has she rather strange eyes, a little yellow, but very pretty, and a nose a little arched?"

"I can't tell you all that; I have n't seen her. She's staying with Mrs. Steuben. She only came a day or two ago, and Mrs. Steuben's to bring her. When she wrote to me to ask leave she told me what I tell you. They have n't come yet."

Vogelstein felt a quick hope that the subject of this correspondence might indeed be the young lady he had parted from on the dock at New York, but the indications seemed to point another way, and he had no wish to cherish an illusion. It did n't seem to him probable that the energetic girl who had introduced him to Mr. Lansing would have the entrée of the best house in Washington; besides, Mrs. Bonnycastle's guest was described as a beauty and belonging to the brilliant city.

"What's the social position of Mrs. Steuben?" it occurred to him to ask while he meditated. He had an earnest artless literal way of putting such a question as that; you could see from it that he was very thorough.

Mrs. Bonnycastle met it, however, but with mocking laughter. "I'm sure I don't know! What's your own?" — and she left him to turn to her other guests, to several of whom she repeated his question. Could they tell her what was the social position of Mrs. Steuben? There was Count Vogelstein who wanted to know. He instantly became aware of course that he ought n't so to have expressed himself. Was n't the lady's place in the scale sufficiently indicated by Mrs. Bonnycastle's acquaintance with her? Still there were fine degrees, and he felt a little unduly snubbed. It was perfectly true, as he told his hostess, that with the quick wave of new impressions that had rolled over him after his arrival in America the image of Pandora was almost completely effaced; he had seen innumerable things that were quite as remarkable in their way as the heroine of the *Donau*, but at the touch of the idea that he might see her and hear her again at any moment she became as vivid in his mind as if they had parted the day before: he remembered the exact shade of the eyes he had described to Mrs. Bonnycastle as yellow, the tone of her voice when at the last she expressed the hope he might judge America correctly. Had he judged America correctly? If he were to meet her again she doubtless would try to ascertain. It would be going much too far to say that the idea of such an ordeal was terrible to Count Otto; but it may at least be said that the thought of meeting Pandora Day made him nervous. The fact is certainly singular, but I shall not take on myself to explain it; there are some things that even the most philosophic historian is n't bound to account for.

He wandered into another room, and there, at the end of five minutes, he was introduced by Mrs. Bonny-castle to one of the young ladies of whom she had spoken. This was a very intelligent girl who came from Boston and showed much acquaintance with Spielhagen's novels. "Do you like them?" Vogel-stein asked rather vaguely, not taking much interest in the matter, as he read works of fiction only in case of a sea-voyage. The young lady from Boston looked pensive and concentrated; then she answered that she liked *some* of them *very* much, but that there were others she did n't like — and she enumerated the works that came under each of these heads. Spiel-hagen is a voluminous writer, and such a catalogue took some time; at the end of it moreover Vogelstein's question was not answered, for he could n't have told us whether she liked Spielhagen or not.

On the next topic, however, there was no doubt about her feelings. They talked about Washington as people talk only in the place itself, revolving about the subject in widening and narrowing circles, perch-ing successively on its many branches, considering it from every point of view. Our young man had been long enough in America to discover that after half a century of social neglect Washington had become the fashion and enjoyed the great advantage of being a new resource in conversation. This was especially the case in the months of spring, when the inhabitants of the commercial cities came so far southward to escape, after the long winter, that final affront. They were all agreed that Washington was fascinating, and none of them were better prepared

to talk it over than the Bostonians. Vogelstein originally had been rather out of step with them; he had
n't seized their point of view, had n't known with
what they compared this object of their infatuation.
But now he knew everything; he had settled down to
the pace; there was n't a possible phase of the discussion that could find him at a loss. There was a
kind of Hegelian element in it; in the light of these
considerations the American capital took on the
semblance of a monstrous mystical infinite *Werden*.
But they fatigued Vogelstein a little, and it was his
preference, as a general thing, not to engage the same
evening with more than one new-comer, one visitor
in the freshness of initiation. This was why Mrs.
Bonnycastle's expression of a wish to introduce him
to three young ladies had startled him a little; he saw
a certain process, in which he flattered himself that he
had become proficient, but which was after all tolerably exhausting, repeated for each of the damsels.
After separating from his judicious Bostonian he
rather evaded Mrs. Bonnycastle, contenting himself
with the conversation of old friends, pitched for the
most part in a lower and easier key.

At last he heard it mentioned that the President
had arrived, had been some half-hour in the house,
and he went in search of the illustrious guest, whose
whereabouts at Washington parties was never indicated by a cluster of courtiers. He made it a point,
whenever he found himself in company with the President, to pay him his respects, and he had not been
discouraged by the fact that there was no association
of ideas in the eye of the great man as he put out his

hand presidentially and said "Happy to meet you, sir." Count Otto felt himself taken for a mere loyal subject, possibly for an office-seeker; and he used to reflect at such moments that the monarchical form had its merits: it provided a line of heredity for the faculty of quick recognition. He had now some difficulty in finding the chief magistrate, and ended by learning that he was in the tea-room, a small apartment devoted to light refection near the entrance of the house. Here our young man presently perceived him seated on a sofa and in conversation with a lady. There were a number of people about the table, eating, drinking, talking; and the couple on the sofa, which was not near it but against the wall, in a shallow recess, looked a little withdrawn, as if they had sought seclusion and were disposed to profit by the diverted attention of the others. The President leaned back; his gloved hands, resting on either knee, made large white spots. He looked eminent, but he looked relaxed, and the lady beside him ministered freely and without scruple, it was clear, to this effect of his comfortably unbending. Vogelstein caught her voice as he approached. He heard her say "Well now, remember; I consider it a promise." She was beautifully dressed, in rose-colour; her hands were clasped in her lap and her eyes attached to the presidential profile.

"Well, madam, in that case it's about the fiftieth promise I've given to-day."

It was just as he heard these words, uttered by her companion in reply, that Count Otto checked himself, turned away and pretended to be looking for a cup of tea. It wasn't usual to disturb the President,

even simply to shake hands, when he was sitting on
a sofa with a lady, and the young secretary felt it in
this case less possible than ever to break the rule, for
the lady on the sofa was none otheɪ than Pandora
Day. He had recognised her without her appearing
to see him, and even with half an eye, as they said,
had taken in that she was now a person to be reckoned
with. She had an air of elation, of success; she shone,
to intensity, in her rose-coloured dress; she was
extracting promises from the ruler of fifty millions of
people. What an odd place to meet her, her old ship-
mate thought, and how little one could tell, after all,
in America, who people were! He did n't want to
speak to her yet; he wanted to wait a little and learn
more; but meanwhile there was something attractive
in the fact that she was just behind him, a few yards
off, that if he should turn he might see her again. It
was she Mrs. Bonnycastle had meant, it was she who
was so much admired in New York. Her face was the
same, yet he had made out in a moment that she was
vaguely prettier; he had recognised the arch of her
nose, which suggested a fine ambition. He took some
tea, which he had n't desired, in order not to go away.
He remembered her *entourage* on the steamer; her
father and mother, the silent senseless burghers, so
little "of the world," her infant sister, so much of it,
her humorous brother with his tall hat and his influence in the smoking-room. He remembered Mrs.
Dangerfield's warnings — yet her perplexities too —
and the letter from Mr. Bellamy, and the introduction
to Mr. Lansing, and the way Pandora had stooped
down on the dirty dock, laughing and talking, mistress

of the situation, to open her trunk for the Customs. He was pretty sure she had paid no duties that day; this would naturally have been the purpose of Mr. Bellamy's letter. Was she still in correspondence with that gentleman, and had he got over the sickness interfering with their reunion? These images and these questions coursed through Count Otto's mind, and he saw it must be quite in Pandora's line to be mistress of the situation, for there was evidently nothing on the present occasion that could call itself her master. He drank his tea and as he put down his cup heard the President, behind him, say: "Well, I guess my wife will wonder why I don't come home."

"Why didn't you bring her with you?" Pandora benevolently asked.

"Well, she doesn't go out much. Then she has got her sister staying with her — Mrs. Runkle, from Natchez. She's a good deal of an invalid, and my wife doesn't like to leave her."

"She must be a very kind woman" — and there was a high mature competence in the way the girl sounded the note of approval.

"Well, I guess she isn't spoiled — yet."

"I should like very much to come and see her," said Pandora.

"Do come round. Couldn't you come some night?" the great man responded.

"Well, I'll come some time. And I shall remind you of your promise."

"All right. There's nothing like keeping it up. Well," said the President, "I must bid good-bye to these bright folks."

Vogelstein heard him rise from the sofa with his companion; after which he gave the pair time to pass out of the room before him. They did it with a certain impressive deliberation, people making way for the ruler of fifty millions and looking with a certain curiosity at the striking pink person at his side. When a little later he followed them across the hall, into one of the other rooms, he saw the host and hostess accompany the President to the door and two foreign ministers and a judge of the Supreme Court address themselves to Pandora Day. He resisted the impulse to join this circle: if he should speak to her at all he would somehow wish it to be in more privacy. She continued nevertheless to occupy him, and when Mrs. Bonnycastle came back from the hall he immediately approached her with an appeal. "I wish you'd tell me something more about that girl — that one opposite and in pink."

"The lovely Day — that's what they call her, I believe? I wanted you to talk with her."

"I find she *is* the one I've met. But she seems to be so different here. I can't make it out," said Count Otto.

There was something in his expression that again moved Mrs. Bonnycastle to mirth. "How we do puzzle you Europeans! You look quite bewildered."

"I'm sorry I look so — I try to hide it. But of course we're very simple. Let me ask then a simple earnest childlike question. Are her parents also in society?"

"Parents in society? D'où tombez-vous? Did you

ever hear of the parents of a triumphant girl in rose-colour, with a nose all her own, in society?"

"Is she then all alone?" he went on with a strain of melancholy in his voice.

Mrs. Bonnycastle launched at him all her laughter. "You're too pathetic. Don't you know what she is? I supposed of course you knew."

"It's exactly what I'm asking you."

"Why she's the new type. It has only come up lately. They have had articles about it in the papers. That's the reason I told Mrs. Steuben to bring her."

"The new type? *What* new type, Mrs. Bonny-castle?" he returned pleadingly — so conscious was he that all types in America were new.

Her laughter checked her reply a moment, and by the time she had recovered herself the young lady from Boston, with whom Vogelstein had been talking, stood there to take leave. This, for an American type, was an old one, he was sure; and the process of parting between the guest and her hostess had an ancient elaboration. Count Otto waited a little; then he turned away and walked up to Pandora Day, whose group of interlocutors had now been re-enforced by a gentleman who had held an important place in the cabinet of the late occupant of the presidential chair. He had asked Mrs. Bonnycastle if she were "all alone"; but there was nothing in her present situation to show her for solitary. She wasn't suf-ficiently alone for our friend's taste; but he was im-patient and he hoped she'd give him a few words to himself. She recognised him without a moment's hesitation and with the sweetest smile, a smile matching to a shade the tone in which she said: "I was watching you. I wondered if you were n't going to speak to me."

"Miss Day was watching him!" one of the foreign ministers exclaimed; "and we flattered ourselves that her attention was all with us."

"I mean before," said the girl, "while I was talking with the President."

At which the gentlemen began to laugh, one of them remarking that this was the way the absent were sacrificed, even the great; while another put on record that he hoped Vogelstein was duly flattered.

"Oh I was watching the President too," said Pandora. "I 've got to watch *him*. He has promised me something."

"It must be the mission to England," the judge of the Supreme Court suggested. "A good position for a lady; they 've got a lady at the head over there."

"I wish they would send you to *my* country," one of the foreign ministers suggested. "I 'd immediately get recalled."

"Why perhaps in your country I would n't speak to you! It 's only because you 're here," the ex-heroine of the *Donau* returned with a gay familiarity which evidently ranked with her but as one of the arts of defence. "You 'll see what mission it is when it comes out. But I 'll speak to Count Vogelstein anywhere," she went on. "He 's an older friend than any right here. I 've known him in difficult days."

"Oh yes, on the great ocean," the young man smiled. "On the watery waste, in the tempest!"

"Oh I don't mean that so much; we had a beautiful voyage and there was n't any tempest. I mean when I was living in Utica. That's a watery waste if you like, and a tempest there would have been a pleasant variety."

"Your parents seemed to me so peaceful!" her associate in the other memories sighed with a vague wish to say something sympathetic.

"Oh you have n't seen them ashore! At Utica they were very lively. But that's no longer our natural home. Don't you remember I told you I was working for New York? Well, I worked — I had to work hard. But we've moved."

Count Otto clung to his interest. "And I hope they're happy."

"My father and mother? Oh they will be, in time. I must give them time. They're very young yet, they've years before them. And you've been always in Washington?" Pandora continued. "I suppose you've found out everything about everything."

"Oh no — there are some things I *can't* find out."

"Come and see me and perhaps I can help you. I'm very different from what I was in that phase. I've advanced a great deal since then."

"Oh how was Miss Day in that phase?" asked a cabinet minister of the last administration.

"She was delightful of course," Count Otto said.

"He's very flattering; I did n't open my mouth!" Pandora cried. "Here comes Mrs. Steuben to take me to some other place. I believe it's a literary party near the Capitol. Everything seems so separate in Washington. Mrs. Steuben's going to read a poem. I wish she'd read it here; would n't it do as well?"

PANDORA

This lady, arriving, signified to her young friend the necessity of their moving on. But Miss Day's companions had various things to say to her before giving her up. She had a vivid answer for each, and it was brought home to Vogelstein while he listened that this would be indeed, in her development, as she said, another phase. Daughter of small burghers as she might be she was really brilliant. He turned away a little and while Mrs. Steuben waited put her a question. He had made her half an hour before the subject of that enquiry to which Mrs. Bonnycastle returned so ambiguous an answer; but this was n't because he failed of all direct acquaintance with the amiable woman or of any general idea of the esteem in which she was held. He had met her in various places and had been at her house. She was the widow of a commodore, was a handsome mild soft swaying person, whom every one liked, with glossy bands of black hair and a little ringlet depending behind each ear. Some one had said that she looked like the *vieux jeu* idea of the queen in "Hamlet." She had written verses which were admired in the South, wore a full-length portrait of the commodore on her bosom and spoke with the accent of Savannah. She had about her a positive strong odour of Washington. It had certainly been very superfluous in our young man to question Mrs. Bonnycastle about her social position.

"Do kindly tell me," he said, lowering his voice, "what 's the type to which that young lady belongs? Mrs. Bonnycastle tells me it 's a new one."

Mrs. Steuben for a moment fixed her liquid eyes on the secretary of legation. She always seemed to

145

be translating the prose of your speech into the finer rhythms with which her own mind was familiar. "Do you think anything 's really new?" she then began to flute. "I 'm very fond of the old; you know that 's a weakness of we Southerners." The poor lady, it will be observed, had another weakness as well. "What we often take to be the new is simply the old under some novel form. Were there not remarkable natures in the past? If you doubt it you should visit the South, where the past still lingers."

Vogelstein had been struck before this with Mrs. Steuben's pronunciation of the word by which her native latitudes were designated; transcribing it from her lips you would have written it (as the nearest approach) the Sooth. But at present he scarce heeded this peculiarity; he was wondering rather how a woman could be at once so copious and so uninforming. What did he care about the past or even about the Sooth? He was afraid of starting her again. He looked at her, discouraged and helpless, as bewildered almost as Mrs. Bonnycastle had found him half an hour before; looked also at the commodore, who, on her bosom, seemed to breathe again with his widow's respirations. "Call it an old type then if you like," he said in a moment. "All I want to know is what type it *is!* It seems impossible," he gasped, "to find out."

"You can find out in the newspapers. They 've had articles about it. They write about everything now. But it is n't true about Miss Day. It 's one of the first families. Her great-grandfather was in the Revolution." Pandora by this time had given her attention again to Mrs. Steuben. She seemed to signify that she was ready to move on. "Was n't your great-grandfather in the Revolution?" the elder lady asked. "I 'm telling Count Vogelstein about him."

"Why are you asking about my ancestors?" the girl demanded of the young German with untempered brightness. "Is that the thing you said just now that you can't find out? Well, if Mrs. Steuben will only be quiet you never will."

Mrs. Steuben shook her head rather dreamily. "Well, it 's no trouble for we of the Sooth to be quiet. There 's a kind of languor in our blood. Besides, we have to be to-day. But I 've got to show some energy to-night. I 've got to get you to the end of Pennsylvania Avenue."

Pandora gave her hand to Count Otto and asked him if he thought they should meet again. He answered that in Washington people were always meeting again and that at any rate he should n't fail to wait upon her. Hereupon, just as the two ladies were detaching themselves, Mrs. Steuben remarked that if the Count and Miss Day wished to meet again the picnic would be a good chance — the picnic she was getting up for the following Thursday. It was to consist of about twenty bright people, and they 'd go down the Potomac to Mount Vernon. The Count answered that if Mrs. Steuben thought him bright enough he should be delighted to join the party; and he was told the hour for which the tryst was taken.

He remained at Mrs. Bonnycastle's after every one had gone, and then he informed this lady of his reason for waiting. Would she have mercy on him and let

him know, in a single word, before he went to rest —
for without it rest would be impossible — what was
this famous type to which Pandora Day belonged?

"Gracious, you don't mean to say you've not
found out that type yet!" Mrs. Bonnycastle exclaimed with a return of her hilarity. "What have
you been doing all the evening? You Germans may
be thorough, but you certainly are not quick!"

It was Alfred Bonnycastle who at last took pity on
him. "My dear Vogelstein, she's the latest freshest
fruit of our great American evolution. She's the self-
made girl!"

Count Otto gazed a moment. "The fruit of the
great American Revolution? Yes, Mrs. Steuben told
me her great-grandfather —" but the rest of his sentence was lost in a renewed explosion of Mrs. Bonnycastle's sense of the ridiculous. He bravely pushed his
advantage, such as it was, however, and, desiring his
host's definition to be defined, enquired what the self-
made girl might be.

"Sit down and we'll tell you all about it," Mrs.
Bonnycastle said. "I like talking this way, after a
party's over. You can smoke if you like, and Alfred
will open another window. Well, to begin with, the
self-made girl's a new feature. That, however, you
know. In the second place she is n't self-made at all.
We all help to make her — we take such an interest in
her."

"That's only after she's made!" Alfred Bonnycastle broke in. "But it's Vogelstein that takes an
interest. What on earth has started you up so on the
subject of Miss Day?"

PANDORA

The visitor explained as well as he could that it was merely the accident of his having crossed the ocean in the steamer with her; but he felt the inadequacy of this account of the matter, felt it more than his hosts, who could know neither how little actual contact he had had with her on the ship, how much he had been affected by Mrs. Dangerfield's warnings, nor how much observation at the same time he had lavished on her. He sat there half an hour, and the warm dead stillness of the Washington night — nowhere are the nights so silent — came in at the open window, mingled with a soft sweet earthy smell, the smell of growing things and in particular, as he thought, of Mrs. Steuben's Sooth. Before he went away he had heard all about the self-made girl, and there was something in the picture that strongly impressed him. She was possible doubtless only in America; American life had smoothed the way for her. She was not fast, nor emancipated, nor crude, nor loud, and there was n't in her, of necessity at least, a grain of the stuff of which the adventuress is made. She was simply very successful, and her success was entirely personal. She had n't been born with the silver spoon of social opportunity; she had grasped it by honest exertion. You knew her by many different signs, but chiefly, infallibly, by the appearance of her parents. It was her parents who told her story; you always saw how little her parents could have made her. Her attitude with regard to them might vary in different ways. As the great fact on her own side was that she had lifted herself from a lower social plane, done it all herself, and done it by the simple lever of her personality, it was naturally to

149

be expected that she would leave the authors of her
mere material being in the shade. Sometimes she had
them in her wake, lost in the bubbles and the foam
that showed where she had passed; sometimes, as
Alfred Bonnycastle said, she let them slide altogether;
sometimes she kept them in close confinement, resort-
ing to them under cover of night and with every precaution; sometimes she exhibited them to the public in
discreet glimpses, in prearranged attitudes. But the
general characteristic of the self-made girl was that,
though it was frequently understood that she was
privately devoted to her kindred, she never attempted
to impose them on society, and it was striking that,
though in some of her manifestations a bore, she was
at her worst less of a bore than they. They were almost
always solemn and portentous, and they were for the
most part of a deathly respectability. She was n't
necessarily snobbish, unless it was snobbish to want
the best. She did n't cringe, she did n't make herself
smaller than she was; she took on the contrary a
stand of her own and attracted things to herself. Naturally she was possible only in America — only in a
country where whole ranges of competition and comparison were absent. The natural history of this interesting creature was at last completely laid bare to the
earnest stranger, who, as he sat there in the animated
stillness, with the fragrant breath of the Western world
in his nostrils, was convinced of what he had already
suspected, that conversation in the great Republic was
more yearningly, not to say gropingly, psychological
than elsewhere. Another thing, as he learned, that
you knew the self-made girl by was her culture, which

was perhaps a little too restless and obvious. She had usually got into society more or less by reading, and her conversation was apt to be garnished with literary allusions, even with familiar quotations. Vogelstein had n't had time to observe this element as a developed form in Pandora Day; but Alfred Bonnycastle hinted that he would n't trust her to keep it under in a *tête-à-tête*. It was needless to say that these young persons had always been to Europe; that was usually the first place they got to. By such arts they sometimes entered society on the other side before they did so at home; it was to be added at the same time that this resource was less and less valuable, for Europe, in the American world, had less and less prestige and people in the Western hemisphere now kept a watch on that roundabout road. All of which quite applied to Pandora Day — the journey to Europe, the culture (as exemplified in the books she read on the ship), the relegation, the effacement, of the family. The only thing that was exceptional was the rapidity of her march; for the jump she had taken since he left her in the hands of Mr. Lansing struck Vogelstein, even after he had made all allowance for the abnormal homogeneity of the American mass, as really considerable. It took all her cleverness to account for such things. When she "moved" from Utica — mobilised her commissariat — the battle appeared virtually to have been gained.

Count Otto called the next day, and Mrs. Steuben's blackamoor informed him, in the communicative manner of his race, that the ladies had gone out to pay some visits and look at the Capitol. Pandora apparently had not hitherto examined this monument, and our young man wished he had known, the evening before, of her omission, so that he might have offered to be her initiator. There is too obvious a connexion for us to fail of catching it between his regret and the fact that in leaving Mrs. Steuben's door he reminded himself that he wanted a good walk, and that he thereupon took his way along Pennsylvania Avenue. His walk had become fairly good by the time he reached the great white edifice that unfolds its repeated colonnades and uplifts its isolated dome at the end of a long vista of saloons and tobacco-shops. He slowly climbed the great steps, hesitating a little, even wondering why he had come. The superficial reason was obvious enough, but there was a real one behind it that struck him as rather wanting in the solidity which should characterise the motives of an emissary of Prince Bismarck. The superficial reason was a belief that Mrs. Steuben would pay her visit first — it was probably only a question of leaving cards — and bring her young friend to the Capitol at the hour when the yellow afternoon light would give a tone to the blankness of its marble walls. The Capitol was a splendid building, but it was rather wanting in tone. Vogelstein's curiosity about Pandora Day had been much more quickened than checked by the revelations made to him in Mrs. Bonnycastle's drawing-room. It was a relief to have the creature classified; but he had a desire, of which he had not been conscious before, to see really to the end how well, in other words how completely and artistically, a girl could make herself. His calculations had been just, and he had wandered about the rotunda for only ten minutes, looking again at the paintings, commemorative of the national annals, which occupy its lower spaces, and at the simulated sculptures, so touchingly characteristic of early American taste, which adorn its upper reaches, when the charming women he had been counting on presented themselves in charge of a licensed guide. He went to meet them and did n't conceal from them that he had marked them for his very own. The encounter was happy on both sides, and he accompanied them through the queer and endless interior, through labyrinths of bleak bare development, into legislative and judicial halls. He thought it a hideous place; he had seen it all before and asked himself what senseless game he was playing. In the lower House were certain bedaubed walls, in the basest style of imitation, which made him feel faintly sick, not to speak of a lobby adorned with artless prints and photographs of eminent defunct Congressmen that was all too serious for a joke and too comic for a Valhalla. But Pandora was greatly interested; she thought the Capitol very fine; it was easy to criticise the details, but as a whole it was the most impressive building she had ever seen. She proved a charming fellow tourist; she had constantly something to say, but never said it too much; it was impossible to drag in the wake of a *cicerone* less of a lengthening or an irritating chain. Vogelstein could see too that she wished to improve her mind; she looked at the historical pictures, at the uncanny statues of local worthies, presented by the different States — they were of different sizes, as if they had been "numbered," in a shop — she asked questions of the guide and in the chamber of the Senate requested him to show her the chairs of the gentlemen from New York. She sat down in one of them, though Mrs. Steuben told her *that* Senator (she mistook the chair, dropping into another State) was a horrid old thing.

Throughout the hour he spent with her Vogelstein seemed to see how it was she had made herself. They walked about afterwards on the splendid terrace that surrounds the Capitol, the great marble floor on which it stands, and made vague remarks — Pandora's were the most definite — about the yellow sheen of the Potomac, the hazy hills of Virginia, the far-gleaming pediment of Arlington, the raw confused-looking country. Washington was beneath them, bristling and geometrical; the long lines of its avenues seemed to stretch into national futures. Pandora asked Count Otto if he had ever been to Athens and, on his admitting so much, sought to know whether the eminence on which they stood did n't give him an idea of the Acropolis in its prime. Vogelstein deferred the satisfaction of this appeal to their next meeting; he was glad — in spite of the appeal — to make pretexts for seeing her again. He did so on the morrow; Mrs. Steuben's picnic was still three days distant. He called on Pandora a second time, also met her each evening in the Washington world. It took very little of this to remind him that he was forgetting both Mrs. Dangerfield's warnings and the admonitions — long familiar to him — of his own conscience. Was he in peril of love? Was he to be sacrificed on the altar of the American girl, an altar at which those other poor fellows had poured out some of the bluest blood in Germany and he had himself taken oath he would never seriously worship? He decided that he was n't in real danger, that he had rather clinched his precautions. It was true that a young person who had succeeded so well for herself might be a great help to her husband; but this diplomatic aspirant preferred on the whole that his success should be his own: it would n't please him to have the air of being pushed by his wife. Such a wife as that would wish to push him, and he could hardly admit to himself that this was what fate had in reserve for him — to be propelled in his career by a young lady who would perhaps attempt to talk to the Kaiser as he had heard her the other night talk to the President. Would she consent to discontinue relations with her family, or would she wish still to borrow plastic relief from that domestic background? That her family was so impossible was to a certain extent an advantage; for if they had been a little better the question of a rupture would be less easy. He turned over these questions in spite of his security, or perhaps indeed because of it. The security made them speculative and disinterested.

They haunted him during the excursion to Mount Vernon, which took place according to traditions long established. Mrs. Steuben's confederates assembled on the steamer and were set afloat on the big brown stream which had already seemed to our special traveller to have too much bosom and too little bank. Here and there, however, he became conscious of a shore where there was something to look at, even though conscious at the same time that he had of old lost great opportunities of an idyllic cast in not having managed to be more "thrown with" a certain young lady on the deck of the North German Lloyd. The two turned round together to hang over Alexandria, which for Pandora, as she declared, was a picture of Old Virginia. She told Vogelstein that she was always hearing about it during the Civil War, ages before. Little girl as she had been at the time she remembered all the names that were on people's lips during those years of reiteration. This historic spot had a touch of the romance of rich decay, a reference to older things, to a dramatic past. The past of Alexandria appeared in the vista of three or four short streets sloping up a hill and lined with poor brick warehouses erected for merchandise that had ceased to come or go. It looked hot and blank and sleepy, down to the shabby waterside where tattered darkies dangled their bare feet from the edge of rotting wharves. Pandora was even more interested in Mount Vernon — when at last its wooded bluff began to command the river — than she had been in the Capitol, and after they had disembarked and ascended to the celebrated mansion she insisted on going into every room it contained. She "claimed for it," as she said — some of her turns were so characteristic both of her nationality and her own style — the finest situation in the world, and was distinct as to the shame of their not giving it to the President for his country-seat. Most of her companions had seen the house often, and were now coupling themselves in the grounds according to their sympathies, so that it was easy for Vogelstein to offer the benefit of his own experience to

156

the most inquisitive member of the party. They were not to lunch for another hour, and in the interval the young man roamed with his first and fairest acquaintance. The breath of the Potomac, on the boat, had been a little harsh, but on the softly-curving lawn, beneath the clustered trees, with the river relegated to a mere shining presence far below and in the distance, the day gave out nothing but its mildness, the whole scene became noble and genial.

Count Otto could joke a little on great occasions, and the present one was worthy of his humour. He maintained to his companion that the shallow painted mansion resembled a false house, a "wing" or structure of daubed canvas, on the stage; but she answered him so well with certain economical palaces she had seen in Germany, where, as she said, there was nothing but china stoves and stuffed birds, that he was obliged to allow the home of Washington to be after all really *gemüthlich*. What he found so in fact was the soft texture of the day, his personal situation, the sweetness of his suspense. For suspense had decidedly become his portion; he was under a charm that made him feel he was watching his own life and that his susceptibilities were beyond his control. It hung over him that things might take a turn, from one hour to the other, which would make them very different from what they had been yet; and his heart certainly beat a little faster as he wondered what that turn might be. Why did he come to picnics on fragrant April days with American girls who might lead him too far? Would n't such girls be glad to marry a Pomeranian count? And *would* they, after all, talk that way to the Kaiser? If

157

he were to marry one of them he should have to give
her several thorough lessons.

In their little tour of the house our young friend and
his companion had had a great many fellow visitors,
who had also arrived by the steamer and who had
hitherto not left them an ideal privacy. But the others
gradually dispersed; they circled about a kind of
showman who was the authorised guide, a big slow
genial vulgar heavily-bearded man, with a whimsical
edifying patronising tone, a tone that had immense
success when he stopped here and there to make his
points — to pass his eyes over his listening flock, then
fix them quite above it with a meditative look and
bring out some ancient pleasantry as if it were a sudden inspiration. He made a cheerful thing, an echo of
the platform before the booth of a country fair, even
of a visit to the tomb of the *pater patriæ*. It is enshrined in a kind of grotto in the grounds, and Vogelstein remarked to Pandora that he was a good man
for the place, but was too familiar. "Oh he'd have
been familiar with Washington," said the girl with the
bright dryness with which she often uttered amusing
things. Vogelstein looked at her a moment, and it
came over him, as he smiled, that she herself probably
would n't have been abashed even by the hero with
whom history has taken fewest liberties. "You look
as if you could hardly believe that," Pandora went on.
"You Germans are always in such awe of great people." And it occurred to her critic that perhaps after
all Washington would have liked her manner, which
was wonderfully fresh and natural. The man with the
beard was an ideal minister to American shrines; he

played on the curiosity of his little band with the touch
of a master, drawing them at the right moment away
to see the classic ice-house where the old lady had been
found weeping in the belief it was Washington's grave.
While this monument was under inspection our interesting couple had the house to themselves, and they
spent some time on a pretty terrace where certain
windows of the second floor opened — a little roofless
verandah which overhung, in a manner, obliquely, all
the magnificence of the view; the immense sweep of
the river, the artistic plantations, the last-century garden with its big box hedges and remains of old espa-
liers. They lingered here for nearly half an hour, and
it was in this retirement that Vogelstein enjoyed the
only approach to intimate conversation appointed for
him, as was to appear, with a young woman in whom
he had been unable to persuade himself that he was
not absorbed. It's not necessary, and it's not possible, that I should reproduce this colloquy; but I may
mention that it began — as they leaned against the
parapet of the terrace and heard the cheerful voice of
the showman wafted up to them from a distance —
with his saying to her rather abruptly that he could n't
make out why they had n't had more talk together
when they crossed the Atlantic.

"Well, I can if you can't," said Pandora. "I'd have
talked quick enough if you had spoken to me. I spoke
to you first."

"Yes, I remember that " — and it affected him
awkwardly.

"You listened too much to Mrs. Dangerfield."

He feigned a vagueness. "To Mrs. Dangerfield?"

"That woman you were always sitting with; she told you not to speak to me. I've seen her in New York; she speaks to me now herself. She recommended you to have nothing to do with me."

"Oh how can you say such dreadful things?" Count Otto cried with a very becoming blush.

"You know you can't deny it. You were n't attracted by my family. They're charming people when you know them. I don't have a better time anywhere than I have at home," the girl went on loyally. "But what does it matter? My family are very happy. They're getting quite used to New York. Mrs. Dangerfield's a vulgar wretch — next winter she'll call on me."

"You are unlike any Mädchen I've ever seen — I don't understand you," said poor Vogelstein with the colour still in his face.

"Well, you never *will* understand me — probably; but what difference does it make?"

He attempted to tell her what difference, but I've no space to follow him here. It's known that when the German mind attempts to explain things it does n't always reduce them to simplicity, and Pandora was first mystified, then amused, by some of the Count's revelations. At last I think she was a little frightened, for she remarked irrelevantly, with some decision, that luncheon would be ready and that they ought to join Mrs. Steuben. Her companion walked slowly, on purpose, as they left the house together, for he knew the pang of a vague sense that he was losing her.

"And shall you be in Washington many days yet?" he appealed as they went.

"It will all depend. I'm expecting important news. What I shall do will be influenced by that."

The way she talked about expecting news — and important! — made him feel somehow that she had a career, that she was active and independent, so that he could scarcely hope to stop her as she passed. It was certainly true that he had never seen any girl like her. It would have occurred to him that the news she was expecting might have reference to the favour she had begged of the President, if he hadn't already made up his mind — in the calm of meditation after that talk with the Bonnycastles — that this favour must be a pleasantry. What she had said to him had a discouraging, a somewhat chilling effect; nevertheless it was not without a certain ardour that he enquired of her whether, so long as she stayed in Washington, he might n't pay her certain respectful attentions.

"As many as you like — and as respectful ones; but you won't keep them up for ever!"

"You try to torment me," said Count Otto.

She waited to explain. "I mean that I may have some of my family."

"I shall be delighted to see them again."

Again she just hung fire. "There are some you 've never seen."

In the afternoon, returning to Washington on the steamer, Vogelstein received a warning. It came from Mrs. Bonnycastle and constituted, oddly enough, the second juncture at which an officious female friend had, while sociably afloat with him, advised him on the subject of Pandora Day.

"There's one thing we forgot to tell you the other

161

night about the self-made girl," said the lady of infinite mirth. "It's never safe to fix your affections on her, because she has almost always an impediment somewhere in the background."

He looked at her askance, but smiled and said: "I should understand your information — for which I'm so much obliged — a little better if I knew what you mean by an impediment."

"Oh I mean she's always engaged to some young man who belongs to her earlier phase."

"Her earlier phase?"

"The time before she had made herself — when she lived unconscious of her powers. A young man from Utica, say. They usually have to wait; he's probably in a store. It's a long engagement."

Count Otto somehow preferred to understand as little as possible. "Do you mean a betrothal — to take effect?"

"I don't mean anything German and moonstruck. I mean that piece of peculiarly American enterprise a premature engagement — to take effect, 'ut too complacently, at the end of time."

Vogelstein very properly reflected that it was no use his having entered the diplomatic career if he were n't able to bear himself as if this interesting generalisation had no particular message for him. He did Mrs. Bonnycastle moreover the justice to believe that she would n't have approached the question with such levity if she had supposed she should make him wince. The whole thing was, like everything else, but for her to laugh at, and the betrayal moreover of a good intention. "I see, I see — the self-made girl has of course always had a past. Yes, and the young man in the store — from Utica — is part of her past."

"You express it perfectly," said Mrs. Bonnycastle. "I could n't say it better myself."

"But with her present, with her future, when they change like this young lady's, I suppose everything else changes. How do you say it in America? She lets him slide."

"We don't say it at all!" Mrs. Bonnycastle cried. "She does nothing of the sort; for what do you take her? She sticks to him; that at least is what we *expect* her to do," she added with less assurance. "As I tell you, the type 's new and the case under consideration. We have n't yet had time for complete study."

"Oh of course I hope she sticks to him," Vogelstein declared simply and with his German accent more audible, as it always was when he was slightly agitated.

For the rest of the trip he was rather restless. He wandered about the boat, talking little with the returning picnickers. Toward the last, as they drew near Washington and the white dome of the Capitol hung aloft before them, looking as simple as a suspended snowball, he found himself, on the deck, in proximity to Mrs. Steuben. He reproached himself with having rather neglected her during an entertainment for which he was indebted to her bounty, and he sought to repair his omission by a proper deference. But the only act of homage that occurred to him was to ask her as by chance whether Miss Day were, to her knowledge, engaged.

Mrs. Steuben turned her Southern eyes upon him

163

with a look of almost romantic compassion. "To my knowledge? Why of course I'd know! I should think you'd know too. Did n't you know she was engaged? Why she has been engaged since she was sixteen."

Count Otto gazed at the dome of the Capitol. "To a gentleman from Utica?"

"Yes, a native of her place. She's expecting him soon."

"I'm so very glad to hear it," said Vogelstein, who decidedly, for his career, had promise. "And is she going to marry him?"

"Why what do people fall in love with each other *for?* I presume they'll marry when she gets round to it. Ah if she had only been from the Sooth —!"

At this he broke quickly in: "But why have they never brought it off, as you say, in so many years?"

"Well, at first she was too young, and then she thought her family ought to see Europe — of course they could see it better *with* her — and they spent some time there. And then Mr. Bellamy had some business difficulties that made him feel as if he did n't want to marry just then. But he has given up business and I presume feels more free. Of course it's rather long, but all the while they've been engaged. It's a true, true love," said Mrs. Steuben, whose sound of the adjective was that of a feeble flute.

"Is his name Mr. Bellamy?" the Count asked with his haunting reminiscence. "D. F. Bellamy, so? And has he been in a store?"

"I don't know what kind of business it was: it was some kind of business in Utica. I think he had a branch in New York. He's one of the leading gentle-

men of Utica and very highly educated. He's a good
deal older than Miss Day. He's a very fine man — I
presume a college man. He stands very high in Utica.
I don't know why you look as if you doubted it."

Vogelstein assured Mrs. Steuben that he doubted
nothing, and indeed what she told him was probably the more credible for seeming to him eminently
strange. Bellamy had been the name of the gentleman who, a year and a half before, was to have met
Pandora on the arrival of the German steamer; it was
in Bellamy's name that she had addressed herself with
such effusion to Bellamy's friend, the man in the straw
hat who was about to fumble in her mother's old
clothes. This was a fact that seemed to Count Otto
to finish the picture of her contradictions; it wanted at
present no touch to be complete. Yet even as it hung
there before him it continued to fascinate him, and he
stared at it, detached from surrounding things and
feeling a little as if he had been pitched out of an over-
turned vehicle, till the boat bumped against one of the
outstanding piles of the wharf at which Mrs. Steuben's
party was to disembark. There was some delay in getting the steamer adjusted to the dock, during which
the passengers watched the process over its side and
extracted what entertainment they might from the
appearance of the various persons collected to receive
it. There were darkies and loafers and hackmen, and
also vague individuals, the loosest and blankest he had
ever seen anywhere, with tufts on their chins, tooth-
picks in their mouths, hands in their pockets, rumina-
tion in their jaws and diamond pins in their shirt-
fronts, who looked as if they had sauntered over from

Pennsylvania Avenue to while away half an hour, for-
saking for that interval their various slanting postures
in the porticoes of the hotels and the doorways of the
saloons.

"Oh I'm so glad! How sweet of you to come
down!" It was a voice close to Count Otto's shoulder
that spoke these words, and he had no need to turn to
see from whom it proceeded. It had been in his ears
the greater part of the day, though, as he now perceived, without the fullest richness of expression of
which it was capable. Still less was he obliged to turn
to discover to whom it was addressed, for the few
simple words I have quoted had been flung across the
narrowing interval of water, and a gentleman who had
stepped to the edge of the dock without our young
man's observing him tossed back an immediate reply.

"I got here by the three o'clock train. They told
me in K Street where you were, and I thought I'd
come down and meet you."

"Charming attention!" said Pandora Day with
the laugh that seemed always to invite the whole of
any company to partake in it; though for some moments after this she and her interlocutor appeared to
continue the conversation only with their eyes. Meanwhile Vogelstein's also were not idle. He looked at her
visitor from head to foot, and he was aware that she
was quite unconscious of his own proximity. The gentleman before him was tall, good-looking, well-dressed;
evidently he would stand well not only at Utica, but,
judging from the way he had planted himself on the
dock, in any position that circumstances might com-
pel him to take up. He was about forty years old; he

had a black moustache and he seemed to look at the
world over some counter-like expanse on which he
invited it all warily and pleasantly to put down first
its idea of the terms of a transaction. He waved a
gloved hand at Pandora as if, when she exclaimed
"Gracious, ain't they long!" to urge her to be patient.
She was patient several seconds and then asked him
if he had any news. He looked at her briefly, in
silence, smiling, after which he drew from his pocket
a large letter with an official-looking seal and shook it
jocosely above his head. This was discreetly, covertly
done. No one but our young man appeared aware of
how much was taking place — and poor Count Otto
mainly felt it in the air. The boat was touching the
wharf and the space between the pair inconsiderable.

"Department of State?" Pandora very prettily and
soundlessly mouthed across at him.

"That's what they call it."

"Well, what country?"

"What's your opinion of the Dutch?" the gentleman asked for answer.

"Oh gracious!" cried Pandora.

"Well, are you going to wait for the return trip?"
said the gentleman.

Our silent sufferer turned away, and presently Mrs.
Steuben and her companion disembarked together.
When this lady entered a carriage with Miss Day the
gentleman who had spoken to the girl followed them;
the others scattered, and Vogelstein, declining with
thanks a "lift" from Mrs. Bonnycastle, walked home
alone and in some intensity of meditation. Two days
later he saw in a newspaper an announcement that

the President had offered the post of Minister to Holland to Mr. D. F. Bellamy of Utica; and in the course of a month he heard from Mrs. Steuben that Pandora, a thousand other duties performed, had finally "got round" to the altar of her own nuptials. He communicated this news to Mrs. Bonnycastle, who had not heard it but who, shrieking at the queer face he showed her, met it with the remark that there was now ground for a new induction as to the self-made girl.

THE PATAGONIA

THE PATAGONIA

I

THE houses were dark in the August night and the
perspective of Beacon Street, with its double chain
of lamps, was a foreshortened desert. The club on
the hill alone, from its semi-cylindrical front, projected a glow upon the dusky vagueness of the Common, and as I passed it I heard in the hot stillness the
click of a pair of billiard-balls. As "every one" was
out of town perhaps the servants, in the extravagance
of their leisure, were profaning the tables. The heat
was insufferable and I thought with joy of the morrow, of the deck of the steamer, the freshening breeze,
the sense of getting out to sea. I was even glad of
what I had learned in the afternoon at the office of
the company — that at the eleventh hour an old ship
with a lower standard of speed had been put on in
place of the vessel in which I had taken my passage.
America was roasting, England might very well be
stuffy, and a slow passage (which at that season of
the year would probably also be a fine one) was a
guarantee of ten or twelve days of fresh air.

I strolled down the hill without meeting a creature,
though I could see through the palings of the Common that that recreative expanse was peopled with
dim forms. I remembered Mrs. Nettlepoint's house
— she lived in those days (they are not so distant, but

there have been changes) on the water-side, a little
way beyond the spot at which the Public Garden
terminates; and I reflected that like myself she would
be spending the night in Boston if it were true that,
as had been mentioned to me a few days before at
Mount Desert, she was to embark on the morrow for
Liverpool. I presently saw this appearance confirmed
by a light above her door and in two or three of her
windows, and I determined to ask for her, having
nothing to do till bedtime. I had come out simply
to pass an hour, leaving my hotel to the blaze of its
gas and the perspiration of its porters; but it occurred
to me that my old friend might very well not know of
the substitution of the *Patagonia* for the *Scandinavia*,
so that I should be doing her a service to prepare her
mind. Besides, I could offer to help her, to look after
her in the morning: lone women are grateful for support in taking ship for far countries.

It came to me indeed as I stood on her door-step
that as she had a son she might not after all be so
lone; yet I remembered at the same time that Jasper
Nettlepoint was not quite a young man to lean upon,
having — as I at least supposed — a life of his own
and tastes and habits which had long since diverted
him from the maternal side. If he did happen just
now to be at home my solicitude would of course
seem officious; for in his many wanderings — I believed he had roamed all over the globe — he would
certainly have learned how to manage. None the less,
in fine, I was very glad to show Mrs. Nettlepoint I
thought of her. With my long absence I had lost sight
of her; but I had liked her of old, she had been a

172

THE PATAGONIA

good friend to my sisters, and I had in regard to her
that sense which is pleasant to those who in general
have gone astray or got detached, the sense that she
at least knew all about me. I could trust her at
any time to tell people I was respectable. Perhaps I
was conscious of how little I deserved this indulgence
when it came over me that I had n't been near her
for ages. The measure of that neglect was given by
my vagueness of mind about Jasper. However, I
really belonged nowadays to a different generation;
I was more the mother's contemporary than the son's.

Mrs. Nettlepoint was at home: I found her in her
back drawing-room, where the wide windows opened
to the water. The room was dusky — it was too hot
for lamps — and she sat slowly moving her fan and
looking out on the little arm of the sea which is so
pretty at night, reflecting the lights of Cambridgeport
and Charlestown. I supposed she was musing on the
loved ones she was to leave behind, her married
daughters, her grandchildren; but she struck a note
more specifically Bostonian as she said to me, pointing
with her fan to the Back Bay: "I shall see nothing
more charming than that over there, you know!"
She made me very welcome, but her son had told her
about the *Patagonia*, for which she was sorry, as this
would mean a longer voyage. She was a poor creature
in any boat and mainly confined to her cabin even in
weather extravagantly termed fine — as if any
weather could be fine at sea.

"Ah then your son's going with you?" I asked.

"Here he comes, he'll tell you for himself much
better than I can pretend to." Jasper Nettlepoint at

that moment joined us, dressed in white flannel and carrying a large fan. "Well, my dear, have you decided?" his mother continued with no scant irony. "He has n't yet made up his mind, and we sail at ten o'clock!"

"What does it matter when my things are put up?" the young man said. "There's no crowd at this moment; there will be cabins to spare. I'm waiting for a telegram — that will settle it. I just walked up to the club to see if it was come — they'll send it there because they suppose this house unoccupied. Not yet, but I shall go back in twenty minutes."

"Mercy, how you rush about in this temperature!" the poor lady exclaimed while I reflected that it was perhaps *his* billiard-balls I had heard ten minutes before. I was sure he was fond of billiards.

"Rush? not in the least. I take it uncommon easy."

"Ah I'm bound to say you do!" Mrs. Nettlepoint returned with inconsequence. I guessed at a certain tension between the pair and a want of consideration on the young man's part, arising perhaps from selfishness. His mother was nervous, in suspense, wanting to be at rest as to whether she should have his company on the voyage or be obliged to struggle alone. But as he stood there smiling and slowly moving his fan he struck me somehow as a person on whom this fact would n't sit too heavily. He was of the type of those whom other people worry about, not of those who worry about other people. Tall and strong, he had a handsome face, with a round head and close-curling hair; the whites of his eyes and the enamel of his teeth, under his brown moustache, gleamed

174

vaguely in the lights of the Back Bay. I made out
that he was sunburnt, as if he lived much in the open
air, and that he looked intelligent but also slightly
brutal, though not in a morose way. His brutality,
if he had any, was bright and finished. I had to tell
him who I was, but even then I saw how little he
placed me and that my explanations gave me in his
mind no great identity or at any rate no great importance. I foresaw that he would in intercourse make me
feel sometimes very young and sometimes very old,
caring himself but little which. He mentioned, as if
to show our companion that he might safely be left
to his own devices, that he had once started from
London to Bombay at three quarters of an hour's
notice.

"Yes, and it must have been pleasant for the people
you were with!"

"Oh the people I was with —!" he returned; and
his tone appeared to signify that such people would
always have to come off as they could. He asked if
there were no cold drinks in the house, no lemonade,
no iced syrups; in such weather something of that sort
ought always to be kept going. When his mother
remarked that surely at the club they *were* kept going
he went on: "Oh yes, I had various things there;
but you know I 've walked down the hill since. One
should have something at either end. May I ring and
see?" He rang while Mrs. Nettlepoint observed that
with the people they had in the house, an establishment reduced naturally at such a moment to its simplest expression — they were burning up candle-ends
and there were no luxuries — she would n't answer

for the service. The matter ended in her leaving the room in quest of cordials with the female domestic who had arrived in response to the bell and in whom Jasper's appeal aroused no visible intelligence.

She remained away some time and I talked with her son, who was sociable but desultory and kept moving over the place, always with his fan, as if he were properly impatient. Sometimes he seated himself an instant on the window-sill, and then I made him out in fact thoroughly good-looking — a fine brown clean young athlete. He failed to tell me on what special contingency his decision depended; he only alluded familiarly to an expected telegram, and I saw he was probably fond at no time of the trouble of explanations. His mother's absence was a sign that when it might be a question of gratifying him she had grown used to spare no pains, and I fancied her rummaging in some close storeroom, among old preserve-pots, while the dull maid-servant held the candle awry. I don't know whether this same vision was in his own eyes; at all events it did n't prevent his saying suddenly, as he looked at his watch, that I must excuse him — he should have to go back to the club. He would return in half an hour — or in less. He walked away and I sat there alone, conscious, on the dark dismantled simplified scene, in the deep silence that rests on American towns during the hot season — there was now and then a far cry or a plash in the water, and at intervals the tinkle of the bells of the horse-cars on the long bridge, slow in the suffocating night — of the strange influence, half-sweet, half-sad, that abides in houses uninhabited or about to become

176

so, in places muffled and bereaved, where the un-
heeded sofas and patient belittered tables seem (like
the disconcerted dogs, to whom everything is alike
sinister) to recognise the eve of a journey.

After a while I heard the sound of voices, of steps,
the rustle of dresses, and I looked round, supposing
these things to denote the return of Mrs. Nettlepoint
and her handmaiden with the refection prepared for
her son. What I saw however was two other female
forms, visitors apparently just admitted, and now
ushered into the room. They were not announced —
the servant turned her back on them and rambled
off to our hostess. They advanced in a wavering
tentative unintroduced way — partly, I could see,
because the place was dark and partly because their
visit was in its nature experimental, a flight of imagination or a stretch of confidence. One of the ladies
was stout and the other slim, and I made sure in a
moment that one was talkative and the other reserved. It was further to be discerned that one was
elderly and the other young, as well as that the fact
of their unlikeness did n't prevent their being mother
and daughter. Mrs. Nettlepoint reappeared in a very
few minutes, but the interval had sufficed to establish
a communication — really copious for the occasion —
between the strangers and the unknown gentleman
whom they found in possession, hat and stick in
hand. This was not my doing — for what had I to
go upon? — and still less was it the doing of the
younger and the more indifferent, or less courageous,
lady. She spoke but once — when her companion
informed me that she was going out to Europe the

next day to be married. Then she protested "Oh mother!" in a tone that struck me in the darkness as doubly odd, exciting my curiosity to see her face.

It had taken the elder woman but a moment to come to that, and to various other things, after I had explained that I myself was waiting for Mrs. Nettlepoint, who would doubtless soon come back.

"Well, she won't know me — I guess she has n't ever heard much about me," the good lady said; "but I've come from Mrs. Allen and I guess that will make it all right. I presume you know Mrs. Allen?"

I was unacquainted with this influential personage, but I assented vaguely to the proposition. Mrs. Allen's emissary was good-humoured and familiar, but rather appealing than insistent (she remarked that if her friend *had* found time to come in the afternoon — she had so much to do, being just up for the day, that she could n't be sure — it would be all right); and somehow even before she mentioned Merrimac Avenue (they had come all the way from there) my imagination had associated her with that indefinite social limbo known to the properly-constituted Boston mind as the South End — a nebulous region which condenses here and there into a pretty face, in which the daughters are an "improvement" on the mothers and are sometimes acquainted with gentlemen more gloriously domiciled, gentlemen whose wives and sisters are in turn not acquainted with them.

When at last Mrs. Nettlepoint came in, accompanied by candles and by a tray laden with glasses of coloured fluid which emitted a cool tinkling, I was in a position to officiate as master of the ceremonies, to introduce Mrs. Mavis and Miss Grace Mavis, to represent that Mrs. Allen had recommended them — nay, had urged them — just to come that way, informally and without fear; Mrs. Allen who had been prevented only by the pressure of occupations so characteristic of her (especially when up from Mattapoisett for a few hours' desperate shopping) from herself calling in the course of the day to explain who they were and what was the favour they had to ask of her benevolent friend. Good-natured women understand each other even when so divided as to sit residentially above and below the salt, as who should say; by which token our hostess had quickly mastered the main facts: Mrs. Allen's visit that morning in Merrimac Avenue to talk of Mrs. Amber's great idea, the classes at the public schools in vacation (she was interested with an equal charity to that of Mrs. Mavis — even in such weather! — in those of the South End) for games and exercises and music, to keep the poor unoccupied children out of the streets; then the revelation that it had suddenly been settled almost from one hour to the other that Grace should sail for Liverpool, Mr. Porterfield at last being ready. He was taking a little holiday; his mother was with him, they had come over from Paris to see some of the celebrated old buildings in England, and he had telegraphed to say that if Grace would start right off they would just finish it up and be married. It often happened that when things had dragged on that way for years they were all huddled up at the end. Of course in such a case she, Mrs. Mavis, had had to fly round. Her daughter's passage was taken, but it seemed too dreadful she should make her journey all alone, the first time she had ever been at sea, without any companion or escort. *She* could n't go — Mr. Mavis was too sick : she had n't even been able to get him off to the seaside.

"Well, Mrs. Nettlepoint's going in that ship," Mrs. Allen had said; and she had represented that nothing was simpler than to give her the girl in charge. When Mrs. Mavis had replied that this was all very well but that she did n't know the lady, Mrs. Allen had declared that that did n't make a speck of difference, for Mrs. Nettlepoint was kind enough for anything. It was easy enough to *know* her, if that was all the trouble! All Mrs. Mavis would have to do would be to go right up to her next morning, when she took her daughter to the ship (she would see her there on the deck with her party) and tell her fair and square what she wanted. Mrs. Nettlepoint had daughters herself and would easily understand. Very likely she'd even look after Grace a little on the other side, in such a queer situation, going out alone to the gentleman she was engaged to : she'd just help her, like a good Samaritan, to turn round before she was married. Mr. Porterfield seemed to think they would n't wait long, once she was there : they would have it right over at the American consul's. Mrs. Allen had said it would perhaps be better still to go and see Mrs. Nettlepoint beforehand, that day, to tell her what they wanted : then they would n't seem to spring it on her just as she was leaving. She herself (Mrs. Allen) would call and say a word for them if she could save ten minutes before catching her train. If she had n't come it was because she had n't saved her ten minutes; but she had made them feel that they must come all the same. Mrs. Mavis liked that better, because on the ship in the morning there would be such a confusion. She did n't think her daughter would be any trouble — conscientiously she did n't. It was just to have some one to speak to her and not sally forth like a servant-girl going to a situation.

"I see, I'm to act as a sort of bridesmaid and to give her away," Mrs. Nettlepoint obligingly said. Kind enough in fact for anything, she showed on this occasion that it was easy enough to know her. There is notoriously nothing less desirable than an imposed aggravation of effort at sea, but she accepted without betrayed dismay the burden of the young lady's dependence and allowed her, as Mrs. Mavis said, to hook herself on. She evidently had the habit of patience, and her reception of her visitors' story reminded me afresh — I was reminded of it whenever I returned to my native land — that my dear compatriots are the people in the world who most freely take mutual accommodation for granted. They have always had to help themselves, and have rather magnanimously failed to learn just where helping others is distinguishable from that. In no country are there fewer forms and more reciprocities.

It was doubtless not singular that the ladies from Merrimac Avenue should n't feel they were importunate: what was striking was that Mrs. Nettlepoint did n't appear to suspect it. However, she would in any case have thought it inhuman to show this — though I could see that under the surface she was amused at everything the more expressive of the pilgrims from the South End took for granted. I scarce know whether the attitude of the younger visitor added or not to the merit of her good nature. Mr. Porterfield's intended took no part in the demonstration, scarcely spoke, sat looking at the Back Bay and the lights on the long bridge. She declined the lemonade and the other mixtures which, at Mrs. Nettlepoint's request, I offered her, while her mother partook freely of everything and I reflected — for I as freely drained a glass or two in which the ice tinkled —that Mr. Jasper had better hurry back if he wished to enjoy these luxuries.

Was the effect of the young woman's reserve meanwhile ungracious, or was it only natural that in her particular situation she should n't have a flow of compliment at her command ? I noticed that Mrs. Nettlepoint looked at her often, and certainly though she was undemonstrative Miss Mavis was interesting. The candle-light enabled me to see that though not in the very first flower of her youth she was still fresh and handsome. Her eyes and hair were dark, her face was pale, and she held up her head as if, with its thick braids and everything else involved in it, it were an appurtenance she was n't ashamed of. If her mother was excellent and common she was not common — not at least flagrantly so — and perhaps also not excellent. At all events she would n't be, in appearance at least, a dreary appendage; which in the case of a person "hooking on" was always something gained. Was it because something of a romantic or pathetic interest usually attaches to a good creature who has been the victim of a "long engagement" that this

young lady made an impression on me from the first
— favoured as I had been so quickly with this glimpse
of her history ? I could charge her certainly with no
positive appeal; she only held her tongue and smiled,
and her smile corrected whatever suggestion might
have forced itself upon me that the spirit within her
was dead — the spirit of that promise of which she
found herself doomed to carry out the letter.

What corrected it less, I must add, was an odd
recollection which gathered vividness as I listened to
it — a mental association evoked by the name of Mr.
Porterfield. Surely I had a personal impression, over-
smeared and confused, of the gentleman who was
waiting at Liverpool, or who presently would be, for
Mrs. Nettlepoint's protégée. I had met him, known
him, some time, somewhere, somehow, on the other
side. Was n't he studying something, very hard,
somewhere — probably in Paris — ten years before,
and did n't he make extraordinarily neat drawings,
linear and architectural ? Did n't he go to a table
d'hôte, at two francs twenty-five, in the Rue Bona-
parte, which I then frequented, and did n't he wear
spectacles and a Scotch plaid arranged in a manner
which seemed to say "I've trustworthy information
that that's the way they do it in the Highlands" ?
Was n't he exemplary to positive irritation, and very
poor, poor to positive oppression, so that I supposed
he had no overcoat and his tartan would be what he
slept under at night ? Was n't he working very hard
still, and would n't he be, in the natural course, not
yet satisfied that he had found his feet or knew enough
to launch out ? He would be a man of long prepara-

tions — Miss Mavis's white face seemed to speak to one of that. It struck me that if I had been in love with her I should n't have needed to lay such a train for the closer approach. Architecture was his line and he was a pupil of the Ecole des Beaux Arts. This reminiscence grew so much more vivid with me that at the end of ten minutes I had an odd sense of knowing — by implication — a good deal about the young lady.

Even after it was settled that Mrs. Nettlepoint would do everything possible for her the other visitor sat sipping our iced liquid and telling how "low" Mr. Mavis had been. At this period the girl's silence struck me as still more conscious, partly perhaps because she deprecated her mother's free flow — she was enough of an "improvement" to measure that — and partly because she was too distressed by the idea of leaving her infirm, her perhaps dying father. It was n't indistinguishable that they were poor and that she would take out a very small purse for her trousseau. For Mr. Porterfield to make up the sum his own case would have had moreover greatly to change. If he had enriched himself by the successful practice of his profession I had encountered no edifice he had reared — his reputation had n't come to my ears.

Mrs. Nettlepoint notified her new friends that she was a very inactive person at sea : she was prepared to suffer to the full with Miss Mavis, but not prepared to pace the deck with her, to struggle with her, to accompany her to meals. To this the girl replied that she would trouble her little, she was sure : she was convinced she should prove a wretched sailor and spend the voyage on her back. Her mother scoffed at this picture, prophesying perfect weather and a lovely time, and I interposed to the effect that if I might be trusted, as a tame bachelor fairly sea-seasoned, I should be delighted to give the new member of our party an arm or any other countenance whenever she should require it. Both the ladies thanked me for this — taking my professions with no sort of abatement — and the elder one declared that we were evidently going to be such a sociable group that it was too bad to have to stay at home. She asked Mrs. Nettlepoint if there were any one else in our party, and when our hostess mentioned her son — there was a chance of his embarking but (was n't it absurd ?) he had n't decided yet — she returned with extraordinary candour : "Oh dear, I do hope he 'll go : that would be so lovely for Grace."

Somehow the words made me think of poor Mr. Porterfield's tartan, especially as Jasper Nettlepoint strolled in again at that moment. His mother at once challenged him : it was ten o'clock; had he by chance made up his great mind ? Apparently he failed to hear her, being in the first place surprised at the strange ladies and then struck with the fact that one of them was n't strange. The young man, after a slight hesitation, greeted Miss Mavis with a handshake and a "Oh good-evening, how do you do ? " He did n't utter her name — which I could see he must have forgotten; but she immediately pronounced his, availing herself of the American girl's discretion to "present" him to her mother.

"Well, you might have told me you knew him all

this time!" that lady jovially cried. Then she had an equal confidence for Mrs. Nettlepoint. "It would have saved me a worry—an acquaintance already begun."

"Ah my son's acquaintances —!" our hostess murmured.

"Yes, and my daughter's too!" Mrs. Mavis gaily echoed. "Mrs. Allen did n't tell us *you* were going," she continued to the young man.

"She 'd have been clever if she had been able to!" Mrs. Nettlepoint sighed.

"Dear mother, I have my telegram," Jasper remarked, looking at Grace Mavis.

"I know you very little," the girl said, returning his observation.

"I 've danced with you at some ball — for some sufferers by something or other."

"I think it was an inundation or a big fire," she a little languidly smiled. "But it was a long time ago — and I have n't seen you since."

"I 've been in far countries — to my loss. I should have said it was a big fire."

"It was at the Horticultural Hall. I did n't remember your name," said Grace Mavis.

"That 's very unkind of you, when I recall vividly that you had a pink dress."

"Oh I remember that dress — your strawberry tarletan : you looked lovely in it!" Mrs. Mavis broke out. "You must get another just like it — on the other side."

"Yes, your daughter looked charming in it," said Jasper Nettlepoint. Then he added to the girl : "Yet you mentioned my name to your mother."

"It came back to me — seeing you here. I had no idea this was your home."

"Well, I confess it is n't, much. Oh there are some drinks!" — he approached the tray and its glasses.

"Indeed there are and quite delicious" — Mrs. Mavis largely wiped her mouth.

"Won't you have another then ? — a pink one, like your daughter's gown."

"With pleasure, sir. Oh do see them over," Mrs. Mavis continued, accepting from the young man's hand a third tumbler.

"My mother and that gentleman ? Surely they can take care of themselves," he freely pleaded.

"Then my daughter — she has a claim as an old friend."

But his mother had by this time interposed. " Jasper, what does your telegram say ?"

He paid her no heed: he stood there with his glass in his hand, looking from Mrs. Mavis to Miss Grace.

"Ah leave her to me, madam; I'm quite competent," I said to Mrs. Mavis.

Then the young man gave me his attention. The next minute he asked of the girl: "Do you mean you're going to Europe?"

"Yes, to-morrow. In the same ship as your mother."

"That's what we've come here for, to see all about it," said Mrs. Mavis.

"My son, take pity on me and tell me what light your telegram throws," Mrs. Nettlepoint went on.

"I will, dearest, when I've quenched my thirst." And he slowly drained his glass.

"Well, I declare you're worse than Gracie," Mrs. Mavis commented. "She was first one thing and then the other — but only about up to three o'clock yesterday."

"Excuse me—won't you take something?" Jasper enquired of Gracie; who however still declined, as if to make up for her mother's copious *consommation*. I found myself quite aware that the two ladies would do well to take leave, the question of Mrs. Nettlepoint's good will being so satisfactorily settled and the meeting of the morrow at the ship so near at hand; and I went so far as to judge that their protracted stay, with their hostess visibly in a fidget, gave the last proof of their want of breeding. Miss Grace after all then was not such an improvement on her mother, for she easily might have taken the initiative of departure, in spite of Mrs. Mavis's evident "game" of making her own absorption of refreshment last as long as possible. I watched the girl with increasing interest; I could n't help asking myself a question or two about her and even perceiving already (in a dim and general way) that rather marked embarrassment, or at least anxiety attended her. Was n't it complicating that she should have needed, by remaining long enough, to assuage a certain suspense, to learn whether or no Jasper were going to sail? Had n't something particular passed between them on the occasion or at the period to which we had caught their allusion, and did n't she really not know her mother was bringing her to *his* mother's, though she apparently had thought it well not to betray knowledge? Such things were symptomatic — though indeed one scarce knew of what — on the part of a young lady betrothed to that curious cross-barred phantom of a Mr. Porterfield. But I am bound to add that she gave me no further warrant for wonder than was conveyed in her all tacitly and covertly encouraging her mother to linger. Somehow I had a sense that *she* was conscious of the indecency of this. I got up myself to go, but Mrs. Nettlepoint detained me after seeing that my movement would n't be taken as a hint, and I felt she wished me not to leave my fellow visitors on her hands. Jasper complained of the closeness of the room, said that it was not a night to sit in a room — one ought to be out in the air, under the sky. He denounced the windows that overlooked the water for not opening upon a balcony or a terrace, until his mother, whom he had n't yet satisfied about his telegram, reminded him that there was a beautiful balcony in front, with room for a dozen people. She assured him we would go and sit there if it would please him.

"It will be nice and cool to-morrow, when we steam into the great ocean," said Miss Mavis, expressing with more vivacity than she had yet thrown into any of her utterances my own thought of half an hour before. Mrs. Nettlepoint replied that it would probably be freezing cold, and her son murmured that he would go and try the drawing-room balcony and report upon it. Just as he was turning away he said, smiling, to Miss Mavis: "Won't you come with me and see if it's pleasant?"

"Oh well, we had better not stay all night!" her mother exclaimed, but still without moving. The girl moved, after a moment's hesitation; she rose and accompanied Jasper to the other room. I saw how her slim tallness showed to advantage as she walked and that she looked well as she passed, with her head thrown back, into the darkness of the other part of the house. There was something rather marked, rather surprising — I scarcely knew why, for the act in itself was simple enough — in her acceptance of such a plea, and perhaps it was our sense of this that held the rest of us somewhat stiffly silent as she remained away. I was waiting for Mrs. Mavis to go, so that I myself might go; and Mrs. Nettlepoint was waiting for her to go so that I might n't. This doubtless made the young lady's absence appear to us longer than it really was — it was probably very brief. Her mother moreover, I think, had now a vague lapse from ease. Jasper Nettlepoint presently returned to the back drawing-room to serve his companion with our lucent syrup, and he took occasion to remark that it was lovely on the balcony: one really got some air, the breeze being from that quarter. I remembered, as he went away with his tinkling tumbler, that from *my* hand, a few minutes before, Miss Mavis had not been willing to accept this innocent offering. A little later Mrs. Nettlepoint said: "Well, if it's so pleasant there we had better go ourselves." So we passed to the front and in the other room met the two young people coming in from the balcony. I was to wonder, in the light of later things, exactly how long they had occupied together a couple of the set of cane chairs garnishing the place in summer. If it had been but five minutes that only made subsequent events more curi-

ous. "We must go, mother," Miss Mavis immediately
said; and a moment after, with a little renewal of
chatter as to our general meeting on the ship, the
visitors had taken leave. Jasper went down with them
to the door and as soon as they had got off Mrs.
Nettlepoint quite richly exhaled her impression. "Ah
but she'll be a bore — she'll be a bore of bores!"

"Not through talking too much, surely."

"An affectation of silence is as bad. I hate that
particular *pose;* it's coming up very much now; an
imitation of the English, like everything else. A girl
who tries to be statuesque at sea — that will act on
one's nerves!"

"I don't know what she tries to be, but she succeeds
in being very handsome."

"So much the better for you. I'll leave her to you,
for I shall be shut up. I like her being placed under
my 'care'!" my friend cried.

"She'll be under Jasper's," I remarked.

"Ah he won't go," she wailed — "I want it too
much!"

"But I did n't see it that way. I have an idea he'll
go."

"Why did n't he tell me so then — when he came
in?"

"He was diverted by that young woman — a
beautiful unexpected girl sitting there."

"Diverted from his mother and her fond hope? —
his mother trembling for his decision?"

"Well" — I pieced it together — "she's an old
friend, older than we know. It was a meeting after
a long separation."

"Yes, such a lot of them as he does know!" Mrs. Nettlepoint sighed.

"Such a lot of them?"

"He has so many female friends — in the most varied circles."

"Well, we can close round her then," I returned; "for I on my side know, or used to know, her young man."

"Her intended?" — she had a light of relief for this.

"The very one she's going out to. He can't, by the way," it occurred to me, "be very young now."

"How odd it sounds — her muddling after him!" said Mrs. Nettlepoint.

I was going to reply that it wasn't odd if you knew Mr. Porterfield, but I reflected that that perhaps only made it odder. I told my companion briefly who he was — that I had met him in the old Paris days, when I believed for a fleeting hour that I could learn to paint, when I lived with the *jeunesse des écoles;* and her comment on this was simply: "Well, he had better have come out for her!"

"Perhaps so. She looked to me as she sat there as if she might change her mind at the last moment."

"About her marriage?"

"About sailing. But she won't change now."

Jasper came back, and his mother instantly challenged him. "Well, *are* you going?"

"Yes, I shall go" — he was finally at peace about it. "I've got my telegram."

"Oh your telegram!" — I ventured a little to jeer. "That charming girl's your telegram."

192

THE PATAGONIA

He gave me a look, but in the dusk I could n't make out very well what it conveyed. Then he bent over his mother, kissing her. "My news is n't particularly satisfactory. I 'm going for *you*."

"Oh you humbug!" she replied. But she was of course delighted.

II

PEOPLE usually spend the first hours of a voyage in squeezing themselves into their cabins, taking their little precautions, either so excessive or so inadequate, wondering how they can pass so many days in such a hole and asking idiotic questions of the stewards, who appear in comparison rare men of the world. My own initiations were rapid, as became an old sailor, and so, it seemed, were Miss Mavis's, for when I mounted to the deck at the end of half an hour I found her there alone, in the stern of the ship, her eyes on the dwindling continent. It dwindled very fast for so big a place. I accosted her, having had no conversation with her amid the crowd of leave-takers and the muddle of farewells before we put off; we talked a little about the boat, our fellow passengers and our prospects, and then I said: "I think you mentioned last night a name I know — that of Mr. Porterfield."

"Oh no I did n't!" she answered very straight while she smiled at me through her closely-drawn veil.

"Then it was your mother."

"Very likely it was my mother." And she continued to smile as if I ought to have known the difference.

"I venture to allude to him because I've an idea I used to know him," I went on.

"Oh I see." And beyond this remark she appeared

194

to take no interest; she left it to me to make any connexion.

"That is if it's the same one." It struck me as feeble to say nothing more; so I added "My Mr. Porterfield was called David."

"Well, so is ours." "Ours" affected me as clever.

"I suppose I shall see him again if he's to meet you at Liverpool," I continued.

"Well, it will be bad if he does n't."

It was too soon for me to have the idea that it would be bad if he did: that only came later. So I remarked that, not having seen him for so many years, it was very possible I should n't know him.

"Well, I've not seen him for a considerable time, but I expect I shall know him all the same."

"Oh with you it's different," I returned with harmlessly bright significance. "Has n't he been back since those days?"

"I don't know," she sturdily professed, "what days you mean."

"When I knew him in Paris — ages ago. He was a pupil of the Ecole des Beaux Arts. He was studying architecture."

"Well, he's studying it still," said Grace Mavis.

"Has n't he learned it yet?"

"I don't know what he has learned. I shall see." Then she added for the benefit of my perhaps undue levity: "Architecture's very difficult and he's tremendously thorough."

"Oh yes, I remember that. He was an admirable worker. But he must have become quite a foreigner if it's so many years since he has been at home."

She seemed to regard this proposition at first as complicated; but she did what she could for me. "Oh he's not changeable. If he were changeable —" Then, however, she paused. I dare say she had been going to observe that if he were changeable he would long ago have given her up. After an instant she went on: "He would n't have stuck so to his profession. You can't make much by it."

I sought to attenuate her rather odd maidenly grimness. "It depends on what you call much."

"It does n't make you rich."

"Oh of course you 've got to practise it — and to practise it long."

"Yes — so Mr. Porterfield says."

Something in the way she uttered these words made me laugh — they were so calm an implication that the gentleman in question did n't live up to his principles. But I checked myself, asking her if she expected to remain in Europe long — to what one might call settle.

"Well, it will be a good while if it takes me as long to come back as it has taken me to go out."

"And I think your mother said last night that it was your first visit."

Miss Mavis, in her deliberate way, met my eyes. "Did n't mother talk!"

"It was all very interesting."

She continued to look at me. "You don't think that," she then simply stated.

"What have I to gain then by saying it?"

"Oh men have always something to gain."

"You make me in that case feel a terrible failure!

I hope at any rate that it gives you pleasure," I went on, "the idea of seeing foreign lands."

"Mercy — I should think so!"

This was almost genial, and it cheered me proportionately. "It's a pity our ship's not one of the fast ones, if you're impatient."

She was silent a little; after which she brought out: "Oh I guess it'ill be fast enough!"

That evening I went in to see Mrs. Nettlepoint and sat on her sea-trunk, which was pulled out from under the berth to accommodate me. It was nine o'clock but not quite dark, as our northward course had already taken us into the latitude of the longer days. She had made her nest admirably and now rested from her labours; she lay upon her sofa in a dressing-gown and a cap that became her. It was her regular practice to spend the voyage in her cabin, which smelt positively good — such was the refinement of her art; and she had a secret peculiar to herself for keeping her port open without shipping seas. She hated what she called the mess of the ship and the idea, if she should go above, of meeting stewards with plates of supererogatory food. She professed to be content with her situation — we promised to lend each other books and I assured her familiarly that I should be in and out of her room a dozen times a day — pitying me for having to mingle in society. She judged this a limited privilege, for on the deck before we left the wharf she had taken a view of our fellow passengers.

"Oh I'm an inveterate, almost a professional observer," I replied, "and with that vice I'm as well occupied as an old woman in the sun with her knitting. It makes me, in any situation, just inordinately and submissively *see* things. I shall see them even here and shall come down very often and tell you about them. You're not interested to-day, but you will be to-morrow, for a ship's a great school of gossip. You won't believe the number of researches and problems you'll be engaged in by the middle of the voyage."

"I? Never in the world!—lying here with my nose in a book and not caring a straw."

"You'll participate at second hand. You'll see through my eyes, hang upon my lips, take sides, feel passions, all sorts of sympathies and indignations. I've an idea," I further developed, "that your young lady's the person on board who will interest me most."

"'Mine' indeed! She has n't been near me since we left the dock."

"There you are — you do feel she owes you something. Well," I added, "she's very curious."

"You've such cold-blooded terms!" Mrs. Nettlepoint wailed. "Elle ne sait pas se conduire; she ought to have come to ask about me."

"Yes, since you're under her care," I laughed. "As for her not knowing how to behave — well, that's exactly what we shall see."

"You will, but not I! I wash my hands of her."

"Don't say that — don't say that."

Mrs. Nettlepoint looked at me a moment. "Why do you speak so solemnly?"

In return I considered her. "I'll tell you before we land. And have you seen much of your son?"

"Oh yes, he has come in several times. He seems very much pleased. He has got a cabin to himself."

"That's great luck," I said, "but I've an idea he's always in luck. I was sure I should have to offer him the second berth in my room."

"And you would n't have enjoyed that, because you don't like him," she took upon herself to say.

"What put that into your head?"

"It is n't in my head — it's in my heart, my *cœur de mère*. We guess those things. You think he's selfish. I could see it last night."

"Dear lady," I contrived promptly enough to reply, "I've no general ideas about him at all. He's just one of the phenomena I am going to observe. He seems to me a very fine young man. However," I added, "since you've mentioned last night I'll admit that I thought he rather tantalised you. He played with your suspense."

"Why he came at the last just to please me," said Mrs. Nettlepoint.

I was silent a little. "Are you sure it was for your sake?"

"Ah, perhaps it was for yours!"

I bore up, however, against this thrust, characteristic of perfidious woman when you presume to side with her against a fond tormentor. "When he went out on the balcony with that girl," I found assurance to suggest, "perhaps she asked him to come for *hers*."

"Perhaps she did. But why should he do everything she asks him — such as she is?"

"I don't know yet, but perhaps I shall know later. Not that he'll tell me — for he'll never tell me anything: he's not," I consistently opined, "one of those who tell."

"If she did n't ask him, what you say is a great wrong to her," said Mrs. Nettlepoint.

"Yes, if she did n't. But you say that to protect Jasper — not to protect her," I smiled.

"You *are* cold-blooded—it 's uncanny!" my friend exclaimed.

"Ah this is nothing yet! Wait a while — you 'll see. At sea in general I 'm awful — I exceed the limits. If I 've outraged her in thought I 'll jump overboard. There are ways of asking — a man does n't need to tell a woman that — without the crude words."

"I don't know what you imagine between them," said Mrs. Nettlepoint.

"Well, nothing," I allowed, "but what was visible on the surface. It transpired, as the newspapers say, that they were old friends."

"He met her at some promiscuous party — I asked him about it afterwards. She 's not a person" — my hostess was confident — "whom he could ever think of seriously."

"That 's exactly what I believe."

"You don't observe — you know — you imagine," Mrs. Nettlepoint continued to argue. "How do you reconcile her laying a trap for Jasper with her going out to Liverpool on an errand of love?"

Oh I was n't to be caught that way! "I don't for an instant suppose she laid a trap; I believe she acted on the impulse of the moment. She 's going out to Liverpool on an errand of marriage; that 's not necessarily the same thing as an errand of love, especially for one who happens to have had a personal impression of the gentleman she 's engaged to."

"Well, there are certain decencies which in such a situation the most abandoned of her sex would still observe. You apparently judge her capable — on no evidence — of violating them."

"Ah you don't understand the shades of things," I returned. "Decencies and violations, dear lady — there's no need for such heavy artillery! I can perfectly imagine that without the least immodesty she should have said to Jasper on the balcony, in fact if not in words : ' I 'm in dreadful spirits, but if you come I shall feel better, and that will be pleasant for you too.' "

"And why is she in dreadful spirits ?"

"She is n't!" I replied, laughing.

My poor friend wondered. "What then is she doing ?"

"She's walking with your son."

Mrs. Nettlepoint for a moment said nothing; then she treated me to another inconsequence. "Ah she's horrid!"

"No, she's charming!" I protested.

"You mean she's 'curious'?"

"Well, for me it's the same thing!"

This led my friend of course to declare once more that I was cold-blooded. On the afternoon of the morrow we had another talk, and she told me that in the morning Miss Mavis had paid her a long visit. She knew nothing, poor creature, about anything, but her intentions were good and she was evidently in her own eyes conscientious and decorous. And Mrs. Nettlepoint concluded these remarks with the sigh: "Unfortunate person!"

"You think she's a good deal to be pitied then?"

"Well, her story sounds dreary — she told me a good deal of it. She fell to talking little by little and went from one thing to another. She's in that situation when a girl *must* open herself — to some woman."

"Hasn't she got Jasper?" I asked.

"He isn't a woman. You strike me as jealous of him," my companion added.

"I dare say *he* thinks so — or will before the end. Ah no — ah no!" And I asked Mrs. Nettlepoint if our young lady struck her as, very grossly, a flirt. She gave me no answer, but went on to remark that she found it odd and interesting to see the way a girl like Grace Mavis resembled the girls of the kind she herself knew better, the girls of "society," at the same time that she differed from them; and the way the differences and resemblances were so mixed up that on certain questions you couldn't tell where you'd find her. You'd think she'd feel as you did because you had found her feeling so, and then suddenly, in regard to some other matter — which was yet quite the same — she'd be utterly wanting. Mrs. Nettlepoint proceeded to observe — to such idle speculations does the vacancy of sea-hours give encouragement — that she wondered whether it were better to be an ordinary girl very well brought up or an extraordinary girl not brought up at all.

"Oh I go in for the extraordinary girl under all circumstances."

"It's true that if you're *very* well brought up you're not, you can't be, ordinary," said Mrs. Nettlepoint,

202

smelling her strong salts. "You're a lady, at any rate."

"And Miss Mavis is fifty miles out — is that what you mean?"

"Well — you've seen her mother."

"Yes, but I think your contention would be that among such people the mother does n't count."

"Precisely, and that's bad."

"I see what you mean. But is n't it rather hard? If your mother does n't know anything it's better you should be independent of her, and yet if you are that constitutes a bad note." I added that Mrs. Mavis had appeared to count sufficiently two nights before. She had said and done everything she wanted, while the girl sat silent and respectful. Grace's attitude, so far as her parent was concerned, had been eminently decent.

"Yes, but she 'squirmed' for her," said Mrs. Nettlepoint.

"Ah if you know it I may confess she has told me as much."

My friend stared. "Told *you?* There's one of the things they do!"

"Well, it was only a word. Won't you let me know whether you do think her a flirt?"

"Try her yourself — that's better than asking another woman; especially as you pretend to study folk."

"Oh your judgement would n't probably at all determine mine. It's as bearing on *you* I ask it." Which, however, demanded explanation, so that I was duly frank; confessing myself curious as to how far maternal immorality would go.

It made her at first but repeat my words. "Maternal immorality?"

"You desire your son to have every possible distraction on his voyage, and if you can make up your mind in the sense I refer to that will make it all right. He'll have no responsibility."

"Heavens, how you analyse!" she cried. "I have n't in the least your passion for making up my mind."

"Then if you chance it," I returned, "you'll be more immoral still."

"Your reasoning's strange," said Mrs. Nettlepoint; "when it was you who tried to put into my head yesterday that she had asked him to come."

"Yes, but in good faith."

"What do you mean, in such a case, by that?"

"Why, as girls of that sort do. Their allowance and measure in such matters," I expounded, "is much larger than that of young persons who have been, as you say, *very* well brought up; and yet I'm not sure that on the whole I don't think them thereby the more innocent. Miss Mavis is engaged, and she's to be married next week, but it's an old old story, and there's no more romance in it than if she were going to be photographed. So her usual life proceeds, and her usual life consists — and that of *ces demoiselles* in general — in having plenty of gentlemen's society. Having it I mean without having any harm from it."

Mrs. Nettlepoint had given me due attention. "Well, if there's no harm from it what are you talking about and why am I immoral?"

I hesitated, laughing. "I retract — you're sane

and clear. I'm sure she thinks there won't be any harm," I added. "That's the great point."

"The great point?"

"To be settled, I mean."

"Mercy, we're not trying them!" cried my friend. "How can *we* settle it?"

"I mean of course in our minds. There will be nothing more interesting these next ten days for our minds to exercise themselves upon."

"Then they'll get terribly tired of it," said Mrs. Nettlepoint.

"No, no — because the interest will increase and the plot will thicken. It simply can't *not*," I insisted. She looked at me as if she thought me more than Mephistophelean, and I went back to something she had lately mentioned. "So she told you everything in her life was dreary?"

"Not everything, but most things. And she did n't tell me so much as I guessed it. She'll tell me more the next time. She'll behave properly now about coming in to see me; I told her she ought to."

"I'm glad of that," I said. "Keep her with you as much as possible."

"I don't follow you closely," Mrs. Nettlepoint replied, "but so far as I do I don't think your remarks in the best taste."

"Well, I'm too excited, I lose my head in these sports," I had to recognise — "cold-blooded as you think me. Does n't she like Mr. Porterfield?"

"Yes, that's the worst of it."

I kept making her stare. "The worst of it?"

"He's so good — there's no fault to be found with

205

him. Otherwise she'd have thrown it all up. It has dragged on since she was eighteen: she became engaged to him before he went abroad to study. It was one of those very young and perfectly needless blunders that parents in America might make so much less possible than they do. The thing is to insist on one's daughter's waiting, on the engagement's being long; and then, after you've got that started, to take it on every occasion as little seriously as possible — to make it die out. You can easily tire it to death," Mrs. Nettlepoint competently stated. "However," she concluded, "Mr. Porterfield has taken this one seriously for some years. He has done his part to keep it alive. She says he adores her."

"His part? Surely his part would have been to marry her by this time."

"He has really no money." My friend was even more confidently able to report it than I had been.

"He ought to have got some, in seven years," I audibly reflected.

"So I think she thinks. There are some sorts of helplessness that are contemptible. However, a small difference has taken place. That's why he won't wait any longer. His mother has come out, she has something — a little — and she's able to assist him. She'll live with them and bear some of the expenses, and after her death the son will have what there is."

"How old is she?" I cynically asked.

"I haven't the least idea. But it doesn't, on his part, sound very heroic — or very inspiring for our friend here. He hasn't been to America since he first went out."

"That's an odd way of adoring her," I observed.

"I made that objection mentally, but I did n't express it to her. She met it indeed a little by telling me that he had had other chances to marry."

"That surprises me," I remarked. "But did she say," I asked, "that *she* had had ?"

"No, and that's one of the things I thought nice in her; for she must have had. She did n't try to make out that he had spoiled her life. She has three other sisters and there's very little money at home. She has tried to make money; she has written little things and painted little things — and dreadful little things they must have been; too bad to think of. Her father has had a long illness and has lost his place — he was in receipt of a salary in connexion with some waterworks — and one of her sisters has lately become a widow, with children and without means. And so as in fact she never has married any one else, whatever opportunities she may have encountered, she appears to have just made up her mind to go out to Mr. Porterfield as the least of her evils. But it is n't very amusing."

"Well," I judged after all, "that only makes her doing it the more honourable. She'll go through with it, whatever it costs, rather than disappoint him after he has waited so long. It's true," I continued, "that when a woman acts from a sense of honour — !"

"Well, when she does ?" said Mrs. Nettlepoint, for I hung back perceptibly.

"It's often so extravagant and unnatural a proceeding as to entail heavy costs on some one."

"You're very impertinent. We all have to pay for

each other all the while; and for each other's virtues as well as vices."

"That's precisely why I shall be sorry for Mr. Porterfield when she steps off the ship with her little bill. I mean with her teeth clenched."

"Her teeth are not in the least clenched. She's quite at her ease now" — Mrs. Nettlepoint could answer for that.

"Well, we must try and keep her so," I said. "You must take care that Jasper neglects nothing."

I scarce know what reflexions this innocent pleasantry of mine provoked on the good lady's part; the upshot of them at all events was to make her say: "Well, I never asked her to come; I'm very glad of that. It's all their own doing."

"'Their' own — you mean Jasper's and hers?"

"No indeed. I mean her mother's and Mrs. Allen's; the girl's too of course. They put themselves on us by main force."

"Oh yes, I can testify to that. Therefore I'm glad too. We should have missed it, I think."

"How seriously you take it!" Mrs. Nettlepoint amusedly cried.

"Ah wait a few days!" — and I got up to leave her.

III

THE *Patagonia* was slow, but spacious and comfortable, and there was a motherly decency in her long nursing rock and her rustling old-fashioned gait, the multitudinous swish, in her wake, as of a thousand proper petticoats. It was as if she wished not to present herself in port with the splashed eagerness of a young creature. We were n't numerous enough quite to elbow each other and yet were n't too few to support — with that familiarity and relief which figures and objects acquire on the great bare field of the ocean and under the great bright glass of the sky. I had never liked the sea so much before, indeed I had never liked it at all; but now I had a revelation of how in a midsummer mood it could please. It was darkly and magnificently blue and imperturbably quiet — save for the great regular swell of its heart-beats, the pulse of its life; and there grew to be something so agreeable in the sense of floating there in infinite isolation and leisure that it was a positive godsend the *Patagonia* was no racer. One had never thought of the sea as the great place of safety, but now it came over one that there 's no place so safe from the land. When it does n't confer trouble it takes trouble away — takes away letters and telegrams and newspapers and visits and duties and efforts, all the complications, all the superfluities and superstitions that we have stuffed into our terrene life. The simple absence of the post, when the particular conditions enable you to enjoy the great fact by which it's produced, becomes in itself a positive bliss, and the clean boards of the deck turn to the stage of a play that amuses, the personal drama of the voyage, the movement and interaction, in the strong sea-light, of figures that end by representing something — something moreover of which the interest is never, even in its keenness, too great to suffer you to slumber. I at any rate dozed to excess, stretched on my rug with a French novel, and when I opened my eyes I generally saw Jasper Nettlepoint pass with the young woman confided to his mother's care on his arm. Somehow at these moments, between sleeping and waking, I inconsequently felt that my French novel had set them in motion. Perhaps this was because I had fallen into the trick, at the start, of regarding Grace Mavis almost as a married woman, which, as every one knows, is the necessary status of the heroine of such a work. Every revolution of our engine at any rate would contribute to the effect of making her one.

In the saloon, at meals, my neighbour on the right was a certain little Mrs. Peck, a very short and very round person whose head was enveloped in a "cloud" (a cloud of dirty white wool) and who promptly let me know that she was going to Europe for the education of her children. I had already perceived — an hour after we left the dock — that some energetic measure was required in their interest, but as we were not in Europe yet the redemption of the four little Pecks was stayed. Enjoying untrammelled leisure they swarmed about the ship as if they had been pirates boarding her, and their mother was as powerless to check their licence as if she had been gagged and stowed away in the hold. They were especially to be trusted to dive between the legs of the stewards when these attendants arrived with bowls of soup for the languid ladies. Their mother was too busy counting over to her fellow passengers all the years Miss Mavis had been engaged. In the blank of our common detachment things that were nobody's business very soon became everybody's, and this was just one of those facts that are propagated with mysterious and ridiculous speed. The whisper that carries them is very small, in the great scale of things, of air and space and progress, but it's also very safe, for there's no compression, no sounding-board, to make speakers responsible. And then repetition at sea is somehow not repetition; monotony is in the air, the mind is flat and everything recurs — the bells, the meals, the stewards' faces, the romp of children, the walk, the clothes, the very shoes and buttons of passengers taking their exercise. These things finally grow at once so circumstantial and so arid that, in comparison, lights on the personal history of one's companions become a substitute for the friendly flicker of the lost fireside.

Jasper Nettlepoint sat on my left hand when he was not upstairs seeing that Miss Mavis had her repast comfortably on deck. His mother's place would have been next mine had she shown herself, and then that of the young lady under her care. These companions, in other words, would have been between us, Jasper marking the limit of the party in that quarter. Miss Mavis was present at luncheon the first day, but din-

ner passed without her coming in, and when it was
half over Jasper remarked that he would go up and
look after her.

"Is n't that young lady coming — the one who was
here to lunch?" Mrs. Peck asked of me as he left the
saloon.

"Apparently not. My friend tells me she does n't
like the saloon."

"You don't mean to say she's sick, do you?"

"Oh no, not in this weather. But she likes to be
above."

"And is that gentleman gone up to her?"

"Yes, she's under his mother's care."

"And is his mother up there, too?" asked Mrs.
Peck, whose processes were homely and direct.

"No, she remains in her cabin. People have different tastes. Perhaps that's one reason why Miss Mavis
does n't come to table," I added — "her chaperon not
being able to accompany her."

"Her chaperon?" my fellow passenger echoed.

"Mrs. Nettlepoint — the lady under whose protection she happens to be."

"Protection?" Mrs. Peck stared at me a moment,
moving some valued morsel in her mouth; then she
exclaimed familiarly "Pshaw!" I was struck with this
and was on the point of asking her what she meant by
it when she continued: "Ain't we going to see Mrs.
Nettlepoint?"

"I'm afraid not. She vows she won't stir from her
sofa."

"Pshaw!" said Mrs. Peck again. "That's quite a
disappointment."

"Do you know her then?"

"No, but I know all about her." Then my companion added: "You don't mean to say she's any real relation?"

"Do you mean to me?"

"No, to Grace Mavis."

"None at all. They're very new friends, as I happen to know. Then you're acquainted with our young lady?" I had n't noticed the passage of any recognition between them at luncheon.

"Is she your young lady too?" asked Mrs. Peck with high significance.

"Ah when people are in the same boat — literally — they belong a little to each other."

"That's so," said Mrs. Peck. "I don't know Miss Mavis, but I know all about her — I live opposite to her on Merrimac Avenue. I don't know whether you know that part."

"Oh yes — it's very beautiful."

The consequence of this remark was another "Pshaw!" But Mrs. Peck went on: "When you've lived opposite to people like that for a long time you feel as if you had some rights in them — tit for tat! But she did n't take it up to-day; she did n't speak to me. She knows who I am as well as she knows her own mother."

"You had better speak to her first — she's constitutionally shy," I remarked.

"Shy? She's constitutionally tough! Why she's thirty years old," cried my neighbour. "I suppose you know where she's going."

"Oh yes — we all take an interest in that."

"That young man, I suppose, particularly." And then as I feigned a vagueness: "The handsome one who sits *there*. Did n't you tell me he 's Mrs. Nettlepoint's son?"

"Oh yes — he acts as her deputy. No doubt he does all he can to carry out her function."

Mrs. Peck briefly brooded. I had spoken jocosely, but she took it with a serious face. "Well, she might let him eat his dinner in peace!" she presently put forth.

"Oh he 'll come back!" I said, glancing at his place. The repast continued and when it was finished I screwed my chair round to leave the table. Mrs. Peck performed the same movement and we quitted the saloon together. Outside of it was the usual vestibule, with several seats, from which you could descend to the lower cabins or mount to the promenade-deck. Mrs. Peck appeared to hesitate as to her course and then solved the problem by going neither way. She dropped on one of the benches and looked up at me.

"I thought you said he 'd come back."

"Young Nettlepoint? Yes, I see he did n't. Miss Mavis then has given him half her dinner."

"It 's very kind of her! She has been engaged half her life."

"Yes, but that will soon be over."

"So I suppose — as quick as ever we land. Every one knows it on Merrimac Avenue," Mrs. Peck pursued. "Every one there takes a great interest in it."

"Ah of course — a girl like that has many friends."

But my informant discriminated. "I mean even people who don't know her."

"I see," I went on: "she's so handsome that she attracts attention — people enter into her affairs."

Mrs. Peck spoke as from the commanding centre of these. "She *used* to be pretty, but I can't say I think she's anything remarkable to-day. Anyhow, if she attracts attention she ought to be all the more careful what she does. You had better tell her that."

"Oh it's none of my business!" I easily made out, leaving the terrible little woman and going above. This profession, I grant, was not perfectly attuned to my real idea, or rather my real idea was not quite in harmony with my profession. The very first thing I did on reaching the deck was to notice that Miss Mavis was pacing it on Jasper Nettlepoint's arm and that whatever beauty she might have lost, according to Mrs. Peck's insinuation, she still kept enough to make one's eyes follow her. She had put on a crimson hood, which was very becoming to her and which she wore for the rest of the voyage. She walked very well, with long steps, and I remember that at this moment the sea had a gentle evening swell which made the great ship dip slowly, rhythmically, giving a movement that was graceful to graceful pedestrians and a more awkward one to the awkward. It was the loveliest hour of a fine day, the clear early evening, with the glow of the sunset in the air and a purple colour on the deep. It was always present to me that so the waters ploughed by the Homeric heroes must have looked. I became conscious on this particular occasion moreover that Grace Mavis would for the rest of the voyage be the most visible thing in one's range, the figure that would count most in the composition of groups. She could n't help it, poor girl; nature had made her conspicuous — important, as the painters say. She paid for it by the corresponding exposure, the danger that people would, as I had said to Mrs. Peck, enter into her affairs.

Jasper Nettlepoint went down at certain times to see his mother, and I watched for one of these occasions — on the third day out — and took advantage of it to go and sit by Miss Mavis. She wore a light blue veil drawn tightly over her face, so that if the smile with which she greeted me rather lacked intensity I could account for it partly by that.

"Well, we 're getting on — we 're getting on," I said cheerfully, looking at the friendly twinkling sea.

"Are we going very fast ?"

"Not fast, but steadily. *Ohne Hast, ohne Rast —* do you know German ?"

"Well, I 've studied it — some."

"It will be useful to you over there when you travel."

"Well yes, if we do. But I don't suppose we shall much. Mr. Nettlepoint says we ought," my young woman added in a moment.

"Ah of course *he* thinks so. He has been all over the world."

"Yes, he has described some of the places. They must be wonderful. I did n't know I should like it so much."

"But it is n't 'Europe' yet!" I laughed.

Well, she did n't care if it was n't. "I mean going on this way. I could go on for ever — for ever and ever."

"Ah you know it's not always like this," I hastened to mention.

"Well, it's better than Boston."

"It is n't so good as Paris," I still more portentously noted.

"Oh I know all about Paris. There's no freshness in that. I feel as if I had been there all the time."

"You mean you've heard so much of it?"

"Oh yes, nothing else for ten years."

I had come to talk with Miss Mavis because she was attractive, but I had been rather conscious of the absence of a good topic, not feeling at liberty to revert to Mr. Porterfield. She had n't encouraged me, when I spoke to her as we were leaving Boston, to go on with the history of my acquaintance with this gentleman; and yet now, unexpectedly, she appeared to imply — it was doubtless one of the disparities mentioned by Mrs. Nettlepoint — that he might be glanced at without indelicacy.

"I see — you mean by letters," I remarked.

"We won't live in a good part. I know enough to know that," she went on.

"Well, it is n't as if there were any very bad ones," I answered reassuringly.

"Why Mr. Nettlepoint says it's regular mean."

"And to what does he apply that expression?"

She eyed me a moment as if I were elegant at her expense, but she answered my question. "Up there in the Batignolles. I seem to make out it's worse than Merrimac Avenue."

"Worse — in what way?"

217

"Why, even less where the nice people live."

"He ought n't to say that," I returned. And I ventured to back it up. "Don't you call Mr. Porterfield a nice person?"

"Oh it does n't make any difference." She watched me again a moment through her veil, the texture of which gave her look a suffused prettiness. "Do you know him very little?" she asked.

"Mr. Porterfield?"

"No, Mr. Nettlepoint."

"Ah very little. He's very considerably my junior, you see."

She had a fresh pause, as if almost again for my elegance; but she went on: "He's younger than me too." I don't know what effect of the comic there could have been in it, but the turn was unexpected and it made me laugh. Neither do I know whether Miss Mavis took offence at my sensibility on this head, though I remember thinking at the moment with compunction that it had brought a flush to her cheek. At all events she got up, gathering her shawl and her books into her arm. "I 'm going down — I 'm tired."

"Tired of me, I 'm afraid."

"No, not yet."

"I 'm like you," I confessed. "I should like it to go on and on."

She had begun to walk along the deck to the companionway and I went with her. "Well, I guess I would n't, after all!"

I had taken her shawl from her to carry it, but at the top of the steps that led down to the cabins I had to give it back. "Your mother would be glad if she could know," I observed as we parted.

But she was proof against my graces. "If she could know what?"

"How well you're getting on." I refused to be discouraged. "And that good Mrs. Allen."

"Oh mother, mother! She made me come, she pushed me off." And almost as if not to say more she went quickly below.

I paid Mrs. Nettlepoint a morning visit after luncheon and another in the evening, before she "turned in." That same day, in the evening, she said to me suddenly: "Do you know what I've done? I've asked Jasper."

"Asked him what?"

"Why, if *she* asked him, you understand."

I wondered. "*Do* I understand?"

"If you don't it's because you 'regular' won't, as she says. If that girl really asked him — on the balcony — to sail with us."

"My dear lady, do you suppose that if she did he'd tell you?"

She had to recognise my acuteness. "That's just what he says. But he says she did n't."

"And do you consider the statement valuable?" I asked, laughing out. "You had better ask your young friend herself."

Mrs. Nettlepoint stared. "I could n't do that."

On which I was the more amused that I had to explain I was only amused. "What does it signify now?"

"I thought you thought everything signified. You were so full," she cried, "of signification!"

219

"Yes, but we're further out now, and somehow in mid-ocean everything becomes absolute."

"What else *can* he do with decency?" Mrs. Nettlepoint went on. "If, as my son, he were never to speak to her it would be very rude and you'd think that stranger still. Then *you* would do what he does, and where would be the difference?"

"How do you know what he does? I have n't mentioned him for twenty-four hours."

"Why, she told me herself. She came in this afternoon."

"What an odd thing to tell you!" I commented.

"Not as she says it. She says he's full of attention, perfectly devoted — looks after her all the time. She seems to want me to know it, so that I may approve him for it."

"That's charming; it shows her good conscience."

"Yes, or her great cleverness."

Something in the tone in which Mrs. Nettlepoint said this caused me to return in real surprise: "Why what do you suppose she has in her mind?"

"To get hold of him, to make him go so far he can't retreat. To marry him perhaps."

"To marry him? And what will she do with Mr. Porterfield?"

"She'll ask me just to make it all right to him — or perhaps you."

"Yes, as an old friend!" — and for a moment I felt it awkwardly possible. But I put to her seriously: "*Do* you see Jasper caught like that?"

"Well, he's only a boy — he's younger at least than she."

220

"Precisely; she regards him as a child. She remarked to me herself to-day, that is, that he's so much younger."

Mrs. Nettlepoint took this in. "Does she talk of it with you? That shows she has a plan, that she has thought it over!"

I've sufficiently expressed — for the interest of my anecdote — that I found an oddity in one of our young companions, but I was far from judging her capable of laying a trap for the other. Moreover my reading of Jasper was n't in the least that he was catchable — could be made to do a thing if he did n't want to do it. Of course it was n't impossible that he might be inclined, that he might take it — or already have taken it — into his head to go further with his mother's charge; but to believe this I should require still more proof than his always being with her. He wanted at most to "take up with her" for the voyage. "If you've questioned him perhaps you've tried to make him feel responsible," I said to my fellow critic.

"A little, but it's very difficult. Interference makes him perverse. One has to go gently. Besides, it's too absurd — think of her age. If she can't take care of herself!" cried Mrs. Nettlepoint.

"Yes, let us keep thinking of her age, though it's not so prodigious. And if things get very bad you've one resource left," I added.

She wondered. "To lock her up in her cabin?"

"No — to come out of yours."

"Ah never, never! If it takes that to save her she

221

must be lost. Besides, what good would it do? If I were to go above she could come below."

"Yes, but you could keep Jasper with you."

"*Could* I?" Mrs. Nettlepoint demanded in the manner of a woman who knew her son.

In the saloon the next day, after dinner, over the red cloth of the tables, beneath the swinging lamps and the racks of tumblers, decanters and wine-glasses, we sat down to whist, Mrs. Peck, to oblige, taking a hand in the game. She played very badly and talked too much, and when the rubber was over assuaged her discomfiture (though not mine — we had been partners) with a Welsh rabbit and a tumbler of something hot. We had done with the cards, but while she waited for this refreshment she sat with her elbows on the table shuffling a pack.

"She has n't spoken to me yet — she won't do it," she remarked in a moment.

"Is it possible there's any one on the ship who has n't spoken to you?"

"Not that girl — she knows too well!" Mrs. Peck looked round our little circle with a smile of intelligence — she had familiar communicative eyes. Several of our company had assembled, according to the wont, the last thing in the evening, of those who are cheerful at sea, for the consumption of grilled sardines and devilled bones.

"What then does she know?"

"Oh she knows *I* know."

"Well, we know what Mrs. Peck knows," one of the ladies of the group observed to me with an air of privilege.

"Well, you would n't know if I had n't told you — from the way she acts," said our friend with a laugh of small charm.

"She's going out to a gentleman who lives over there — he's waiting there to marry her," the other lady went on, in the tone of authentic information. I remember that her name was Mrs. Gotch and that her mouth looked always as if she were whistling.

"Oh he knows — I've told him," said Mrs. Peck.

"Well, I presume every one knows," Mrs. Gotch contributed.

"Dear madam, is it every one's business ?" I asked.

"Why, don't you think it's a peculiar way to act ?" — and Mrs. Gotch was evidently surprised at my little protest.

"Why it's right there — straight in front of you, like a play at the theatre — as if you had paid to see it," said Mrs. Peck. "If you don't call it public —!"

"Are n't you mixing things up ? What do you call public ?"

"Why the way they go on. They're up there now."

"They cuddle up there half the night," said Mrs. Gotch. "I don't know when they come down. Any hour they like. When all the lights are out they're up there still."

"Oh you can't tire them out. They don't want relief — like the ship's watch !" laughed one of the gentlemen.

"Well, if they enjoy each other's society what's the harm ?" another asked. "They'd do just the same on land."

"They would n't do it on the public streets, I presume," said Mrs. Peck. "And they would n't do it if Mr. Porterfield was round!"

"Is n't that just where your confusion comes in?" I made answer. "It's public enough that Miss Mavis and Mr. Nettlepoint are always together, but it is n't in the least public that she's going to be married."

"Why how can you say — when the very sailors know it! The Captain knows it and all the officers know it. They see them there, especially at night, when they're sailing the ship."

"I thought there was some rule —!" submitted Mrs. Gotch.

"Well, there is — that you've got to behave yourself," Mrs. Peck explained. "So the Captain told me — he said they have some rule. He said they have to have, when people are too undignified."

"Is that the term he used?" I enquired.

"Well, he may have said when they attract too much attention."

I ventured to discriminate. "It's we who attract the attention — by talking about what does n't concern us and about what we really don't know."

"She said the Captain said he'd tell on her as soon as ever we arrive," Mrs. Gotch none the less serenely pursued.

"*She* said —?" I repeated, bewildered.

"Well, he did say so, that he'd think it his duty to inform Mr. Porterfield when he comes on to meet her — if they keep it up in the same way," said Mrs. Peck.

"Oh they'll keep it up, don't you fear!" one of the gentlemen exclaimed.

"Dear madam, the Captain's having his joke on you," was, however, my own congruous reply.

"No, he ain't — he's right down scandalised. He says he regards us all as a real family and wants the family not to be downright coarse." I felt Mrs. Peck irritated by my controversial tone: she challenged me with considerable spirit. "How can you say I don't know it when all the street knows it and has known it for years — for years and years?" She spoke as if the girl had been engaged at least for twenty. "What's she going out for if not to marry him?"

"Perhaps she's going to see how he looks," suggested one of the gentlemen.

"He'd look queer — if he knew."

"Well, I guess he'll know," said Mrs. Gotch.

"She'd tell him herself — she wouldn't be afraid," the gentleman went on.

"Well she might as well kill him. He'll jump overboard," Mrs. Peck could foretell.

"Jump overboard?" cried Mrs. Gotch as if she hoped then that Mr. Porterfield would be told.

"He has just been waiting for this — for long, long years," said Mrs. Peck.

"Do you happen to know him?" I asked.

She replied at her convenience. "No, but I know a lady who does. Are you going up?"

I had risen from my place — I had not ordered supper. "I'm going to take a turn before going to bed."

"Well then you'll see!"

Outside the saloon I hesitated, for Mrs. Peck's admonition made me feel for a moment that if I went up I should have entered in a manner into her little conspiracy. But the night was so warm and splendid that I had been intending to smoke a cigar in the air before going below, and I did n't see why I should deprive myself of this pleasure in order to seem not to mind Mrs. Peck. I mounted accordingly and saw a few figures sitting or moving about in the darkness. The ocean looked black and small, as it is apt to do at night, and the long mass of the ship, with its vague dim wings, seemed to take up a great part of it. There were more stars than one saw on land and the heavens struck one more than ever as larger than the earth. Grace Mavis and her companion were not, so far as I perceived at first, among the few passengers who lingered late, and I was glad, because I hated to hear her talked about in the manner of the gossips I had left at supper. I wished there had been some way to prevent it, but I could think of none but to recommend her privately to reconsider her rule of discretion. That would be a very delicate business, and perhaps it would be better to begin with Jasper, though that would be delicate too. At any rate one might let him know, in a friendly spirit, to how much remark he exposed the young lady — leaving this revelation to work its way upon him. Unfortunately I could n't altogether believe that the pair were unconscious of the observation and the opinion of the passengers. They were n't boy and girl; they had a certain social perspective in their eye. I was meanwhile at any rate in no possession of the details of that behaviour which had made them — according to the version of my good friends in the saloon — a scandal to the ship; for though I had taken due note of them, as will already

have been gathered, I had taken really no such ferocious, or at least such competent, note as Mrs. Peck.
Nevertheless the probability was that they knew what
was thought of them — what naturally would be —
and simply did n't care. That made our heroine out
rather perverse and even rather shameless; and yet
somehow if these were her leanings I did n't dislike her
for them. I don't know what strange secret excuses I
found for her. I presently indeed encountered, on the
spot, a need for any I might have at call, since, just as I
was on the point of going below again, after several
restless turns and — within the limit where smoking
was allowed — as many puffs at a cigar as I cared for,
I became aware of a couple of figures settled together
behind one of the lifeboats that rested on the deck.
They were so placed as to be visible only to a person
going close to the rail and peering a little sidewise. I
don't think I peered, but as I stood a moment beside
the rail my eye was attracted by a dusky object that
protruded beyond the boat and that I saw at a second glance to be the tail of a lady's dress. I bent forward an instant, but even then I saw very little more;
that scarcely mattered however, as I easily concluded
that the persons tucked away in so snug a corner were
Jasper Nettlepoint and Mr. Porterfield's intended.
Tucked away was the odious right expression, and I
deplored the fact so betrayed for the pitiful bad taste in
it. I immediately turned away, and the next moment
found myself face to face with our vessel's skipper.
I had already had some conversation with him — he
had been so good as to invite me, as he had invited
Mrs. Nettlepoint and her son and the young lady

travelling with them, and also Mrs. Peck, to sit at his table — and had observed with pleasure that his seamanship had the grace, not universal on the Atlantic liners, of a fine-weather manner.

"They don't waste much time — your friends in there," he said, nodding in the direction in which he had seen me looking.

"Ah well, they have n't much to lose."

"That's what I mean. I'm told *she* has n't."

I wanted to say something exculpatory, but scarcely knew what note to strike. I could only look vaguely about me at the starry darkness and the sea that seemed to sleep. "Well, with these splendid nights and this perfect air people are beguiled into late hours."

"Yes, we want a bit of a blow," the Captain said.

I demurred. "How much of one?"

"Enough to clear the decks!"

He was after all rather dry and he went about his business. He had made me uneasy, and instead of going below I took a few turns more. The other walkers dropped off pair by pair — they were all men — till at last I was alone. Then after a little I quitted the field. Jasper and his companion were still behind their lifeboat. Personally I greatly preferred our actual conditions, but as I went down I found myself vaguely wishing, in the interest of I scarcely knew what, unless it had been a mere superstitious delicacy, that we might have half a gale.

Miss Mavis turned out, in sea-phrase, early; for the next morning I saw her come up only a short time after I had finished my breakfast, a ceremony over which I contrived not to dawdle. She was alone and Jasper Nettlepoint, by a rare accident, was not on deck to help her. I went to meet her — she was encumbered as usual with her shawl, her sun-umbrella and a book — and laid my hands on her chair, placing it near the stern of the ship, where she liked best to be. But I proposed to her to walk a little before she sat down, and she took my arm after I had put her accessories into the chair. The deck was clear at that hour and the morning light gay; one had an extravagant sense of good omens and propitious airs. I forget what we spoke of first, but it was because I felt these things pleasantly, and not to torment my companion nor to test her, that I could n't help exclaiming cheerfully after a moment, as I have mentioned having done the first day: "Well, we 're getting on, we 're getting on!"

"Oh yes, I count every hour."

"The last days always go quicker," I said, "and the last hours —!"

"Well, the last hours?" she asked; for I had instinctively checked myself.

"Oh one 's so glad then that it 's almost the same as if one had arrived. Yet we ought to be grateful when the elements have been so kind to us," I added. "I hope you 'll have enjoyed the voyage."

She hesitated ever so little. "Yes, much more than I expected."

"Did you think it would be very bad?"

"Horrible, horrible!"

The tone of these words was strange, but I had n't much time to reflect upon it, for turning round at that moment I saw Jasper Nettlepoint come toward us.

229

He was still distant by the expanse of the white deck, and I could n't help taking him in from head to foot as he drew nearer. I don't know what rendered me on this occasion particularly sensitive to the impression, but it struck me that I saw him as I had never seen him before, saw him, thanks to the intense sea-light, inside and out, in his personal, his moral totality. It was a quick, a vivid revelation; if it only lasted a moment it had a simplifying certifying effect. He was intrinsically a pleasing apparition, with his handsome young face and that marked absence of any drop in his personal arrangements which, more than any one I 've ever seen, he managed to exhibit on shipboard. He had none of the appearance of wearing out old clothes that usually prevails there, but dressed quite straight, as I heard some one say. This gave him an assured, almost a triumphant air, as of a young man who would come best out of any awkwardness. I expected to feel my companion's hand loosen itself on my arm, as an indication that now she must go to him, and I was almost surprised she did n't drop me. We stopped as we met and Jasper bade us a friendly good-morning. Of course the remark that we had another lovely day was already indicated, and it led him to exclaim, in the manner of one to whom criticism came easily, "Yes, but with this sort of thing consider what one of the others would do!"

"One of the other ships?"

"We should be there now, or at any rate to-morrow."

"Well then I 'm glad it is n't one of the others " — and I smiled at the young lady on my arm. My words

230

offered her a chance to say something appreciative, and gave him one even more; but neither Jasper nor Grace Mavis took advantage of the occasion. What they did do, I noticed, was to look at each other rather fixedly an instant; after which she turned her eyes silently to the sea. She made no movement and uttered no sound, contriving to give me the sense that she had all at once become perfectly passive, that she somehow declined responsibility. We remained standing there with Jasper in front of us, and if the contact of her arm did n't suggest I should give her up, neither did it intimate that we had better pass on. I had no idea of giving her up, albeit one of the things I seemed to read just then into Jasper's countenance was a fine implication that she was his property. His eyes met mine for a moment, and it was exactly as if he had said to me "I know what you think, but I don't care a rap." What I really thought was that he was selfish beyond the limits: that was the substance of my little revelation. Youth is almost always selfish, just as it is almost always conceited, and, after all, when it 's combined with health and good parts, good looks and good spirits, it has a right to be, and I easily forgive it if it be really youth. Still it's a question of degree, and what stuck out of Jasper Nettlepoint — if, of course, one had the intelligence for it — was that his egotism had a hardness, his love of his own way an avidity. These elements were jaunty and prosperous, they were accustomed to prevail. He was fond, very fond, of women; they were necessary to him — that was in his type; but he was n't in the least in love with Grace Mavis. Among the reflexions I quickly made this was the one that was most to the point. There was a degree of awkwardness, after a minute, in the way we were planted there, though the apprehension of it was doubtless not in the least with himself. To dissimulate my own share in it, at any rate, I asked him how his mother might be.

His answer was unexpected. "You had better go down and see."

"Not till Miss Mavis is tired of me."

She said nothing to this and I made her walk again. For some minutes she failed to speak; then, rather abruptly, she began: "I've seen you talking to that lady who sits at our table — the one who has so many children."

"Mrs. Peck? Oh yes, one has inevitably talked with Mrs. Peck."

"Do you know her very well?"

"Only as one knows people at sea. An acquaintance makes itself. It does n't mean very much."

"She does n't speak to me — she might if she wanted."

"That's just what she says of you — that you might speak to her."

"Oh if she's waiting for that —!" said my companion with a laugh. Then she added: "She lives in our street, nearly opposite."

"Precisely. That's the reason why she thinks you coy or haughty. She has seen you so often and seems to know so much about you."

"What does she know about me?"

"Ah you must ask her — I can't tell you!"

"I don't care what she knows," said my young lady.

232

After a moment she went on: "She must have seen I ain't very sociable." And then, "What are you laughing at?" she asked.

"Well" — my amusement was difficult to explain — "you're not very sociable, and yet somehow you are. Mrs. Peck is, at any rate, and thought that ought to make it easy for you to enter into conversation with her."

"Oh I don't care for her conversation — I know what it amounts to." I made no reply — I scarcely knew what reply to make — and the girl went on: "I know what she thinks and I know what she says." Still I was silent, but the next moment I saw my discretion had been wasted, for Miss Mavis put to me straight: "Does she make out that she knows Mr. Porterfield?"

"No, she only claims she knows a lady who knows him."

"Yes, that's it — Mrs. Jeremie. Mrs. Jeremie's an idiot!" I wasn't in a position to controvert this, and presently my young lady said she would sit down. I left her in her chair — I saw that she preferred it — and wandered to a distance. A few minutes later I met Jasper again, and he stopped of his own accord to say: "We shall be in about six in the evening of our eleventh day — they promise it."

"If nothing happens, of course."

"Well, what's going to happen?"

"That's just what I'm wondering!" And I turned away and went below with the foolish but innocent satisfaction of thinking I had mystified him.

IV

"I DON'T know what to do, and you must help me,"
Mrs. Nettlepoint said to me, that evening, as soon as
I looked in.

"I 'll do what I can — but what 's the matter?"

"She has been crying here and going on — she has
quite upset me."

"Crying? She does n't look like that."

"Exactly, and that 's what startled me. She came
in to see me this afternoon, as she has done before,
and we talked of the weather and the run of the ship
and the manners of the stewardess and other such
trifles, and then suddenly, in the midst of it, as she
sat there, on no visible pretext, she burst into tears.
I asked her what ailed her and tried to comfort her,
but she did n't explain; she said it was nothing, the
effect of the sea, of the monotony, of the excitement,
of leaving home. I asked her if it had anything to do
with her prospects, with her marriage; whether she
finds as this draws near that her heart is n't in it.
I told her she must n't be nervous, that I could enter
into that — in short I said what I could. All she
replied was that she *is* nervous, very nervous, but
that it was already over; and then she jumped up and
kissed me and went away. Does she look as if she
has been crying?" Mrs. Nettlepoint wound up.

"How can I tell, when she never quits that horrid
veil? It 's as if she were ashamed to show her face."

234

"She's keeping it for Liverpool. But I don't like such incidents," said Mrs. Nettlepoint. "I think I ought to go above."

"And is that where you want me to help you?"

"Oh with your arm and that sort of thing, yes. But I may have to look to you for something more. I feel as if something were going to happen."

"That's exactly what I said to Jasper this morning."

"And what did he say?"

"He only looked innocent — as if he thought I meant a fog or a storm."

"Heaven forbid — it is n't that! I shall never be good-natured again," Mrs. Nettlepoint went on; "never have a girl put on me that way. You always pay for it — there are always tiresome complications. What I'm afraid of is after we get there. She'll throw up her engagement; there will be dreadful scenes; I shall be mixed up with them and have to look after her and keep her with me. I shall have to stay there with her till she can be sent back, or even take her up to London. Do you see all that?"

I listened respectfully; after which I observed: "You're afraid of your son."

She also had a pause. "It depends on how you mean it."

"There are things you might say to him — and with your manner; because you have one, you know, when you choose."

"Very likely, but what's my manner to his? Besides, I *have* said everything to him. That is I've said the great thing — that he's making her immensely talked about."

"And of course in answer to that he has asked you how you know, and you 've told him you have it from me."

"I 've had to tell him; and he says it 's none of your business."

"I wish he 'd say that," I remarked, "to my face."

"He 'll do so perfectly if you give him a chance. That 's where you can help me. Quarrel with him — he 's rather good at a quarrel; and that will divert him and draw him off."

"Then I 'm ready," I returned, "to discuss the matter with him for the rest of the voyage."

"Very well; I count on you. But he 'll ask you, as he asks me, what the deuce you want him to do."

"To go to bed!" — and I 'm afraid I laughed.

"Oh it is n't a joke."

I did n't want to be irritating, but I made my point. "That 's exactly what I told you at first."

"Yes, but don't exult; I hate people who exult. Jasper asks of me," she went on, "why he should mind her being talked about if she does n't mind it herself."

"I 'll tell him why," I replied; and Mrs. Nettlepoint said she should be exceedingly obliged to me and repeated that she would indeed take the field.

I looked for Jasper above that same evening, but circumstances did n't favour my quest. I found him — that is I gathered he was again ensconced behind the lifeboat with Miss Mavis; but there was a needless violence in breaking into their communion, and I put off our interview till the next day. Then I took the first opportunity, at breakfast, to make sure of it. He

236

was in the saloon when I went in and was preparing to leave the table; but I stopped him and asked if he would give me a quarter of an hour on deck a little later — there was something particular I wanted to say to him. He said "Oh yes, if you like" — with just a visible surprise, but I thought with plenty of assurance. When I had finished my breakfast I found him smoking on the forward-deck and I immediately began: "I'm going to say something you won't at all like; to ask you a question you'll probably denounce for impertinent."

"I certainly shall if I find it so," said Jasper Nettle-point.

"Well, of course my warning has meant that I don't care if you do. I'm a good deal older than you and I'm a friend — of many years — of your mother. There's nothing I like less than to be meddlesome, but I think these things give me a certain right — a sort of privilege. Besides which my enquiry will speak for itself."

"Why so many damned preliminaries?" my young man asked through his smoke.

We looked into each other's eyes a moment. What indeed was his mother's manner — her best manner — compared with his? "Are you prepared to be responsible?"

"To you?"

"Dear no — to the young lady herself. I'm speaking of course of Miss Mavis."

"Ah yes, my mother tells me you have her greatly on your mind."

"So has your mother herself — now."

237

"She's so good as to say so — to oblige you."

"She'd oblige me a great deal more by reassuring me. I know perfectly of your knowing I've told her that Miss Mavis is greatly talked about."

"Yes, but what on earth does it matter?"

"It matters as a sign."

"A sign of what?"

"That she's in a false position."

Jasper puffed his cigar with his eyes on the horizon, and I had, a little unexpectedly, the sense of producing a certain effect on him. "I don't know whether it's *your* business, what you're attempting to discuss; but it really strikes me it's none of mine. What have I to do with the tattle with which a pack of old women console themselves for not being sea-sick?"

"Do you call it tattle that Miss Mavis is in love with you?"

"Drivelling."

"Then," I retorted, "you're very ungrateful. The tattle of a pack of old women has this importance, that she suspects, or she knows, it exists, and that decent girls are for the most part very sensitive to that sort of thing. To be prepared not to heed it in this case she must have a reason, and the reason must be the one I've taken the liberty to call your attention to."

"In love with me in six days, just like that?" — and he still looked away through narrowed eyelids.

"There's no accounting for tastes, and six days at sea are equivalent to sixty on land. I don't want to make you too proud. Of course if you recognise your responsibility it's all right and I've nothing to say."

"I don't see what you mean," he presently returned.

"Surely you ought to have thought of that by this time. She's engaged to be married, and the gentleman she's engaged to is to meet her at Liverpool. The whole ship knows it — though *I* did n't tell them! — and the whole ship's watching her. It's impertinent if you like, just as I am myself, but we make a little world here together and we can't blink its conditions. What I ask you is whether you're prepared to allow her to give up the gentleman I've just mentioned for your sake."

Jasper spoke in a moment as if he did n't understand. "For my sake?"

"To marry her if she breaks with him."

He turned his eyes from the horizon to my own, and I found a strange expression in them. "Has Miss Mavis commissioned you to go into that?"

"Not in the least."

"Well then, I don't quite see — !"

"It is n't as from another I make it. Let it come from yourself — *to* yourself."

"Lord, you must think I lead myself a life!" he cried as in compassion for my simplicity. "That's a question the young lady may put to me any moment it pleases her."

"Let me then express the hope that she will. But what will you answer?"

"My dear sir, it seems to me that in spite of all the titles you've enumerated you've no reason to expect I'll tell you." He turned away, and I dedicated in perfect sincerity a deep sore sigh to the thought of our young woman. At this, under the impression of it,

he faced me again and, looking at me from head
to foot, demanded: "What is it you want me to
do?"

"I put it to your mother that you ought to go to
bed."

"You had better do that yourself!" he replied.

This time he walked off, and I reflected rather dolefully that the only clear result of my undertaking
would probably have been to make it vivid to him
that she was in love with him. Mrs. Nettlepoint came
up as she had announced, but the day was half over:
it was nearly three o'clock. She was accompanied by
her son, who established her on deck, arranged her
chair and her shawls, saw she was protected from sun
and wind, and for an hour was very properly attentive.
While this went on Grace Mavis was not visible, nor
did she reappear during the whole afternoon. I had
n't observed that she had as yet been absent from the
deck for so long a period. Jasper left his mother, but
came back at intervals to see how she got on, and when
she asked where Miss Mavis might be answered that
he had n't the least idea. I sat with my friend at her
particular request: she told me she knew that if I
did n't Mrs. Peck and Mrs. Gotch would make their
approach, so that I must act as a watch-dog. She was
flurried and fatigued with her migration, and I think
that Grace Mavis's choosing this occasion for retirement suggested to her a little that she had been made
a fool of. She remarked that the girl's not being there
showed her for the barbarian she only could be, and
that she herself was really very good so to have put
herself out; her charge was a mere bore: that was

the end of it. I could see that my companion's advent quickened the speculative activity of the other ladies; they watched her from the opposite side of the deck, keeping their eyes fixed on her very much as the man at the wheel kept his on the course of the ship. Mrs. Peck plainly had designs, and it was from this danger that Mrs. Nettlepoint averted her face.

"It's just as we said," she remarked to me as we sat there. "It's like the buckets in the well. When I come up everything else goes down."

"No, not at all everything else—since Jasper remains here."

"Remains? I don't see him."

"He comes and goes — it's the same thing."

"He goes more than he comes. But *n'en parlons plus;* I have n't gained anything. I don't admire the sea at all — what is it but a magnified water-tank? I shan't come up again."

"I've an idea she'll stay in her cabin now," I said. "She tells me she has one to herself." Mrs. Nettlepoint replied that she might do as she liked, and I repeated to her the little conversation I had had with Jasper.

She listened with interest, but "Marry her? Mercy!" she exclaimed. "I like the fine freedom with which you give my son away."

"You would n't accept that?"

"Why in the world should I?"

"Then I don't understand your position."

"Good heavens, I *have* none! It is n't a position to be tired of the whole thing."

"You would n't accept it even in the case I put to

241

him — that of her believing she had been encouraged
to throw over poor Porterfield?"

"Not even — not even. Who can know what she
believes?"

It brought me back to where we had started from.
"Then you do exactly what I said you would — you
show me a fine example of maternal immorality."

"Maternal fiddlesticks! It was she who began it."

"Then why did you come up to-day?" I asked.

"To keep you quiet."

Mrs. Nettlepoint's dinner was served on deck, but
I went into the saloon. Jasper was there, but not
Grace Mavis, as I had half-expected. I sought to
learn from him what had become of her, if she were
ill — he must have thought I had an odious pertin-
acity — and he replied that he knew nothing whatever about her. Mrs. Peck talked to me — or tried
to — of Mrs. Nettlepoint, expatiating on the great
interest it had been to see her; only it was a pity she
did n't seem more sociable. To this I made answer
that she was to be excused on the score of health.

"You don't mean to say she's sick on this pond?"

"No, she's unwell in another way."

"I guess I know the way!" Mrs. Peck laughed.
And then she added: "I suppose she came up to look
after her pet."

"Her pet?" I set my face.

"Why Miss Mavis. We've talked enough about
that."

"Quite enough. I don't know what that has had
to do with it. Miss Mavis, so far as I've noticed,
has n't been above to-day."

"Oh it goes on all the same."

"It goes on?"

"Well, it's too late."

"Too late?"

"Well, you'll see. There'll be a row."

This was n't comforting, but I did n't repeat it on deck. Mrs. Nettlepoint returned early to her cabin, professing herself infinitely spent. I did n't know what "went on," but Grace Mavis continued not to show. I looked in late, for a good-night to my friend, and learned from her that the girl had n't been to her. She had sent the stewardess to her room for news, to see if she were ill and needed assistance, and the stewardess had come back with mere mention of her not being there. I went above after this; the night was not quite so fair and the deck almost empty. In a moment Jasper Nettlepoint and our young lady moved past me together. "I hope you're better!" I called after her; and she tossed me over her shoulder— "Oh yes, I had a headache; but the air now does me good!"

I went down again — I was the only person there but they, and I wanted not to seem to dog their steps — and, returning to Mrs. Nettlepoint's room, found (her door was open to the little passage) that she was still sitting up.

"She's all right!" I said. "She's on the deck with Jasper."

The good lady looked up at me from her book. "I did n't know you called that all right."

"Well, it's better than something else."

"Than what else?"

"Something I was a little afraid of." Mrs. Nettlepoint continued to look at me; she asked again what
that might be. "I'll tell you when we're ashore," I
said.

The next day I waited on her at the usual hour of
my morning visit, and found her not a little dis-
traught. "The scenes have begun," she said; "you
know I told you I should n't get through without
them! You made me nervous last night — I have n't
the least idea what you meant; but you made me horribly nervous. She came in to see me an hour ago, and
I had the courage to say to her: 'I don't know why I
should n't tell you frankly that I've been scolding my
son about you.' Of course she asked what I meant by
that, and I let her know. 'It seems to me he drags you
about the ship too much for a girl in your position.
He has the air of not remembering that you belong to
some one else. There's a want of taste and even a
want of respect in it.' That brought on an outbreak:
she became very violent."

"Do you mean indignant?"

"Yes, indignant, and above all flustered and excited — at my presuming to suppose her relations with
my son not the very simplest in the world. I might
scold him as much as I liked — that was between ourselves; but she did n't see why I should mention such
matters to herself. Did I think she allowed him to
treat her with disrespect? That idea was n't much of
a compliment to either of them! He had treated her
better and been kinder to her than most other people
— there were very few on the ship who had n't been
insulting. She should be glad enough when she got off

244

it, to her own people, to some one whom nobody would have a right to speak of. What was there in her position that was n't perfectly natural ? what was the idea of making a fuss about her position ? Did I mean that she took it too easily — that she did n't think as much as she ought about Mr. Porterfield ? Did n't I believe she was attached to him — did n't I believe she was just counting the hours till she saw him ? That would be the happiest moment of her life. It showed how little I knew her if I thought anything else."

"All that must have been rather fine — I should have liked to hear it," I said after quite hanging on my friend's lips. "And what did you reply ?"

"Oh I grovelled; I assured her that I accused her — as regards my son — of nothing worse than an excess of good nature. She helped him to pass his time — he ought to be immensely obliged. Also that it would be a very happy moment for me too when I should hand her over to Mr. Porterfield."

"And will you come up to-day ?"

"No indeed — I think she'll do beautifully now."

I heaved this time a sigh of relief. "All's well that ends well !"

Jasper spent that day a great deal of time with his mother. She had told me how much she had lacked hitherto proper opportunity to talk over with him their movements after disembarking. Everything changes a little the last two or three days of a voyage; the spell is broken and new combinations take place. Grace Mavis was neither on deck nor at dinner, and I drew Mrs. Peck's attention to the extreme propriety with which she now conducted herself. She had spent the day in meditation and judged it best to continue to meditate.

"Ah she's afraid," said my implacable neighbour.

"Afraid of what?"

"Well, that we'll tell tales when we get there."

"Whom do you mean by 'we'?"

"Well, there are plenty — on a ship like this."

"Then I think," I returned, "we won't."

"Maybe we won't have the chance," said the dreadful little woman.

"Oh at that moment" — I spoke from a full experience — "universal geniality reigns."

Mrs. Peck however knew little of any such law. "I guess she's afraid all the same."

"So much the better!"

"Yes — so much the better!"

All the next day too the girl remained invisible, and Mrs. Nettlepoint told me she hadn't looked in. She herself had accordingly enquired by the stewardess if she might be received in Miss Mavis's own quarters, and the young lady had replied that they were littered up with things and unfit for visitors: she was packing a trunk over. Jasper made up for his devotion to his mother the day before by now spending a great deal of his time in the smoking-room. I wanted to say to him "This is much better," but I thought it wiser to hold my tongue. Indeed I had begun to feel the emotion of prospective arrival — the sense of the return to Europe always kept its intensity — and had thereby the less attention for other matters. It will doubtless

246

appear to the critical reader that my expenditure of interest had been out of proportion to the vulgar appearances of which my story gives an account, but to this I can only reply that the event was to justify me. We sighted land, the dim yet rich coast of Ireland, about sunset, and I leaned on the bulwark and took it in. "It does n't look like much, does it?" I heard a voice say, beside me; whereupon, turning, I found Grace Mavis at hand. Almost for the first time she had her veil up, and I thought her very pale.

"It will be more to-morrow," I said.

"Oh yes, a great deal more."

"The first sight of land, at sea, changes everything," I went on. "It always affects me as waking up from a dream. It 's a return to reality."

For a moment she made me no response; then she said "It does n't look very real yet."

"No, and meanwhile, this lovely evening, one can put it that the dream 's still present."

She looked up at the sky, which had a brightness, though the light of the sun had left it and that of the stars had n't begun. "It *is* a lovely evening."

"Oh yes, with this we shall do."

She stood some moments more, while the growing dusk effaced the line of the land more rapidly than our progress made it distinct. She said nothing more, she only looked in front of her; but her very quietness prompted me to something suggestive of sympathy and service. It was difficult indeed to strike the right note — some things seemed too wide of the mark and others too importunate. At last, unexpectedly, she appeared to give me my chance. Irrelevantly, abruptly she broke out: "Did n't you tell me you knew Mr. Porterfield?"

"Dear me, yes — I used to see him. I've often wanted to speak to you of him."

She turned her face on me and in the deepened evening I imagined her more pale. "What good would that do?"

"Why it would be a pleasure," I replied rather foolishly.

"Do you mean for you?"

"Well, yes — call it that," I smiled.

"Did you know him so well?"

My smile became a laugh and I lost a little my confidence. "You 're not easy to make speeches to."

"I hate speeches!" The words came from her lips with a force that surprised me; they were loud and hard. But before I had time to wonder she went on a little differently. "Shall you know him when you see him?"

"Perfectly, I think." Her manner was so strange that I had to notice it in some way, and I judged the best way was jocularly; so I added: "Shan't you?"

"Oh perhaps you 'll point him out!" And she walked quickly away. As I looked after her there came to me a perverse, rather a provoking consciousness of having during the previous days, and especially in speaking to Jasper Nettlepoint, interfered with her situation in some degree to her loss. There was an odd pang for me in seeing her move about alone; I felt somehow responsible for it and asked myself why I could n't have kept my hands off. I had seen Jasper in the smoking-room more than once that day, as I

248

passed it, and half an hour before this had observed, through the open door, that he was there. He had been with her so much that without him she now struck one as bereaved and forsaken. This was really better, no doubt, but superficially it moved — and I admit with the last inconsequence — one's pity. Mrs. Peck would doubtless have assured me that their separation was gammon: they did n't show together on deck and in the saloon, but they made it up elsewhere. The secret places on shipboard are not numerous; Mrs. Peck's "elsewhere" would have been vague, and I know not what licence her imagination took. It was distinct that Jasper had fallen off, but of course what had passed between them on this score was n't so and could never be. Later on, through his mother, I had *his* version of that, but I may remark that I gave it no credit. Poor Mrs. Nettlepoint, on the other hand, was of course to give it all. I was almost capable, after the girl had left me, of going to my young man and saying: "After all, do return to her a little, just till we get in! It won't make any difference after we land." And I don't think it was the fear he would tell me I was an idiot that prevented me. At any rate the next time I passed the door of the smoking-room I saw he had left it. I paid my usual visit to Mrs. Nettlepoint that night, but I troubled her no further about Miss Mavis. She had made up her mind that everything was smooth and settled now, and it seemed to me I had worried her, and that she had worried herself, in sufficiency. I left her to enjoy the deepening foretaste of arrival, which had taken possession of her mind. Before turning in I went above and

249

found more passengers on deck than I had ever seen so late. Jasper moved about among them alone, but I forbore to join him. The coast of Ireland had disappeared, but the night and the sea were perfect. On the way to my cabin, when I came down, I met the stewardess in one of the passages, and the idea entered my head to say to her: "Do you happen to know where Miss Mavis is?"

"Why she's in her room, sir, at this hour."

"Do you suppose I could speak to her?" It had come into my mind to ask her why she had wanted to know of me if I should recognise Mr. Porterfield.

"No sir," said the stewardess; "she has gone to bed."

"That's all right." And I followed the young lady's excellent example.

The next morning, while I dressed, the steward of my side of the ship came to me as usual to see what I wanted. But the first thing he said to me was: "Rather a bad job, sir — a passenger missing." And while I took I scarce know what instant chill from it, "A lady, sir," he went on — "whom I think you knew. Poor Miss Mavis, sir."

"*Missing?*" I cried — staring at him and horror-stricken.

"She's not on the ship. They can't find her."

"Then where to God is she?"

I recall his queer face. "Well sir, I suppose you know that as well as I."

"Do you mean she has jumped overboard?"

"Some time in the night, sir — on the quiet. But it's beyond every one, the way she escaped notice.

They usually sees 'em, sir. It must have been about half-past two. Lord, but she was sharp, sir. She did n't so much as make a splash. They say she *'ad* come against her will, sir."

I had dropped upon my sofa — I felt faint. The man went on, liking to talk as persons of his class do when they have something horrible to tell. She usually rang for the stewardess early, but this morning of course there had been no ring. The stewardess had gone in all the same about eight o'clock and found the cabin empty. That was about an hour previous. Her things were there in confusion — the things she usually wore when she went above. The stewardess thought she had been a bit odd the night before, but had waited a little and then gone back. Miss Mavis had n't turned up — and she did n't turn up. The stewardess began to look for her — she had n't been seen on deck or in the saloon. Besides, she was n't dressed — not to show herself; all her clothes were in her room. There was another lady, an old lady, Mrs. Nettlepoint — I would know her — that she was sometimes with, but the stewardess had been with *her* and knew Miss Mavis had n't come near her that morning. She had spoken to *him* and they had taken a quiet look — they had hunted everywhere. A ship's a big place, but you did come to the end of it, and if a person was n't there why there it was. In short an hour had passed and the young lady was not accounted for: from which I might judge if she ever would be. The watch could n't account for her, but no doubt the fishes in the sea could — poor miserable pitiful lady! The stewardess and he had of course thought it their duty to speak at once to the Doctor, and the Doctor had spoken immediately to the Captain. The Captain did n't like it — they never did, but he 'd try to keep it quiet — they always did.

By the time I succeeded in pulling myself together and getting on, after a fashion, the rest of my clothes I had learned that Mrs. Nettlepoint would n't yet have been told, unless the stewardess had broken it to her within the previous few minutes. Her son knew, the young gentleman on the other side of the ship — he had the other steward; my man had seen him come out of his cabin and rush above, just before he came in to me. He *had* gone above, my man was sure; he had n't gone to the old lady's cabin. I catch again the sense of my dreadfully seeing something at that moment, catch the wild flash, under the steward's words, of Jasper Nettlepoint leaping, with a mad compunction in his young agility, over the side of the ship. I hasten to add, however, that no such incident was destined to contribute its horror to poor Grace Mavis's unwitnessed and unlighted tragic act. What followed was miserable enough, but I can only glance at it. When I got to Mrs. Nettlepoint's door she was there with a shawl about her; the stewardess had just told her and she was dashing out to come to me. I made her go back — I said I would go for Jasper. I went for him but I missed him, partly no doubt because it was really at first the Captain I was after. I found this personage and found him highly scandalised, but he gave me no hope that we were in error, and his displeasure, expressed with seamanlike strength, was a definite settlement of the question. From the deck, where I merely turned round and looked, I saw the light of another summer day, the coast of Ireland green and near and the sea of a more charming colour than it had shown at all. When I came below again Jasper had passed back; he had gone to his cabin and his mother had joined him there. He remained there till we reached Liverpool — I never saw him. His mother, after a little, at his request, left him alone. All the world went above to look at the land and chatter about our tragedy, but the poor lady spent the day, dismally enough, in her room. It seemed to me, the dreadful day, intolerably long; I was thinking so of vague, of inconceivable yet inevitable Porterfield, and of my having to face him somehow on the morrow. Now of course I knew why she had asked me if I should recognise him; she had delegated to me mentally a certain pleasant office. I gave Mrs. Peck and Mrs. Gotch a wide berth — I could n't talk to them. I could, or at least I did a little, to Mrs. Nettlepoint, but with too many reserves for comfort on either side, since I quite felt how little it would now make for ease to mention Jasper to her. I was obliged to assume by my silence that he had had nothing to do with what had happened; and of course I never really ascertained what he *had* had to do. The secret of what passed between him and the strange girl who would have sacrificed her marriage to him on so short an acquaintance remains shut up in his breast. His mother, I know, went to his door from time to time, but he refused her admission. That evening, to be human at a venture, I requested the steward to go in and ask him if he should care to see me, and the good man returned with an answer which he candidly transmitted. "Not in the least!" — Jasper apparently was almost as scandalised as the Captain.

At Liverpool, at the dock, when we had touched, twenty people came on board and I had already made out Mr. Porterfield at a distance. He was looking up at the side of the great vessel with disappointment written — for my strained eyes — in his face; disappointment at not seeing the woman he had so long awaited lean over it and wave her handkerchief to him. Every one was looking at him, every one but she — his identity flew about in a moment — and I wondered if it did n't strike him. He used to be gaunt and angular, but had grown almost fat and stooped a little. The interval between us diminished — he was on the plank and then on the deck with the jostling agents of the Customs; too soon for my equanimity. I met him instantly, however, to save him from exposure — laid my hand on him and drew him away, though I was sure he had no impression of having seen me before. It was not till afterwards that I thought this rather characteristically dull of him. I drew him far away — I was conscious of Mrs. Peck and Mrs. Gotch, looking at us as we passed — into the empty stale smoking-room: he remained speechless, and that struck me as like him. I had to speak first, he could n't even relieve me by saying "Is anything the matter?" I broke ground by putting it, feebly, that she was ill. It was a dire moment.

THE MARRIAGES

THE MARRIAGES

I

"WON'T you stay a little longer?" the hostess asked while she held the girl's hand and smiled. "It's too early for every one to go — it's too absurd." Mrs. Churchley inclined her head to one side and looked gracious; she flourished about her face, in a vaguely protecting sheltering way, an enormous fan of red feathers. Everything in her composition, for Adela Chart, was enormous. She had big eyes, big teeth, big shoulders, big hands, big rings and bracelets, big jewels of every sort and many of them. The train of her crimson dress was longer than any other; her house was huge; her drawing-room, especially now that the company had left it, looked vast, and it offered to the girl's eyes a collection of the largest sofas and chairs, pictures, mirrors, clocks, that she had ever beheld. Was Mrs. Churchley's fortune also large, to account for so many immensities? Of this Adela could know nothing, but it struck her, while she smiled sweetly back at their entertainer, that she had better try to find out. Mrs. Churchley had at least a high-hung carriage drawn by the tallest horses, and in the Row she was to be seen perched on a mighty hunter. She was high and extensive herself, though not exactly fat; her bones were big, her limbs were long, and her loud hurrying voice resembled the bell of a steamboat. While she spoke to his daughter she had the air of hiding from Colonel Chart, a little shyly, behind the wide ostrich fan. But Colonel Chart was not a man to be either ignored or eluded.

"Of course every one's going on to something else," he said. "I believe there are a lot of things to-night."

"And where are *you* going?" Mrs. Churchley asked, dropping her fan and turning her bright hard eyes on the Colonel.

"Oh I don't do that sort of thing!"—he used a tone of familiar resentment that fell with a certain effect on his daughter's ear. She saw in it that he thought Mrs. Churchley might have done him a little more justice. But what made the honest soul suppose her a person to look to for a perception of fine shades? Indeed the shade was one it might have been a little difficult to seize — the difference between "going on" and coming to a dinner of twenty people. The pair were in mourning; the second year had maintained it for Adela, but the Colonel had n't objected to dining with Mrs. Churchley, any more than he had objected at Easter to going down to the Millwards', where he had met her and where the girl had her reasons for believing him to have known he should meet her. Adela was n't clear about the occasion of their original meeting, to which a certain mystery attached. In Mrs. Churchley's exclamation now there was the fullest concurrence in Colonel Chart's idea; she did n't say "Ah yes, dear friend, I understand!" but this was the note of sympathy she plainly wished to sound. It immediately made Adela say to her "Surely you must be going on somewhere yourself."

"Yes, you must have a lot of places," the Colonel concurred, while his view of her shining raiment had an invidious directness. Adela could read the tacit implication: "You're not in sorrow, in desolation."

Mrs. Churchley turned away from her at this and just waited before answering. The red fan was up again, and this time it sheltered her from Adela. "I'll give everything up — for *you*," were the words that issued from behind it. "*Do* stay a little. I always think this is such a nice hour. One can really talk," Mrs. Churchley went on. The Colonel laughed; he said it wasn't fair. But their hostess pressed his daughter. "Do sit down; it's the only time to have any talk." The girl saw her father sit down, but she wandered away, turning her back and pretending to look at a picture. She was so far from agreeing with Mrs. Churchley that it was an hour she particularly disliked. She was conscious of the queerness, the shyness, in London, of the gregarious flight of guests after a dinner, the general *sauve qui peut* and panic fear of being left with the host and hostess. But personally she always felt the contagion, always conformed to the rush. Besides, she knew herself turn red now, flushed with a conviction that had come over her and that she wished not to show.

Her father sat down on one of the big sofas with Mrs. Churchley; fortunately he was also a person with a presence that could hold its own. Adela didn't care to sit and watch them while they made love, as she crudely imaged it, and she cared still less to join in their strange commerce. She wandered further away, went into another of the bright "handsome,"

rather nude rooms — they were like women dressed
for a ball — where the displaced chairs, at awkward
angles to each other, seemed to retain the attitudes of
bored talkers. Her heart beat as she had seldom
known it, but she continued to make a pretence of
looking at the pictures on the walls and the ornaments
on the tables, while she hoped that, as she preferred
it, it would be also the course her father would like
best. She hoped "awfully," as she would have said,
that he would n't think her rude. She was a person
of courage, and he was a kind, an intensely good-
natured man; nevertheless she went in some fear of
him. At home it had always been a religion with them
to be nice to the people he liked. How, in the old days,
her mother, her incomparable mother, so clever, so
unerring, so perfect, how in the precious days her
mother had practised that art! Oh her mother, her
irrecoverable mother! One of the pictures she was
looking at swam before her eyes. Mrs. Churchley, in
the natural course, would have begun immediately
to climb staircases. Adela could see the high bony
shoulders and the long crimson tail and the universal
coruscating nod wriggle their horribly practical way
through the rest of the night. Therefore she *must*
have had her reasons for detaining them. There were
mothers who thought every one wanted to marry their
eldest son, and the girl sought to be clear as to whether
she herself belonged to the class of daughters who
thought every one wanted to marry their father. Her
companions left her alone; and though she did n't
want to be near them it angered her that Mrs. Churchley did n't call her. That proved she was conscious

of the situation. She would have called her, only Colonel Chart had perhaps dreadfully murmured "Don't, love, don't." This proved he also was conscious. The time was really not long — ten minutes at the most elapsed — when he cried out gaily, pleasantly, as if with a small jocular reproach, "I say, Adela, we must release this dear lady!" He spoke of course as if it had been Adela's fault that they lingered. When they took leave she gave Mrs. Churchley, without intention and without defiance, but from the simple sincerity of her pain, a longer look into the eyes than she had ever given her before. Mrs. Churchley's onyx pupils reflected the question as distant dark windows reflect the sunset; they seemed to say: "Yes, I *am*, if that's what you want to know!"

What made the case worse, what made the girl more sure, was the silence preserved by her companion in the brougham on their way home. They rolled along in the June darkness from Prince's Gate to Seymour Street, each looking out of a window in conscious prudence; watching but not seeing the hurry of the London night, the flash of lamps, the quick roll on the wood of hansoms and other broughams. Adela had expected her father would say something about Mrs. Churchley; but when he said nothing it affected her, very oddly, still more as if he had spoken. In Seymour Street he asked the footman if Mr. Godfrey had come in, to which the servant replied that he had come in early and gone straight to his room. Adela had gathered as much, without saying so, from a lighted window on the second floor; but she contributed no remark to the question. At the foot of the stairs her father halted as if he had something on his mind; but what it amounted to seemed only the dry "Good-night" with which he presently ascended. It was the first time since her mother's death that he had bidden her good-night without kissing her. They were a kissing family, and after that dire event the habit had taken a fresh spring. She had left behind her such a general passion of regret that in kissing each other they felt themselves a little to be kissing her. Now, as, standing in the hall, with the stiff watching footman — she could have said to him angrily "Go away!" — planted near her, she looked with unspeakable pain at her father's back while he mounted, the effect was of his having withheld from another and a still more slighted cheek the touch of his lips.

He was going to his room, and after a moment she heard his door close. Then she said to the servant "Shut up the house" — she tried to do everything her mother had done, to be a little of what she had been, conscious only of falling woefully short — and took her own way upstairs. After she had reached her room she waited, listening, shaken by the apprehension that she should hear her father come out again and go up to Godfrey. He would go up to tell him, to have it over without delay, precisely because it would be so difficult. She asked herself indeed why he should tell Godfrey when he had n't taken the occasion — their drive home being an occasion — to tell herself. However, she wanted no announcing, no telling; there was such a horrible clearness in her mind that what she now waited for was only to be

sure her father would n't proceed as she had imagined.
At the end of the minutes she saw this particular
danger was over, upon which she came out and made
her own way to her brother. Exactly what she wanted
to say to him first, if their parent counted on the boy's
greater indulgence, and before he could say anything,
was: "Don't forgive him; don't, don't!"

He was to go up for an examination, poor lad, and
during these weeks his lamp burned till the small
hours. It was for the Foreign Office, and there was
to be some frightful number of competitors; but Adela
had great hopes of him — she believed so in his
talents and saw with pity how hard he worked. This
would have made her spare him, not trouble his night,
his scanty rest, if anything less dreadful had been at
stake. It was a blessing however that one could count
on his coolness, young as he was — his bright good-
looking discretion, the thing that already made him
half a man of the world. Moreover he was the one
who would care most. If Basil was the eldest son —
he had as a matter of course gone into the army and
was in India, on the staff, by good luck, of a governor-
general — it was exactly this that would make him
comparatively indifferent. His life was elsewhere,
and his father and he had been in a measure military
comrades, so that he would be deterred by a certain
delicacy from protesting; he would n't have liked any
such protest in an affair of *his*. Beatrice and Muriel
would care, but they were too young to speak, and
this was just why her own responsibility was so great.

Godfrey was in working-gear — shirt and trousers
and slippers and a beautiful silk jacket. His room

felt hot, though a window was open to the summer night; the lamp on the table shed its studious light over a formidable heap of text-books and papers, the bed moreover showing how he had flung himself down to think out a problem. As soon as she got in she began. "Father's going to marry Mrs. Churchley, you know."

She saw his poor pink face turn pale. "How do you know?"

"I've seen with my eyes. We've been dining there — we've just come home. He's in love with her. She's in love with *him*. They'll arrange it."

"Oh I say!" Godfrey exclaimed, incredulous.

"He will, he will, he will!" cried the girl; and with it she burst into tears.

Godfrey, who had a cigarette in his hand, lighted it at one of the candles on the mantelpiece as if he were embarrassed. As Adela, who had dropped into his armchair, continued to sob, he said after a moment: "He ought n't to — he ought n't to."

"Oh think of mamma — think of mamma!" she wailed almost louder than was safe.

"Yes, he ought to think of mamma." With which Godfrey looked at the tip of his cigarette.

"To such a woman as that — after *her!*"

"Dear old mamma!" said Godfrey while he smoked.

Adela rose again, drying her eyes. "It's like an insult to her; it's as if he denied her." Now that she spoke of it she felt herself rise to a height. "He rubs out at a stroke all the years of their happiness."

"They were awfully happy," Godfrey agreed.

"Think what she was — think how no one else will ever again be like her!" the girl went on.

"I suppose he's not very happy now," her brother vaguely contributed.

"Of course he is n't, any more than you and I are; and it's dreadful of him to want to be."

"Well, don't make yourself miserable till you're sure," the young man said.

But Adela showed him confidently that she *was* sure, from the way the pair had behaved together and from her father's attitude on the drive home. If Godfrey had been there he would have seen everything; it could n't be explained, but he would have felt. When he asked at what moment the girl had first had her suspicion she replied that it had all come at once, that evening; or that at least she had had no conscious fear till then. There had been signs for two or three weeks, but she had n't understood them — ever since the day Mrs. Churchley had dined in Seymour Street. Adela had on that occasion thought it odd her father should have wished to invite her, given the quiet way they were living; she was a person they knew so little. He had said something about her having been very civil to him, and that evening, already, she had guessed that he must have frequented their portentous guest herself more than there had been signs of. To-night it had come to her clearly that he would have called on her every day since the time of her dining with them; every afternoon about the hour he was ostensibly at his club. Mrs. Churchley *was* his club — she was for all the world just like one. At this Godfrey laughed; he wanted to know what his sister knew about clubs. She was slightly disappointed in his laugh, even wounded by it, but she knew perfectly what she meant: she meant that Mrs. Churchley was public and florid, promiscuous and mannish.

"Oh I dare say she's all right," he said as if he wanted to get on with his work. He looked at the clock on the mantel-shelf; he would have to put in another hour.

"All right to come and take darling mamma's place — to sit where *she* used to sit, to lay her horrible hands on *her* things?" Adela was appalled — all the more that she had n't expected it — at her brother's apparent acceptance of such a prospect.

He coloured; there was something in her passionate piety that scorched him. She glared at him with tragic eyes — he might have profaned an altar. "Oh I mean that nothing will come of it."

"Not if we do our duty," said Adela. And then as he looked as if he had n't an idea of what that could be: "You must speak to him — tell him how we feel; that we shall never forgive him, that we can't endure it."

"He 'll think I 'm cheeky," her brother returned, looking down at his papers with his back to her and his hands in his pockets.

"Cheeky to plead for *her* memory?"

"He 'll say it 's none of my business."

"Then you believe he 'll do it?" cried the girl.

"Not a bit. Go to bed!"

"*I 'll* speak to him" — she had turned as pale as a young priestess.

"Don't cry out till you 're hurt; wait till he speaks to *you*."

"He won't, he won't!" she declared. "He'll do it without telling us."

Her brother had faced round to her again; he started a little at this, and again, at one of the candles, lighted his cigarette, which had gone out. She looked at him a moment; then he said something that surprised her. "Is Mrs. Churchley very rich?"

"I have n't the least idea. What on earth has that to do with it?"

Godfrey puffed his cigarette. "Does she live as if she were?"

"She has a lot of hideous showy things."

"Well, we must keep our eyes open," he concluded. "And now you *must* let me get on." He kissed his visitor as if to make up for dismissing her, or for his failure to take fire; and she held him a moment, burying her head on his shoulder.

A wave of emotion surged through her, and again she quavered out: "Ah why did she leave us? Why did she leave us?"

"Yes, why indeed?" the young man sighed, disengaging himself with a movement of oppression.

II

ADELA was so far right as that by the end of the week, though she remained certain, her father had still not made the announcement she dreaded. What convinced her was the sense of her changed relations with him — of there being between them something unexpressed, something she was aware of as she would have been of an open wound. When she spoke of this to Godfrey he said the change was of her own making — also that she was cruelly unjust to the governor. She suffered even more from her brother's unexpected perversity; she had had so different a theory about him that her disappointment was almost an humiliation and she needed all her fortitude to pitch her faith lower. She wondered what had happened to him and why he so failed her. She would have trusted him to feel right about anything, above all about such a question. Their worship of their mother's memory, their recognition of her sacred place in their past, her exquisite influence in their father's life, his fortune, his career, in the whole history of the family and welfare of the house — accomplished clever gentle good beautiful and capable as she had been, a woman whose quiet distinction was universally admired, so that on her death one of the Princesses, the most august of her friends, had written Adela such a note about her as princesses were understood very seldom to write : their hushed tenderness over all this was like a religion, and was also an attributive honour, to fall away from which was a form of treachery. This was n't the way people usually felt in London, she knew; but strenuous ardent observant girl as she was, with secrecies of sentiment and dim originalities of attitude, she had already made up her mind that London was no treasure-house of delicacies. Remembrance there was hammered thin — to be faithful was to make society gape. The patient dead were sacrificed; they had no shrines, for people were literally ashamed of mourning. When they had hustled all sensibility out of their lives they invented the fiction that they felt too much to utter. Adela said nothing to her sisters; this reticence was part of the virtue it was her idea to practise for them. *She* was to be their mother, a direct deputy and representative. Before the vision of that other woman parading in such a character she felt capable of ingenuities, of deep diplomacies. The essence of these indeed was just tremulously to watch her father. Five days after they had dined together at Mrs. Churchley's he asked her if she had been to see that lady.

"No indeed, why should I ?" Adela knew that he knew she had n't been, since Mrs. Churchley would have told him.

"Don't you call on people after you dine with them ?" said Colonel Chart.

"Yes, in the course of time. I don't rush off within the week."

Her father looked at her, and his eyes were colder than she had ever seen them, which was probably, she reflected, just the way hers appeared to himself. "Then you 'll please rush off to-morrow. She 's to dine with us on the 12th, and I shall expect your sisters to come down."

Adela stared. "To a dinner-party?"

"It's not to be a dinner-party. I want them to know Mrs. Churchley."

"Is there to be nobody else?"

"Godfrey of course. A family party," he said with an assurance before which she turned cold.

The girl asked her brother that evening if *that* was n't tantamount to an announcement. He looked at her queerly and then said: "*I've* been to see her."

"What on earth did you do that for?"

"Father told me he wished it."

"Then he *has* told you?"

"Told me what?" Godfrey asked while her heart sank with the sense of his making difficulties for her.

"That they 're engaged, of course. What else can all this mean?"

"He did n't tell me that, but I like her."

"*Like* her!" the girl shrieked.

"She 's very kind, very good."

"To thrust herself upon us when we hate her? Is that what you call kind? Is that what you call decent?"

"Oh *I* don't hate her" — and he turned away as if she bored him.

She called the next day on Mrs. Churchley, designing to break out somehow, to plead, to appeal — "Oh spare us! have mercy on us! let him alone! go away!" But that was n't easy when they were face to face. Mrs. Churchley had every intention of getting, as she would have said — she was perpetually using the expression — into touch; but her good intentions were as depressing as a tailor's misfits. She could never understand that they had no place for her vulgar charity, that their life was filled with a fragrance of perfection for which she had no sense fine enough. She was as undomestic as a shop-front and as out of tune as a parrot. She would either make them live in the streets or bring the streets into their life — it was the same thing. She had evidently never read a book, and she used intonations that Adela had never heard, as if she had been an Australian or an American. She understood everything in a vulgar sense; speaking of Godfrey's visit to her and praising him according to her idea, saying horrid things about him — that he was awfully good-looking, a perfect gentleman, the kind she liked. How could her father, who was after all in everything else such a dear, listen to a woman, or endure her, who thought she pleased him when she called the son of his dead wife a perfect gentleman? What would he have been, pray? Much she knew about what any of them were! When she told Adela she wanted her to like her the girl thought for an instant her opportunity had come — the chance to plead with her and beg her off. But she presented such an impenetrable surface that it would have been like giving a message to a varnished door. She was n't a woman, said Adela; she was an address.

When she dined in Seymour Street the "children," as the girl called the others, including Godfrey, liked her. Beatrice and Muriel stared shyly and silently at the wonders of her apparel (she was brutally over-dressed) without of course guessing the danger that

271

tainted the air. They supposed her in their innocence to be amusing, and they did n't know, any more than she did herself, how she patronised them. When she was upstairs with them after dinner Adela could see her look round the room at the things she meant to alter — their mother's things, not a bit like her own and not good enough for her. After a quarter of an hour of this our young lady felt sure she was deciding that Seymour Street would n't do at all, the dear old home that had done for their mother those twenty years. Was she plotting to transport them all to her horrible Prince's Gate ? Of one thing at any rate Adela was certain : her father, at that moment alone in the dining-room with Godfrey, pretending to drink another glass of wine to make time, was coming to the point, was telling the news. When they reappeared they both, to her eyes, looked unnatural : the news had been told.

She had it from Godfrey before Mrs. Churchley left the house, when, after a brief interval, he followed her out of the drawing-room on her taking her sisters to bed. She was waiting for him at the door of her room. Her father was then alone with his *fiancée* — the word was grotesque to Adela ; it was already as if the place were her home.

"What did you say to him ?" our young woman asked when her brother had told her.

"I said nothing." Then he added, colouring — the expression of her face was such — "There was nothing to say."

"Is that how it strikes you ?" — and she stared at the lamp.

"He asked me to speak to her," Godfrey went on.

"In what hideous sense?"

"To tell her I was glad."

"And did you?" Adela panted.

"I don't know. I said something. She kissed me."

"Oh how *could* you?" shuddered the girl, who covered her face with her hands.

"He says she's very rich," her brother returned.

"Is that why you kissed her?"

"I did n't kiss her. Good-night." And the young man, turning his back, went out.

When he had gone Adela locked herself in as with the fear she should be overtaken or invaded, and during a sleepless feverish memorable night she took counsel of her uncompromising spirit. She saw things as they were, in all the indignity of life. The levity, the mockery, the infidelity, the ugliness, lay as plain as a map before her; it was a world of gross practical jokes, a world *pour rire;* but she cried about it all the same. The morning dawned early, or rather it seemed to her there had been no night, nothing but a sickly creeping day. But by the time she heard the house stirring again she had determined what to do. When she came down to the breakfast-room her father was already in his place with newspapers and letters; and she expected the first words he would utter to be a rebuke to her for having disappeared the night before without taking leave of Mrs. Churchley. Then she saw he wished to be intensely kind, to make every allowance, to conciliate and console her. He knew she had heard from Godfrey, and he got up and kissed her. He told her as quickly as possible, to have it over, stammering

273

a little, with an "I've a piece of news for you that will probably shock you," yet looking even exaggeratedly grave and rather pompous, to inspire the respect he did n't deserve. When he kissed her she melted, she burst into tears. He held her against him, kissing her again and again, saying tenderly "Yes, yes, I know, I know." But he did n't know else he could n't have done it. Beatrice and Muriel came in, frightened when they saw her crying, and still more scared when she turned to them with words and an air that were terrible in their comfortable little lives : "Papa 's going to be married; he 's going to marry Mrs. Churchley!" After staring a moment and seeing their father look as strange, on his side, as Adela, though in a different way, the children also began to cry, so that when the servants arrived with tea and boiled eggs these functionaries were greatly embarrassed with their burden, not knowing whether to come in or hang back. They all scraped together a decorum, and as soon as the things had been put on table the Colonel banished the men with a glance. Then he made a little affectionate speech to Beatrice and Muriel, in which he described Mrs. Churchley as the kindest, the most delightful of women, only wanting to make them happy, only wanting to make *him* happy, and convinced that he would be if they were and that they would be if he was.

"What do such words mean?" Adela asked herself. She declared privately that they meant nothing, but she was silent, and every one was silent, on account of the advent of Miss Flynn the governess, before whom Colonel Chart preferred not to discuss the situation. Adela recognised on the spot that if things were to go as he wished his children would practically never again be alone with him. He would spend all his time with Mrs. Churchley till they were married, and then Mrs. Churchley would spend all her time with him. Adela was ashamed of him, and that was horrible — all the more that every one else would be, all his other friends, every one who had known her mother. But the public dishonour to that high memory should n't be enacted; he should n't do as he wished.

After breakfast her father remarked to her that it would give him pleasure if in a day or two she would take her sisters to see their friend, and she replied that he should be obeyed. He held her hand a moment, looking at her with an argument in his eyes which presently hardened into sternness. He wanted to know that she forgave him, but also wanted to assure her that he expected her to mind what she did, to go straight. She turned away her eyes; she was indeed ashamed of him.

She waited three days and then conveyed her sisters to the *repaire*, as she would have been ready to term it, of the lioness. That queen of beasts was surrounded with callers, as Adela knew she would be; it was her "day" and the occasion the girl preferred. Before this she had spent all her time with her companions, talking to them about their mother, playing on their memory of her, making them cry and making them laugh, reminding them of blest hours of their early childhood, telling them anecdotes of her own. None the less she confided to them that she believed there was no harm at all in Mrs. Churchley, and that when the time should come she would probably take them out immensely. She saw with smothered irritation that they enjoyed their visit at Prince's Gate; they had never been at anything so "grown-up," nor seen so many smart bonnets and brilliant complexions. Moreover they were considered with interest, quite as if, being minor elements, yet perceptible ones, of Mrs. Churchley's new life, they had been described in advance and were the heroines of the occasion. There were so many ladies present that this personage did n't talk to them much; she only called them her "chicks" and asked them to hand about tea-cups and bread and butter. All of which was highly agreeable and indeed intensely exciting to Beatrice and Muriel, who had little round red spots in *their* cheeks when they came away. Adela quivered with the sense that her mother's children were now Mrs. Churchley's "chicks" and a part of the furniture of Mrs. Churchley's dreadful consciousness.

It was one thing to have made up her mind, however; it was another thing to make her attempt. It was when she learned from Godfrey that the day was fixed, the 20th of July, only six weeks removed, that she felt the importance of prompt action. She learned everything from Godfrey now, having decided it would be hypocrisy to question her father. Even her silence was hypocritical, but she could n't weep and wail. Her father showed extreme tact; taking no notice of her detachment, treating it as a moment of *bouderie* he was bound to allow her and that would pout itself away. She debated much as to whether she should take Godfrey into her confidence; she would have done so without hesitation if he had n't disappointed her. He was so little what she might have expected, and so perversely preoccupied that she could explain it only by the high pressure at which he was living, his anxiety about his "exam." He was in a fidget, in a fever, putting on a spurt to come in first; sceptical moreover about his success and cynical about everything else. He appeared to agree to the general axiom that they did n't want a strange woman thrust into their life, but he found Mrs. Churchley "very jolly as a person to know." He had been to see her by himself — he had been to see her three times. He in fact gave it out that he would make the most of her now; he should probably be so little in Seymour Street after these days. What Adela at last determined to give him was her assurance that the marriage would never take place. When he asked what she meant and who was to prevent it she replied that the interesting couple would abandon the idea of themselves, or that Mrs. Churchley at least would after a week or two back out of it.

"That will be really horrid then," Godfrey pronounced. "The only respectable thing, at the point they 've come to, is to put it through. Charming for poor Dad to have the air of being 'chucked'!"

This made her hesitate two days more, but she found answers more valid than any objections. The many-voiced answer to everything — it was like the autumn wind round the house — was the affront that fell back on her mother. Her mother was dead, but it killed her again. So one morning at eleven o'clock, when she knew her father was writing letters, she went out quietly and, stopping the first hansom she met, drove to Prince's Gate. Mrs. Churchley was at home, and she was shown into the drawing-room with the request that she would wait five minutes. She waited without the sense of breaking down at the last, and the impulse to run away, which were what she had expected to have. In the cab and at the door her heart had beat terribly, but now suddenly, with the game really to play, she found herself lucid and calm. It was a joy to her to feel later that this was the way Mrs. Churchley found her; not confused, not stammering nor prevaricating, only a little amazed at her own courage, conscious of the immense responsibility of her step and wonderfully older than her years. Her hostess sounded her at first with suspicious eyes, but eventually, to Adela's surprise, burst into tears. At this the girl herself cried, and with the secret happiness of believing they were saved. Mrs. Churchley said she would think over what she had been told, and she promised her young friend, freely enough and very firmly, not to betray the secret of the latter's step to the Colonel. They were saved — they were saved: the words sung themselves in the girl's soul as she came downstairs. When the door opened for her she saw her brother on the step, and they looked at each other in surprise, each finding it on the part of the other an odd hour for Prince's Gate. Godfrey remarked that Mrs. Churchley would have enough of the family, and Adela answered that she would perhaps have too much. None the less the young man went in while his sister took her way home.

III

SHE saw nothing of him for nearly a week; he had more and more his own times and hours, adjusted to his tremendous responsibilities, and he spent whole days at his crammer's. When she knocked at his door late in the evening he was regularly not in his room. It was known in the house how much he was worried; he was horribly nervous about his ordeal. It was to begin on the 23d of June, and his father was as worried as himself. The wedding had been arranged in relation to this; they wished poor Godfrey's fate settled first, though they felt the nuptials would be darkened if it should n't be settled right.

Ten days after that performance of her private undertaking Adela began to sniff, as it were, a difference in the general air; but as yet she was afraid to exult. It was n't in truth a difference for the better, so that there might be still a great tension. Her father, since the announcement of his intended marriage, had been visibly pleased with himself, but that pleasure now appeared to have undergone a check. She had the impression known to the passengers on a great steamer when, in the middle of the night, they feel the engines stop. As this impression may easily sharpen to the sense that something serious has happened, so the girl asked herself what had actually occurred. She had expected something serious; but it was as if she could n't keep still in her cabin — she

279

wanted to go up and see. On the 20th, just before breakfast, her maid brought her a message from her brother. Mr. Godfrey would be obliged if she would speak to him in his room. She went straight up to him, dreading to find him ill, broken down on the eve of his formidable week. This was not the case however — he rather seemed already at work, to have been at work since dawn. But he was very white and his eyes had a strange and new expression. Her beautiful young brother looked older; he looked haggard and hard. He met her there as if he had been waiting for her, and he said at once: "Please tell me this, Adela — what was the purpose of your visit the other morning to Mrs. Churchley, the day I met you at her door?"

She stared — she cast about. "The purpose? What's the matter? Why do you ask?"

"They've put it off — they've put it off a month."

"Ah thank God!" said Adela.

"Why the devil do you thank God?" Godfrey asked with a strange impatience.

She gave a strained intense smile. "You know I think it all wrong."

He stood looking at her up and down. "What did you do there? How did you interfere?"

"Who told you I interfered?" she returned with a deep flush.

"You said something — you did something. I knew you had done it when I saw you come out."

"What I did was my own business."

"Damn your own business!" cried the young man.

She had never in her life been so spoken to, and in

280

advance, had she been given the choice, would have said that she'd rather die than be so handled by Godfrey. But her spirit was high, and for a moment she was as angry as if she had been cut with a whip. She escaped the blow but felt the insult. "And *your* business then?" she asked. "I wondered what that was when I saw *you*."

He stood a moment longer scowling at her; then with the exclamation "You've made a pretty mess!" he turned away from her and sat down to his books.

They had put it off, as he said; her father was dry and stiff and official about it. "I suppose I had better let you know we've thought it best to postpone our marriage till the end of the summer — Mrs. Churchley has so many arrangements to make": he was not more expansive than that. She neither knew nor greatly cared whether she but vainly imagined or correctly observed him to watch her obliquely for some measure of her receipt of these words. She flattered herself that, thanks to Godfrey's forewarning, cruel as the form of it had been, she was able to repress any crude sign of elation. She had a perfectly good conscience, for she could now judge what odious elements Mrs. Churchley, whom she had not seen since the morning in Prince's Gate, had already introduced into their dealings. She gathered without difficulty that her father had n't concurred in the postponement, for he was more restless than before, more absent and distinctly irritable. There was naturally still the question of how much of this condition was to be attributed to his solicitude about Godfrey. That young man took occasion to say a horrible thing to his sister:

"If I don't pass it will be your fault." These were
dreadful days for the girl, and she asked herself how
she could have borne them if the hovering spirit of
her mother had n't been at her side. Fortunately she
always felt it there, sustaining, commending, sancti-
fying. Suddenly her father announced to her that he
wished her to go immediately, with her sisters, down
to Brinton, where there was always part of a household and where for a few weeks they would manage
well enough. The only explanation he gave of this
desire was that he wanted them out of the way. "Out
of the way of what?" she queried, since there were
to be for the time no preparations in Seymour Street.
She was willing to take it for out of the way of his
nerves.

She never needed urging however to go to Brinton,
the dearest old house in the world, where the happiest
days of her young life had been spent and the silent
nearness of her mother always seemed greatest. She
was happy again, with Beatrice and Muriel and Miss
Flynn, with the air of summer and the haunted rooms
and her mother's garden and the talking oaks and the
nightingales. She wrote briefly to her father, giving
him, as he had requested, an account of things; and
he wrote back that since she was so contented — she
did n't recognise having told him that — she had better not return to town at all. The fag-end of the London season would be unimportant to her, and he was
getting on very well. He mentioned that Godfrey
had passed his tests, but, as she knew, there would
be a tiresome wait before news of results. The poor
chap was going abroad for a month with young Sher-

ard — he had earned a little rest and a little fun. He went abroad without a word to Adela, but in his beautiful little hand he took a chaffing leave of Beatrice. The child showed her sister the letter, of which she was very proud and which contained no message for any one else. This was the worst bitterness of the whole crisis for that somebody — its placing in so strange a light the creature in the world whom, after her mother, she had loved best.

Colonel Chart had said he would "run down" while his children were at Brinton, but they heard no more about it. He only wrote two or three times to Miss Flynn on matters in regard to which Adela was surprised he should n't have communicated with herself. Muriel accomplished an upright little letter to Mrs. Churchley — her eldest sister neither fostered nor discouraged the performance — to which Mrs. Churchley replied, after a fortnight, in a meagre and, as Adela thought, illiterate fashion, making no allusion to the approach of any closer tie. Evidently the situation had changed; the question of the marriage was dropped, at any rate for the time. This idea gave our young woman a singular and almost intoxicating sense of power; she felt as if she were riding a great wave of confidence. She had decided and acted — the greatest could do no more than that. The grand thing was to see one's results, and what else was she doing? These results were in big rich conspicuous lives; the stage was large on which she moved her figures. Such a vision was exciting, and as they had the use of a couple of ponies at Brinton she worked off her excitement by a long gallop. A day or two after this however came news of which the effect was to rekindle it. Godfrey had come back, the list had been published, he had passed first. These happy tidings proceeded from the young man himself; he announced them by a telegram to Beatrice, who had never in her life before received such a missive and was proportionately inflated. Adela reflected that she herself ought to have felt snubbed, but she was too happy. They were free again, they were themselves, the nightmare of the previous weeks was blown away, the unity and dignity of her father's life restored, and, to round off her sense of success, Godfrey had achieved his first step toward high distinction. She wrote him the next day as frankly and affectionately as if there had been no estrangement between them, and besides telling him how she rejoiced in his triumph begged him in charity to let them know exactly how the case stood with regard to Mrs. Churchley.

Late in the summer afternoon she walked through the park to the village with her letter, posted it and came back. Suddenly, at one of the turns of the avenue, halfway to the house, she saw a young man hover there as if awaiting her — a young man who proved to be Godfrey on his pedestrian progress over from the station. He had seen her as he took his short cut, and if he had come down to Brinton it was n't apparently to avoid her. There was nevertheless none of the joy of his triumph in his face as he came a very few steps to meet her; and although, stiffly enough, he let her kiss him and say "I'm so glad — I'm so glad!" she felt this tolerance as not quite the mere calm of the rising diplomatist. He turned toward the

284

house with her and walked on a short distance while she uttered the hope that he had come to stay some days.

"Only till to-morrow morning. They're sending me straight to Madrid. I came down to say good-bye; there's a fellow bringing my bags."

"To Madrid? How awfully nice! And it's awfully nice of you to have come," she said as she passed her hand into his arm.

The movement made him stop, and, stopping, he turned on her in a flash a face of something more than suspicion — of passionate reprobation. "What I really came for — you might as well know without more delay — is to ask you a question."

"A question?" — she echoed it with a beating heart.

They stood there under the old trees in the lingering light, and, young and fine and fair as they both were, formed a complete superficial harmony with the peaceful English scene. A near view, however, would have shown that Godfrey Chart hadn't taken so much trouble only to skim the surface. He looked deep into his sister's eyes. "What was it you said that morning to Mrs. Churchley?"

She fixed them on the ground a moment, but at last met his own again. "If she has told you, why do you ask?"

"She has told me nothing. I've seen for myself."

"What have you seen?"

"She has broken it off. Everything's over. Father's in the depths."

"In the depths?" the girl quavered.

"Did you think it would make him jolly?" he went on.

She had to choose what to say. "He'll get over it. He'll be glad."

"That remains to be seen. You interfered, you invented something, you got round her. I insist on knowing what you did."

Adela felt that if it was a question of obstinacy there was something within her she could count on; in spite of which, while she stood looking down again a moment, she said to herself "I could be dumb and dogged if I chose, but I scorn to be." She wasn't ashamed of what she had done, but she wanted to be clear. "Are you absolutely certain it's broken off?"

"He is, and she is; so that's as good."

"What reason has she given?"

"None at all — or half a dozen; it's the same thing. She has changed her mind — she mistook her feelings — she can't part with her independence. Moreover he has too many children."

"Did he tell you this?" the girl asked.

"Mrs. Churchley told me. She has gone abroad for a year."

"And she did n't tell you what I said to her?"

Godfrey showed an impatience. "Why should I take this trouble if she had?"

"You might have taken it to make me suffer," said Adela. "That appears to be what you want to do."

"No, I leave that to *you* — it's the good turn you've done me!" cried the young man with hot tears in his eyes.

She stared, aghast with the perception that there was some dreadful thing she did n't know; but he walked on, dropping the question angrily and turning his back to her as if he could n't trust himself. She read his disgust in his averted face, in the way he squared his shoulders and smote the ground with his stick, and she hurried after him and presently overtook him. She kept by him for a moment in silence; then she broke out: "What do you mean? What in the world have I done to you?"

"She would have helped me. She was all ready to help me," Godfrey portentously said.

"Helped you in what?" She wondered what he meant; if he had made debts that he was afraid to confess to his father and — of all horrible things — had been looking to Mrs. Churchley to pay. She turned red with the mere apprehension of this and, on the heels of her guess, exulted again at having perhaps averted such a shame.

"Can't you just see I'm in trouble? Where are your eyes, your senses, your sympathy, that you talk so much about? Have n't you seen these six months that I've a curst worry in my life?"

She seized his arm, made him stop, stood looking up at him like a frightened little girl. "What's the matter, Godfrey? — what *is* the matter?"

"You've gone against me so — I could strangle you!" he growled. This image added nothing to her dread; her dread was that he had done some wrong, was stained with some guilt. She uttered it to him with clasped hands, begging him to tell her the worst; but, still more passionately, he cut her short with his

287

own cry: "In God's name, satisfy me! What infernal thing did you do?"

"It was n't infernal — it was right. I told her mamma had been wretched," said Adela.

"Wretched? You told her such a lie?"

"It was the only way, and she believed me."

"Wretched how? — wretched when? — wretched where?" the young man stammered.

"I told her papa had made her so, and that *she* ought to know it. I told her the question troubled me unspeakably, but that I had made up my mind it was my duty to initiate her." Adela paused, the light of bravado in her face, as if, though struck while the words came with the monstrosity of what she had done, she was incapable of abating a jot of it. "I notified her that he had faults and peculiarities that made mamma's life a long worry — a martyrdom that she hid wonderfully from the world, but that we saw and that I had often pitied. I told her what they were, these faults and peculiarities; I put the dots on the *i*'s. I said it was n't fair to let another person marry him without a warning. I warned her; I satisfied my conscience. She could do as she liked. My responsibility was over."

Godfrey gazed at her; he listened with parted lips, incredulous and appalled. "You invented such a tissue of falsities and calumnies, and you talk about your conscience? You stand there in your senses and proclaim your crime?"

"I'd have committed any crime that would have rescued us."

"You insult and blacken and ruin your own father?" Godfrey kept on.

"He'll never know it; she took a vow she would n't tell him."

"Ah I'll be damned if *I* won't tell him!" he rang out.

Adela felt sick at this, but she flamed up to resent the treachery, as it struck her, of such a menace. "I did right — I did right!" she vehemently declared. "I went down on my knees to pray for guidance, and I saved mamma's memory from outrage. But if I had n't, if I had n't" — she faltered an instant — "I'm not worse than you, and I'm not so bad, for you've done something that you're ashamed to tell me."

He had taken out his watch; he looked at it with quick intensity, as if not hearing nor heeding her. Then, his calculating eyes raised, he fixed her long enough to exclaim with unsurpassable horror and contempt: "You raving maniac!" He turned away from her; he bounded down the avenue in the direction from which they had come, and, while she watched him, strode away, across the grass, toward the short cut to the station.

IV

His bags, by the time she got home, had been brought to the house, but Beatrice and Muriel, immediately informed of this, waited for their brother in vain. Their sister said nothing to them of her having seen him, and she accepted after a little, with a calmness that surprised herself, the idea that he had returned to town to denounce her. She believed this would make no difference now — she had done what she had done. She had somehow a stiff faith in Mrs. Churchley. Once that so considerable mass had received its impetus it would n't, it could n't pull up. It represented a heavy-footed person, incapable of further agility. Adela recognised too how well it might have come over her that there were too many children. Lastly the girl fortified herself with the reflexion, grotesque in the conditions and conducing to prove her sense of humour not high, that her father was after all not a man to be played with. It seemed to her at any rate that if she *had* baffled his unholy purpose she could bear anything — bear imprisonment and bread and water, bear lashes and torture, bear even his lifelong reproach. What she could bear least was the wonder of the inconvenience she had inflicted on Godfrey. She had time to turn this over, very vainly, for a succession of days — days more numerous than she had expected, which passed without bringing her from London any summons to come up and take her punishment. She sounded the possible, she compared the degrees of the probable; feeling however that as a cloistered girl she was poorly equipped for speculation. She tried to imagine the calamitous things young men might do, and could only feel that such things would naturally be connected either with borrowed money or with bad women. She became conscious that after all she knew almost nothing about either of those interests. The worst woman she knew was Mrs. Churchley herself. Meanwhile there was no reverberation from Seymour Street — only a sultry silence.

At Brinton she spent hours in her mother's garden, where she had grown up, where she considered that she was training for old age, since she meant not to depend on whist. She loved the place as, had she been a good Catholic, she would have loved the smell of her parish church; and indeed there was in her passion for flowers something of the respect of a religion. They seemed to her the only things in the world that really respected themselves, unless one made an exception for Nutkins, who had been in command all through her mother's time, with whom she had had a real friendship and who had been affected by their pure example. He was the person left in the world with whom on the whole she could speak most intimately of the dead. They never had to name her together — they only said "she"; and Nutkins freely conceded that she had taught him everything he knew. When Beatrice and Muriel said "she" they referred to Mrs. Churchley. Adela had reason to believe she should never marry, and that some day she should have about a thousand a year. This made her see in the far future a little garden of her own, under a hill, full of rare and exquisite things, where she would spend most of her old age on her knees with an apron and stout gloves, with a pair of shears and a trowel, steeped in the comfort of being thought mad.

One morning ten days after her scene with Godfrey, on coming back into the house shortly before lunch, she was met by Miss Flynn with the notification that a lady in the drawing-room had been waiting for her for some minutes. "A lady" suggested immediately Mrs. Churchley. It came over Adela that the form in which her penalty was to descend would be a personal explanation with that misdirected woman. The lady had given no name, and Miss Flynn had n't seen Mrs. Churchley; nevertheless the governess was certain Adela's surmise was wrong.

"Is she big and dreadful?" the girl asked.

Miss Flynn, who was circumspection itself, took her time. "She's dreadful, but she's not big." She added that she was n't sure she ought to let Adela go in alone; but this young lady took herself throughout for a heroine, and it was n't in a heroine to shrink from any encounter. Was n't she every instant in transcendent contact with her mother? The visitor might have no connexion whatever with the drama of her father's frustrated marriage; but everything to-day for Adela was part of that.

Miss Flynn's description had prepared her for a considerable shock, but she was n't agitated by her first glimpse of the person who awaited her. A youngish well-dressed woman stood there, and silence was between them while they looked at each other. Before either had spoken however Adela began to see what Miss Flynn had intended. In the light of the drawing-room window the lady was five-and-thirty years of age and had vivid yellow hair. She also had a blue cloth suit with brass buttons, a stick-up collar like a gentleman's, a necktie arranged in a sailor's knot, a golden pin in the shape of a little lawn-tennis racket, and pearl-grey gloves with big black stitchings. Adela's second impression was that she was an actress, and her third that no such person had ever before crossed that threshold.

"I'll tell you what I've come for," said the apparition. "I've come to ask you to intercede." She wasn't an actress; an actress would have had a nicer voice.

"To intercede?" Adela was too bewildered to ask her to sit down.

"With your father, you know. He does n't know, but he'll have to." Her "have" sounded like "'ave." She explained, with many more such sounds, that she was Mrs. Godfrey, that they had been married seven mortal months. If Godfrey was going abroad she must go with him, and the only way she could go with him would be for his father to do something. He was afraid of his father — that was clear; he was afraid even to tell him. What she had come down for was to see some other member of the family face to face — "fice to fice" Mrs. Godfrey called it — and try if he could n't be approached by another side. If no one else would act then she would just have to act herself. The Colonel would have to do something — that was the only way out of it.

293

What really happened Adela never quite understood; what seemed to be happening was that the room went round and round. Through the blur of perception accompanying this effect the sharp stabs of her visitor's revelation came to her like the words heard by a patient "going off" under ether. She afterwards denied passionately even to herself that she had done anything so abject as to faint; but there was a lapse in her consciousness on the score of Miss Flynn's intervention. This intervention had evidently been active, for when they talked the matter over, later in the day, with bated breath and infinite dissimulation for the school-room quarter, the governess had more lurid truths, and still more, to impart than to receive. She was at any rate under the impression that she had athletically contended, in the drawing-room, with the yellow hair — this after removing Adela from the scene and before inducing Mrs. Godfrey to withdraw. Miss Flynn had never known a more thrilling day, for all the rest of it too was pervaded with agitations and conversations, precautions and alarms. It was given out to Beatrice and Muriel that their sister had been taken suddenly ill, and the governess ministered to her in her room. Indeed Adela had never found herself less at ease, for this time she had received a blow that she could n't return. There was nothing to do but to take it, to endure the humiliation of her wound.

At first she declined to take it — having, as might appear, the much more attractive resource of regarding her visitant as a mere masquerading person, an impudent impostor. On the face of the matter moreover it was n't fair to believe till one heard; and to hear in such a case was to hear Godfrey himself. Whatever she had tried to imagine about him she had n't arrived at anything so belittling as an idiotic secret marriage with a dyed and painted hag. Adela repeated this last word as if it gave her comfort; and indeed where everything was so bad fifteen years of seniority made the case little worse. Miss Flynn was portentous, for Miss Flynn had had it out with the wretch. She had cross-questioned her and had not broken her down. This was the most uplifted hour of Miss Flynn's life; for whereas she usually had to content herself with being humbly and gloomily in the right she could now be magnanimously and showily so. Her only perplexity was as to what she ought to do — write to Colonel Chart or go up to town to see him. She bloomed with alternatives — she resembled some dull garden-path which under a copious downpour has begun to flaunt with colour. Toward evening Adela was obliged to recognise that her brother's worry, of which he had spoken to her, had appeared bad enough to consist even of a low wife, and to remember that, so far from its being inconceivable a young man in his position should clandestinely take one, she had been present, years before, during her mother's lifetime, when Lady Molesley declared gaily, over a cup of tea, that this was precisely what she expected of her eldest son. The next morning it was the worst possibilities that seemed clearest; the only thing left with a tatter of dusky comfort being the ambiguity of Godfrey's charge that her own action had "done" for him. That was a matter by itself, and she racked her brains for a connecting link between Mrs. Churchley and

295

Mrs. Godfrey. At last she made up her mind that they were related by blood; very likely, though differing in fortune, they were cousins or even sisters. But even then what did the wretched boy mean?

Arrested by the unnatural fascination of opportunity, Miss Flynn received before lunch a telegram from Colonel Chart — an order for dinner and a vehicle; he and Godfrey were to arrive at six o'clock. Adela had plenty of occupation for the interval, since she was pitying her father when she was n't rejoicing that her mother had gone too soon to know. She flattered herself she made out the providential reason of that cruelty now. She found time however still to wonder for what purpose, given the situation, Godfrey was to be brought down. She was n't unconscious indeed that she had little general knowledge of what usually was done with young men in that predicament. One talked about the situation, but the situation was an abyss. She felt this still more when she found, on her father's arrival, that nothing apparently was to happen as she had taken for granted it would. There was an inviolable hush over the whole affair, but no tragedy, no publicity, nothing ugly. The tragedy had been in town — the faces of the two men spoke of it in spite of their other perfunctory aspects; and at present there was only a family dinner, with Beatrice and Muriel and the governess — with almost a company tone too, the result of the desire to avoid publicity. Adela admired her father; she knew what he was feeling if Mrs. Godfrey had been at him, and yet she saw him positively gallant. He was mildly austere, or rather even — what was it? — august; just as, coldly equivocal, he never looked at his son, so that at moments he struck her as almost sick with sadness. Godfrey was equally inscrutable and therefore wholly different from what he had been as he stood before her in the park. If he was to start on his career (with such a wife! — would n't she utterly blight it?) he was already professional enough to know how to wear a mask.

Before they rose from table she felt herself wholly bewildered, so little were such large causes traceable in their effects. She had nerved herself for a great ordeal, but the air was as sweet as an anodyne. It was perfectly plain to her that her father was deadly sore — as pathetic as a person betrayed. He was broken, but he showed no resentment; there was a weight on his heart, but he had lightened it by dressing as immaculately as usual for dinner. She asked herself what immensity of a row there could have been in town to have left his anger so spent. He went through everything, even to sitting with his son after dinner. When they came out together he invited Beatrice and Muriel to the billiard-room, and as Miss Flynn discreetly withdrew Adela was left alone with Godfrey, who was completely changed and not now in the least of a rage. He was broken too, but not so pathetic as his father. He was only very correct and apologetic; he said to his sister: "I'm awfully sorry *you* were annoyed — it was something I never dreamed of."

She could n't think immediately what he meant; then she grasped the reference to her extraordinary invader. She was uncertain, however, what tone to take; perhaps his father had arranged with him that

297

they were to make the best of it. But she spoke her own despair in the way she murmured "Oh Godfrey, Godfrey, is it true?"

"I've been the most unutterable donkey — you can say what you like to me. You can't say anything worse than I've said to myself."

"My brother, my brother!"—his words made her wail it out. He hushed her with a movement and she asked: "What has father said?"

He looked very high over her head. "He'll give her six hundred a year."

"Ah the angel!" — it was too splendid.

"On condition" — Godfrey scarce blinked — "she never comes near me. She has solemnly promised, and she'll probably leave me alone to get the money. If she does n't — in diplomacy — I'm lost." He had been turning his eyes vaguely about, this way and that, to avoid meeting hers; but after another instant he gave up the effort and she had the miserable confession of his glance. "I've been living in hell."

"My brother, my brother!" she yearningly repeated.

"I'm not an idiot; yet for her I've behaved like one. Don't ask me — you must n't know. It was all done in a day, and since then fancy my condition; fancy my work in such a torment; fancy my coming through at all."

"Thank God you passed!" she cried. "You were wonderful!"

"I'd have shot myself if I had n't been. I had an awful day yesterday with the governor; it was late at night before it was over. I leave England next

week. He brought me down here for it to look well —
so that the children shan't know."

"*He's* wonderful too!" Adela murmured.

"Wonderful too!" Godfrey echoed.

"Did *she* tell him?" the girl went on.

"She came straight to Seymour Street from here.
She saw him alone first; then he called me in. *That*
luxury lasted about an hour."

"Poor, poor father!" Adela moaned at this; on
which her brother remained silent. Then after he had
alluded to it as the scene he had lived in terror of all
through his cramming, and she had sighed forth again
her pity and admiration for such a mixture of anxie-
ties and such a triumph of talent, she pursued: "Have
you told him?"

"Told him what?"

"What you said you would — what *I* did."

Godfrey turned away as if at present he had very
little interest in that inferior tribulation. "I was angry
with you, but I cooled off. I held my tongue."

She clasped her hands. "You thought of mamma!"

"Oh don't speak of mamma!" he cried as in rueful
tenderness.

It was indeed not a happy moment, and she murmured: "No; if you *had* thought of her —!"

This made Godfrey face her again with a small
flare in his eyes. "Oh *then* it did n't prevent. I
thought that woman really good. I believed in
her."

"Is she *very* bad?"

"I shall never mention her to you again," he returned with dignity.

299

"You may believe *I* won't speak of her! So father does n't know?" the girl added.

"Does n't know what?"

"That I said what I did to Mrs. Churchley."

He had a momentary pause. "I don't think so, but you must find out for yourself."

"I shall find out," said Adela. "But what had Mrs. Churchley to do with it?"

"With *my* misery? I told her. I had to tell some one."

"Why did n't you tell me?"

He appeared — though but after an instant — to know exactly why. "Oh you take things so beastly hard — you make such rows." Adela covered her face with her hands and he went on: "What I wanted was comfort — not to be lashed up. I thought I should go mad. I wanted Mrs. Churchley to break it to father, to intercede for me and help him to meet it. She was awfully kind to me, she listened and she understood; she could fancy how it had happened. Without her I should n't have pulled through. She liked me, you know," he further explained, and as if it were quite worth mentioning — all the more that it was pleasant to him. "She said she'd do what she could for me. She was full of sympathy and re-source. I really leaned on her. But when *you* cut in of course it spoiled everything. That's why I was so furious with you. She could n't do anything then."

Adela dropped her hands, staring; she felt she had walked in darkness. "So that he had to meet it alone?"

"Dame!" said Godfrey, who had got up his French tremendously.

Muriel came to the door to say papa wished the two others to join them, and the next day Godfrey returned to town. His father remained at Brinton, without an intermission, the rest of the summer and the whole of the autumn, and Adela had a chance to find out, as she had said, whether he knew she had interfered. But in spite of her chance she never found out. He knew Mrs. Churchley had thrown him over and he knew his daughter rejoiced in it, but he appeared not to have divined the relation between the two facts. It was strange that one of the matters he was clearest about — Adela's secret triumph — should have been just the thing which from this time on justified less and less such a confidence. She was too sorry for him to be consistently glad. She watched his attempts to wind himself up on the subject of shorthorns and drainage, and she favoured to the utmost of her ability his intermittent disposition to make a figure in orchids. She wondered whether they might n't have a few people at Brinton; but when she mentioned the idea he asked what in the world there would be to attract them. It was a confoundedly stupid house, he remarked — with all respect to *her* cleverness. Beatrice and Muriel were mystified; the prospect of going out immensely had faded so utterly away. They were apparently not to go out at all. Colonel Chart was aimless and bored; he paced up and down and went back to smoking, which was bad for him, and looked drearily out of windows as if on the bare chance that something might arrive. Did he expect Mrs. Churchley to arrive, did he expect her to relent on finding she could n't live without him ? It was Adela's belief that she gave no sign. But the girl thought it really remarkable of her not to have betrayed her ingenious young visitor. Adela's judgement of human nature was perhaps harsh, but she believed that most women, given the various facts, would n't have been so forbearing. This lady's conception of the point of honour placed her there in a finer and purer light than had at all originally promised to shine about her.

She meanwhile herself could well judge how heavy her father found the burden of Godfrey's folly and how he was incommoded at having to pay the horrible woman six hundred a year. Doubtless he was having dreadful letters from her; doubtless she threatened them all with hideous exposure. If the matter should be bruited Godfrey's prospects would collapse on the spot. He thought Madrid very charming and curious, but Mrs. Godfrey was in England, so that his father had to face the music. Adela took a dolorous comfort in her mother's being out of *that* — it would have killed her; but this did n't blind her to the fact that the comfort for her father would perhaps have been greater if he had had some one to talk to about his trouble. He never dreamed of doing so to her, and she felt she could n't ask him. In the family life he wanted utter silence about it. Early in the winter he went abroad for ten weeks, leaving her with her sisters in the country, where it was not to be denied that at this time existence had very little savour. She half-expected her sister-in-law would again descend

on her; but the fear was n't justified, and the quiet-
ude of the awful creature seemed really to vibrate
with the ring of gold-pieces. There were sure to be
extras. Adela winced at the extras. Colonel Chart
went to Paris and to Monte Carlo and then to Madrid
to see his boy. His daughter had the vision of his
perhaps meeting Mrs. Churchley somewhere, since,
if she had gone for a year, she would still be on the
Continent. If he should meet her perhaps the affair
would come on again: she caught herself musing over
this. But he brought back no such appearance, and,
seeing him after an interval, she was struck afresh
with his jilted and wasted air. She did n't like it —
she resented it. A little more and she would have said
that that was no way to treat so faithful a man.

They all went up to town in March, and on one of
the first days of April she saw Mrs. Churchley in the
Park. She herself remained apparently invisible to
that lady — she herself and Beatrice and Muriel,
who sat with her in their mother's old bottle-green
landau. Mrs. Churchley, perched higher than ever,
rode by without a recognition; but this did n't prevent
Adela's going to her before the month was over. As
on her great previous occasion she went in the morning, and she again had the good fortune to be admitted. This time, however, her visit was shorter,
and a week after making it — the week was a desolation — she addressed to her brother at Madrid
a letter containing these words: "I could endure it
no longer — I confessed and retracted; I explained
to her as well as I could the falsity of what I said
to her ten months ago and the benighted purity of

303

my motives for saying it. I besought her to regard it as unsaid, to forgive me, not to despise me too much, to take pity on poor *perfect* papa and come back to him. She was more good-natured than you might have expected — indeed she laughed extravagantly. She had never believed me — it was too absurd; she had only, at the time, disliked me. She found me utterly false — she was very frank with me about this — and she told papa she really thought me horrid. She said she could never live with such a girl, and as I would certainly never marry I must be sent away — in short she quite loathed me. Papa defended me, he refused to sacrifice me, and this led practically to their rupture. Papa gave her up, as it were, for *me*. Fancy the angel, and fancy what I must try to be to him for the rest of his life! Mrs. Churchley can never come back — she's going to marry Lord Dovedale."

THE REAL THING

THE REAL THING

I

WHEN the porter's wife, who used to answer the house-bell, announced "A gentleman and a lady, sir," I had, as I often had in those days — the wish being father to the thought — an immediate vision of sitters. Sitters my visitors in this case proved to be; but not in the sense I should have preferred. There was nothing at first however to indicate that they might n't have come for a portrait. The gentleman, a man of fifty, very high and very straight, with a moustache slightly grizzled and a dark grey walking-coat admirably fitted, both of which I noted professionally — I don't mean as a barber or yet as a tailor — would have struck me as a celebrity if celebrities often were striking. It was a truth of which I had for some time been conscious that a figure with a good deal of frontage was, as one might say, almost never a public institution. A glance at the lady helped to remind me of this paradoxical law: she also looked too distinguished to be a "personality." Moreover one would scarcely come across two variations together.

Neither of the pair immediately spoke — they only prolonged the preliminary gaze suggesting that each wished to give the other a chance. They were visibly shy; they stood there letting me take them in — which, as I afterwards perceived, was the most practical thing they could have done. In this way their embarrassment served their cause. I had seen people painfully reluctant to mention that they desired anything so gross as to be represented on canvas; but the scruples of my new friends appeared almost insurmountable. Yet the gentleman might have said "I should like a portrait of my wife," and the lady might have said "I should like a portrait of my husband." Perhaps they were n't husband and wife — this naturally would make the matter more delicate. Perhaps they wished to be done together — in which case they ought to have brought a third person to break the news.

"We come from Mr. Rivet," the lady finally said with a dim smile that had the effect of a moist sponge passed over a "sunk" piece of painting, as well as of a vague allusion to vanished beauty. She was as tall and straight, in her degree, as her companion, and with ten years less to carry. She looked as sad as a woman could look whose face was not charged with expression; that is her tinted oval mask showed waste as an exposed surface shows friction. The hand of time had played over her freely, but to an effect of elimination. She was slim and stiff, and so well-dressed, in dark blue cloth, with lappets and pockets and buttons, that it was clear she employed the same tailor as her husband. The couple had an indefinable air of prosperous thrift — they evidently got a good deal of luxury for their money. If I was to be one of their luxuries it would behove me to consider my terms.

"Ah Claude Rivet recommended me?" I echoed;

and I added that it was very kind of him, though I could reflect that, as he only painted landscape, this was n't a sacrifice.

The lady looked very hard at the gentleman, and the gentleman looked round the room. Then staring at the floor a moment and stroking his moustache, he rested his pleasant eyes on me with the remark: "He said you were the right one."

"I try to be, when people want to sit."

"Yes, we should like to," said the lady anxiously.

"Do you mean together?"

My visitors exchanged a glance. "If you could do anything with *me* I suppose it would be double," the gentleman stammered.

"Oh yes, there's naturally a higher charge for two figures than for one."

"We should like to make it pay," the husband confessed.

"That's very good of you," I returned, appreciating so unwonted a sympathy — for I supposed he meant pay the artist.

A sense of strangeness seemed to dawn on the lady. "We mean for the illustrations — Mr. Rivet said you might put one in."

"Put in — an illustration?" I was equally confused.

"Sketch her off, you know," said the gentleman, colouring.

It was only then that I understood the service Claude Rivet had rendered me; he had told them how I worked in black-and-white, for magazines, for story-books, for sketches of contemporary life, and consequently had copious employment for models. These things were true, but it was not less true — I may confess it now; whether because the aspiration was to lead to everything or to nothing I leave the reader to guess — that I could n't get the honours, to say nothing of the emoluments, of a great painter of portraits out of my head. My "illustrations" were my pot-boilers; I looked to a different branch of art — far and away the most interesting it had always seemed to me — to perpetuate my fame. There was no shame in looking to it also to make my fortune; but that fortune was by so much further from being made from the moment my visitors wished to be "done" for nothing. I was disappointed; for in the pictorial sense I had immediately *seen* them. I had seized their type — I had already settled what I would do with it. Something that would n't absolutely have pleased them, I afterwards reflected.

"Ah you 're — you 're — a — ?" I began as soon as I had mastered my surprise. I could n't bring out the dingy word "models" : it seemed so little to fit the case.

"We have n't had much practice," said the lady.

"We 've got to *do* something, and we 've thought that an artist in your line might perhaps make something of us," her husband threw off. He further mentioned that they did n't know many artists and that they had gone first, on the off-chance — he painted views of course, but sometimes put in figures; perhaps I remembered — to Mr. Rivet, whom they had met a few years before at a place in Norfolk where he was sketching.

310

"We used to sketch a little ourselves," the lady hinted.

"It's very awkward, but we absolutely *must* do something," her husband went on.

"Of course we're not so *very* young," she admitted with a wan smile.

With the remark that I might as well know something more about them the husband had handed me a card extracted from a neat new pocket-book — their appurtenances were all of the freshest — and inscribed with the words "Major Monarch." Impressive as these words were they didn't carry my knowledge much further; but my visitor presently added: "I've left the army and we've had the misfortune to lose our money. In fact our means are dreadfully small."

"It's awfully trying — a regular strain," said Mrs. Monarch.

They evidently wished to be discreet — to take care not to swagger because they were gentlefolk. I felt them willing to recognise this as something of a drawback, at the same time that I guessed at an underlying sense — their consolation in adversity — that they *had* their points. They certainly had; but these advantages struck me as preponderantly social; such for instance as would help to make a drawing-room look well. However, a drawing-room was always, or ought to be, a picture.

In consequence of his wife's allusion to their age Major Monarch observed: "Naturally it's more for the figure that we thought of going in. We can still hold ourselves up." On the instant I saw that the figure was indeed their strong point. His "naturally" did n't sound vain, but it lighted up the question. "*She* has the best one," he continued, nodding at his wife with a pleasant after-dinner absence of circumlocution. I could only reply, as if we were in fact sitting over our wine, that this did n't prevent his own from being very good; which led him in turn to make answer: "We thought that if you ever have to do people like us we might be something like it. *She* particularly — for a lady in a book, you know."

I was so amused by them that, to get more of it, I did my best to take their point of view; and though it was an embarrassment to find myself appraising physically, as if they were animals on hire or useful blacks, a pair whom I should have expected to meet only in one of the relations in which criticism is tacit, I looked at Mrs. Monarch judicially enough to be able to exclaim after a moment with conviction: "Oh yes, a lady in a book!" She was singularly like a bad illustration.

"We 'll stand up, if you like," said the Major; and he raised himself before me with a really grand air.

I could take his measure at a glance — he was six feet two and a perfect gentleman. It would have paid any club in process of formation and in want of a stamp to engage him at a salary to stand in the principal window. What struck me at once was that in coming to me they had rather missed their vocation; they could surely have been turned to better account for advertising purposes. I could n't of course see the thing in detail, but I could see them make somebody's fortune — I don't mean their own. There was something in them for a waistcoat-maker, an hotel-keeper or a soap-vendor. I could imagine "We always use it" pinned on their bosoms with the greatest effect; I had a vision of the brilliancy with which they would launch a table d'hôte.

Mrs. Monarch sat still, not from pride but from shyness, and presently her husband said to her: "Get up, my dear, and show how smart you are." She obeyed, but she had no need to get up to show it. She walked to the end of the studio and then came back blushing, her fluttered eyes on the partner of her appeal. I was reminded of an incident I had accidentally had a glimpse of in Paris — being with a friend there, a dramatist about to produce a play, when an actress came to him to ask to be entrusted with a part. She went through her paces before him, walked up and down as Mrs. Monarch was doing. Mrs. Monarch did it quite as well, but I abstained from applauding. It was very odd to see such people apply for such poor pay. She looked as if she had ten thousand a year. Her husband had used the word that described her: she was in the London current jargon essentially and typically "smart." Her figure was, in the same order of ideas, conspicuously and irreproachably "good." For a woman of her age her waist was surprisingly small; her elbow moreover had the orthodox crook. She held her head at the conventional angle, but why did she come to *me*? She ought to have tried on jackets at a big shop. I feared my visitors were not only destitute but "artistic" — which would be a great complication. When she sat down again I thanked her, observing that what a draughtsman most valued in his model was the faculty of keeping quiet.

"Oh *she* can keep quiet," said Major Monarch. Then he added jocosely: "I've always kept her quiet."

"I'm not a nasty fidget, am I?" It was going to wring tears from me, I felt, the way she hid her head, ostrich-like, in the other broad bosom.

The owner of this expanse addressed his answer to me. "Perhaps it isn't out of place to mention — because we ought to be quite business-like, ought n't we? — that when I married her she was known as the Beautiful Statue."

"Oh dear!" said Mrs. Monarch ruefully.

"Of course I should want a certain amount of expression," I rejoined.

"Of *course!*" — and I had never heard such unanimity.

"And then I suppose you know that you'll get awfully tired."

"Oh we *never* get tired!" they eagerly cried.

"Have you had any kind of practice?"

They hesitated — they looked at each other. "We've been photographed — *immensely*," said Mrs. Monarch.

"She means the fellows have asked us themselves," added the Major.

"I see — because you're so good-looking."

"I don't know what they thought, but they were always after us."

"We always got our photographs for nothing," smiled Mrs. Monarch.

"We might have brought some, my dear," her husband remarked.

314

"I'm not sure we have any left. We've given quantities away," she explained to me.

"With our autographs and that sort of thing," said the Major.

"Are they to be got in the shops?" I enquired as a harmless pleasantry.

"Oh yes, *hers* — they used to be."

"Not now," said Mrs. Monarch with her eyes on the floor.

II

I COULD fancy the "sort of thing" they put on the presentation copies of their photographs, and I was sure they wrote a beautiful hand. It was odd how quickly I was sure of everything that concerned them. If they were now so poor as to have to earn shillings and pence they could never have had much of a margin. Their good looks had been their capital, and they had good-humouredly made the most of the career that this resource marked out for them. It was in their faces, the blankness, the deep intellectual repose of the twenty years of country-house visiting that had given them pleasant intonations. I could see the sunny drawing-rooms, sprinkled with periodicals she did n't read, in which Mrs. Monarch had continuously sat; I could see the wet shrubberies in which she had walked, equipped to admiration for either exercise. I could see the rich covers the Major had helped to shoot and the wonderful garments in which, late at night, he repaired to the smoking-room to talk about them. I could imagine their leggings and waterproofs, their knowing tweeds and rugs, their rolls of sticks and cases of tackle and neat umbrellas; and I could evoke the exact appearance of their servants and the compact variety of their luggage on the platforms of country stations.

They gave small tips, but they were liked; they did n't do anything themselves, but they were welcome. They looked so well everywhere; they gratified

the general relish for stature, complexion and "form."
They knew it without fatuity or vulgarity, and they
respected themselves in consequence. They were n't
superficial; they were thorough and kept themselves
up — it had been their line. People with such a taste
for activity had to have some line. I could feel how
even in a dull house they could have been counted on
for the joy of life. At present something had happened
— it did n't matter what, their little income had grown
less, it had grown least — and they had to do something for pocket-money. Their friends could like
them, I made out, without liking to support them.
There was something about them that represented
credit — their clothes, their manners, their type; but
if credit is a large empty pocket in which an occasional
chink reverberates, the chink at least must be audible.
What they wanted of me was to help to make it so.
Fortunately they had no children — I soon divined
that. They would also perhaps wish our relations to
be kept secret: this was why it was "for the figure"
— the reproduction of the face would betray them.

I liked them — I felt, quite as their friends must have
done — they were so simple; and I had no objection
to them if they would suit. But somehow with all their
perfections I did n't easily believe in them. After all
they were amateurs, and the ruling passion of my life
was the detestation of the amateur. Combined with
this was another perversity — an innate preference
for the represented subject over the real one: the defect
of the real one was so apt to be a lack of representation. I liked things that appeared; then one was sure.
Whether they *were* or not was a subordinate and

almost always a profitless question. There were other considerations, the first of which was that I already had two or three recruits in use, notably a young person with big feet, in alpaca, from Kilburn, who for a couple of years had come to me regularly for my illustrations and with whom I was still — perhaps ignobly — satisfied. I frankly explained to my visitors how the case stood, but they had taken more precautions than I supposed. They had reasoned out their opportunity, for Claude Rivet had told them of the projected *édition de luxe* of one of the writers of our day — the rarest of the novelists — who, long neglected by the multitudinous vulgar and dearly prized by the attentive (need I mention Philip Vincent?) had had the happy fortune of seeing, late in life, the dawn and then the full light of a higher criticism; an estimate in which on the part of the public there was something really of expiation. The edition preparing, planned by a publisher of taste, was practically an act of high reparation; the wood-cuts with which it was to be enriched were the homage of English art to one of the most independent representatives of English letters. Major and Mrs. Monarch confessed to me they had hoped I might be able to work *them* into my branch of the enterprise. They knew I was to do the first of the books, "Rutland Ramsay," but I had to make clear to them that my participation in the rest of the affair— this first book was to be a test — must depend on the satisfaction I should give. If this should be limited my employers would drop me with scarce common forms. It was therefore a crisis for me, and naturally I was making special preparations, looking about for

318

new people, should they be necessary, and securing the best types. I admitted however that I should like to settle down to two or three good models who would do for everything.

"Should we have often to — a — put on special clothes?" Mrs. Monarch timidly demanded.

"Dear yes — that's half the business."

"And should we be expected to supply our own costumes?"

"Oh no; I've got a lot of things. A painter's models put on — or put off — anything he likes."

"And you mean — a — the same?"

"The same?"

Mrs. Monarch looked at her husband again.

"Oh she was just wondering," he explained, "if the costumes are in *general* use." I had to confess that they were, and I mentioned further that some of them — I had a lot of genuine greasy last-century things — had served their time, a hundred years ago, on living world-stained men and women; on figures not perhaps so far removed, in that vanished world, from *their* type, the Monarchs', *quoi!* of a breeched and be-wigged age. "We'll put on anything that *fits*," said the Major.

"Oh I arrange that — they fit in the pictures."

"I'm afraid I should do better for the modern books. I'd come as you like," said Mrs. Monarch.

"She has got a lot of clothes at home: they might do for contemporary life," her husband continued.

"Oh I can fancy scenes in which you'd be quite natural." And indeed I could see the slipshod rear-rangements of stale properties — the stories I tried to

produce pictures for without the exasperation of reading them — whose sandy tracts the good lady might
help to people. But I had to return to the fact that for
this sort of work — the daily mechanical grind — I
was already equipped : the people I was working with
were fully adequate.

"We only thought we might be more like *some*
characters," said Mrs. Monarch mildly, getting up.

Her husband also rose; he stood looking at me with
a dim wistfulness that was touching in so fine a man.
"Would n't it be rather a pull sometimes to have —
a — to have — ?" He hung fire; he wanted me to
help him by phrasing what he meant. But I could n't
— I did n't know. So he brought it out awkwardly:
"The *real* thing; a gentleman, you know, or a lady."
I was quite ready to give a general assent — I admitted
that there was a great deal in that. This encouraged
Major Monarch to say, following up his appeal with
an unacted gulp: "It's awfully hard — we've tried
everything." The gulp was communicative; it proved
too much for his wife. Before I knew it Mrs. Monarch
had dropped again upon a divan and burst into tears.
Her husband sat down beside her, holding one of her
hands; whereupon she quickly dried her eyes with the
other, while I felt embarrassed as she looked up at me.
"There is n't a confounded job I have n't applied for
— waited for — prayed for. You can fancy we'd be
pretty bad first. Secretaryships and that sort of thing ?
You might as well ask for a peerage. I'd be *anything*
— I'm strong; a messenger or a coalheaver. I'd put
on a gold-laced cap and open carriage-doors in front of
the haberdasher's; I'd hang about a station to carry

portmanteaux; I'd be a postman. But they won't *look* at you; there are thousands as good as yourself already on the ground. *Gentlemen*, poor beggars, who've drunk their wine, who've kept their hunters!"

I was as reassuring as I knew how to be, and my visitors were presently on their feet again while, for the experiment, we agreed on an hour. We were discussing it when the door opened and Miss Churm came in with a wet umbrella. Miss Churm had to take the omnibus to Maida Vale and then walk half a mile. She looked a trifle blowsy and slightly splashed. I scarcely ever saw her come in without thinking afresh how odd it was that, being so little in herself, she should yet be so much in others. She was a meagre little Miss Churm, but was such an ample heroine of romance. She was only a freckled cockney, but she could represent everything, from a fine lady to a shepherdess; she had the faculty as she might have had a fine voice or long hair. She couldn't spell and she loved beer, but she had two or three "points," and practice, and a knack, and mother-wit, and a whimsical sensibility, and a love of the theatre, and seven sisters, and not an ounce of respect, especially for the *h*. The first thing my visitors saw was that her umbrella was wet, and in their spotless perfection they visibly winced at it. The rain had come on since their arrival.

"I'm all in a soak; there *was* a mess of people in the 'bus. I wish you lived near a styion," said Miss Churm. I requested her to get ready as quickly as possible, and she passed into the room in which she always changed her dress. But before going out she asked me what she was to get into this time.

"It's the Russian princess, don't you know?" I answered; "the one with the 'golden eyes,' in black velvet, for the long thing in the *Cheapside*."

"Golden eyes? I *say!*" cried Miss Churm, while my companions watched her with intensity as she withdrew. She always arranged herself, when she was late, before I could turn round; and I kept my visitors a little on purpose, so that they might get an idea, from seeing her, what would be expected of themselves. I mentioned that she was quite my notion of an excellent model — she was really very clever.

"Do you think she looks like a Russian princess?" Major Monarch asked with lurking alarm.

"When I make her, yes."

"Oh if you have to *make* her —!" he reasoned, not without point.

"That's the most you can ask. There are so many who are not makeable."

"Well now, *here's* a lady" — and with a persuasive smile he passed his arm into his wife's — "who's already made!"

"Oh I'm not a Russian princess," Mrs. Monarch protested a little coldly. I could see she had known some and did n't like them. There at once was a complication of a kind I never had to fear with Miss Churm.

This young lady came back in black velvet — the gown was rather rusty and very low on her lean shoulders — and with a Japanese fan in her red hands. I reminded her that in the scene I was doing she had to look over some one's head. "I forget whose it is; but it does n't matter. Just look over a head."

322

"I'd rather look over a stove," said Miss Churm; and she took her station near the fire. She fell into position, settled herself into a tall attitude, gave a certain backward inclination to her head and a certain forward droop to her fan, and looked, at least to my prejudiced sense, distinguished and charming, foreign and dangerous. We left her looking so while I went downstairs with Major and Mrs. Monarch.

"I believe I could come about as near it as that," said Mrs. Monarch.

"Oh you think she's shabby, but you must allow for the alchemy of art."

However, they went off with an evident increase of comfort founded on their demonstrable advantage in being the real thing. I could fancy them shuddering over Miss Churm. She was very droll about them when I went back, for I told her what they wanted.

"Well, if *she* can sit I'll tyke to bookkeeping," said my model.

"She's very ladylike," I replied as an innocent form of aggravation.

"So much the worse for *you*. That means she can't turn round."

"She'll do for the fashionable novels."

"Oh yes, she'll *do* for them!" my model humorously declared. "Ain't they bad enough without her?" I had often sociably denounced them to Miss Churm.

III

IT was for the elucidation of a mystery in one of these works that I first tried Mrs. Monarch. Her husband came with her, to be useful if necessary — it was sufficiently clear that as a general thing he would prefer to come with her. At first I wondered if this were for "propriety's" sake — if he were going to be jealous and meddling. The idea was too tiresome, and if it had been confirmed it would speedily have brought our acquaintance to a close. But I soon saw there was nothing in it and that if he accompanied Mrs. Monarch it was — in addition to the chance of being wanted — simply because he had nothing else to do. When they were separate his occupation was gone and they never *had* been separate. I judged rightly that in their awkward situation their close union was their main comfort and that this union had no weak spot. It was a real marriage, an encouragement to the hesitating, a nut for pessimists to crack. Their address was humble — I remember afterwards thinking it had been the only thing about them that was really professional — and I could fancy the lamentable lodgings in which the Major would have been left alone. He could sit there more or less grimly with his wife — he could n't sit there anyhow without her.

He had too much tact to try and make himself agreeable when he could n't be useful; so when I was too absorbed in my work to talk he simply sat and waited. But I liked to hear him talk — it made my work, when not interrupting it, less mechanical, less special. To listen to him was to combine the excitement of going out with the economy of staying at home. There was only one hindrance — that I seemed not to know any of the people this brilliant couple had known. I think he wondered extremely, during the term of our intercourse, whom the deuce I *did* know. He had n't a stray sixpence of an idea to fumble for, so we did n't spin it very fine; we confined ourselves to questions of leather and even of liquor — saddlers and breeches-makers and how to get excellent claret cheap — and matters like "good trains" and the habits of small game. His lore on these last subjects was astonishing — he managed to interweave the station-master with the ornithologist. When he could n't talk about greater things he could talk cheerfully about smaller, and since I could n't accompany him into reminiscences of the fashionable world he could lower the conversation without a visible effort to my level.

So earnest a desire to please was touching in a man who could so easily have knocked one down. He looked after the fire and had an opinion on the draught of the stove without my asking him, and I could see that he thought many of my arrangements not half knowing. I remember telling him that if I were only rich I'd offer him a salary to come and teach me how to live. Sometimes he gave a random sigh of which the essence might have been: "Give me even such a bare old barrack as *this*, and I'd do something with it!" When I wanted to use him he came alone; which was an illustration of the superior courage of women. His wife could bear her solitary second floor, and she was in general more discreet; showing by various small reserves that she was alive to the propriety of keeping our relations markedly professional — not letting them slide into sociability. She wished it to remain clear that she and the Major were employed, not cultivated, and if she approved of me as a superior, who could be kept in his place, she never thought me quite good enough for an equal.

She sat with great intensity, giving the whole of her mind to it, and was capable of remaining for an hour almost as motionless as before a photographer's lens. I could see she had been photographed often, but somehow the very habit that made her good for that purpose unfitted her for mine. At first I was extremely pleased with her ladylike air, and it was a satisfaction, on coming to follow her lines, to see how good they were and how far they could lead the pencil. But after a little skirmishing I began to find her too insurmountably stiff; do what I would with it my drawing looked like a photograph or a copy of a photograph. Her figure had no variety of expression — she herself had no sense of variety. You may say that this was my business and was only a question of placing her. Yet I placed her in every conceivable position and she managed to obliterate their differences. She was always a lady certainly, and into the bargain was always the same lady. She was the real thing, but always the same thing. There were moments when I rather writhed under the serenity of her confidence that she *was* the real thing. All her dealings with me

and all her husband's were an implication that this
was lucky for *me*. Meanwhile I found myself trying to
invent types that approached her own, instead of making her own transform itself — in the clever way that
was not impossible for instance to poor Miss Churm.
Arrange as I would and take the precautions I would,
she always came out, in my pictures, too tall — landing me in the dilemma of having represented a fascinating woman as seven feet high, which (out of respect
perhaps to my own very much scantier inches) was far
from my idea of such a personage.

The case was worse with the Major — nothing I
could do would keep *him* down, so that he became
useful only for the representation of brawny giants.
I adored variety and range, I cherished human accidents, the illustrative note; I wanted to characterise
closely, and the thing in the world I most hated was
the danger of being ridden by a type. I had quar-
relled with some of my friends about it; I had parted
company with them for maintaining that one *had* to
be, and that if the type was beautiful — witness
Raphael and Leonardo — the servitude was only a
gain. I was neither Leonardo nor Raphael — I might
only be a presumptuous young modern searcher; but
I held that everything was to be sacrificed sooner than
character. When they claimed that the obsessional
form could easily *be* character I retorted, perhaps
superficially, "Whose?" It could n't be everybody's
— it might end in being nobody's.

After I had drawn Mrs. Monarch a dozen times I
felt surer even than before that the value of such a
model as Miss Churm resided precisely in the fact

that she had no positive stamp, combined of course with the other fact that what she did have was a curious and inexplicable talent for imitation. Her usual appearance was like a curtain which she could draw up at request for a capital performance. This performance was simply suggestive; but it was a word to the wise — it was vivid and pretty. Sometimes even I thought it, though she was plain herself, too insipidly pretty; I made it a reproach to her that the figures drawn from her were monotonously (*bêtement*, as we used to say) graceful. Nothing made her more angry: it was so much her pride to feel she could sit for characters that had nothing in common with each other. She would accuse me at such moments of taking away her "reputytion."

It suffered a certain shrinkage, this queer quantity, from the repeated visits of my new friends. Miss Churm was greatly in demand, never in want of employment, so I had no scruple in putting her off occasionally, to try them more at my ease. It was certainly amusing at first to do the real thing — it was amusing to do Major Monarch's trousers. They *were* the real thing, even if he did come out colossal. It was amusing to do his wife's back hair — it was so mathematically neat — and the particular "smart" tension of her tight stays. She lent herself especially to positions in which the face was somewhat averted or blurred; she abounded in ladylike back views and *profils perdus*. When she stood erect she took naturally one of the attitudes in which court-painters represent queens and princesses; so that I found myself wondering whether, to draw out this accomplishment, I

328

could n't get the editor of the *Cheapside* to publish a really royal romance, "A Tale of Buckingham Palace." Sometimes however the real thing and the make-believe came into contact; by which I mean that Miss Churm, keeping an appointment or coming to make one on days when I had much work in hand, encountered her invidious rivals. The encounter was not on their part, for they noticed her no more than if she had been the housemaid; not from intentional loftiness, but simply because as yet, professionally, they did n't know how to fraternise, as I could imagine they would have liked — or at least that the Major would. They could n't talk about the omnibus — they always walked; and they did n't know what else to try — she was n't interested in good trains or cheap claret. Besides, they must have felt — in the air — that she was amused at them, secretly derisive of their ever knowing how. She was n't a person to conceal the limits of her faith if she had had a chance to show them. On the other hand Mrs. Monarch did n't think her tidy; for why else did she take pains to say to me — it was going out of the way, for Mrs. Monarch — that she did n't like dirty women?

One day when my young lady happened to be present with my other sitters — she even dropped in, when it was convenient, for a chat — I asked her to be so good as to lend a hand in getting tea, a service with which she was familiar and which was one of a class that, living as I did in a small way, with slender domestic resources, I often appealed to my models to render. They liked to lay hands on my property, to break the sitting, and sometimes the china — it made

329

them feel Bohemian. The next time I saw Miss Churm after this incident she surprised me greatly by making a scene about it — she accused me of having wished to humiliate her. She had n't resented the outrage at the time, but had seemed obliging and amused, enjoying the comedy of asking Mrs. Monarch, who sat vague and silent, whether she would have cream and sugar, and putting an exaggerated simper into the question. She had tried intonations — as if she too wished to pass for the real thing — till I was afraid my other visitors would take offence.

Oh they were determined not to do this, and their touching patience was the measure of their great need. They would sit by the hour, uncomplaining, till I was ready to use them; they would come back on the chance of being wanted and would walk away cheerfully if it failed. I used to go to the door with them to see in what magnificent order they retreated. I tried to find other employment for them — I introduced them to several artists. But they did n't "take," for reasons I could appreciate, and I became rather anxiously aware that after such disappointments they fell back upon me with a heavier weight. They did me the honour to think me most *their* form. They were n't romantic enough for the painters, and in those days there were few serious workers in black-and-white. Besides, they had an eye to the great job I had mentioned to them — they had secretly set their hearts on supplying the right essence for my pictorial vindication of our fine novelist. They knew that for this undertaking I should want no costume-effects, none of the frippery of past ages — that it was a case in which everything would be contemporary and satirical and presumably genteel. If I could work them into it their future would be assured, for the labour would of course be long and the occupation steady.

One day Mrs. Monarch came without her husband — she explained his absence by his having had to go to the City. While she sat there in her usual relaxed majesty there came at the door a knock which I immediately recognised as the subdued appeal of a model out of work. It was followed by the entrance of a young man whom I at once saw to be a foreigner and who proved in fact an Italian acquainted with no English word but my name, which he uttered in a way that made it seem to include all others. I had n't then visited his country, nor was I proficient in his tongue; but as he was not so meanly constituted — what Italian is? — as to depend only on that member for expression he conveyed to me, in familiar but graceful mimicry, that he was in search of exactly the employment in which the lady before me was engaged. I was not struck with him at first, and while I continued to draw I dropped few signs of interest or encouragement. He stood his ground however — not importunately, but with a dumb dog-like fidelity in his eyes that amounted to innocent impudence, the manner of a devoted servant — he might have been in the house for years — unjustly suspected. Suddenly it struck me that this very attitude and expression made a picture; whereupon I told him to sit down and wait till I should be free. There was another picture in the way he obeyed me, and I observed as I worked that there were others still in the way he looked wonderingly, with his head thrown back, about the high studio. He might have been crossing himself in Saint Peter's. Before I finished I said to myself "The fellow's a bankrupt orange-monger, but a treasure."

When Mrs. Monarch withdrew he passed across the room like a flash to open the door for her, standing there with the rapt pure gaze of the young Dante spellbound by the young Beatrice. As I never insisted, in such situations, on the blankness of the British domestic, I reflected that he had the making of a servant — and I needed one, but could n't pay him to be only that — as well as of a model; in short I resolved to adopt my bright adventurer if he would agree to officiate in the double capacity. He jumped at my offer, and in the event my rashness — for I had really known nothing about him — was n't brought home to me. He proved a sympathetic though a desultory ministrant, and had in a wonderful degree the *sentiment de la pose*. It was uncultivated, instinctive, a part of the happy instinct that had guided him to my door and helped him to spell out my name on the card nailed to it. He had had no other introduction to me than a guess, from the shape of my high north window, seen outside, that my place was a studio and that as a studio it would contain an artist. He had wandered to England in search of fortune, like other itinerants, and had embarked, with a partner and a small green hand-cart, on the sale of penny ices. The ices had melted away and the partner had dissolved in their train. My young man wore tight yellow trousers with reddish stripes and his name was

THE REAL THING

Oronte. He was sallow but fair, and when I put him into some old clothes of my own he looked like an Englishman. He was as good as Miss Churm, who could look, when requested, like an Italian.

IV

I THOUGHT Mrs. Monarch's face slightly convulsed when, on her coming back with her husband, she found Oronte installed. It was strange to have to recognise in a scrap of a lazzarone a competitor to her magnificent Major. It was she who scented danger first, for the Major was anecdotically unconscious. But Oronte gave us tea, with a hundred eager confusions — he had never been concerned in so queer a process — and I think she thought better of me for having at last an "establishment." They saw a couple of drawings that I had made of the establishment, and Mrs. Monarch hinted that it never would have struck her he had sat for them. "Now the drawings you make from *us*, they look exactly like us," she reminded me, smiling in triumph; and I recognised that this was indeed just their defect. When I drew the Monarchs I could n't anyhow get away from them — get into the character I wanted to represent; and I had n't the least desire my model should be discoverable in my picture. Miss Churm never was, and Mrs. Monarch thought I hid her, very properly, because she was vulgar; whereas if she was lost it was only as the dead who go to heaven are lost — in the gain of an angel the more.

By this time I had got a certain start with "Rutland Ramsay," the first novel in the great projected series; that is I had produced a dozen drawings, several with the help of the Major and his wife, and I had sent them in for approval. My understanding with the publishers, as I have already hinted, had been that I was to be left to do my work, in this particular case, as I liked, with the whole book committed to me; but my connexion with the rest of the series was only contingent. There were moments when, frankly, it *was* a comfort to have the real thing under one's hand; for there were characters in "Rutland Ramsay" that were very much like it. There were people presumably as erect as the Major and women of as good a fashion as Mrs. Monarch. There was a great deal of country-house life — treated, it is true, in a fine fanciful ironical generalised way — and there was a considerable implication of knickerbockers and kilts. There were certain things I had to settle at the outset; such things for instance as the exact appearance of the hero and the particular bloom and figure of the heroine. The author of course gave me a lead, but there was a margin for interpretation. I took the Monarchs into my confidence, I told them frankly what I was about, I mentioned my embarrassments and alternatives. "Oh take *him!*" Mrs. Monarch murmured sweetly, looking at her husband; and "What could you want better than my wife?" the Major enquired with the comfortable candour that now prevailed between us.

I was n't obliged to answer these remarks — I was only obliged to place my sitters. I was n't easy in mind, and I postponed a little timidly perhaps the solving of my question. The book was a large canvas, the other figures were numerous, and I worked off at first some of the episodes in which the hero and the heroine were not concerned. When once I had set *them* up I should have to stick to them — I could n't make my young man seven feet high in one place and five feet nine in another. I inclined on the whole to the latter measurement, though the Major more than once reminded me that *he* looked about as young as any one. It was indeed quite possible to arrange him, for the figure, so that it would have been difficult to detect his age. After the spontaneous Oronte had been with me a month, and after I had given him to understand several times over that his native exuberance would presently constitute an insurmountable barrier to our further intercourse, I waked to a sense of his heroic capacity. He was only five feet seven, but the remaining inches were latent. I tried him almost secretly at first, for I was really rather afraid of the judgement my other models would pass on such a choice. If they regarded Miss Churm as little better than a snare what would they think of the representation by a person so little the real thing as an Italian street-vendor of a protagonist formed by a public school ?

If I went a little in fear of them it was n't because they bullied me, because they had got an oppressive foothold, but because in their really pathetic decorum and mysteriously permanent newness they counted on me so intensely. I was therefore very glad when Jack Hawley came home : he was always of such good counsel. He painted badly himself, but there was no one like him for putting his finger on the place. He had been absent from England for a year ; he had been somewhere — I don't remember where — to get a fresh eye. I was in a good deal of dread of any such organ, but we were old friends; he had been away for months and a sense of emptiness was creeping into my life. I had n't dodged a missile for a year.

He came back with a fresh eye, but with the same old black velvet blouse, and the first evening he spent in my studio we smoked cigarettes till the small hours. He had done no work himself, he had only got the eye; so the field was clear for the production of my little things. He wanted to see what I had produced for the *Cheapside*, but he was disappointed in the exhibition. That at least seemed the meaning of two or three comprehensive groans which, as he lounged on my big divan, his leg folded under him, looking at my latest drawings, issued from his lips with the smoke of the cigarette.

"What's the matter with you?" I asked.

"What's the matter with *you*?"

"Nothing save that I'm mystified."

"You are indeed. You're quite off the hinge. What's the meaning of this new fad?" And he tossed me, with visible irreverence, a drawing in which I happened to have depicted both my elegant models. I asked if he did n't think it good, and he replied that it struck him as execrable, given the sort of thing I had always represented myself to him as wishing to arrive at; but I let that pass — I was so anxious to see exactly what he meant. The two figures in the picture looked colossal, but I supposed this was *not* what he meant, inasmuch as, for aught he knew to the contrary, I might have been trying for some such effect.

337

I maintained that I was working exactly in the same way as when he last had done me the honour to tell me I might do something some day. "Well, there's a screw loose somewhere," he answered; "wait a bit and I'll discover it." I depended upon him to do so: where else was the fresh eye? But he produced at last nothing more luminous than "I don't know — I don't like your types." This was lame for a critic who had never consented to discuss with me anything but the question of execution, the direction of strokes and the mystery of values.

"In the drawings you've been looking at I think my types are very handsome."

"Oh they won't do!"

"I've been working with new models."

"I see you have. *They* won't do."

"Are you very sure of that?"

"Absolutely — they're stupid."

"You mean *I* am — for I ought to get round that."

"You *can't* — with such people. Who are they?"

I told him, so far as was necessary, and he concluded heartlessly: "Ce sont des gens qu'il faut mettre à la porte."

"You've never seen them; they're awfully good" — I flew to their defence.

"Not seen them? Why all this recent work of yours drops to pieces with them. It's all I want to see of them."

"No one else has said anything against it — the *Cheapside* people are pleased."

"Every one else is an ass, and the *Cheapside* people the biggest asses of all. Come, don't pretend at this time of day to have pretty illusions about the public, especially about publishers and editors. It's not for *such* animals you work — it's for those who know, *coloro che sanno;* so keep straight for *me* if you can't keep straight for yourself. There was a certain sort of thing you used to try for — and a very good thing it was. But this twaddle is n't *in* it." When I talked with Hawley later about "Rutland Ramsay" and its possible successors he declared that I must get back into my boat again or I should go to the bottom. His voice in short was the voice of warning.

I noted the warning, but I did n't turn my friends out of doors. They bored me a good deal; but the very fact that they bored me admonished me not to sacrifice them — if there was anything to be done with them — simply to irritation. As I look back at this phase they seem to me to have pervaded my life not a little. I have a vision of them as most of the time in my studio, seated against the wall on an old velvet bench to be out of the way, and resembling the while a pair of patient courtiers in a royal ante-chamber. I'm convinced that during the coldest weeks of the winter they held their ground because it saved them fire. Their newness was losing its gloss, and it was impossible not to feel them objects of charity. Whenever Miss Churm arrived they went away, and after I was fairly launched in "Rutland Ramsay" Miss Churm arrived pretty often. They managed to express to me tacitly that they supposed I wanted her for the low life of the book, and I let them suppose it, since they had attempted to study the work — it was lying about the studio — without discovering that it dealt only with the highest circles. They had dipped into the most brilliant of our novelists without deciphering many passages. I still took an hour from them, now and again, in spite of Jack Hawley's warning: it would be time enough to dismiss them, if dismissal should be necessary, when the rigour of the season was over. Hawley had made their acquaintance — he had met them at my fireside — and thought them a ridiculous pair. Learning that he was a painter they tried to approach him, to show him too that they were the real thing; but he looked at them, across the big room, as if they were miles away: they were a compendium of everything he most objected to in the social system of his country. Such people as that, all convention and patent-leather, with ejaculations that stopped conversation, had no business in a studio. A studio was a place to learn to see, and how could you see through a pair of feather-beds?

The main inconvenience I suffered at their hands was that at first I was shy of letting it break upon them that my artful little servant had begun to sit to me for "Rutland Ramsay." They knew I had been odd enough — they were prepared by this time to allow oddity to artists — to pick a foreign vagabond out of the streets when I might have had a person with whiskers and credentials; but it was some time before they learned how high I rated his accomplishments. They found him in an attitude more than once, but they never doubted I was doing him as an organ-grinder. There were several things they never guessed, and one of them was that for a striking scene in the novel, in which a footman briefly figured, it occurred to me to make use of Major Monarch as the menial. I kept putting this off, I did n't like to ask him to don the livery — besides the difficulty of finding a livery to fit him. At last, one day late in the winter, when I was at work on the despised Oronte, who caught one's idea on the wing, and was in the glow of feeling myself go very straight, they came in, the Major and his wife, with their society laugh about nothing (there was less and less to laugh at); came in like country-callers — they always reminded me of that — who have walked across the park after church and are presently persuaded to stay to luncheon. Luncheon was over, but they could stay to tea — I knew they wanted it. The fit was on me, however, and I could n't let my ardour cool and my work wait, with the fading daylight, while my model prepared it. So I asked Mrs. Monarch if she would mind laying it out — a request which for an instant brought all the blood to her face. Her eyes were on her husband's for a second, and some mute telegraphy passed between them. Their folly was over the next instant; his cheerful shrewd-ness put an end to it. So far from pitying their wounded pride, I must add, I was moved to give it as complete a lesson as I could. They bustled about together and got out the cups and saucers and made the kettle boil. I know they felt as if they were wait-ing on my servant, and when the tea was prepared I said : "He 'll have a cup, please — he 's tired." Mrs. Monarch brought him one where he stood, and he took it from her as if he had been a gentleman at a party squeezing a crush-hat with an elbow.

Then it came over me that she had made a great

effort for me — made it with a kind of nobleness — and that I owed her a compensation. Each time I saw her after this I wondered what the compensation could be. I could n't go on doing the wrong thing to oblige them. Oh it *was* the wrong thing, the stamp of the work for which they sat — Hawley was not the only person to say it now. I sent in a large number of the drawings I had made for "Rutland Ramsay," and I received a warning that was more to the point than Hawley's. The artistic adviser of the house for which I was working was of opinion that many of my illustrations were not what had been looked for. Most of these illustrations were the subjects in which the Monarchs had figured. Without going into the question of what *had* been looked for, I had to face the fact that at this rate I should n't get the other books to do. I hurled myself in despair on Miss Churm — I put her through all her paces. I not only adopted Oronte publicly as my hero, but one morning when the Major looked in to see if I did n't require him to finish a *Cheapside* figure for which he had begun to sit the week before, I told him I had changed my mind — I 'd do the drawing from my man. At this my visitor turned pale and stood looking at me. "Is *he* your idea of an English gentleman ?" he asked.

I was disappointed, I was nervous, I wanted to get on with my work; so I replied with irritation: "Oh my dear Major — I can't be ruined for *you!*"

It was a horrid speech, but he stood another moment — after which, without a word, he quitted the studio. I drew a long breath, for I said to myself that I should n't see him again. I had n't told him definitely that I was in danger of having my work rejected, but I was vexed at his not having felt the catastrophe in the air, read with me the moral of our fruitless collaboration, the lesson that in the deceptive atmosphere of art even the highest respectability may fail of being plastic.

I did n't owe my friends money, but I did see them again. They reappeared together three days later, and, given all the other facts, there was something tragic in that one. It was a clear proof they could find nothing else in life to do. They had threshed the matter out in a dismal conference — they had digested the bad news that they were not in for the series. If they were n't useful to me even for the *Cheapside* their function seemed difficult to determine, and I could only judge at first that they had come, forgivingly, decorously, to take a last leave. This made me rejoice in secret that I had little leisure for a scene; for I had placed both my other models in position together and I was pegging away at a drawing from which I hoped to derive glory. It had been suggested by the passage in which Rutland Ramsay, drawing up a chair to Artemisia's piano-stool, says extraordinary things to her while she ostensibly fingers out a difficult piece of music. I had done Miss Churm at the piano before — it was an attitude in which she knew how to take on an absolutely poetic grace. I wished the two figures to "compose" together with intensity, and my little Italian had entered perfectly into my conception. The pair were vividly before me, the piano had been pulled out; it was a charming show of blended youth and murmured love, which I had only to catch and keep.

343

My visitors stood and looked at it, and I was friendly to them over my shoulder.

They made no response, but I was used to silent company and went on with my work, only a little disconcerted — even though exhilarated by the sense that *this* was at least the ideal thing — at not having got rid of them after all. Presently I heard Mrs. Monarch's sweet voice beside or rather above me: "I wish her hair were a little better done." I looked up and she was staring with a strange fixedness at Miss Churm, whose back was turned to her. "Do you mind my just touching it?" she went on — a question which made me spring up for an instant as with the instinctive fear that she might do the young lady a harm. But she quieted me with a glance I shall never forget — I confess I should like to have been able to paint *that* — and went for a moment to my model. She spoke to her softly, laying a hand on her shoulder and bending over her; and as the girl, understanding, gratefully assented, she disposed her rough curls, with a few quick passes, in such a way as to make Miss Churm's head twice as charming. It was one of the most heroic personal services I've ever seen rendered. Then Mrs. Monarch turned away with a low sigh and, looking about her as if for something to do, stooped to the floor with a noble humility and picked up a dirty rag that had dropped out of my paint-box.

The Major meanwhile had also been looking for something to do, and, wandering to the other end of the studio, saw before him my breakfast-things neglected, unremoved. "I say, can't I be useful *here?*" he called out to me with an irrepressible quaver. I

assented with a laugh that I fear was awkward, and
for the next ten minutes, while I worked, I heard the
light clatter of china and the tinkle of spoons and
glass. Mrs. Monarch assisted her husband — they
washed up my crockery, they put it away. They wandered off into my little scullery, and I afterwards found
that they had cleaned my knives and that my slender
stock of plate had an unprecedented surface. When it
came over me, the latent eloquence of what they were
doing, I confess that my drawing was blurred for a
moment — the picture swam. They had accepted
their failure, but they could n't accept their fate.
They had bowed their heads in bewilderment to the
perverse and cruel law in virtue of which the real thing
could be so much less precious than the unreal; but
they did n't want to starve. If my servants were my
models, then my models might be my servants. They
would reverse the parts — the others would sit for the
ladies and gentlemen and *they* would do the work.
They would still be in the studio — it was an intense
dumb appeal to me not to turn them out. "Take us
on," they wanted to say — "we'll do *anything*."

My pencil dropped from my hand; my sitting was
spoiled and I got rid of my sitters, who were also evidently rather mystified and awestruck. Then, alone
with the Major and his wife I had a most uncomfort-
able moment. He put their prayer into a single sentence: "I say, you know — just let *us* do for you, can't
you?" I could n't — it was dreadful to see them
emptying my slops; but I pretended I could, to oblige
them, for about a week. Then I gave them a sum of
money to go away, and I never saw them again. I ob-

tained the remaining books, but my friend Hawley repeats that Major and Mrs. Monarch did me a permanent harm, got me into false ways. If it be true I'm content to have paid the price — for the memory.

BROOKSMITH

BROOKSMITH

WE are scattered now, the friends of the late Mr. Oliver Offord; but whenever we chance to meet I think we are conscious of a certain esoteric respect for each other. "Yes, you too have been in Arcadia," we seem not too grumpily to allow. When I pass the house in Mansfield Street I remember that Arcadia was there. I don't know who has it now, and don't want to know; it's enough to be so sure that if I should ring the bell there would be no such luck for me as that Brooksmith should open the door. Mr. Offord, the most agreeable, the most attaching of bachelors, was a retired diplomatist, living on his pension and on something of his own over and above; a good deal confined, by his infirmities, to his fireside and delighted to be found there any afternoon in the year, from five o'clock on, by such visitors as Brooksmith allowed to come up. Brooksmith was his butler and his most intimate friend, to whom we all stood, or I should say sat, in the same relation in which the subject of the sovereign finds himself to the prime minister. By having been for years, in foreign lands, the most delightful Englishman any one had ever known, Mr. Offord had in my opinion rendered signal service to his country. But I suppose he had been too much liked — liked even by those who did n't like *it* — so that as people of that sort never get titles or dotations for the horrid things they 've *not* done, his principal reward was simply that we went to see him.

BROOKSMITH

Oh we went perpetually, and it was not our fault if he was not overwhelmed with this particular honour. Any visitor who came once came again; to come merely once was a slight nobody, I 'm sure, had ever put upon him. His circle therefore was essentially composed of habitués, who were habitués for each other as well as for him, as those of a happy salon should be. I remember vividly every element of the place, down to the intensely Londonish look of the grey opposite houses, in the gap of the white curtains of the high windows, and the exact spot where, on a particular afternoon, I put down my tea-cup for Brooksmith, lingering an instant, to gather it up as if he were plucking a flower. Mr. Offord's drawing-room was indeed Brooksmith's garden, his pruned and tended human parterre, and if we all flourished there and grew well in our places it was largely owing to his supervision.

Many persons have heard much, though most have doubtless seen little, of the famous institution of the salon, and many are born to the depression of knowing that this finest flower of social life refuses to bloom where the English tongue is spoken. The explanation is usually that our women have not the skill to cultivate it — the art to direct through a smiling land, between suggestive shores, a sinuous stream of talk. My affectionate, my pious memory of Mr. Offord contradicts this induction only, I fear, more insidiously to confirm it. The sallow and slightly smoked drawing-room in which he spent so large a portion of the last years of his life certainly deserved the distinguished name; but on the other hand it could n't be said at all to owe its stamp to any intervention throwing into relief the fact that there was no Mrs. Offord. The dear man had indeed, at the most, been capable of one of those sacrifices to which women are deemed peculiarly apt: he had recognised — under the influence, in some degree, it is true, of physical infirmity — that if you wish people to find you at home you must manage not to be out. He had in short accepted the truth which many dabblers in the social art are slow to learn, that you must really, as they say, take a line, and that the only way as yet discovered of being at home is to stay at home. Finally his own fireside had become a summary of his habits. Why should he ever have left it? — since this would have been leaving what was notoriously pleasantest in London, the compact charmed cluster (thinning away indeed into casual couples) round the fine old last-century chimney-piece which, with the exception of the remarkable collection of miniatures, was the best thing the place contained. Mr. Offord was n't rich; he had nothing but his pension and the use for life of the somewhat superannuated house.

When I 'm reminded by some opposed discomfort of the present hour how perfectly we were all handled there, I ask myself once more what had been the secret of such perfection. One had taken it for granted at the time, for anything that is supremely good produces more acceptance than surprise. I felt we were all happy, but I did n't consider how our happiness was managed. And yet there were questions to be asked, questions that strike me as singularly obvious now that there 's nobody to answer them. Mr. Offord had solved the insoluble; he had, without feminine help —

save in the sense that ladies were dying to come to him and that he saved the lives of several — established a salon; but I might have guessed that there was a method in his madness, a law in his success. He had n't hit it off by a mere fluke. There was an art in it all, and how was the art so hidden? Who indeed if it came to that was the occult artist? Launching this enquiry the other day I had already got hold of the tail of my reply. I was helped by the very wonder of some of the conditions that came back to me — those that used to seem as natural as sunshine in a fine climate.

How was it for instance that we never were a crowd, never either too many or too few, always the right people *with* the right people — there must really have been no wrong people at all — always coming and going, never sticking fast nor overstaying, yet never popping in or out with an indecorous familiarity? How was it that we all sat where we wanted and moved when we wanted and met whom we wanted and escaped whom we wanted; joining, according to the accident of inclination, the general circle or falling in with a single talker on a convenient sofa? Why were all the sofas so convenient, the accidents so happy, the talkers so ready, the listeners so willing, the subjects presented to you in a rotation as quickly foreordained as the courses at dinner? A dearth of topics would have been as unheard of as a lapse in the service. These speculations could n't fail to lead me to the fundamental truth that Brooksmith had been somehow at the bottom of the mystery. If he had n't established the salon at least he had carried it on. Brooksmith in short was the artist!

BROOKSMITH

We felt this covertly at the time, without formulating it, and were conscious, as an ordered and prosperous community, of his evenhanded justice, all untainted with flunkeyism. He had none of that vulgarity — his touch was infinitely fine. The delicacy of it was clear to me on the first occasion my eyes rested, as they were so often to rest again, on the domestic revealed, in the turbid light of the street, by the opening of the house-door. I saw on the spot that though he had plenty of school he carried it without arrogance — he had remained articulate and human. *L'Ecole Anglaise* Mr. Offord used laughingly to call him when, later on, it happened more than once that we had some conversation about him. But I remember accusing Mr. Offord of not doing him quite ideal justice. That he was n't one of the giants of the school, however, was admitted by my old friend, who really understood him perfectly and was devoted to him, as I shall show; which doubtless poor Brooksmith had himself felt, to his cost, when his value in the market was originally determined. The utility of his class in general is estimated by the foot and the inch, and poor Brooksmith had only about five feet three to put into circulation. He acknowledged the inadequacy of this provision, and I'm sure was penetrated with the everlasting fitness of the relation between service and stature. If *he* had been Mr. Offord he certainly would have found Brooksmith wanting, and indeed the laxity of his employer on this score was one of many things he had had to condone and to which he had at last indulgently adapted himself.

I remember the old man's saying to me: "Oh my

servants, if they can live with me a fortnight they can live with me for ever. But it's the first fortnight that tries 'em." It was in the first fortnight for instance that Brooksmith had had to learn that he was exposed to being addressed as "my dear fellow" and "my poor child." Strange and deep must such a probation have been to him, and he doubtless emerged from it tempered and purified. This was written to a certain extent in his appearance; in his spare brisk little person, in his cloistered white face and extraordinarily polished hair, which told of responsibility, looked as if it were kept up to the same high standard as the plate; in his small clear anxious eyes, even in the permitted, though not exactly encouraged, tuft on his chin. "He thinks me rather mad, but I've broken him in, and now he likes the place, he likes the company," said the old man. I embraced this fully after I had become aware that Brooksmith's main characteristic was a deep and shy refinement, though I remember I was rather puzzled when, on another occasion, Mr. Offord remarked: "What he likes is the talk — mingling in the conversation." I was conscious I had never seen Brooksmith permit himself this freedom, but I guessed in a moment that what Mr. Offord alluded to was a participation more intense than any speech could have represented — that of being perpetually present on a hundred legitimate pretexts, errands, necessities, and breathing the very atmosphere of criticism, the famous criticism of life. "Quite an education, sir, isn't it, sir?" he said to me one day at the foot of the stairs when he was letting me out; and I've always remembered the words and the tone as the first sign of the quickening drama of poor Brooksmith's fate. It was indeed an education, but to what was this sensitive young man of thirty-five, of the servile class, being educated ?

Practically and inevitably, for the time, to companionship, to the perpetual, the even exaggerated reference and appeal of a person brought to dependence by his time of life and his infirmities and always addicted moreover — this was the exaggeration — to the art of giving you pleasure by letting you do things for him. There were certain things Mr. Offord was capable of pretending he liked you to do even when he did n't — this, I mean, if he thought *you* liked them. If it happened that you did n't either — which was rare, yet might be — of course there were crosspurposes; but Brooksmith was there to prevent their going very far. This was precisely the way he acted as moderator; he averted misunderstandings or cleared them up. He had been capable, strange as it may appear, of acquiring for this purpose an insight into the French tongue, which was often used at Mr. Offord's; for besides being habitual to most of the foreigners, and they were many, who haunted the place or arrived with letters — letters often requiring a little worried consideration, of which Brooksmith always had cognisance — it had really become the primary language of the master of the house. I don't know if all the *malentendus* were in French, but almost all the explanations were, and this did n't a bit prevent Brooksmith's following them. I know Mr. Offord used to read passages to him from Montaigne and Saint-Simon, for he read perpetually when alone —

when *they* were alone, that is — and Brooksmith was always about. Perhaps you'll say no wonder Mr. Offord's butler regarded him as "rather mad." However, if I'm not sure what he thought about Montaigne I'm convinced he admired Saint-Simon. A certain feeling for letters must have rubbed off on him from the mere handling of his master's books, which he was always carrying to and fro and putting back in their places.

I often noticed that if an anecdote or a quotation, much more a lively discussion, was going forward, he would, if busy with the fire or the curtains, the lamp or the tea, find a pretext for remaining in the room till the point should be reached. If his purpose was to catch it you weren't discreet, you were in fact scarce human, to call him off, and I shall never forget a look, a hard stony stare — I caught it in its passage — which, one day when there were a good many people in the room, he fastened upon the footman who was helping him in the service and who, in an undertone, had asked him some irrelevant question. It was the only manifestation of harshness I ever observed on Brooksmith's part, and I at first wondered what was the matter. Then I became conscious that Mr. Offord was relating a very curious anecdote, never before perhaps made so public, and imparted to the narrator by an eye-witness of the fact, bearing on Lord Byron's life in Italy. Nothing would induce me to reproduce it here, but Brooksmith had been in danger of losing it. If I ever should venture to reproduce it I shall feel how much I lose in not having my fellow auditor to refer to.

BROOKSMITH

The first day Mr. Offord's door was closed was therefore a dark date in contemporary history. It was raining hard and my umbrella was wet, but Brooksmith received it from me exactly as if this were a preliminary for going upstairs. I observed however that instead of putting it away he held it poised and trickling over the rug, and I then became aware that he was looking at me with deep acknowledging eyes — his air of universal responsibility. I immediately understood — there was scarce need of question and answer as they passed between us. When I took in that our good friend had given up as never before, though only for the occasion, I exclaimed dolefully: "What a difference it will make — and to how many people!"

"I shall be one of them, sir!" said Brooksmith; and that was the beginning of the end.

Mr. Offord came down again, but the spell was broken, the great sign being that the conversation was for the first time not directed. It wandered and stumbled, a little frightened, like a lost child — it had let go the nurse's hand. "The worst of it is that now we shall talk about my health — c'est la fin de tout," Mr. Offord said when he reappeared; and then I recognised what a note of change that would be — for he had never tolerated anything so provincial. We "ran" to each other's health as little as to the daily weather. The talk became ours, in a word — not his; and as ours, even when *he* talked, it could only be inferior. In this form it was a distress to Brooksmith, whose attention now wandered from it altogether: he had so much closer a vision of his master's intimate

357

conditions than our superficialities represented. There were better hours, and he was more in and out of the room, but I could see he was conscious of the decline, almost of the collapse, of our great institution. He seemed to wish to take counsel with me about it, to feel responsible for its going on in some form or other. When for the second period — the first had lasted several days — he had to tell me that his employer did n't receive, I half-expected to hear him say after a moment "Do you think I ought to, sir, in his place?" — as he might have asked me, with the return of autumn, if I thought he had better light the drawing-room fire.

He had a resigned philosophic sense of what his guests — our guests, as I came to regard them in our colloquies — would expect. His feeling was that he would n't absolutely have approved of himself as a substitute for Mr. Offord; but he was so saturated with the religion of habit that he would have made, for our friends, the necessary sacrifice to the divinity. He would take them on a little further and till they could look about them. I think I saw him also mentally confronted with the opportunity to deal — for once in his life — with some of his own dumb preferences, his limitations of sympathy, *weeding* a little in prospect and returning to a purer tradition. It was not unknown to me that he considered that toward the end of our host's career a certain laxity of selection had crept in.

At last it came to be the case that we all found the closed door more often than the open one; but even when it was closed Brooksmith managed a crack for me to squeeze through; so that practically I never turned away without having paid a visit. The difference simply came to be that the visit was to Brooksmith. It took place in the hall, at the familiar foot of the stairs, and we did n't sit down, at least Brooksmith did n't; moreover it was devoted wholly to one topic and always had the air of being already over — beginning, so to say, at the end. But it was always interesting — it always gave me something to think about. It's true that the subject of my meditation was ever the same — ever "It's all very well, but what *will* become of Brooksmith?" Even my private answer to this question left me still unsatisfied. No doubt Mr. Offord would provide for him, but *what* would he provide? — that was the great point. He could n't provide society; and society had become a necessity of Brooksmith's nature. I must add that he never showed a symptom of what I may call sordid solicitude — anxiety on his own account. He was rather livid and intensely grave, as befitted a man before whose eyes the "shade of that which once was great" was passing away. He had the solemnity of a person winding up, under depressing circumstances, a long-established and celebrated business; he was a kind of social executor or liquidator. But his manner seemed to testify exclusively to the uncertainty of *our* future. I could n't in those days have afforded it — I lived in two rooms in Jermyn Street and did n't "keep a man"; but even if my income had permitted I should n't have ventured to say to Brooksmith (emulating Mr. Offord) "My dear fellow, I'll take you on." The whole tone of our intercourse was so much more an implication that it was *I* who should now want a lift. Indeed there was a tacit assurance in Brooksmith's whole attitude that he should have me on his mind.

One of the most assiduous members of our circle had been Lady Kenyon, and I remember his telling me one day that her ladyship had in spite of her own infirmities, lately much aggravated, been in person to enquire. In answer to this I remarked that she would feel it more than any one. Brooksmith had a pause before saying in a certain tone — there's no reproducing some of his tones — "I'll go and see her." I went to see her myself and learned he had waited on her; but when I said to her, in the form of a joke but with a core of earnest, that when all was over some of us ought to combine, to club together, and set Brooksmith up on his own account, she replied a trifle disappointingly: "Do you mean in a public-house?" I looked at her in a way that I think Brooksmith himself would have approved, and then I answered: "Yes, the Offord Arms." What I had meant of course was that for the love of art itself we ought to look to it that such a peculiar faculty and so much acquired experience should n't be wasted. I really think that if we had caused a few black-edged cards to be struck off and circulated — "Mr. Brooksmith will continue to receive on the old premises from four to seven; business carried on as usual during the alterations" — the greater number of us would have rallied.

Several times he took me upstairs — always by his own proposal — and our dear old friend, in bed (in a curious flowered and brocaded casaque which made

him, especially as his head was tied up in a handkerchief to match, look, to my imagination, like the
dying Voltaire) held for ten minutes a sadly shrunken
little salon. I felt indeed each time as if I were attending the last *coucher* of some social sovereign. He was
royally whimsical about his sufferings and not at all
concerned — quite as if the Constitution provided
for the case — about his successor. He glided over
our sufferings charmingly, and none of his jokes — it
was a gallant abstention, some of them would have
been so easy — were at our expense. Now and again,
I confess, there was one at Brooksmith's, but so
pathetically sociable as to make the excellent man
look at me in a way that seemed to say: "Do exchange
a glance with me, or I shan't be able to stand it."
What he was n't able to stand was not what Mr.
Offord said about him, but what he was n't able to
say in return. His idea of conversation for himself
was giving you the convenience of speaking to him;
and when he went to "see" Lady Kenyon for instance
it was to carry her the tribute of his receptive silence.
Where would the speech of his betters have been if
proper service had been a manifestation of sound?
In that case the fundamental difference would have
had to be shown by *their* dumbness, and many of
them, poor things, were dumb enough without that
provision. Brooksmith took an unfailing interest in
the preservation of the fundamental difference; it was
the thing he had most on his conscience.

What had become of it however when Mr. Offord
passed away like any inferior person — was relegated
to eternal stillness after the manner of a butler above-

stairs ? His aspect on the event — for the several suc-
cessive days — may be imagined, and the multiplica-
tion by funereal observance of the things he did n't
say. When everything was over — it was late the
same day — I knocked at the door of the house of
mourning as I so often had done before. I could never
call on Mr. Offord again, but I had come literally to
call on Brooksmith. I wanted to ask him if there was
anything I could do for him, tainted with vagueness
as this enquiry could only be. My presumptuous
dream of taking him into my own service had died
away : my service was n't worth his being taken into.
My offer could only be to help him to find another
place, and yet there was an indelicacy, as it were, in
taking for granted that his thoughts would immediately be fixed on another. I had a hope that he
would be able to give his life a different form —
though certainly not the form, the frequent result of
such bereavements, of his setting up a little shop.
That would have been dreadful; for I should have
wished to forward any enterprise he might embark in, yet how could I have brought myself to go
and pay him shillings and take back coppers over a
counter ? My visit then was simply an intended compliment. He took it as such, gratefully and with all
the tact in the world. He knew I really could n't help
him and that I knew he knew I could n't; but we
discussed the situation — with a good deal of elegant
generality — at the foot of the stairs, in the hall
already dismantled, where I had so often discussed
other situations with him. The executors were in
possession, as was still more apparent when he made

me pass for a few minutes into the dining-room, where various objects were muffled up for removal.

Two definite facts, however, he had to communicate; one being that he was to leave the house for ever that night (servants, for some mysterious reason, seem always to depart by night), and the other — he mentioned it only at the last and with hesitation — that he was already aware his late master had left him a legacy of eighty pounds. "I'm very glad," I said, and Brooksmith was of the same mind: "It was so like him to think of me." This was all that passed between us on the subject, and I know nothing of his judgement of Mr. Offord's memento. Eighty pounds are always eighty pounds, and no one has ever left *me* an equal sum; but, all the same, for Brooksmith, I was disappointed. I don't know what I had expected, but it was almost a shock. Eighty pounds might stock a small shop — a *very* small shop; but, I repeat, I could n't bear to think of that. I asked my friend if he had been able to save a little, and he replied: "No, sir; I've had to do things." I did n't enquire what things they might have been; they were his own affair, and I took his word for them as assentingly as if he had had the greatness of an ancient house to keep up; especially as there was something in his manner that seemed to convey a prospect of further sacrifice.

"I shall have to turn round a bit, sir — I shall have to look about me," he said; and then he added indulgently, magnanimously: "If you should happen to hear of anything for me —"

I could n't let him finish; this was, in its essence, too much in the really grand manner. It would be a help to my getting him off my mind to be able to pretend I *could* find the right place, and that help he wished to give me, for it was doubtless painful to him to see me in so false a position. I interposed with a few words to the effect of how well aware I was that wherever he should go, whatever he should do, he would miss our old friend terribly — miss him even more than I should, having been with him so much more. This led him to make the speech that has remained with me as the very text of the whole episode.

"Oh sir, it's sad for *you*, very sad indeed, and for a great many gentlemen and ladies; that it is, sir. But for me, sir, it is, if I may say so, still graver even than that: it's just the loss of something that was everything. For me, sir," he went on with rising tears, "he was just *all*, if you know what I mean, sir. You have others, sir, I dare say — not that I would have you understand me to speak of them as in any way tantamount. But you have the pleasures of society, sir; if it's only in talking about him, sir, as I dare say you do freely — for all his blest memory has to fear from it — with gentlemen and ladies who have had the same honour. That's not for me, sir, and I've to keep my associations to myself. Mr. Offord was *my* society, and now, you see, I just haven't any. You go back to conversation, sir, after all, and I go back to my place," Brooksmith stammered, without exaggerated irony or dramatic bitterness, but with a flat unstudied veracity and his hand on the knob of the street-door. He turned it to let me out and then he added: "I just go downstairs, sir, again, and I stay there."

"My poor child," I replied in my emotion, quite as Mr. Offord used to speak, "my dear fellow, leave it to me: *we'll* look after you, we'll all do something for you."

"Ah if you could give me some one *like* him! But there ain't two such in the world," Brooksmith said as we parted.

He had given me his address — the place where he would be to be heard of. For a long time I had no occasion to make use of the information: he proved on trial so very difficult a case. The people who knew him and had known Mr. Offord did n't want to take him, and yet I could n't bear to try to thrust him among strangers — strangers to his past when not to his present. I spoke to many of our old friends about him and found them all governed by the odd mixture of feelings of which I myself was conscious — as well as disposed, further, to entertain a suspicion that he was "spoiled," with which I then would have nothing to do. In plain terms a certain embarrassment, a sensible awkwardness when they thought of it, attached to the idea of using him as a menial: they had met him so often in society. Many of them would have asked him, and did ask him, or rather did ask me to ask him, to come and see them; but a mere visiting-list was not what I wanted for him. He was too short for people who were very particular; nevertheless I heard of an opening in a diplomatic household which led me to write him a note, though I was looking much less for something grand than for something human. Five days later I heard from him. The secretary's wife had decided, after keeping him waiting till then, that she could n't take a servant out of a house in which there had n't been a lady. The note had a P.S.: "It's a good job there was n't, sir, such a lady as some."

A week later he came to see me and told me he was "suited," committed to some highly respectable people — they were something quite immense in the City — who lived on the Bayswater side of the Park. "I dare say it will be rather poor, sir," he admitted; "but I've seen the fireworks, have n't I, sir? — it can't be fireworks *every* night. After Mansfield Street there ain't much choice." There was a certain amount, however, it seemed; for the following year, calling one day on a country cousin, a lady of a certain age who was spending a fortnight in town with some friends of her own, a family unknown to me and resident in Chester Square, the door of the house was opened, to my surprise and gratification, by Brooksmith in person. When I came out I had some conversation with him from which I gathered that he had found the large City people too dull for endurance, and I guessed, though he did n't say it, that he had found them vulgar. as well. I don't know what judgement he would have passed on his actual patrons if my relative had n't been their friend; but in view of that connexion he abstained from comment.

None was necessary, however, for before the lady in question brought her visit to a close they honoured me with an invitation to dinner, which I accepted. There was a largeish party on the occasion, but I confess I thought of Brooksmith rather more than of the seated company. They required no depth of attention —

they were all referable to usual irredeemable inevitable types. It was the world of cheerful commonplace and conscious gentility and prosperous density, a full-fed material insular world, a world of hideous florid plate and ponderous order and thin conversation. There was n't a word said about Byron, or even about a minor bard then much in view. Nothing would have induced me to look at Brooksmith in the course of the repast, and I felt sure that not even my overturning the wine would have induced him to meet my eye. We were in intellectual sympathy — we felt, as regards each other, a degree of social responsibility. In short we had been in Arcadia together, and we had both come to *this!* No wonder we were ashamed to be confronted. When he had helped on my overcoat, as I was going away, we parted, for the first time since the earliest days of Mansfield Street, in silence. I thought he looked lean and wasted, and I guessed that his new place was n't more "human" than his previous one. There was plenty of beef and beer, but there was no reciprocity. The question for him to have asked before accepting the position would n't have been "How many footmen are kept?" but "How much imagination?"

The next time I went to the house — I confess it was n't very soon — I encountered his successor, a personage who evidently enjoyed the good fortune of never having quitted his natural level. Could any be higher? he seemed to ask — over the heads of three footmen and even of some visitors. He made me feel as if Brooksmith were dead; but I did n't dare to enquire — I could n't have borne his "I have n't the least idea, sir." I dispatched a note to the address that worthy had given me after Mr. Offord's death, but I received no answer. Six months later however I was favoured with a visit from an elderly dreary dingy person who introduced herself to me as Mr. Brooksmith's aunt and from whom I learned that he was out of place and out of health and had allowed her to come and say to me that if I could spare half an hour to look in at him he would take it as a rare honour.

I went the next day — his messenger had given me a new address — and found my friend lodged in a short sordid street in Marylebone, one of those corners of London that wear the last expression of sickly meanness. The room into which I was shown was above the small establishment of a dyer and cleaner who had inflated kid gloves and discoloured shawls in his shopfront. There was a great deal of grimy infant life up and down the place, and there was a hot moist smell within, as of the "boiling" of dirty linen. Brooksmith sat with a blanket over his legs at a clean little window where, from behind stiff bluish-white curtains, he could look across at a huckster's and a tinsmith's and a small greasy public-house. He had passed through an illness and was convalescent, and his mother, as well as his aunt, was in attendance on him. I liked the nearer relative, who was bland and intensely humble, but I had my doubts of the remoter, whom I connected perhaps unjustly with the opposite public-house — she seemed somehow greasy with the same grease — and whose furtive eye followed every movement of my hand as to see if it were n't going into my pocket. It did n't take this direction — I could n't, unsolicited, put myself at that sort of ease with Brooksmith. Several times the door of the room opened and mysterious old women peeped in and shuffled back again. I don't know who they were; poor Brooksmith seemed encompassed with vague prying beery females.

He was vague himself, and evidently weak, and much embarrassed, and not an allusion was made between us to Mansfield Street. The vision of the salon of which he had been an ornament hovered before me however, by contrast, sufficiently. He assured me he was really getting better, and his mother remarked that he would come round if he could only get his spirits up. The aunt echoed this opinion, and I became more sure that in her own case she knew where to go for such a purpose. I'm afraid I was rather weak with my old friend, for I neglected the opportunity, so exceptionally good, to rebuke the levity which had led him to throw up honourable positions — fine stiff steady berths in Bayswater and Belgravia, with morning prayers, as I knew, attached to one of them. Very likely his reasons had been profane and sentimental; he did n't want morning prayers, he wanted to be somebody's dear fellow; but I could n't be the person to rebuke him. He shuffled these episodes out of sight — I saw he had no wish to discuss them. I noted further, strangely enough, that it would probably be a questionable pleasure for him to see me again: he doubted now even of my power to condone his aberrations. He did n't wish to have to explain; and his behaviour was likely in future to need explanation. When I bade him farewell he looked at me a moment with eyes that said everything: "How can I talk about those exquisite years in this place, before these people, with the old women poking their heads in? It was very good of you to come to see me; it was n't my idea — *she* brought you. We 've said everything; it 's over; you 'll lose all patience with me, and I 'd rather you should n't see the rest." I sent him some money in a letter the next day, but I saw the rest only in the light of a barren sequel.

A whole year after my visit to him I became aware once, in dining out, that Brooksmith was one of the several servants who hovered behind our chairs. He had n't opened the door of the house to me, nor had I recognised him in the array of retainers in the hall. This time I tried to catch his eye, but he never gave me a chance, and when he handed me a dish I could only be careful to thank him audibly. Indeed I partook of two *entrées* of which I had my doubts, subsequently converted into certainties, in order not to snub him. He looked well enough in health, but much older, and wore in an exceptionally marked degree the glazed and expressionless mask of the British domestic *de race*. I saw with dismay that if I had n't known him I should have taken him, on the showing of his countenance, for an extravagant illustration of irresponsive servile gloom. I said to myself that he had become a reactionary, gone over to the Philistines, thrown himself into religion, the religion of his "place," like a foreign lady *sur le retour*. I divined moreover that he was only engaged for the evening — he had become a mere waiter, had joined the band of the white-waistcoated who "go out." There was something pathetic in this fact — it was a terrible vulgarisation of Brooksmith. It was the mercenary prose of butlerhood; he had given up the struggle for the poetry. If reciprocity was what he had missed where was the reciprocity now? Only in the bottoms of the wine-glasses and the five shillings — or whatever they get — clapped into his hand by the permanent man. However, I supposed he had taken up a precarious branch of his profession because it after all sent him less downstairs. His relations with London society were more superficial, but they were of course more various. As I went away on this occasion I looked out for him eagerly among the four or five attendants whose perpendicular persons, fluting the walls of London passages, are supposed to lubricate the process of departure; but he was not on duty. I asked one of the others if he were not in the house, and received the prompt answer: "Just left, sir. Anything I can do for you, sir?" I wanted to say "Please give him my kind regards"; but I abstained — I did n't want to compromise him; and I never came across him again.

Often and often, in dining out, I looked for him, sometimes accepting invitations on purpose to multiply the chances of my meeting him. But always in vain; so that as I met many other members of the casual class over and over again I at last adopted the theory that he always procured a list of expected guests beforehand and kept away from the banquets which he thus learned I was to grace. At last I gave up hope, and one day at the end of three years I received another visit from his aunt. She was drearier and dingier, almost squalid, and she was in great tribulation and want. Her sister, Mrs. Brooksmith, had been dead a year, and three months later her nephew had disappeared. He had always looked after her a bit — since her troubles; I never knew what her troubles had been — and now she had n't so much as a petticoat to pawn. She had also a niece, to whom she had been everything before her troubles, but the niece had treated her most shameful. These were details; the great and romantic fact was Brooksmith's final evasion of his fate. He had gone out to wait one evening as usual, in a white waistcoat she had done up for him with her own hands — being due at a large party up Kensington way. But he had never come home again and had never arrived at the large party, nor at any party that any one could make out. No trace of him had come to light — no gleam of the white waistcoat had pierced the obscurity of his doom. This news was a sharp shock to me, for I had my ideas about his real destination. His aged relative had promptly, as she said, guessed the worst. Somehow and somewhere he had got out of the way altogether, and now I trust that, with characteristic deliberation, he is changing the plates of the immortal gods. As my depressing visitant also said, he never *had* got his spirits up. I was fortunately able to dismiss her with her own somewhat improved. But the dim ghost of poor Brooksmith is one of those that I see. He had indeed been spoiled.

THE BELDONALD HOLBEIN

THE BELDONALD HOLBEIN

I

MRS. MUNDEN had not yet been to my studio on so good a pretext as when she first intimated that it would be quite open to me — should I only care, as she called it, to throw the handkerchief — to paint her beautiful sister-in-law. I need n't go here more than is essential into the question of Mrs. Munden, who would really, by the way, be a story in herself. She has a manner of her own of putting things, and some of those she has put to me —! Her implication was that Lady Beldonald had n't only seen and admired certain examples of my work, but had literally been prepossessed in favour of the painter's "personality." Had I been struck with this sketch I might easily have imagined her ladyship was throwing *me* the handkerchief. "She has n't done," my visitor said, "what she ought."

"Do you mean she has done what she ought n't?"

"Nothing horrid — oh dear no." And something in Mrs. Munden's tone, with the way she appeared to muse a moment, even suggested to me that what she "ought n't" was perhaps what Lady Beldonald had too much neglected. "She has n't got on."

"What's the matter with her?"

"Well, to begin with, she's American."

"But I thought that was the way of ways to get on."

375

"It's one of them. But it's one of the ways of being awfully out of it too. There are so many!"

"So many Americans?" I asked.

"Yes, plenty of *them*," Mrs. Munden sighed. "So many ways, I mean, of being one."

"But if your sister-in-law's way is to be beautiful — ?"

"Oh there are different ways of that too."

"And she hasn't taken the right way?"

"Well," my friend returned as if it were rather difficult to express, "she hasn't done with it —"

"I see," I laughed; "what she oughtn't!"

Mrs. Munden in a manner corrected me, but it *was* difficult to express. "My brother at all events was certainly selfish. Till he died she was almost never in London; they wintered, year after year, for what he supposed to be his health — which it didn't help, since he was so much too soon to meet his end — in the south of France and in the dullest holes he could pick out, and when they came back to England he always kept her in the country. I must say for her that she always behaved beautifully. Since his death she has been more in London, but on a stupidly unsuccessful footing. I don't think she quite understands. She hasn't what *I* should call a life. It may be of course that she doesn't want one. That's just what I can't exactly find out. I can't make out how much she knows."

"I can easily make out," I returned with hilarity, "how much *you* do!"

"Well, you're very horrid. Perhaps she's too old."

"Too old for what?" I persisted.

"For anything. Of course she's no longer even a little young; only preserved — oh but preserved, like bottled fruit, in syrup! I want to help her if only because she gets on my nerves, and I really think the way of it would be just the right thing of yours at the Academy and on the line."

"But suppose," I threw out, "she should give on *my* nerves?"

"Oh she will. But isn't that all in the day's work, and don't great beauties always — ?"

"*You* don't," I interrupted; but I at any rate saw Lady Beldonald later on — the day came when her kinswoman brought her, and then I saw how her life must have its centre in her own idea of her appearance. Nothing else about her mattered — one knew her all when one knew that. She's indeed in one particular, I think, sole of her kind — a person whom vanity has had the odd effect of keeping positively safe and sound. This passion is supposed surely, for the most part, to be a principle of perversion and of injury, leading astray those who listen to it and landing them sooner or later in this or that complication; but it has landed her ladyship nowhere whatever — it has kept her from the first moment of full consciousness, one feels, exactly in the same place. It has protected her from every danger, has made her absolutely proper and prim. If she's "preserved," as Mrs. Munden originally described her to me, it's her vanity that has beautifully done it — putting her years ago in a plate-glass case and closing up the receptacle against every breath of air. How shouldn't she be preserved when you might smash your knuckles on this transparency before you could crack it? And she *is* — oh amazingly! Preservation is scarce the word for the rare condition of her surface. She looks *naturally* new, as if she took out every night her large lovely varnished eyes and put them in water. The thing was to paint her, I perceived, *in* the glass case — a most tempting attaching feat; render to the full the shining interposing plate and the general show-window effect.

It was agreed, though it was n't quite arranged, that she should sit to me. If it was n't quite arranged this was because, as I was made to understand from an early stage, the conditions from our start must be such as should exclude all elements of disturbance, such, in a word, as she herself should judge absolutely favourable. And it seemed that these conditions were easily imperilled. Suddenly, for instance, at a moment when I was expecting her to meet an appointment — the first — that I had proposed, I received a hurried visit from Mrs. Munden, who came on her behalf to let me know that the season happened just not to be propitious and that our friend could n't be quite sure, to the hour, when it would again become so. She felt nothing would make it so but a total absence of worry.

"Oh a 'total absence,'" I said, "is a large order! We live in a worrying world."

"Yes; and she feels exactly that — more than you 'd think. It 's in fact just why she must n't have, as she has now, a particular distress on at the very moment. She wants of course to look her best, and such things tell on her appearance."

I shook my head. "Nothing tells on her appearance. Nothing reaches it in any way; nothing gets *at* it. However, I can understand her anxiety. But what's her particular distress?"

"Why the illness of Miss Dadd."

"And who in the world's Miss Dadd?"

"Her most intimate friend and constant companion — the lady who was with us here that first day."

"Oh the little round black woman who gurgled with admiration?"

"None other. But she was taken ill last week, and it may very well be that she'll gurgle no more. She was very bad yesterday and is no better to-day, and Nina's much upset. If anything happens to Miss Dadd she'll have to get another, and, though she has had two or three before, that won't be so easy."

"Two or three Miss Dadds? Is it possible? And still wanting another!" I recalled the poor lady completely now. "No; I should n't indeed think it would be easy to get another. But why is a succession of them necessary to Lady Beldonald's existence?"

"Can't you guess?" Mrs. Munden looked deep, yet impatient. "They help."

"Help what? Help whom?"

"Why every one. You and me for instance. To do what? Why to think Nina beautiful. She has them for that purpose; they serve as foils, as accents serve on syllables, as terms of comparison. They make her 'stand out.' It's an effect of contrast that must be familiar to you artists; it's what a woman does when she puts a band of black velvet under a pearl ornament that may require, as she thinks, a little showing off."

I wondered. "Do you mean she always has them black?"

"Dear no; I've seen them blue, green, yellow. They may be what they like, so long as they're always one other thing."

"Hideous?"

Mrs. Munden made a mouth for it. "Hideous is too much to say; she does n't really require them as bad as that. But consistently, cheerfully, loyally plain. It's really a most happy relation. She loves them for it."

"And for what do they love *her?*"

"Why just for the amiability that they produce in her. Then also for their 'home.' It's a career for them."

"I see. But if that's the case," I asked, "why are they so difficult to find?"

"Oh they must be safe; it's all in that: her being able to depend on them to keep to the terms of the bargain and never have moments of rising — as even the ugliest woman will now and then (say when she's in love) — superior to themselves."

I turned it over. "Then if they can't inspire passions the poor things may n't even at least feel them?"

"She distinctly deprecates it. That's why such a man as you may be after all a complication."

I continued to brood. "You're very sure Miss Dadd's ailment is n't an affection that, being smothered, has struck in?" My joke, however, was n't well timed, for I afterwards learned that the unfortunate lady's state had been, even while I spoke, such as to forbid all hope. The worst symptoms had appeared; she was destined not to recover; and a week later I heard from Mrs. Munden that she would in fact "gurgle" no more.

II

ALL this had been for Lady Beldonald an agitation so
great that access to her apartment was denied for a
time even to her sister-in-law. It was much more out
of the question of course that she should unveil her
face to a person of my special business with it; so that
the question of the portrait was by common consent
left to depend on that of the installation of a successor
to her late companion. Such a successor, I gathered
from Mrs. Munden, widowed childless and lonely, as
well as inapt for the minor offices, she had absolutely
to have; a more or less humble *alter ego* to deal with
the servants, keep the accounts, make the tea and
watch the window-blinds. Nothing seemed more natural than that she should marry again, and obviously
that might come; yet the predecessors of Miss Dadd
had been contemporaneous with a first husband, so
that others formed in her image might be contemporaneous with a second. I was much occupied in those
months at any rate, and these questions and their ram-
ifications losing themselves for a while to my view, I
was only brought back to them by Mrs. Munden's arrival one day with the news that we were all right again
— her sister-in-law was once more "suited." A certain Mrs. Brash, an American relative whom she
had n't seen for years, but with whom she had continued to communicate, was to come out to her immediately; and this person, it appeared, could be quite
trusted to meet the conditions. She was ugly — ugly

enough, without abuse of it, and was unlimitedly good. The position offered her by Lady Beldonald was moreover exactly what she needed; widowed also, after many troubles and reverses, with her fortune of the smallest and her various children either buried or placed about, she had never had time or means to visit England, and would really be grateful in her declining years for the new experience and the pleasant light work involved in her cousin's hospitality. They had been much together early in life and Lady Beldonald was immensely fond of her — would in fact have tried to get hold of her before had n't Mrs. Brash been always in bondage to family duties, to the variety of her tribulations. I dare say I laughed at my friend's use of the term "position" — the position, one might call it, of a candlestick or a sign-post, and I dare say I must have asked if the special service the poor lady was to render had been made clear to her. Mrs. Munden left me in any case with the rather droll image of her faring forth across the sea quite consciously and resignedly to perform it.

The point of the communication had however been that my sitter was again looking up and would doubtless, on the arrival and due initiation of Mrs. Brash, be in form really to wait on me. The situation must further, to my knowledge, have developed happily, for I arranged with Mrs. Munden that our friend, now all ready to begin, but wanting first just to see the things I had most recently done, should come once more, as a final preliminary, to my studio. A good foreign friend of mine, a French painter, Paul Outreau, was at the moment in London, and I had proposed, as he was much interested in types, to get together for his amusement a small afternoon party. Every one came, my big room was full, there was music and a modest spread; and I've not forgotten the light of admiration in Outreau's expressive face as at the end of half an hour he came up to me in his enthusiasm. "Bonté divine, mon cher — que cette vieille est donc belle ! "

I had tried to collect all the beauty I could, and also all the youth, so that for a moment I was at a loss. I had talked to many people and provided for the music, and there were figures in the crowd that were still lost to me. "What old woman do you mean ? "

"I don't know her name — she was over by the door a moment ago. I asked somebody and was told, I think, that she's American."

I looked about and saw one of my guests attach a pair of fine eyes to Outreau very much as if she knew he must be talking of her. "Oh Lady Beldonald! Yes, she's handsome; but the great point about her is that she has been 'put up' to keep, and that she would n't be flattered if she knew you spoke of her as old. A box of sardines is 'old' only after it has been opened. Lady Beldonald never has yet been — but I'm going to do it." I joked, but I was somehow disappointed. It was a type that, with his unerring sense for the *banal*, I should n't have expected Outreau to pick out.

"You're going to paint her ? But, my dear man, she *is* painted — and as neither you nor I can do it. Où est-elle donc ? " He had lost her, and I saw I had made a mistake. "She's the greatest of all the great Holbeins."

I was relieved. "Ah then not Lady Beldonald! But do I possess a Holbein of *any* price unawares?"

"There she is — there she is! Dear, dear, dear, what a head!" And I saw whom he meant — and what: a small old lady in a black dress and a black bonnet, both relieved with a little white, who had evidently just changed her place to reach a corner from which more of the room and of the scene was presented to her. She appeared unnoticed and unknown, and I immediately recognised that some other guest must have brought her and, for want of opportunity, had as yet to call my attention to her. But two things, simultaneously with this and with each other, struck me with force; one of them the truth of Outreau's description of her, the other the fact that the person bringing her could only have been Lady Beldonald. She *was* a Holbein — of the first water; yet she was also Mrs. Brash, the imported "foil," the indispensable "accent," the successor to the dreary Miss Dadd! By the time I had put these things together — Outreau's "American" having helped me — I was in just such full possession of her face as I had found myself, on the other first occasion, of that of her patroness. Only with so different a consequence. I could n't look at her enough, and I stared and stared till I became aware she might have fancied me challenging her as a person unpresented. "All the same," Outreau went on, equally held, "c'est une tête à faire. If I were only staying long enough for a crack at her! But I tell you what" — and he seized my arm — "bring her over!"

"Over?"

"To Paris. She'd have a *succès fou.*"

"Ah thanks, my dear fellow," I was now quite in a position to say; "she's the handsomest thing in London, and" — for what I might do with her was already before me with intensity — "I propose to keep her to myself." It was before me with intensity, in the light of Mrs. Brash's distant perfection of a little white old face, in which every wrinkle was the touch of a master; but something else, I suddenly felt, was not less so, for Lady Beldonald, in the other quarter, and though she could n't have made out the subject of our notice, continued to fix us, and her eyes had the challenge of those of the woman of consequence who has missed something. A moment later I was close to her, apologising first for not having been more on the spot at her arrival, but saying in the next breath uncontrollably: "Why my dear lady, it's a Holbein!"

"A Holbein? What?"

"Why the wonderful sharp old face — so extraordinarily, consummately drawn — in the frame of black velvet. That of Mrs. Brash, I mean — is n't it her name? — your companion."

This was the beginning of a most odd matter — the essence of my anecdote; and I think the very first note of the oddity must have sounded for me in the tone in which her ladyship spoke after giving me a silent look. It seemed to come to me out of a distance immeasurably removed from Holbein. "Mrs. Brash is n't my 'companion' in the sense you appear to mean. She's my rather near relation and a very dear old friend. I *love* her — and you must know her."

"Know her? Rather! Why to see her is to want

on the spot to 'go' for her. She also must sit for me."

"*She?* Louisa Brash?" If Lady Beldonald had the theory that her beauty directly showed it when things were n't well with her, this impression, which the fixed sweetness of her serenity had hitherto struck me by no means as justifying, gave me now my first glimpse of its grounds. It was as if I had never before seen her face invaded by anything I should have called an expression. This expression moreover was of the faintest — was like the effect produced on a surface by an agitation both deep within and as yet much confused. "Have you told her so?" she then quickly asked, as if to soften the sound of her surprise.

"Dear no, I've but just noticed her — Outreau a moment ago put me on her. But we 're both so taken, and he also wants — "

"To *paint* her?" Lady Beldonald uncontrollably murmured.

"Don't be afraid we shall fight for her," I returned with a laugh for this tone. Mrs. Brash was still where I could see her without appearing to stare, and she might n't have seen I was looking at her, though her protectress, I 'm afraid, could scarce have failed of that certainty. "We must each take our turn, and at any rate she 's a wonderful thing, so that if you 'll let her go to Paris Outreau promises her there — "

"*There?*" my companion gasped.

"A career bigger still than among *us*, as he considers we have n't half their eye. He guarantees her a *succès fou*."

She could n't get over it. "Louisa Brash? In Paris?"

"They do see," I went on, "more than we; and they live extraordinarily, don't you know, *in* that. But she 'll do something here too."

"And what will she do?"

If frankly now I could n't help giving Mrs. Brash a longer look, so after it I could as little resist sounding my converser. "You 'll see. Only give her time."

She said nothing during the moment in which she met my eyes; but then: "Time, it seems to me, is exactly what you and your friend want. If you have n't talked with her —"

"We have n't seen her? Oh we see bang off — with a click like a steel spring. It 's our trade, it 's our life, and we should be donkeys if we made mistakes. That 's the way I saw you yourself, my lady, if I may say so; that 's the way, with a long pin straight through your body, I 've got you. And just so I 've got *her!*"

All this, for reasons, had brought my guest to her feet; but her eyes had while we talked never once followed the direction of mine. "You call her a Holbein?"

"Outreau did, and I of course immediately recognised it. Don't *you?* She brings the old boy to life! It 's just as I should call you a Titian. You bring *him* to life."

She could n't be said to relax, because she could n't be said to have hardened; but something at any rate on this took place in her — something indeed quite disconnected from what I would have called her. "Don't you understand that she has always been sup-

posed — ?" It had the ring of impatience; nevertheless it stopped short on a scruple.

I knew what it was, however, well enough to say it
for her if she preferred. "To be nothing whatever to
look at? To be unfortunately plain — or even if you
like repulsively ugly? Oh yes, I understand it perfectly, just as I understand — I have to as a part of
my trade — many other forms of stupidity. It's nothing new to one that ninety-nine people out of a hundred have no eyes, no sense, no taste. There are whole
communities impenetrably sealed. I don't say your
friend's a person to make the men turn round in
Regent Street. But it adds to the joy of the few who do
see that they have it so much to themselves. Where in
the world can she have lived? You must tell me all
about that — or rather, if she'll be so good, *she*
must."

"You mean then to speak to her — ?"

I wondered as she pulled up again. "Of her
beauty?"

"Her beauty!" cried Lady Beldonald so loud that
two or three persons looked round.

"Ah with every precaution of respect!" I declared
in a much lower tone. But her back was by this time
turned to me, and in the movement, as it were, one of
the strangest little dramas I've ever known was well
launched.

IT was a drama of small smothered intensely private things, and I knew of but one other person in the secret; yet that person and I found it exquisitely susceptible of notation, followed it with an interest the mutual communication of which did much for our enjoyment, and were present with emotion at its touching catastrophe. The small case — for so small a case — had made a great stride even before my little party separated, and in fact within the next ten minutes.

In that space of time two things had happened; one of which was that I made the acquaintance of Mrs. Brash, and the other that Mrs. Munden reached me, cleaving the crowd, with one of her usual pieces of news. What she had to impart was that, on her having just before asked Nina if the conditions of our sitting had been arranged with me, Nina had replied, with something like perversity, that she did n't propose to arrange them, that the whole affair was "off" again and that she preferred not to be further beset for the present. The question for Mrs. Munden was naturally what had happened and whether I understood. Oh I understood perfectly, and what I at first most understood was that even when I had brought in the name of Mrs. Brash intelligence was n't yet in Mrs. Munden. She was quite as surprised as Lady Beldonald had been on hearing of the esteem in which I

held Mrs. Brash's appearance. She was stupefied at
learning that I had just in my ardour proposed to its
proprietress to sit to me. Only she came round
promptly — which Lady Beldonald really never did.
Mrs. Munden was in fact wonderful; for when I had
given her quickly "Why she's a Holbein, you know,
absolutely," she took it up, after a first fine vacancy,
with an immediate abysmal "Oh *is* she?" that, as a
piece of social gymnastics, did her the greatest honour;
and she was in fact the first in London to spread the
tidings. For a face-about it was magnificent. But she
was also the first, I must add, to see what would really
happen — though this she put before me only a week
or two later. "It will kill her, my dear — that's what
it will do!"

She meant neither more nor less than that it would
kill Lady Beldonald if I were to paint Mrs. Brash; for
at this lurid light had we arrived in so short a space of
time. It was for me to decide whether my æsthetic
need of giving life to my idea was such as to justify me
in destroying it in a woman after all in most eyes so
beautiful. The situation was indeed sufficiently queer;
for it remained to be seen what I should positively
gain by giving up Mrs. Brash. I appeared to have in
any case lost Lady Beldonald, now too "upset" — it
was always Mrs. Munden's word about her and, as I
inferred, her own about herself — to meet me again
on our previous footing. The only thing, I of course
soon saw, was to temporise — to drop the whole question for the present and yet so far as possible keep each
of the pair in view. I may as well say at once that this
plan and this process gave their principal interest to

the next several months. Mrs. Brash had turned up, if I remember, early in the new year, and her little wonderful career was in our particular circle one of the features of the following season. It was at all events for myself the most attaching; it 's not my fault if I am so put together as often to find more life in situations obscure and subject to interpretation than in the gross rattle of the foreground. And there were all sorts of things, things touching, amusing, mystifying — and above all such an instance as I had never yet met — in this funny little fortune of the useful American cousin. Mrs. Munden was promptly at one with me as to the rarity and, to a near and human view, the beauty and interest of the position. We had neither of us ever before seen that degree and that special sort of personal success come to a woman for the first time so late in life. I found it an example of poetic, of absolutely retributive justice; so that my desire grew great to work it, as we say, on those lines. I had seen it all from the original moment at my studio; the poor lady had never known an hour's appreciation — which moreover, in perfect good faith, she had never missed. The very first thing I did after inducing so unintentionally the resentful retreat of her protectress had been to go straight over to her and say almost without preliminaries that I should hold myself immeasurably obliged for a few patient sittings. What I thus came face to face with was, on the instant, her whole unenlightened past and the full, if foreshortened, revelation of what among us all was now unfailingly in store for her. To turn the handle and start that tune came to me on the spot as a temptation. Here was a poor lady who had waited for the approach of old age to find out what she was worth. Here was a benighted being to whom it was to be disclosed in her fifty-seventh year — I was to make that out — that she had something that might pass for a face. She looked much more than her age, and was fairly frightened — as if I had been trying on her some possibly heartless London trick — when she had taken in my appeal. That showed me in what an air she had lived and — as I should have been tempted to put it had I spoken out — among what children of darkness. Later on I did them more justice; saw more that her wonderful points must have been points largely the fruit of time, and even that possibly she might never in all her life have looked so well as at this particular moment. It might have been that if her hour had struck I just happened to be present at the striking. What had occurred, all the same, was at the worst a notable comedy.

The famous "irony of fate" takes many forms, but I had never yet seen it take quite this one. She had been "had over" on an understanding, and she was n't playing fair. She had broken the law of her ugliness and had turned beautiful on the hands of her employer. More interesting even perhaps than a view of the conscious triumph that this might prepare for her, and of which, had I doubted of my own judgement, I could still take Outreau's fine start as the full guarantee — more interesting was the question of the process by which such a history could get itself enacted. The curious thing was that all the while the reasons of her having passed for plain — the reasons for Lady Beldonald's fond calculation, which they quite justified

— were written large in her face, so large that it was easy to understand them as the only ones she herself had ever read. What was it then that actually made the old stale sentence mean something so different ? — into what new combinations, what extraordinary language, unknown but understood at a glance, had time and life translated it ? The only thing to be said was that time and life were artists who beat us all, working with recipes and secrets we could never find out. I really ought to have, like a lecturer or a showman, a chart or a blackboard to present properly the relation, in the wonderful old tender battered blanched face, between the original elements and the exquisite final "style." I could do it with chalks, but I can scarcely do it with words. However, the thing was, for any artist who respected himself, to *feel* it — which I abundantly did; and then not to conceal from *her* I felt it — which I neglected as little. But she was really, to do her complete justice, the last to understand; and I'm not sure that, to the end — for there was an end — she quite made it all out or knew where she was. When you 've been brought up for fifty years on black it must be hard to adjust your organism at a day's notice to gold-colour. Her whole nature had been pitched in the key of her supposed plainness. She had known how to be ugly — it was the only thing she had learnt save, if possible, how not to mind it. Being beautiful took in any case a new set of muscles. It was on the prior conviction, literally, that she had developed her admirable dress, instinctively felicitous, always either black or white and a matter of rather severe squareness and studied line. She was magnificently neat;

everything has showed had a way of looking both old and fresh; and there was on every occasion the same picture in her draped head — draped in low-falling black — and the fine white plaits (of a painter's white, somehow) disposed on her chest. What had happened was that these arrangements, determined by certain considerations, lent themselves in effect much better to certain others. Adopted in mere shy silence they had really only deepened her accent. It was singular, moreover, that, so constituted, there was nothing in her aspect of the ascetic or the nun. She was a good hard sixteenth-century figure, not withered with innocence, bleached rather by life in the open. She was in short just what we had made of her, a Holbein for a great museum; and our position, Mrs. Munden's and mine, rapidly became that of persons having such a treasure to dispose of. The world — I speak of course mainly of the art-world — flocked to see it.

IV

"But has she any idea herself, poor thing?" was the way I had put it to Mrs. Munden on our next meeting after the incident at my studio; with the effect, however, only of leaving my friend at first to take me as alluding to Mrs. Brash's possible prevision of the chatter she might create. I had my own sense of that — this prevision had been *nil;* the question was of her consciousness of the office for which Lady Beldonald had counted on her and for which we were so promptly proceeding to spoil her altogether.

"Oh I think she arrived with a goodish notion," Mrs. Munden had replied when I had explained; "for she's clever too, you know, as well as good-looking, and I don't see how, if she ever really *knew* Nina, she could have supposed for a moment that she wasn't wanted for whatever she might have left to give up. Hasn't she moreover always been made to feel that she's ugly enough for anything?" It was even at this point already wonderful how my friend had mastered the case and what lights, alike for its past and its future, she was prepared to throw on it. "If she has seen herself as ugly enough for anything she has seen herself — and that was the only way — as ugly enough for Nina; and she has had her own manner of showing that she understands without making Nina commit herself to anything vulgar. Women are never without ways for doing such things — both for communicating and receiving knowledge — that I can't explain to you, and that you would n't understand if I could, since you must *be* a woman even to do that. I dare say they've expressed it all to each other simply in the language of kisses. But does n't it at any rate make something rather beautiful of the relation between them as affected by our discovery?"

I had a laugh for her plural possessive. "The point is of course that if there was a conscious bargain, and our action on Mrs. Brash is to deprive her of the sense of keeping her side of it, various things may happen that won't be good either for her or for ourselves. She may conscientiously throw up the position."

"Yes," my companion mused — "for she *is* conscientious. Or Nina, without waiting for that, may cast her forth."

I faced it all. "Then *we* should have to keep her."

"As a regular model?" Mrs. Munden was ready for anything. "Oh that would be lovely!"

But I further worked it out. "The difficulty is that she's *not* a model, hang it — that she's too good for one, that she's the very thing herself. When Outreau and I have each had our go, that will be all; there'll be nothing left for any one else. Therefore it behoves us quite to understand that our attitude's a responsibility. If we can't do for her positively more than Nina does —"

"We must let her alone?" My companion continued to muse. "I see!"

"Yet don't," I returned, "see too much. We *can* do more."

"Than Nina?" She was again on the spot. "It

397

would n't after all be difficult. We only want the directly opposite thing — and which is the only one the poor dear can give. Unless indeed," she suggested, "we simply retract — we back out."

I turned it over. "It 's too late for that. Whether Mrs. Brash's peace is gone I can't say. But Nina's is."

"Yes, and there 's no way to bring it back that won't sacrifice her friend. We can't turn round and say Mrs. Brash *is* ugly, can we ? But fancy Nina's not having *seen!*" Mrs. Munden exclaimed.

"She does n't see now," I answered. "She can't, I 'm certain, make out what we mean. The woman, for *her* still, is just what she always was. But she has nevertheless had her stroke, and her blindness, while she wavers and gropes in the dark, only adds to her discomfort. Her blow was to see the attention of the world deviate."

"All the same I don't think, you know," my interlocutress said, "that Nina will have made her a scene or that, whatever we do, she 'll ever make her one. That is n't the way it will happen, for she 's exactly as conscientious as Mrs. Brash."

"Then what *is* the way ?" I asked.

"It will just happen in silence."

"And what will 'it,' as you call it, be ?"

"Is n't that what we want really to see ?"

"Well," I replied after a turn or two about, "whether we want it or not it 's exactly what we *shall* see; which is a reason the more for fancying, between the pair there — in the quiet exquisite house, and full of superiorities and suppressions as they both are —

the extraordinary situation. If I said just now that it's too late to do anything but assent it's because I've taken the full measure of what happened at my studio. It took but a few moments— but she tasted of the tree."

My companion wondered. "Nina?"

"Mrs. Brash." And to have to put it so ministered, while I took yet another turn, to a sort of agitation. Our attitude *was* a responsibility.

But I had suggested something else to my friend, who appeared for a moment detached. "Should you say she'll hate her worse if she *does n't* see?"

"Lady Beldonald? Does n't see what *we* see, you mean, than if she does? Ah I give *that* up!" I laughed. "But what I can tell you is why I hold that, as I said just now, we can do most. We can do this: we can give to a harmless and sensitive creature hitherto practically disinherited — and give with an unexpectedness that will immensely add to its price — the pure joy of a deep draught of the very pride of life, of an acclaimed personal triumph in our superior sophisticated world."

Mrs. Munden had a glow of response for my sudden eloquence. "Oh it will be beautiful!"

V

WELL, that's what, on the whole and in spite of everything, it really was. It has dropped into my memory a rich little gallery of pictures, a regular panorama of those occasions that were to minister to the view from which I had so for a moment extracted a lyric inspiration. I see Mrs. Brash on each of these occasions practically enthroned and surrounded and more or less mobbed; see the hurrying and the nudging and the pressing and the staring; see the people "making up" and introduced, and catch the word when they have had their turn; hear it above all, the great one — "Ah yes, the famous Holbein!" — passed about with that perfection of promptitude that makes the motions of the London mind so happy a mixture of those of the parrot and the sheep. Nothing would be easier of course than to tell the whole little tale with an eye only for that silly side of it. Great was the silliness, but great also as to this case of poor Mrs. Brash, I will say for it, the good nature. Of course, furthermore, it took in particular "our set," with its positive child-terror of the *banal*, to be either so foolish or so wise; though indeed I've never quite known where our set begins and ends, and have had to content myself on this score with the indication once given me by a lady next whom I was placed at dinner: "Oh it's bounded on the north by Ibsen and on the south by Sargent!" Mrs. Brash never sat to me; she absolutely declined; and when she declared that it was quite enough for her that I had with that fine precipitation invited her, I quite took this as she meant it; before we had gone very far our understanding, hers and mine, was complete. Her attitude was as happy as her success was prodigious. The sacrifice of the portrait was a sacrifice to the true inwardness of Lady Beldonald, and did much, for the time, I divined, toward muffling their domestic tension. All it was thus in her power to say — and I heard of a few cases of her having said it — was that she was sure I would have painted her beautifully if she had n't prevented me. She could n't even tell the truth, which was that I certainly would have done so if Lady Beldonald had n't; and she never could mention the subject at all before that personage. I can only describe the affair, naturally, from the outside, and heaven forbid indeed that I should try too closely to reconstruct the possible strange intercourse of these good friends at home.

My anecdote, however, would lose half the point it may have to show were I to omit all mention of the consummate turn her ladyship appeared gradually to have found herself able to give her deportment. She had made it impossible I should myself bring up our old, our original question, but there was real distinction in her manner of now accepting certain other possibilities. Let me do her that justice; her effort at magnanimity must have been immense. There could n't fail of course to be ways in which poor Mrs. Brash paid for it. How much she had to pay we were in fact soon enough to see; and it 's my intimate conviction that, as a climax, her life at last was the price. But while she lived at least — and it was with an intensity, for those wondrous weeks, of which she had never dreamed — Lady Beldonald herself faced the music. This is what I mean by the possibilities, by the sharp actualities indeed, that she accepted. She took our friend out, she showed her at home, never attempted to hide or to betray her, played her no trick whatever so long as the ordeal lasted. She drank deep, on *her* side too, of the cup — the cup that for her own lips could only be bitterness. There was, I think, scarce a special success of her companion's at which she was n't personally present. Mrs. Munden's theory of the silence in which all this would be muffled for them was none the less, and in abundance, confirmed by our observations. The whole thing was to be the death of one or the other of them, but they never spoke of it at tea. I remember even that Nina went so far as to say to me once, looking me full in the eyes, quite sublimely, "I 've made out what you mean — she *is* a picture." The beauty of this moreover was that, as I 'm persuaded, she had n't really made it out at all — the words were the mere hypocrisy of her reflective endeavour for virtue. She could n't possibly have made it out; her friend was as much as ever "dreadfully plain" to her; she must have wondered to the last what on earth possessed us. Would n't it in fact have been after all just this failure of vision, this supreme stupidity in short, that kept the catastrophe so long at bay? There was a certain sense of greatness for her in seeing so many of us so absurdly mistaken; and I recall that on various occasions, and in particular when she uttered the words just quoted, this high serenity, as a sign of the relief of her soreness, if not of the effort of her conscience, did something quite visible to my eyes, and also quite unprecedented, for the beauty of her face. She got a real lift from it — such a momentary discernible sublimity that I recollect coming out on the spot with a queer crude amused "Do you know I believe I could paint you *now?*"

She was a fool not to have closed with me then and there; for what has happened since has altered everything — what was to happen a little later was so much more than I could swallow. This was the disappearance of the famous Holbein from one day to the other — producing a consternation among us all as great as if the Venus of Milo had suddenly vanished from the Louvre. "She has simply shipped her straight back" — the explanation was given in that form by Mrs. Munden, who added that any cord pulled tight enough would end at last by snapping. At the snap, in any case, we mightily jumped, for the masterpiece we had for three or four months been living with had made us feel its presence as a luminous lesson and a daily need. We recognised more than ever that it had been, for high finish, the gem of our collection — we found what a blank it left on the wall. Lady Beldonald might fill up the blank, but *we* could n't. That she did soon fill it up — and, heaven help us, *how?* — was put before me after an interval of no great length, but during which I had n't seen her. I dined on the Christmas of last year at Mrs. Munden's, and Nina, with a "scratch lot," as our hostess said, was there, so that, the preliminary wait being longish, she could approach me very sweetly. "I'll come to you to-morrow if you like," she said; and the effect of it, after a first stare at her, was to make me look all round. I took in, by these two motions, two things; one of which was that, though now again so satisfied herself of her high state, she could give me nothing comparable to what I should have got had she taken me up at the moment of my meeting her on her distinguished concession; the other that she was "suited" afresh and that Mrs. Brash's successor was fully installed. Mrs. Brash's successor was at the other side of the room, and I became conscious that Mrs. Munden was waiting to see my eyes seek her. I guessed the meaning of the wait; what *was* one, this time, to say? Oh first and foremost assuredly that it was immensely droll, for this time at least there was no mistake. The lady I looked upon, and as to whom my friend, again quite at sea, appealed to me for a formula, was as little a Holbein, or a specimen of any other school, as she was, like Lady Beldonald herself, a Titian. The formula was easy to give, for the amusement was that her prettiness — yes, literally, prodigiously, her prettiness — was distinct. Lady Beldonald had been magnificent — had been almost intelligent. Miss What's-her-name continues pretty, continues even young, and does n't matter a straw! She matters so ideally little that Lady Beldonald is practically safer, I judge, than she has ever been. There has n't been a symptom of chatter about this person, and I believe her protectress is much surprised that we're not more struck.

THE BELDONALD HOLBEIN

It was at any rate strictly impossible to me to make an appointment for the day as to which I have just recorded Nina's proposal; and the turn of events since then has not quickened my eagerness. Mrs. Munden remained in correspondence with Mrs. Brash — to the extent, that is, of three letters, each of which she showed me. They so told to our imagination her terrible little story that we were quite prepared — or thought we were — for her going out like a snuffed candle. She resisted, on her return to her original conditions, less than a year; the taste of the tree, as I had called it, had been fatal to her; what she had contentedly enough lived without before for half a century she could n't now live without for a day. I know nothing of her original conditions — some minor American city — save that for her to have gone back to them was clearly to have stepped out of her frame. We performed, Mrs. Munden and I, a small funeral service for her by talking it all over and making it all out. It was n't — the minor American city — a market for Holbeins, and what had occurred was that the poor old picture, banished from its museum and refreshed by the rise of no new movement to hang it, was capable of the miracle of a silent revolution, of itself turning, in its dire dishonour, its face to the wall. So it stood, without the intervention of the ghost of a critic, till they happened to pull it round again and find it mere dead paint. Well, it had had, if that 's anything, its season of fame, its name on a thousand tongues and printed in capitals in the catalogue. *We* had n't been at fault. I have n't, all the same, the least note of her — not a scratch. And I did her so in

405

intention! Mrs. Munden continues to remind me, however, that this is not the sort of rendering with which, on the other side, after all, Lady Beldonald proposes to content herself. She has come back to the question of her own portrait. Let me settle it then at last. Since she *will* have the real thing — well, hang it, she shall!

THE STORY IN IT

THE STORY IN IT

I

THE weather had turned so much worse that the rest of the day was certainly lost. The wind had risen and the storm gathered force; they gave from time to time a thump at the firm windows and dashed even against those protected by the verandah their vicious splotches of rain. Beyond the lawn, beyond the cliff, the great wet brush of the sky dipped deep into the sea. But the lawn, already vivid with the touch of May, showed a violence of watered green; the budding shrubs and trees repeated the note as they tossed their thick masses, and the cold troubled light, filling the pretty saloon, marked the spring afternoon as sufficiently young. The two ladies seated there in silence could pursue without difficulty — as well as, clearly, without interruption — their respective tasks; a confidence expressed, when the noise of the wind allowed it to be heard, by the sharp scratch of Mrs. Dyott's pen at the table where she was busy with letters.

Her visitor, settled on a small sofa that, with a palm-tree, a screen, a stool, a stand, a bowl of flowers and three photographs in silver frames, had been arranged near the light wood-fire as a choice "corner" — Maud Blessingbourne, her guest, turned audibly, though at intervals neither brief nor regular, the leaves of a book covered in lemon-coloured paper and not yet despoiled of a certain fresh crispness. This effect of the volume, for the eye, would have made it, as presumably the newest French novel — and evidently, from the attitude of the reader, "good" — consort happily with the special tone of the room, a consistent air of selection and suppression, one of the finer æsthetic evolutions. If Mrs. Dyott was fond of ancient French furniture and distinctly difficult about it, her inmates could be fond — with whatever critical cocks of charming dark-braided heads over slender sloping shoulders — of modern French authors. Nothing had passed for half an hour — nothing at least, to be exact, but that each of the companions occasionally and covertly intermitted her pursuit in such a manner as to ascertain the degree of absorption of the other without turning round. What their silence was charged with therefore was not only a sense of the weather, but a sense, so to speak, of its own nature. Maud Blessingbourne, when she lowered her book into her lap, closed her eyes with a conscious patience that seemed to say she waited; but it was nevertheless she who at last made the movement representing a snap of their tension. She got up and stood by the fire, into which she looked a minute; then came round and approached the window as if to see what was really going on. At this Mrs. Dyott wrote with re-freshed intensity. Her little pile of letters had grown, and if a look of determination was compatible with her fair and slightly faded beauty the habit of attending to her business could always keep pace with any excursion of her thought. Yet she was the first who spoke.

"I trust your book has been interesting."

"Well enough; a little mild."

A louder throb of the tempest had blurred the sound of the words. "A little wild?"

"Dear no — timid and tame; unless I've quite lost my sense."

"Perhaps you have," Mrs. Dyott placidly suggested — "reading so many."

Her companion made a motion of feigned despair. "Ah you take away my courage for going to my room, as I was just meaning to, for another."

"Another French one?"

"I'm afraid."

"Do you carry them by the dozen —?"

"Into innocent British homes?" Maud tried to remember. "I believe I brought three — seeing them in a shop-window as I passed through town. It never rains but it pours! But I've already read two."

"And are they the only ones you do read?"

"French ones?" Maud considered. "Oh no. D'Annunzio."

"And what's that?" Mrs. Dyott asked as she affixed a stamp.

"Oh you dear thing!" Her friend was amused, yet almost showed pity. "I know you don't read," Maud went on; "but why should you? *You* live!"

"Yes — wretchedly enough," Mrs. Dyott returned, getting her letters together. She left her place, holding them as a neat achieved handful, and came over to the fire while Mrs. Blessingbourne turned once more to the window, where she was met by another flurry.

Maud spoke then as if moved only by the elements. "Do you expect him through all this?"

Mrs. Dyott just waited, and it had the effect, indescribably, of making everything that had gone before seem to have led up to the question. This effect was even deepened by the way she then said "Whom do you mean?"

"Why I thought you mentioned at luncheon that Colonel Voyt was to walk over. Surely he can't."

"Do you care very much?" Mrs. Dyott asked.

Her friend now hesitated. "It depends on what you call 'much.' If you mean should I like to see him — then certainly."

"Well, my dear, I think he understands you're here."

"So that as he evidently isn't coming," Maud laughed, "it's particularly flattering! Or rather," she added, giving up the prospect again, "it would be, I think, quite extraordinarily flattering if he did. Except that of course," she threw in, "he might come partly for you."

"'Partly' is charming. Thank you for 'partly.' If you *are* going upstairs, will you kindly," Mrs. Dyott pursued, "put these into the box as you pass?"

The younger woman, taking the little pile of letters, considered them with envy. "Nine! You *are* good. You're always a living reproach!"

Mrs. Dyott gave a sigh. "I don't do it on purpose. The only thing, this afternoon," she went on, reverting to the other question, "would be their not having come down."

"And as to that you don't know."

"No — I don't know." But she caught even as she spoke a rat-tat-tat of the knocker, which struck her as a sign. "Ah there!"

"Then I go." And Maud whisked out.

Mrs. Dyott, left alone, moved with an air of selection to the window, and it was as so stationed, gazing out at the wild weather, that the visitor, whose delay to appear spoke of the wiping of boots and the disposal of drenched mackintosh and cap, finally found her. He was tall lean fine, with little in him, on the whole, to confirm the titular in the "Colonel Voyt" by which he was announced. But he had left the army, so that his reputation for gallantry mainly depended now on his fighting Liberalism in the House of Commons. Even these facts, however, his aspect scantily matched; partly, no doubt, because he looked, as was usually said, un-English. His black hair, cropped close, was lightly powdered with silver, and his dense glossy beard, that of an emir or a caliph, and grown for civil reasons, repeated its handsome colour and its somewhat foreign effect. His nose had a strong and shapely arch, and the dark grey of his eyes was tinted with blue. It had been said of him — in relation to these signs — that he would have struck you as a Jew had he not, in spite of his nose, struck you so much as an Irishman. Neither responsibility could in fact have been fixed upon him, and just now, at all events, he was only a pleasant weather-washed wind-battered Briton, who brought in from a struggle with the elements that he appeared quite to have enjoyed a certain amount of unremoved mud and an unusual quantity of easy expression. It was exactly the silence ensuing on the retreat of the servant and the closed door that marked between him and his hostess the degree of this ease. They met, as it were, twice: the first time while the servant was there and the second as soon as he was not. The difference was great between the two encounters, though we must add in justice to the second that its marks were at first mainly negative. This communion consisted only in their having drawn each other for a minute as close as possible — as possible, that is, with no help but the full clasp of hands. Thus they were mutually held, and the closeness was at any rate such that, for a little, though it took account of dangers, it did without words. When words presently came the pair were talking by the fire and she had rung for tea. He had by this time asked if the note he had dispatched to her after breakfast had been safely delivered.

"Yes, before luncheon. But I'm always in a state when — except for some extraordinary reason — you send such things by hand. I knew, without it, that you had come. It never fails. I'm sure when you're there — I'm sure when you're not."

He wiped, before the glass, his wet moustache. "I see. But this morning I had an impulse."

"It was beautiful. But they make me as uneasy, sometimes, your impulses, as if they were calculations; make me wonder what you have in reserve."

"Because when small children are too awfully good they die? Well, I *am* a small child compared to you — but I'm not dead yet. I cling to life."

He had covered her with his smile, but she continued grave. "I'm not half so much afraid when you're nasty."

"Thank you! What then did you do," he asked, "with my note?"

"You deserve that I should have spread it out on my dressing-table — or left it, better still, in Maud Blessingbourne's room."

He wondered while he laughed. "Oh but what does *she* deserve?"

It was her gravity that continued to answer. "Yes — it would probably kill her."

"She believes so in you?"

"She believes so in *you*. So don't be *too* nice to her."

He was still looking, in the chimney-glass, at the state of his beard — brushing from it, with his handkerchief, the traces of wind and wet. "If she also then prefers me when I'm nasty it seems to me I ought to satisfy her. Shall I now at any rate see her?"

"She's so like a pea on a pan over the possibility of it that she's pulling herself together in her room."

"Oh then we must try and keep her together. But why, graceful tender, pretty too — quite or almost as she is — does n't she re-marry?"

Mrs. Dyott appeared — and as if the first time — to look for the reason. "Because she likes too many men."

It kept up his spirits. "And how many *may* a lady like — ?"

"In order not to like any of them too much? Ah

415

that, you know, I never found out — and it's too late now. When," she presently pursued, "did you last see her?"

He really had to think. "Would it have been since last November or so? — somewhere or other where we spent three days."

"Oh at Surredge? I know all about that. I thought you also met afterwards."

He had again to recall. "So we did! Would n't it have been somewhere at Christmas? But it was n't by arrangement!" he laughed, giving with his forefinger a little pleasant nick to his hostess's chin. Then as if something in the way she received this attention put him back to his question of a moment before: "Have you kept my note?"

She held him with her pretty eyes. "Do you want it back?"

"Ah don't speak as if I did take things —!"

She dropped her gaze to the fire. "No, you don't; not even the hard things a really generous nature often would." She quitted, however, as if to forget that, the chimney-place. "I put it *there!*"

"You've burnt it? Good!" It made him easier, but he noticed the next moment on a table the lemon-coloured volume left there by Mrs. Blessingbourne, and, taking it up for a look, immediately put it down. "You might while you were about it have burnt that too."

"You've read it?"

"Dear yes. And you?"

"No," said Mrs. Dyott; "it was n't for me Maud brought it."

It pulled her visitor up. "Mrs. Blessingbourne brought it?"

"For such a day as this." But she wondered. "How you look! Is it so awful?"

"Oh like his others." Something had occurred to him; his thought was already far. "Does she know?"

"Know what?"

"Why anything."

But the door opened too soon for Mrs. Dyott, who could only murmur quickly — "Take care!'

IT was in fact Mrs. Blessingbourne, who had under her arm the book she had gone up for — a pair of covers showing this time a pretty, a candid blue. She was followed next minute by the servant, who brought in tea, the consumption of which, with the passage of greetings, enquiries and other light civilities between the two visitors, occupied a quarter of an hour. Mrs. Dyott meanwhile, as a contribution to so much amenity, mentioned to Maud that her fellow guest wished to scold her for the books she read — a statement met by this friend with the remark that he must first be sure about them. But as soon as he had picked up the new, the blue volume he broke out into a frank "Dear, dear!"

"Have you read that too?" Mrs. Dyott enquired. "How much you'll have to talk over together! The other one," she explained to him, "Maud speaks of as terribly tame."

"Ah I must have that out with her! You don't feel the extraordinary force of the fellow?" Voyt went on to Mrs. Blessingbourne.

And so, round the hearth, they talked — talked soon, while they warmed their toes, with zest enough to make it seem as happy a chance as any of the quieter opportunities their imprisonment might have involved. Mrs. Blessingbourne did feel, it then appeared, the force of the fellow, but she had her reserves and reactions, in which Voyt was much interested. Mrs. Dyott rather detached herself, mainly gazing, as she leaned back, at the fire; she intervened, however, enough to relieve Maud of the sense of being listened to. That sense, with Maud, was too apt to convey that one was listened to for a fool. "Yes, when I read a novel I mostly read a French one," she had said to Voyt in answer to a question about her usual practice; "for I seem with it to get hold more of the real thing — to get more life for my money. Only I'm not so infatuated with them but that sometimes for months and months on end I don't read any fiction at all."

The two books were now together beside them. "Then when you begin again you read a mass?"

"Dear no. I only keep up with three or four authors."

He laughed at this over the cigarette he had been allowed to light. "I like your 'keeping up,' and keeping up in particular with 'authors.'"

"One must keep up with somebody," Mrs. Dyott threw off.

"I dare say I'm ridiculous," Mrs. Blessingbourne conceded without heeding it; "but that's the way we express ourselves in my part of the country."

"I only alluded," said Voyt, "to the tremendous conscience of your sex. It's more than mine can keep up with. You take everything too hard. But if you can't read the novel of British and American manufacture, heaven knows I'm at one with you. It seems really to show our sense of life as the sense of puppies and kittens."

419

"Well," Maud more patiently returned, "I'm told all sorts of people are now doing wonderful things; but somehow I remain outside."

"Ah it's *they*, it's our poor twangers and twaddlers who remain outside. They pick up a living in the street. And who indeed would want them in?"

Mrs. Blessingbourne seemed unable to say, and yet at the same time to have her idea. The subject, in truth, she evidently found, was not so easy to handle. "People lend me things, and I try; but at the end of fifty pages —"

"There you are! Yes — heaven help us!"

"But what I mean," she went on, "is n't that I don't get woefully weary of the eternal French thing. What's *their* sense of life?"

"Ah voilà!" Mrs. Dyott softly sounded.

"Oh but it *is* one; you can make it out," Voyt promptly declared. "They do what they feel, and they feel more things than we. They strike so many more notes, and with so different a hand. When it comes to any account of a relation say between a man and a woman — I mean an intimate or a curious or a suggestive one — where are we compared to them? They don't exhaust the subject, no doubt," he admitted; "but we don't touch it, don't even skim it. It's as if we denied its existence, its possibility. You'll doubtless tell me, however," he went on, "that as all such relations *are* for us at the most much simpler we can only have all round less to say about them."

She met this imputation with the quickest amusement. "I beg your pardon. I don't think I shall tell you anything of the sort. I don't know that I even agree with your premiss."

"About such relations?" He looked agreeably surprised. "You think we make them larger? — or subtler?"

Mrs. Blessingbourne leaned back, not looking, like Mrs. Dyott, at the fire, but at the ceiling. "I don't know what I think."

"It's not that she doesn't know," Mrs. Dyott remarked. "It's only that she doesn't say."

But Voyt had this time no eye for their hostess. For a moment he watched Maud. "It sticks out of you, you know, that you've yourself written something. Haven't you — and published? I've a notion I could read *you*."

"When I do publish," she said without moving, "you'll be the last one I shall tell. I *have*," she went on, "a lovely subject, but it would take an amount of treatment —!"

"Tell us then at least what it is."

At this she again met his eyes. "Oh to tell it would be to express it, and that's just what I can't do. What I meant to say just now," she added, "was that the French, to my sense, give us only again and again, for ever and ever, the same couple. There they are once more, as one has had them to satiety, in that yellow thing, and there I shall certainly again find them in the blue."

"Then why do you keep reading about them?" Mrs. Dyott demanded.

Maud cast about. "I don't!" she sighed. "At all events, I shan't any more. I give it up."

"You've been looking for something, I judge," said Colonel Voyt, "that you're not likely to find. It doesn't exist."

"What is it?" Mrs. Dyott desired to know.

"I never look," Maud remarked, "for anything but an interest."

"Naturally. But your interest," Voyt replied, "is in something different from life."

"Ah not a bit! I *love* life — in art, though I hate it anywhere else. It's the poverty of the life those people show, and the awful bounders, of both sexes, that they represent."

"Oh now we have you!" her interlocutor laughed. "To me, when all's said and done, they seem to be — as near as art can come — in the truth of the truth. It can only take what life gives it, though it certainly may be a pity that that isn't better. Your complaint of their monotony is a complaint of their conditions. When you say we get always the same couple what do you mean but that we get always the same passion? Of course we do!" Voyt pursued. "If what you're looking for is another, that's what you won't anywhere find."

Maud for a while said nothing, and Mrs. Dyott seemed to wait. "Well, I suppose I'm looking, more than anything else, for a decent woman."

"Oh then you mustn't look for her in pictures of passion. That's not her element nor her whereabouts."

Mrs. Blessingbourne weighed the objection. "Doesn't it depend on what you mean by passion?"

"I think I can mean only one thing: the enemy to behaviour."

"Oh I can imagine passions that are on the contrary friends to it."

Her fellow guest thought. "Does n't it depend perhaps on what you mean by behaviour?"

"Dear no. Behaviour 's just behaviour — the most definite thing in the world."

"Then what do you mean by the 'interest' you just now spoke of? The picture of that definite thing?"

"Yes — call it that. Women are n't *always* vicious, even when they 're —"

"When they 're what?" Voyt pressed.

"When they 're unhappy. They can be unhappy and good."

"That one does n't for a moment deny. But can they be 'good' and interesting?"

"That must be Maud's subject!" Mrs. Dyott interposed. "To show a woman who *is*. I 'm afraid, my dear," she continued, "you could only show yourself."

"You 'd show then the most beautiful specimen conceivable" — and Voyt addressed himself to Maud. "But does n't it prove that life is, against your contention, more interesting than art? Life you embellish and elevate; but art would find itself able to do nothing with you, and, on such impossible terms, would ruin you."

The colour in her faint consciousness gave beauty to her stare. "'Ruin' me?"

"He means," Mrs. Dyott again indicated, "that you 'd ruin 'art.'"

"Without on the other hand" — Voyt seemed to assent — "its giving at all a coherent impression of you."

"She wants her romance cheap!" said Mrs. Dyott.

"Oh no — I should be willing to pay for it. I don't see why the romance — since you give it that name — should be all, as the French inveterately make it, for the women who are bad."

"Oh they pay for it!" said Mrs. Dyott.

"*Do* they?"

"So at least" — Mrs. Dyott a little corrected herself — "one has gathered (for I don't read your books, you know!) that they're usually shown as doing."

Maud wondered, but looking at Voyt. "They're shown often, no doubt, as paying for their badness. But are they shown as paying for their romance?"

"My dear lady," said Voyt, "their romance *is* their badness. There isn't any other. It's a hard law, if you will, and a strange, but goodness has to go without that luxury. Isn't to *be* good just exactly, all round, to go without?" He put it before her kindly and clearly — regretfully too, as if he were sorry the truth should be so sad. He and she, his pleasant eyes seemed to say, would, had they had the making of it, have made it better. "One has heard it before — at least *I* have; one has heard your question put. But always, when put to a mind not merely muddled, for an inevitable answer. 'Why don't you, *cher monsieur*, give us the drama of virtue?' 'Because, *chère madame*, the high privilege of virtue is precisely to avoid drama.'

The adventures of the honest lady? The honest lady has n't, can't possibly have, adventures."

Mrs. Blessingbourne only met his eyes at first, smiling with some intensity. "Does n't it depend a little on what you call adventures?"

"My poor Maud," said Mrs. Dyott as if in compassion for sophistry so simple, "adventures are just adventures. That's all you can make of them!"

But her friend talked for their companion and as if without hearing. "Does n't it depend a good deal on what you call drama?" Maud spoke as one who had already thought it out. "Does n't it depend on what you call romance?"

Her listener gave these arguments his very best attention. "Of course you may call things anything you like — speak of them as one thing and mean quite another. But why should it depend on anything? Behind these words we use — the adventure, the novel, the drama, the romance, the situation, in short, as we most comprehensively say — behind them all stands the same sharp fact which they all in their different ways represent."

"Precisely!" Mrs. Dyott was full of approval.

Maud however was full of vagueness. "What great fact?"

"The fact of a relation. The adventure's a relation; the relation's an adventure. The romance, the novel, the drama are the picture of one. The subject the novelist treats is the rise, the formation, the development, the climax and for the most part the decline of one. And what is the honest lady doing on that side of the town?"

Mrs. Dyott was more pointed. "She does n't so much as *form* a relation."

But Maud bore up. "Does n't it depend again on what you call a relation?"

"Oh," said Mrs. Dyott, "if a gentleman picks up her pocket-handkerchief —"

"Ah even that's one," their friend laughed, "if she has thrown it to him. We can only deal with one that *is* one."

"Surely," Maud replied. "But if it's an innocent one —?"

"Does n't it depend a good deal," Mrs. Dyott asked, "on what you call innocent?"

"You mean that the adventures of innocence have so often been the material of fiction? Yes," Voyt replied; "that's exactly what the bored reader complains of. He has asked for bread and been given a stone. What is it but, with absolute directness, a question of interest or, as people say, of the story? What's a situation undeveloped but a subject lost? If a relation stops, where's the story? If it does n't stop, where's the innocence? It seems to me you must choose. It would be very pretty if it were otherwise, but that's how we flounder. Art is our flounderings shown."

Mrs. Blessingbourne — and with an air of deference scarce supported perhaps by its sketchiness — kept her deep eyes on this definition. "But sometimes we flounder out."

It immediately touched in Colonel Voyt the spring of a genial derision. "That's just where I expected *you* would! One always sees it come."

"He has, you notice," Mrs. Dyott parenthesised to Maud, "seen it come so often; and he has always waited for it and met it."

"Met it, dear lady, simply enough! It's the old story, Mrs. Blessingbourne. The relation's innocent that the heroine gets out of. The book's innocent that's the story of her getting out. But what the devil — in the name of innocence — was she doing *in?*"

Mrs. Dyott promptly echoed the question. "You have to be in, you know, to *get* out. So there you are already with your relation. It's the end of your goodness."

"And the beginning," said Voyt, "of your play!"

"Are n't they all, for that matter, even the worst," Mrs. Dyott pursued, "supposed *some* time or other to get out? But if meanwhile they 've been in, however briefly, long enough to adorn a tale —"

"They 've been in long enough to point a moral. That is to point ours!" With which, and as if a sudden flush of warmer light had moved him, Colonel Voyt got up. The veil of the storm had parted over a great red sunset.

Mrs. Dyott also was on her feet, and they stood before his charming antagonist, who, with eyes lowered and a somewhat fixed smile, had not moved. "We 've spoiled her subject!" the elder lady sighed.

"Well," said Voyt, "it's better to spoil an artist's subject than to spoil his reputation. I mean," he explained to Maud with his indulgent manner, "his appearance of knowing what he has got hold of, for that, in the last resort, is his happiness."

She slowly rose at this, facing him with an aspect as handsomely mild as his own. "You can't spoil my happiness."

He held her hand an instant as he took leave. "I wish I could add to it!"

III

WHEN he had quitted them and Mrs. Dyott had candidly asked if her friend had found him rude or crude, Maud replied — though not immediately — that she had feared showing only too much how charming she found him. But if Mrs. Dyott took this it was to weigh the sense. "How could you show it too much?"

"Because I always feel that that's my only way of showing anything. It's absurd, if you like," Mrs. Blessingbourne pursued, "but I never know, in such intense discussions, what strange impression I may give."

Her companion looked amused. "Was it intense?"

"*I* was," Maud frankly confessed.

"Then it's a pity you were so wrong. Colonel Voyt, you know, is right." Mrs. Blessingbourne at this gave one of the slow soft silent headshakes to which she often resorted and which, mostly accompanied by the light of cheer, had somehow, in spite of the small obstinacy that smiled in them, a special grace. With this grace, for a moment, her friend, looking her up and down, appeared impressed, yet not too much so to take the next minute a decision. "Oh my dear, I'm sorry to differ from any one so lovely — for you're awfully beautiful to-night, and your frock's the very nicest I've ever seen you wear. But he's as right as he can be."

Maud repeated her motion. "Not so right, at all events, as he thinks he is. Or perhaps I can say," she

429

went on, after an instant, "that I'm not so wrong. I do know a little what I'm talking about."

Mrs. Dyott continued to study her. "You *are* vexed. You naturally don't like it — such destruction."

"Destruction?"

"Of your illusion."

"I *have* no illusion. If I had moreover it would n't be destroyed. I have on the whole, I think, my little decency."

Mrs. Dyott stared. "Let us grant it for argument. What, then?"

"Well, I've also my little drama."

"An attachment?"

"An attachment."

"That you should n't have?"

"That I should n't have."

"A passion?"

"A passion."

"Shared?"

"Ah thank goodness, no!"

Mrs. Dyott continued to gaze. "The object's unaware — ?"

"Utterly."

Mrs. Dyott turned it over. "Are you sure?"

"Sure."

"That's what you call your decency? But is n't it," Mrs. Dyott asked, "rather *his*?"

"Dear no. It's only his good fortune."

Mrs. Dyott laughed. "But yours, darling — your good fortune: where does *that* come in?"

"Why, in my sense of the romance of it."

"The romance of what? Of his not knowing?"

"Of my not wanting him to. If I did" — Maud had touchingly worked it out — "where would be my honesty?"

The enquiry, for an instant, held her friend; yet only, it seemed, for a stupefaction that was almost amusement. "Can you want or not want as you like? Where in the world, if you don't want, is your romance?"

Mrs. Blessingbourne still wore her smile, and she now, with a light gesture that matched it, just touched the region of her heart. "There!"

Her companion admiringly marvelled. "A lovely place for it, no doubt! — but not quite a place, that I can see, to make the sentiment a relation."

"Why not? What more is required for a relation for *me*?"

"Oh all sorts of things, I should say! And many more, added to those, to make it one for the person you mention."

"Ah that I don't pretend it either should be or *can* be. I only speak for myself."

This was said in a manner that made Mrs. Dyott, with a visible mixture of impressions, suddenly turn away. She indulged in a vague movement or two, as if to look for something; then again found herself near her friend, on whom with the same abruptness, in fact with a strange sharpness, she conferred a kiss that might have represented either her tribute to exalted consistency or her idea of a graceful close of the discussion. "You deserve that one should speak *for* you!"

Her companion looked cheerful and secure. "How *can* you without knowing —?"

"Oh by guessing! It's not —?"

But that was as far as Mrs. Dyott could get. "It's not," said Maud, "any one you've ever seen."

"Ah then I give you up!"

And Mrs. Dyott conformed for the rest of Maud's stay to the spirit of this speech. It was made on a Saturday night, and Mrs. Blessingbourne remained till the Wednesday following, an interval during which, as the return of fine weather was confirmed by the Sunday, the two ladies found a wider range of action. There were drives to be taken, calls made, objects of interest seen at a distance; with the effect of much easy talk and still more easy silence. There had been a question of Colonel Voyt's probable return on the Sunday, but the whole time passed without a sign from him, and it was merely mentioned by Mrs. Dyott, in explanation, that he must have been suddenly called, as he was so liable to be, to town. That this in fact was what had happened he made clear to her on Thursday afternoon, when, walking over again late, he found her alone. The consequence of his Sunday letters had been his taking, that day, the 4.15. Mrs. Voyt had gone back on Thursday, and he now, to settle on the spot the question of a piece of work begun at his place, had rushed down for a few hours in anticipation of the usual collective move for the week's end. He was to go up again by the late train, and had to count a little — a fact accepted by his hostess with the hard pliancy of practice — his present happy moments. Too few as these were, however, he found time to make of her an enquiry or two not directly bearing on their situation. The first was a recall of the question for which Mrs. Blessingbourne's entrance on the previous Saturday had arrested her answer. Had that lady the idea of anything between them?

"No. I'm sure. There's one idea she has got," Mrs. Dyott went on; "but it's quite different and not so very wonderful."

"What then is it?"

"Well, that she's herself in love."

Voyt showed his interest. "You mean she told you?"

"I got it out of her."

He showed his amusement. "Poor thing! And with whom?"

"With you."

His surprise, if the distinction might be made, was less than his wonder. "You got that out of her too?"

"No — it remains in. Which is much the best way for it. For you to know it would be to end it."

He looked rather cheerfully at sea. "Is that then why you tell me?"

"I mean for her to know you know it. Therefore it's in your interest not to let her."

"I see," Voyt after a moment returned. "Your real calculation is that my interest will be sacrificed to my vanity — so that, if your other idea is just, the flame will in fact, and thanks to her morbid conscience, expire by her taking fright at seeing me so pleased. But I promise you," he declared, "that she shan't see it. So there you are!" She kept her eyes on him

433

and had evidently to admit after a little that there she
was. Distinct as he had made the case, however, he
was n't yet quite satisfied. "Why are you so sure
I 'm the man?"

"From the way she denies you."

"You put it to her?"

"Straight. If you had n't been she 'd of course
have confessed to you — to keep me in the dark about
the real one."

Poor Voyt laughed out again. "Oh you dear souls!"

"Besides," his companion pursued, "I was n't in
want of that evidence."

"Then what other had you?"

"Her state before you came — which was what
made me ask you how much you had seen her. And
her state after it," Mrs. Dyott added. "And her
state," she wound up, "while you were here."

"But her state while I was here was charming."

"Charming. That 's just what I say."

She said it in a tone that placed the matter in its
right light — a light in which they appeared kindly,
quite tenderly, to watch Maud wander away into
space with her lovely head bent under a theory rather
too big for it. Voyt's last word, however, was that
there was just enough in it — in the theory — for them
to allow that she had not shown herself, on the occasion of their talk, wholly bereft of sense. Her consciousness, if they let it alone — as they of course after
this mercifully must — *was*, in the last analysis, a
kind of shy romance. Not a romance like their own,
a thing to make the fortune of any author up to the
mark — one who should have the invention or who

could have the courage; but a small scared starved subjective satisfaction that would do her no harm and nobody else any good. Who but a duffer — he stuck to his contention — would see the shadow of a "story" in it?

FLICKERBRIDGE

FLICKERBRIDGE

I

FRANK GRANGER had arrived from Paris to paint a portrait — an order given him, as a young compatriot with a future, whose early work would some day have a price, by a lady from New York, a friend of his own people and also, as it happened, of Addie's, the young woman to whom it was publicly both affirmed and denied that he was engaged. Other young women in Paris — fellow members there of the little tight transpontine world of art-study— professed to know that the pair had "several times" over renewed their fond understanding. This, however, was their own affair; the last phase of the relation, the last time of the times, had passed into vagueness; there was perhaps even an impression that if they were inscrutable to their friends they were not wholly crystalline to each other and themselves. What had occurred for Granger at all events in connexion with the portrait was that Mrs. Bracken, his intending model, whose return to America was at hand, had suddenly been called to London by her husband, occupied there with pressing business, but had yet desired that her displacement should not interrupt her sittings. The young man, at her request, had followed her to England and profited by all she could give him, making shift with a small studio lent him by a London painter whom he had known

439

and liked a few years before in the French *atelier* that then cradled, and that continued to cradle, so many of their kind.

The British capital was a strange grey world to him, where people walked, in more ways than one, by a dim light; but he was happily of such a turn that the impression, just as it came, could nowhere ever fail him, and even the worst of these things was almost as much an occupation — putting it only at that — as the best. Mrs. Bracken moreover passed him on, and while the darkness ebbed a little in the April days he found himself consolingly committed to a couple of fresh subjects. This cut him out work for more than another month, but meanwhile, as he said, he saw a lot — a lot that, with frequency and with much expression, he wrote about to Addie. She also wrote to her absent friend, but in briefer snatches, a meagreness to her reasons for which he had long since assented. She had other play for her pen as well as, fortunately, other remuneration; a regular correspondence for a "prominent Boston paper," fitful connexions with public sheets perhaps also in cases fitful, and a mind above all engrossed at times, to the exclusion of everything else, with the study of the short story. This last was what she had mainly come out to go into, two or three years after he had found himself engulfed in the mystery of Carolus. She was indeed, on her own deep sea, more engulfed than he had ever been, and he had grown to accept the sense that, for progress too, she sailed under more canvas. It had n't been particularly present to him till now that he had in the least got on, but the way in which Addie had — and evidently still more would — was the theme, as it were, of every tongue. She had thirty short stories out and nine descriptive articles. His three or four portraits of fat American ladies — they were all fat, all ladies and all American — were a poor show compared with these triumphs; especially as Addie had begun to throw out that it was about time they should go home. It kept perpetually coming up in Paris, in the trans-pontine world, that, as the phrase was, America had grown more interesting since they left. Addie was attentive to the rumour, and, as full of conscience as she was of taste, of patriotism as of curiosity, had often put it to him frankly, with what he, who was of New York, recognised as her New England emphasis: "I'm not sure, you know, that we do *real* justice to our country." Granger felt he would do it on the day — if the day ever came — he should irrevocably marry her. No other country could possibly have produced her.

II

BUT meanwhile it befell that, in London, he was stricken with influenza and with subsequent sorrow. The attack was short but sharp — had it lasted Addie would certainly have come to his aid; most of a blight really in its secondary stage. The good ladies his sitters — the ladies with the frizzled hair, with the diamond earrings, with the chins tending to the massive — left for him, at the door of his lodgings, flowers, soup and love, so that with their assistance he pulled through; but his convalescence was slow and his weakness out of proportion to the muffled shock. He came out, but he went about lame; it tired him to paint — he felt as if he had been ill three months. He strolled in Kensington Gardens when he should have been at work; he sat long on penny chairs and helplessly mused and mooned. Addie desired him to return to Paris, but there were chances under his hand that he felt he had just wit enough left not to relinquish. He would have gone for a week to the sea — he would have gone to Brighton; but Mrs. Bracken had to be finished — Mrs. Bracken was so soon to sail. He just managed to finish her in time — the day before the date fixed for his breaking ground on a greater business still, the circumvallation of Mrs. Dunn. Mrs. Dunn duly waited on him, and he sat down before her, feeling, however, ere he rose, that he must take a long breath before the attack. While asking himself that

night, therefore, where he should best replenish his
lungs he received from Addie, who had had from Mrs.
Bracken a poor report of him, a communication
which, besides being of sudden and startling interest,
applied directly to his case.

His friend wrote to him under the lively emotion of
having from one day to another become aware of a
new relative, an ancient cousin, a sequestered gentle-
woman, the sole survival of "the English branch of
the family," still resident, at Flickerbridge, in the "old
family home," and with whom, that he might immediately betake himself to so auspicious a quarter for
change of air, she had already done what was proper
to place him, as she said, in touch. What came of it
all, to be brief, was that Granger found himself so
placed almost as he read : he was in touch with Miss
Wenham of Flickerbridge, to the extent of being in
correspondence with her, before twenty-four hours
had sped. And on the second day he was in the train,
settled for a five-hours' run to the door of this amiable
woman who had so abruptly and kindly taken him on
trust and of whom but yesterday he had never so much
as heard. This was an oddity — the whole incident
was — of which, in the corner of his compartment, as
he proceeded, he had time to take the size. But the
surprise, the incongruity, as he felt, could but deepen
as he went. It was a sufficiently queer note, in the
light, or the absence of it, of his late experience, that so
complex a product as Addie should have *any* simple
insular tie; but it was a queerer note still that she
should have had one so long only to remain unprofit-
ably unconscious of it. Not to have done something

with it, used it, worked it, talked about it at least, and perhaps even written — these things, at the rate she moved, represented a loss of opportunity under which, as he saw her, she was peculiarly formed to wince. She was at any rate, it was clear, doing something with it now; using it, working it, certainly, already talking — and, yes, quite possibly writing — about it. She was in short smartly making up what she had missed, and he could take such comfort from his own action as he had been helped to by the rest of the facts, succinctly reported from Paris on the very morning of his start.

It was the singular story of a sharp split — in a good English house — that dated now from years back. A worthy Briton, of the best middling stock, had, during the fourth decade of the century, as a very young man, in Dresden, whither he had been dispatched to qualify in German for a stool in an uncle's counting-house, met, admired, wooed and won an American girl, of due attractions, domiciled at that period with her parents and a sister, who was also attractive, in the Saxon capital. He had married her, taken her to England, and there, after some years of harmony and happiness, lost her. The sister in question had, after her death, come to him and to his young child on a visit, the effect of which, between the pair, eventually defined itself as a sentiment that was not to be resisted. The bereaved husband, yielding to a new attachment and a new response, and finding a new union thus prescribed, had yet been forced to reckon with the unaccommodating law of the land. Encompassed with frowns in his own country however, marriages of this

444

particular type were wreathed in smiles in his sister's-in-law, so that his remedy was not forbidden. Choosing between two allegiances he had let the one go that seemed the least close, and had in brief transplanted his possibilities to an easier air. The knot was tied for the couple in New York, where, to protect the legitimacy of such other children as might come to them, they settled and prospered. Children came, and one of the daughters, growing up and marrying in her turn, was, if Frank rightly followed, the mother of his own Addie, who had been deprived of the knowledge of her indeed, in childhood, by death, and been brought up, though without undue tension, by a step-mother — a character breaking out thus anew.

The breach produced in England by the invidious action, as it was there held, of the girl's grandfather, had not failed to widen — all the more that nothing had been done on the American side to close it. Frigidity had settled, and hostility had been arrested only by indifference. Darkness therefore had fortunately supervened, and a cousinship completely divided. On either side of the impassable gulf, of the impenetrable curtain, each branch had put forth its leaves — a foliage failing, in the American quarter, it was distinct enough to Granger, of no sign or symptom of climate and environment. The graft in New York had taken, and Addie was a vivid, an unmistakeable flower. At Flickerbridge, or wherever, on the other hand, strange to say, the parent stem had had a fortune comparatively meagre. Fortune, it was true, in the vulgarest sense, had attended neither party. Addie's immediate belongings were as poor as they were numerous, and he gathered that Miss Wenham's pretensions to wealth were not so marked as to expose the claim of kinship to the imputation of motive. To this lady's single identity the original stock had at all events dwindled, and our young man was properly warned that he would find her shy and solitary. What was singular was that in these conditions she should desire, she should endure, to receive him. But that was all another story, lucid enough when mastered. He kept Addie's letters, exceptionally copious, in his lap; he conned them at intervals; he held the threads.

He looked out between whiles at the pleasant English land, an April *aquarelle* washed in with wondrous breadth. He knew the French thing, he knew the American, but he had known nothing of this. He saw it already as the remarkable Miss Wenham's setting. The doctor's daughter at Flickerbridge, with nippers on her nose, a palette on her thumb and innocence in her heart, had been the miraculous link. She had become aware even there, in our world of wonders, that the current fashion for young women so equipped was to enter the Parisian lists. Addie had accordingly chanced upon her, on the slopes of Montparnasse, as one of the English girls in one of the thorough-going sets. They had met in some easy collocation and had fallen upon common ground; after which the young woman, restored to Flickerbridge for an interlude and retailing there her adventures and impressions, had mentioned to Miss Wenham, who had known and protected her from babyhood, that that lady's own name of Adelaide was, as well as the surname conjoined with it, borne, to her knowledge, in Paris, by an extra-

ordinary American specimen. She had then recrossed
the Channel with a wonderful message, a courteous
challenge, to her friend's duplicate, who had in turn
granted through her every satisfaction. The duplicate
had in other words bravely let Miss Wenham know
exactly who she was. Miss Wenham, in whose personal tradition the flame of resentment appeared to
have been reduced by time to the palest ashes — for
whom indeed the story of the great schism was now but
a legend only needing a little less dimness to make it
romantic — Miss Wenham had promptly responded
by a letter fragrant with the hope that old threads
might be taken up. It was a relationship that they
must puzzle out together, and she had earnestly
sounded the other party to it on the subject of a possible visit. Addie had met her with a definite promise;
she would come soon, she would come when free, she
would come in July; but meanwhile she sent her
deputy. Frank asked himself by what name she had
described, by what character introduced him to
Flickerbridge. He mainly felt on the whole as if he
were going there to find out if he were engaged to her.
He was at sea really now as to which of the various
views Addie herself took of it. To Miss Wenham she
must definitely have taken one, and perhaps Miss
Wenham would reveal it. This expectation was in fact
his excuse for a possible indiscretion.

III

HE was indeed to learn on arrival to what he had been committed; but that was for a while so much a part of his first general impression that the particular truth took time to detach itself, the first general impression demanding verily all his faculties of response. He almost felt for a day or two the victim of a practical joke, a gross abuse of confidence. He had presented himself with the moderate amount of flutter involved in a sense of due preparation; but he had then found that, however primed with prefaces and prompted with hints, he had n't been prepared at all. How *could* he be, he asked himself, for anything so foreign to his experience, so alien to his proper world, so little to be preconceived in the sharp north light of the newest impressionism, and yet so recognised after all in the event, so noted and tasted and assimilated? It was a case he would scarce have known how to describe — could doubtless have described best with a full clean brush, supplemented by a play of gesture; for it was always his habit to see an occasion, of whatever kind, primarily as a picture, so that he might get it, as he was wont to say, so that he might keep it, well together. He had been treated of a sudden, in this adventure, to one of the sweetest fairest coolest impressions of his life — one moreover visibly complete and homogeneous from the start. Oh it was *there*, if that was all one wanted of a thing! It was so "there" that, as had befallen him in Italy, in Spain, confronted at last, in dusky side-chapel or rich museum, with great things dreamed of or with greater ones unexpectedly presented, he had held his breath for fear of breaking the spell; had almost, from the quick impulse to respect, to prolong, lowered his voice and moved on tiptoe. Supreme beauty suddenly revealed is apt to strike us as a possible illusion playing with our desire — instant freedom with it to strike us as a possible rashness.

This fortunately, however — and the more so as his freedom for the time quite left him — did n't prevent his hostess, the evening of his advent and while the vision was new, from being exactly as queer and rare and *impayable*, as improbable, as impossible, as delightful at the eight o'clock dinner — she appeared to keep these immense hours — as she had overwhelmingly been at the five o'clock tea. She was in the most natural way in the world one of the oddest apparitions, but that the particular means to such an end *could* be natural was an inference difficult to make. He failed in fact to make it for a couple of days; but then — though then only — he made it with confidence. By this time indeed he was sure of everything, luckily including himself. If we compare his impression, with slight extravagance, to some of the greatest he had ever received, this is simply because the image before him was so rounded and stamped. It expressed with pure perfection, it exhausted its character. It was so absolutely and so unconsciously what it was. He had been floated by the strangest of chances out of the rushing stream into a clear still backwater — a deep

449

and quiet pool in which objects were sharply mirrored. He had hitherto in life known nothing that was old except a few statues and pictures; but here everything was old, was immemorial, and nothing so much so as the very freshness itself. Vaguely to have supposed there were such nooks in the world had done little enough, he now saw, to temper the glare of their opposites. It was the fine touches that counted, and these had to be seen to be believed.

Miss Wenham, fifty-five years of age and unappeasably timid, unaccountably strange, had, on her reduced scale, an almost Gothic grotesqueness; but the final effect of one's sense of it was an amenity that accompanied one's steps like wafted gratitude. More flurried, more spasmodic, more apologetic, more completely at a loss at one moment and more precipitately abounding at another, he had never before in all his days seen any maiden lady; yet for no maiden lady he had ever seen had he so promptly conceived a private enthusiasm. Her eyes protruded, her chin receded and her nose carried on in conversation a queer little independent motion. She wore on the top of her head an upright circular cap that made her resemble a caryatid disburdened, and on other parts of her person strange combinations of colours, stuffs, shapes, of metal, mineral and plant. The tones of her voice rose and fell, her facial convulsions, whether tending — one could scarce make out — to expression or *re*pression, succeeded each other by a law of their own; she was embarrassed at nothing and at everything, frightened at everything and at nothing, and she approached objects, subjects, the simplest questions and answers and the whole material of intercourse, either with the indirectness of terror or with the violence of despair. These things, none the less, her refinements of oddity and intensities of custom, her betrayal at once of conventions and simplicities, of ease and of agony, her roundabout retarded suggestions and perceptions, still permitted her to strike her guest as irresistibly charming. He did n't know what to call it; she was a fruit of time. She had a queer distinction. She had been expensively produced and there would be a good deal more of her to come.

The result of the whole quality of her welcome, at any rate, was that the first evening, in his room, before going to bed, he relieved his mind in a letter to Addie, which, if space allowed us to embody it in our text, would usefully perform the office of a "plate." It would enable us to present ourselves as profusely illustrated. But the process of reproduction, as we say, costs. He wished his friend to know how grandly their affair turned out. She had put him in the way of something absolutely special – an old house untouched, untouchable, indescribable, an old corner such as one did n't believe existed, and the holy calm of which made the chatter of studios, the smell of paint, the slang of critics, the whole sense and sound of Paris, come back as so many signs of a huge monkey-cage. He moved about, restless, while he wrote; he lighted cigarettes and, nervous and suddenly scrupulous, put them out again; the night was mild and one of the windows of his large high room, which stood over the garden, was up. He lost himself in the things about him, in the type of the room, the last century with not a chair moved, not a point stretched. He hung over the objects and ornaments, blissfully few and adorably good, perfect pieces all, and never one, for a change, French. The scene was as rare as some fine old print with the best bits down in the corners. Old books and old pictures, allusions remembered and aspects conjectured, reappeared to him; he knew now what anxious islanders had been trying for in their backward hunt for the homely. But the homely at Flickerbridge was all style, even as style at the same time was mere honesty. The larger, the smaller past — he scarce knew which to call it — was at all events so hushed to sleep round him as he wrote that he had almost a bad conscience about having come. How one might love it, but how one might spoil it! To look at it too hard was positively to make it conscious, and to make it conscious was positively to wake it up. Its only safety, of a truth, was to be left still to sleep — to sleep in its large fair chambers and under its high clean canopies.

He added thus restlessly a line to his letter, maundered round the room again, noted and fingered something else, and then, dropping on the old flowered sofa, sustained by the tight cubes of its cushions, yielded afresh to the cigarette, hesitated, stared, wrote a few words more. He wanted Addie to know, that was what he most felt, unless he perhaps felt more how much she herself would want to. Yes, what he supremely saw was all that Addie would make of it. Up to his neck in it there he fairly turned cold at the sense of suppressed opportunity, of the outrage of privation that his correspondent would retrospectively and, as he even divined with a vague shudder, almost vindictively nurse. Well, what had happened was that the acquaintance had been kept for her, like a packet enveloped and sealed for delivery, till her attention was free. He saw her there, heard her and felt her — felt how she would feel and how she would, as she usually said, "rave." Some of her young compatriots called it "yell," and in the reference itself, alas! illustrated their meaning. She would understand the place at any rate, down to the ground; there was n't the slightest doubt of that. Her sense of it would be exactly like his own, and he could see, in anticipation, just the terms of recognition and rapture in which she would abound. He knew just what she would call quaint, just what she would call bland, just what she would call weird, just what she would call wild. She would take it all in with an intelligence much more fitted than his own, in fact, to deal with what he supposed he must regard as its literary relations. She would have read the long-winded obsolete memoirs and novels that both the figures and the setting ought clearly to remind one of; she would know about the past generations — the lumbering country magnates and their turbaned wives and round-eyed daughters, who, in other days, had treated the ruddy sturdy tradeless town, the solid square houses and wide walled gardens, the streets to-day all grass and gossip, as the scene of a local "season." She would have warrant for the assemblies, dinners, deep potations; for the smoked sconces in the dusky parlours; for the long muddy century of family coaches, "holsters," highwaymen. She would put a finger in short, just as he had done, on the vital spot — the rich humility of the whole thing, the fact that neither Flickerbridge in general nor Miss Wenham in particular, nor anything nor any one concerned, had a suspicion of their character and their merit. Addie and he would have to come to let in light.

He let it in then, little by little, before going to bed, through the eight or ten pages he addressed to her; assured her that it was the happiest case in the world, a little picture — yet full of "style" too — absolutely composed and transmitted, with tradition, and tradition only, in every stroke, tradition still noiselessly breathing and visibly flushing, marking strange hours in the tall mahogany clocks that were never wound up and that yet audibly ticked on. All the elements, he was sure he should see, would hang together with a charm, presenting his hostess — a strange iridescent fish for the glazed exposure of an aquarium — as afloat in her native medium. He left his letter open on the table, but, looking it over next morning, felt of a sudden indisposed to send it. He would keep it to add more, for there would be more to know; yet when three days had elapsed he still had not sent it. He sent instead, after delay, a much briefer report, which he was moved to make different and, for some reason, less vivid. Meanwhile he learned from Miss Wenham how Addie had introduced him. It took time to arrive with her at that point, but after the Rubicon was crossed they went far afield.

IV

"Oh yes, she said you were engaged to her. That was why — since I *had* broken out so — she thought I might like to see you; as I assure you I 've been so delighted to. But *are n't* you?" the good lady asked as if she saw in his face some ground for doubt.

"Assuredly — if she says so. It may seem very odd to you, but I have n't known, and yet I 've felt that, being nothing whatever to you directly, I need some warrant for consenting thus to be thrust on you. We *were*," the young man explained, "engaged a year ago; but since then (if you don't mind my telling you such things; I feel now as if I could tell you anything!) I have n't quite known how I stand. It has n't seemed we were in a position to marry. Things are better now, but I have n't quite known how she 'd see them. They were so bad six months ago that I understood her, I thought, as breaking off. I have n't broken; I 've only accepted, for the time — because men must be easy with women — being treated as 'the best of friends.' Well, I try to be. I would n't have come here if I had n't been. I thought it would be charming for her to know you — when I heard from her the extraordinary way you had dawned upon her; and charming therefore if I could help her to it. And if I 'm helping you to know *her*," he went on, "is n't that charming too?"

"Oh I so want to!" Miss Wenham murmured in
455

her unpractical impersonal way. "You're so different!" she wistfully declared.

"It's *you*, if I may respectfully, ecstatically say so,
who are different. That's the point of it all. I'm not
sure that anything so terrible really ought to happen
to you as to know us."

"Well," said Miss Wenham, "I do know you a little
by this time, don't I? And I don't find it terrible. It's
a delightful change for me."

"Oh I'm not sure you ought to have a delightful
change!"

"Why not — if you do?"

"Ah I can bear it. I'm not sure you can. I'm too
bad to spoil — I *am* spoiled. I'm nobody, in short;
I'm nothing. I've no type. You're *all* type. It has
taken delicious long years of security and monotony to
produce you. You fit your frame with a perfection
only equalled by the perfection with which your frame
fits you. So this admirable old house, all time-softened
white within and time-faded red without, so everything that surrounds you here and that has, by some
extraordinary mercy, escaped the inevitable fate of
exploitation: so it all, I say, is the sort of thing that,
were it the least bit to fall to pieces, could never, ah
never more be put together again. I have, dear Miss
Wenham," Granger went on, happy himself in his
extravagance, which was yet all sincere, and happier
still in her deep but altogether pleased mystification —
"I've found, do you know, just the thing one has ever
heard of that you most resemble. You're the Sleeping
Beauty in the Wood."

He still had no compunction when he heard her

bewilderedly sigh: "Oh you're too delightfully droll!"

"No, I only put things just as they are, and as I've also learned a little, thank heaven, to see them — which is n't, I quite agree with you, at all what any one does. You're in the deep doze of the spell that has held you for long years, and it would be a shame, a crime, to wake you up. Indeed I already feel with a thousand scruples that I'm giving you the fatal shake. I say it even though it makes me sound a little as if I thought myself the fairy prince."

She gazed at him with her queerest kindest look, which he was getting used to in spite of a faint fear, at the back of his head, of the strange things that sometimes occurred when lonely ladies, however mature, began to look at interesting young men from over the seas as if the young men desired to flirt. "It's so wonderful," she said, "that you should be so very odd and yet so very good-natured." Well, it all came to the same thing — it was so wonderful that *she* should be so simple and yet so little of a bore. He accepted with gratitude the theory of his languor — which moreover was real enough and partly perhaps why he was so sensitive; he let himself go as a convalescent, let her insist on the weakness always left by fever. It helped him to gain time, to preserve the spell even while he talked of breaking it; saw him through slow strolls and soft sessions, long gossips, fitful hopeless questions — there was so much more to tell than, by any contortion, she *could* — and explanations addressed gallantly and patiently to her understanding, but not, by good fortune, really reaching it. They were perfectly at cross-purposes, and it was all the better, and they wandered together in the silver haze with all communication blurred.

When they sat in the sun in her formal garden he quite knew how little even the tenderest consideration failed to disguise his treating her as the most exquisite of curiosities. The term of comparison most present to him was that of some obsolete musical instrument. The old-time order of her mind and her air had the stillness of a painted spinnet that was duly dusted, gently rubbed, but never tuned nor played on. Her opinions were like dried roseleaves; her attitudes like British sculpture; her voice what he imagined of the possible tone of the old gilded silver-stringed harp in one of the corners of the drawing-room. The lonely little decencies and modest dignities of her life, the fine grain of its conservatism, the innocence of its ignorance, all its monotony of stupidity and salubrity, its cold dulness and dim brightness, were there before him. Meanwhile within him strange things took place. It was literally true that his impression began again, after a lull, to make him nervous and anxious, and for reasons peculiarly confused, almost grotesquely mingled, or at least comically sharp. He was distinctly an agitation and a new taste — that he could see; and he saw quite as much therefore the excitement she already drew from the vision of Addie, an image intensified by the sense of closer kinship and presented to her, clearly, with various erratic enhancements, by her friend the doctor's daughter. At the end of a few days he said to her: "Do you know she wants to come without waiting any longer? She wants to come while

FLICKERBRIDGE

I'm here. I received this morning her letter proposing it, but I've been thinking it over and have waited to speak to you. The thing is, you see, that if she writes to *you* proposing it —"

"Oh I shall be so particularly glad!"

V

THEY were as usual in the garden, and it had n't yet
been so present to him that if he were only a happy cad
there would be a good way to protect her. As she
would n't hear of his being yet beyond precautions she
had gone into the house for a particular shawl that
was just the thing for his knees, and, blinking in the
watery sunshine, had come back with it across the fine
little lawn. He was neither fatuous nor asinine, but he
had almost to put it to himself as a small task to resist
the sense of his absurd advantage with her. It filled
him with horror and awkwardness, made him think of
he did n't know what, recalled something of Maupas-
sant's — the smitten "Miss Harriet" and her tragic
fate. There was a preposterous possibility — yes, he
held the strings quite in his hands — of keeping the
treasure for himself. That was the art of life — what
the real artist would consistently do. He would close
the door on his impression, treat it as a private museum. He would see that he could lounge and linger
there, live with wonderful things there, lie up there to
rest and refit. For himself he was sure that after a little he should be able to paint there — do things in a
key he had never thought of before. When she
brought him the rug he took it from her and made her
sit down on the bench and resume her knitting; then,
passing behind her with a laugh, he placed it over her
own shoulders; after which he moved to and fro

before her, his hands in his pockets and his cigarette in his teeth. He was ashamed of the cigarette — a villainous false note; but she allowed, liked, begged him to smoke, and what he said to her on it, in one of the pleasantries she benevolently missed, was that he did so for fear of doing worse. That only showed how the end was really in sight. "I dare say it will strike you as quite awful, what I'm going to say to you, but I can't help it. I speak out of the depths of my respect for you. It will seem to you horrid disloyalty to poor Addie. Yes — there we are; there *I* am at least in my naked monstrosity." He stopped and looked at her till she might have been almost frightened. "Don't let her come. Tell her not to. I've tried to prevent it, but she suspects."

The poor woman wondered. "Suspects?"

"Well, I drew it, in writing to her, on reflexion, as mild as I could — having been visited in the watches of the night by the instinct of what might happen. Something told me to keep back my first letter — in which, under the first impression, I myself rashly 'raved'; and I concocted instead of it an insincere and guarded report. But guarded as I was I clearly did n't keep you 'down,' as we say, enough. The wonder of your colour — daub you over with grey as I might — must have come through and told the tale. She scents battle from afar — by which I mean she scents 'quaintness.' But keep her off. It's hideous, what I'm saying — but I owe it to you. I owe it to the world. She'll kill you."

"You mean I shan't get on with her?"

"Oh fatally! See how *I* have. And see how you

461

FLICKERBRIDGE

have with *me*. She's intelligent moreover, remarkably
pretty, remarkably good. And she'll adore you."
  "Well then?"
  "Why that will be just how she'll do for you."
  "Oh I can hold my own!" said Miss Wenham with
the headshake of a horse making his sleigh-bells rattle
in frosty air.
  "Ah but you can't hold hers! She'll rave about
you. She'll write about you. You're Niagara before
the first white traveller — and you know, or rather
you can't know, what Niagara became *after* that gentleman. Addie will have discovered Niagara. She'll
understand you in perfection; she'll feel you down to
the ground; not a delicate shade of you will she lose or
let any one else lose. You'll be too weird for words,
but the words will nevertheless come. You'll be too
exactly the real thing and to be left too utterly just as
you are, and all Addie's friends and all Addie's
editors and contributors and readers will cross the
Atlantic and flock to Flickerbridge just in order so —
unanimously, universally, vociferously — to leave you.
You'll be in the magazines with illustrations; you'll
be in the papers with headings; you'll be everywhere
with everything. You don't understand — you think
you do, but you don't. Heaven forbid you *should* understand! That's just your beauty — your 'sleeping'
beauty. But you need n't. You can take me on trust.
Don't have her. Give as a pretext, as a reason anything in the world you like. Lie to her — scare her
away. I'll go away and give you up — I'll sacrifice
everything myself." Granger pursued his exhortation,
convincing himself more and more. "If I saw my way
462

out, my way completely through, *I'd* pile up some fabric of fiction for her — I should only want to be sure of its not tumbling down. One would have, you see, to keep the thing up. But I'd throw dust in her eyes. I'd tell her you don't do at all — that you're not in fact a desirable acquaintance. I'd tell her you're vulgar, improper, scandalous; I'd tell her you're mercenary, designing, dangerous; I'd tell her the only safe course is immediately to let you drop. I'd thus surround you with an impenetrable legend of conscientious misrepresentation, a circle of pious fraud, and all the while privately keep you for myself."

She had listened to him as if he were a band of music and she herself a small shy garden-party. "I should n't like you to go away. I should n't in the least like you not to come again."

"Ah there it is!" he replied. "How can I come again if Addie ruins you?"

"But how will she ruin me — even if she does what you say? I know I'm too old to change and really much too queer to please in any of the extraordinary ways you speak of. If it's a question of quizzing me I don't think my cousin, or any one else, will have quite the hand for it that *you* seem to have. So that if *you* have n't ruined me —!"

"But I *have* — that's just the point!" Granger insisted. "I've undermined you at least. I've left after all terribly little for Addie to do."

She laughed in clear tones. "Well then, we'll admit that you've done everything but frighten me."

He looked at her with surpassing gloom. "No —

that again is one of the most dreadful features. You'll positively like it — what's to come. You'll be caught up in a chariot of fire like the prophet — wasn't there, was there one? — of old. That's exactly why — if one could but have done it — you'd have been to be kept ignorant and helpless. There's something or other in Latin that says it's the finest things that change the most easily for the worse. You already enjoy your dishonour and revel in your shame. It's too late — you're lost!"

VI

ALL this was as pleasant a manner of passing the time as any other, for it did n't prevent his old-world corner from closing round him more entirely, nor stand in the way of his making out from day to day some new source as well as some new effect of its virtue. He was really scared at moments at some of the liberties he took in talk — at finding himself so familiar; for the great note of the place was just that a certain modern ease had never crossed its threshold, that quick intimacies and quick oblivions were a stranger to its air. It had known in all its days no rude, no loud invasion. Serenely unconscious of most contemporary things, it had been so of nothing so much as of the diffused social practice of running in and out. Granger held his breath on occasions to think how Addie would run. There were moments when, more than at others, for some reason, he heard her step on the staircase and her cry in the hall. If he nevertheless played freely with the idea with which we have shown him as occupied it was n't that in all palpable ways he did n't sacrifice so far as mortally possible to stillness. He only hovered, ever so lightly, to take up again his thread. She would n't hear of his leaving her, of his being in the least fit again, as she said, to travel. She spoke of the journey to London — which was in fact a matter of many hours — as an experiment fraught with lurking complications. He added then day to day, yet only hereby, as he reminded her, giving other

465

complications a larger chance to multiply. He kept it before her, when there was nothing else to do, that she must consider; after which he had his times of fear that she perhaps really would make for him this sacrifice.

He knew she had written again to Paris, and knew he must himself again write — a situation abounding for each in the elements of a plight. If he stayed so long why then he was n't better, and if he was n't better Addie might take it into her head —! They must make it clear that he *was* better, so that, suspicious, alarmed at what was kept from her, she should n't suddenly present herself to nurse him. If he was better however, why did he stay so long? If he stayed only for the attraction the sense of the attraction might be contagious. This was what finally grew clearest for him, so that he had for his mild disciple hours of still sharper prophecy. It consorted with his fancy to represent to her that their young friend had been by this time unsparingly warned; but nothing could be plainer than that this was ineffectual so long as he himself resisted the ordeal. To plead that he remained because he was too weak to move was only to throw themselves back on the other horn of their dilemma. If he was too weak to move Addie would bring him her strength — of which, when she got there, she would give them specimens enough. One morning he broke out at breakfast with an intimate conviction. They'd see that she was actually starting — they'd receive a wire by noon. They did n't receive it, but by his theory the portent was only the stronger. It had moreover its grave as well as its gay side, since

FLICKERBRIDGE

Granger's paradox and pleasantry were only the method most open to him of conveying what he felt. He literally heard the knell sound, and in expressing this to Miss Wenham with the conversational freedom that seemed best to pay his way he the more vividly faced the contingency. He could never return, and though he announced it with a despair that did what might be to make it pass as a joke, he saw how, whether or no she at last understood, she quite at last believed him. On this, to his knowledge, she wrote again to Addie, and the contents of her letter excited his curiosity. But that sentiment, though not assuaged, quite dropped when, the day after, in the evening, she let him know she had had a telegram an hour before.

"She comes Thursday."

He showed not the least surprise. It was the deep calm of the fatalist. It *had* to be. "I must leave you then to-morrow."

She looked, on this, as he had never seen her; it would have been hard to say whether what showed in her face was the last failure to follow or the first effort to meet. "And really not to come back?"

"Never, never, dear lady. Why should I come back? You can never be again what you *have* been. I shall have seen the last of you."

"Oh!" she touchingly urged.

"Yes, for I should next find you simply brought to self-consciousness. You'll be exactly what you are, I charitably admit — nothing more or less, nothing different. But you'll be it all in a different way. We live in an age of prodigious machinery, all organised to a single end. That end is publicity — a publicity as fe-

467

rocious as the appetite of a cannibal. The thing therefore is not to have any illusions — fondly to flatter yourself in a muddled moment that the cannibal will spare you. He spares nobody. He spares nothing. It will be all right. You'll have a lovely time. You'll be only just a public character — blown about the world 'for all you're worth' and proclaimed 'for all you're worth' on the house-tops. It will be for *that*, mind, I quite recognise — because Addie is superior — as well as for all you are n't. So good-bye."

He remained however till the next day, and noted at intervals the different stages of their friend's journey; the hour, this time, she would really have started, the hour she'd reach Dover, the hour she'd get to town, where she'd alight at Mrs. Dunn's. Perhaps she'd bring Mrs. Dunn, for Mrs. Dunn would swell the chorus. At the last, on the morrow, as if in anticipation of this, stillness settled between them: he became as silent as his hostess. But before he went she brought out shyly and anxiously, as an appeal, the question that for hours had clearly been giving her thought. "Do you meet her then to-night in London?"

"Dear no. In what position am I, alas! to do that? When can I *ever* meet her again?" He had turned it all over. "If I could meet Addie after this, you know, I could meet *you*. And if I do meet Addie," he lucidly pursued, "what will happen by the same stroke is that I *shall* meet you. And that's just what I've explained to you I dread."

"You mean she and I will be inseparable?"

He hesitated. "I mean she'll tell me all about you. I can hear her and her ravings now."

468

She gave again — and it was infinitely sad — her little whinnying laugh. "Oh but if what you say is true you'll know."

"Ah but Addie won't! Won't, I mean, know that *I* know — or at least won't believe it. Won't believe that any one knows. Such," he added with a strange smothered sigh, "*is* Addie. Do you know," he wound up, "that what, after all, has most definitely happened is that you've made me see her as I've never done before?"

She blinked and gasped, she wondered and despaired. "Oh no, it will be *you*. I've had nothing to do with it. Everything's *all* you!"

But for all it mattered now! "You'll see," he said, "that she's charming. I shall go for to-night to Oxford. I shall almost cross her on the way."

"Then if she's charming what am I to tell her from you in explanation of such strange behaviour as your flying away just as she arrives?"

"Ah you need n't mind about that — you need n't tell her anything."

She fixed him as if as never again. "It's none of my business, of course I feel; but is n't it a little cruel if you're engaged?"

Granger gave a laugh almost as odd as one of her own. "Oh you've cost me that!" — and he put out his hand to her.

She wondered while she took it. "Cost you — ?"

"We're not engaged. Good-bye."

MRS. MEDWIN

MRS. MEDWIN

I

"WELL, we *are* a pair!" the poor lady's visitor broke
out to her at the end of her explanation in a manner
disconcerting enough. The poor lady was Miss
Cutter, who lived in South Audley Street, where she
had an "upper half" so concise that it had to pass
boldly for convenient; and her visitor was her half-
brother, whom she hadn't seen for three years. She
was remarkable for a maturity of which every symptom might have been observed to be admirably controlled, had not a tendency to stoutness just affirmed
its independence. Her present, no doubt, insisted too
much on her past, but with the excuse, sufficiently
valid, that she must certainly once have been prettier.
She was clearly not contented with once — she wished
to be prettier again. She neglected nothing that could
produce that illusion, and, being both fair and fat,
dressed almost wholly in black. When she added a
little colour it was not, at any rate, to her drapery.
Her small rooms had the peculiarity that everything
they contained appeared to testify with vividness to
her position in society, quite as if they had been furn-
ished by the bounty of admiring friends. They were
adorned indeed almost exclusively with objects that
nobody buys, as had more than once been remarked
by spectators of her own sex, for herself, and would

have been luxurious if luxury consisted mainly in photographic portraits slashed across with signatures, in baskets of flowers beribboned with the cards of passing compatriots, and in a neat collection of red volumes, blue volumes, alphabetical volumes, aids to London lucidity, of every sort, devoted to addresses and engagements. To be in Miss Cutter's tiny drawing-room, in short, even with Miss Cutter alone — should you by any chance have found her so — was somehow to be in the world and in a crowd. It was like an agency — it bristled with particulars.

This was what the tall lean loose gentleman lounging there before her might have appeared to read in the suggestive scene over which, while she talked to him, his eyes moved without haste and without rest. "Oh come, Mamie!" he occasionally threw off; and the words were evidently connected with the impression thus absorbed. His comparative youth spoke of waste even as her positive — her too positive — spoke of economy. There was only one thing, that is, to make up in him for everything he had lost, though it was distinct enough indeed that this thing might sometimes serve. It consisted in the perfection of an indifference, an indifference at the present moment directed to the plea — a plea of inability, of pure destitution — with which his sister had met him. Yet it had even now a wider embrace, took in quite sufficiently all consequences of queerness, confessed in advance to the false note that, in such a setting, he almost excruciatingly constituted. He cared as little that he looked at moments all his impudence as that he looked all his shabbiness, all his cleverness, all his

history. These different things were written in him
— in his premature baldness, his seamed strained
face, the lapse from bravery of his long tawny moustache; above all in his easy friendly universally acquainted eye, so much too sociable for mere conversation. What possible relation with him could be
natural enough to meet it? He wore a scant rough
Inverness cape and a pair of black trousers, wanting
in substance and marked with the sheen of time, that
had presumably once served for evening use. He
spoke with the slowness helplessly permitted to Americans — as something too slow to be stopped — and
he repeated that he found himself associated with
Miss Cutter in a harmony calling for wonder. She
had been telling him not only that she could n't possibly give him ten pounds, but that his unexpected
arrival, should he insist on being much in view, might
seriously interfere with arrangements necessary to
her own maintenance; on which he had begun by
replying that he of course knew she had long ago
spent her money, but that he looked to her now exactly because she had, without the aid of that convenience, mastered the art of life.

"I 'd really go away with a fiver, my dear, if you 'd
only tell me how you do it. It 's no use saying only,
as you 've always said, that 'people are very kind to
you.' What the devil are they kind to you *for?*"

"Well, one reason is precisely that no particular inconvenience has hitherto been supposed to attach to
me. I 'm just what I am," said Mamie Cutter; "nothing less and nothing more. It 's awkward to have
to explain to you, which moreover I really need n't

475

in the least. I'm clever and amusing and charming."
She was uneasy and even frightened, but she kept her
temper and met him with a grace of her own. "I don't
think you ought to ask me more questions than I ask
you."

"Ah my dear," said the odd young man, "*I've* no
mysteries. Why in the world, since it was what you
came out for and have devoted so much of your time
to, haven't you pulled it off? Why haven't you
married?"

"Why haven't *you?*" she retorted. "Do you think
that if I had it would have been better for you? —
that my husband would for a moment have put up
with you? Do you mind my asking you if you'll
kindly go *now?*" she went on after a glance at the
clock. "I'm expecting a friend, whom I must see
alone, on a matter of great importance —"

"And my being seen with you may compromise
your respectability or undermine your nerve?" He
sprawled imperturbably in his place, crossing again,
in another sense, his long black legs and showing,
above his low shoes, an absurd reach of parti-coloured
sock. "I take your point well enough, but mayn't
you be after all quite wrong? If you can't do anything for me couldn't you at least do something *with*
me? If it comes to that, I'm clever and amusing and
charming too! I've been such an ass that you don't
appreciate me. But people like me — I assure you
they do. They usually don't know what an ass I've
been; they only see the surface, which" — and he
stretched himself afresh as she looked him up and
down — "you *can* imagine them, can't you, rather

476

taken with? *I'm* 'what I am' too; nothing less and nothing more. That's true of us as a family, you see. We *are* a crew!" He delivered himself serenely. His voice was soft and flat, his pleasant eyes, his simple tones tending to the solemn, achieved at moments that effect of quaintness which is, in certain connexions, socially so known and enjoyed. "English people have quite a weakness for me — more than any others. I get on with them beautifully. I've always been with them abroad. They think me," the young man explained, "diabolically American."

"You!" Such stupidity drew from her a sigh of compassion.

Her companion apparently quite understood it. "Are you homesick, Mamie?" he asked, with wondering irrelevance.

The manner of the question made her for some reason, in spite of her preoccupations, break into a laugh. A shade of indulgence, a sense of other things, came back to her. "You *are* funny, Scott!"

"Well," remarked Scott, "that's just what I claim. But *are* you so homesick?" he spaciously enquired, not as to a practical end, but from an easy play of intelligence.

"I'm just dying of it!" said Mamie Cutter.

"Why so am I!" Her visitor had a sweetness of concurrence.

"We're the only decent people," Miss Cutter declared. "And I know. *You* don't — you can't; and I can't explain. Come in," she continued with a return of her impatience and an increase of her decision, "at seven sharp."

477

She had quitted her seat some time before, and now, to get him into motion, hovered before him while, still motionless, he looked up at her. Something intimate, in the silence, appeared to pass between them — a community of fatigue and failure and, after all, of intelligence. There was a final cynical humour in it. It determined him, in any case, at last, and he slowly rose, taking in again as he stood there the testimony of the room. He might have been counting the photographs, but he looked at the flowers with detachment. "Who's coming?"

"Mrs. Medwin."

"American?"

"Dear no!"

"Then what are you doing for her?"

"I work for every one," she promptly returned.

"For every one who pays? So I suppose. Yet isn't it only we who do pay?"

There was a drollery, not lost on her, in the way his queer presence lent itself to his emphasised plural. "Do you consider that *you* do?"

At this, with his deliberation, he came back to his charming idea. "Only try me, and see if I can't be *made* to. Work me in." On her sharply presenting her back he stared a little at the clock. "If I come at seven may I stay to dinner?"

It brought her round again. "Impossible. I'm dining out."

"With whom?"

She had to think. "With Lord Considine."

"Oh my eye!" Scott exclaimed.

She looked at him gloomily. "Is *that* sort of tone

what makes you pay ? I think you might understand,"
she went on, "that if you're to sponge on me successfully you must n't ruin me. I must have *some* remote
resemblance to a lady."

"Yes ? But why must *I ?*" Her exasperated silence
was full of answers, of which however his inimitable
manner took no account. "You don't understand
my real strength; I doubt if you even understand
your own. You're clever, Mamie, but you're not so
clever as I supposed. However," he pursued, "it's
out of Mrs. Medwin that you'll get it."

"Get what ?"

"Why the cheque that will enable you to assist
me."

On this, for a moment, she met his eyes. "If you'll
come back at seven sharp — not a minute before,
and not a minute after, I'll give you two five-pound
notes."

He thought it over. "Whom are you expecting a
minute after ?"

It sent her to the window with a groan almost of
anguish, and she answered nothing till she had looked
at the street. "If you injure me, you know, Scott,
you'll be sorry."

"I would n't injure you for the world. What I want
to do in fact is really to help you, and I promise you
that I won't leave you — by which I mean won't leave
London — till I've effected something really pleasant
for you. I like you, Mamie, because I like pluck; I
like you much more than you like me. I like you
very, *very* much." He had at last with this reached
the door and opened it, but he remained with his

479

hand on the latch. "What does Mrs. Medwin want of you?" he thus brought out.

She had come round to see him disappear, and in the relief of this prospect she again just indulged him. "The impossible."

He waited another minute. "And you're going to do it?"

"I'm going to do it," said Mamie Cutter.

"Well then that ought to be a haul. Call it *three* fivers!" he laughed. "At seven sharp." And at last he left her alone.

II

Miss Cutter waited till she heard the house-door close; after which, in a sightless mechanical way, she moved about the room readjusting various objects he had not touched. It was as if his mere voice and accent had spoiled her form. But she was not left too long to reckon with these things, for Mrs. Medwin was promptly announced. This lady was not, more than her hostess, in the first flush of her youth; her appearance — the scattered remains of beauty manipulated by taste — resembled one of the light repasts in which the fragments of yesterday's dinner figure with a conscious ease that makes up for the want of presence. She was perhaps of an effect still too immediate to be called interesting, but she was candid, gentle and surprised — not fatiguingly surprised, only just in the right degree; and her white face — it was too white — with the fixed eyes, the somewhat touzled hair and the Louis Seize hat, might at the end of the very long neck have suggested the head of a princess carried on a pike in a revolution. She immediately took up the business that had brought her, with the air however of drawing from the omens then discernible less confidence than she had hoped. The complication lay in the fact that if it was Mamie's part to present the omens, that lady yet had so to

481

colour them as to make her own service large. She perhaps over-coloured, for her friend gave way to momentary despair.

"What you mean is then that it's simply impossible?"

"Oh no," said Mamie with a qualified emphasis. "It's *possible.*"

"But disgustingly difficult?"

"As difficult as you like."

"Then what can I do that I have n't done?"

"You can only wait a little longer."

"But that's just what I *have* done. I've done nothing else. I'm always waiting a little longer!"

Miss Cutter retained, in spite of this pathos, her grasp of the subject. "*The* thing, as I've told you, is for you first to be seen."

"But if people won't look at me?"

"They will."

"They *will?*" Mrs. Medwin was eager.

"They shall," her hostess went on. "It's their only having heard — without having seen."

"But if they stare straight the other way?" Mrs. Medwin continued to object. "You can't simply go up to them and twist their heads about."

"It's just what I can," said Mamie Cutter.

But her charming visitor, heedless for the moment of this attenuation, had found the way to put it. "It's the old story. You can't go into the water till you swim, and you can't swim till you go into the water. I can't be spoken to till I'm seen, but I can't be seen till I'm spoken to."

She met this lucidity, Miss Cutter, with but an

instant's lapse. "You say I can't twist their heads about. But I *have* twisted them."

It had been quietly produced, but it gave her companion a jerk. "They say 'Yes'?"

She summed it up. "All but one. *She* says 'No.'"

Mrs. Medwin thought; then jumped. "Lady Wantridge?"

Miss Cutter, as more delicate, only bowed admission. "I shall see her either this afternoon or late to-morrow. But she has written."

Her visitor wondered again. "May I see her letter?"

"No." She spoke with decision. "But I shall square her."

"Then how?"

"Well" — and Miss Cutter, as if looking upward for inspiration, fixed her eyes a while on the ceiling — "well, it will come to me."

Mrs. Medwin watched her — it was impressive. "And will *they* come to you — the others?" This question drew out the fact that they would — so far at least as they consisted of Lady Edward, Lady Bellhouse and Mrs. Pouncer, who had engaged to muster, at the signal of tea, on the 14th — prepared, as it were, for the worst. There was of course always the chance that Lady Wantridge might take the field in such force as to paralyse them, though that danger, at the same time, seemed inconsistent with her being squared. It did n't perhaps all quite ideally hang together; but what it sufficiently came to was that if she was the one who could do most *for* a person in Mrs. Medwin's position she was also the one who could do most against. It would therefore be distinctly what our friend familiarly spoke of as "collar-work." The effect of these mixed considerations was at any rate that Mamie eventually acquiesced in the idea, handsomely thrown out by her client, that she should have an "advance" to go on with. Miss Cutter confessed that it seemed at times as if one scarce *could* go on; but the advance was, in spite of this delicacy, still more delicately made — made in the form of a banknote, several sovereigns, some loose silver and two coppers, the whole contents of her purse, neatly disposed by Mrs. Medwin on one of the tiny tables. It seemed to clear the air for deeper intimacies, the fruit of which was that Mamie, lonely after all in her crowd and always more helpful than helped, eventually brought out that the way Scott had been going on was what seemed momentarily to overshadow her own power to do so.

"I've had a descent from him." But she had to explain. "My half-brother — Scott Homer. A wretch."

"What kind of a wretch?"

"Every kind. I lose sight of him at times — he disappears abroad. But he always turns up again, worse than ever."

"Violent?"

"No."

"Maudlin?"

"No."

"Only unpleasant?"

"No. Rather pleasant. Awfully clever — awfully travelled and easy."

"Then what's the matter with him?"

Mamie mused, hesitated — seemed to see a wide past. "I don't know."

"Something in the background?" Then as her friend was silent, "Something queer about cards?" Mrs. Medwin threw off.

"I don't know — and I don't want to!"

"Ah well, I'm sure *I* don't," Mrs. Medwin returned with spirit. The note of sharpness was perhaps also a little in the observation she made as she gathered herself to go. "Do you mind my saying something?"

Mamie took her eyes quickly from the money on the little stand. "You may say what you like."

"I only mean that anything awkward you may have to keep out of the way does seem to make more wonderful, does n't it, that you should have got just where you are? I allude, you know, to your position."

"I see." Miss Cutter somewhat coldly smiled. "To my power."

"So awfully remarkable in an American."

"Ah you like us so."

Mrs. Medwin candidly considered. "But we don't, dearest."

Her companion's smile brightened. "Then why do you come to me?"

"Oh I like *you!*" Mrs. Medwin made out.

"Then that's it. There are no 'Americans.' It's always 'you.'"

"Me?" Mrs. Medwin looked lovely, but a little muddled.

"*Me!*" Mamie Cutter laughed. "But if you like me, you dear thing, you can judge if I like *you.*" She gave her a kiss to dismiss her. "I'll see you again when I've seen her."

"Lady Wantridge? I hope so, indeed. I'll turn up late to-morrow, if you don't catch me first. Has it come to you yet?" the visitor, now at the door, went on.

"No; but it will. There's time."

"Oh a little less every day!"

Miss Cutter had approached the table and glanced again at the gold and silver and the note, not indeed absolutely overlooking the two coppers. "The balance," she put it, "the day after?"

"That very night if you like."

"Then count on me."

"Oh if I did n't —!" But the door closed on the dark idea. Yearningly then, and only when it had done so, Miss Cutter took up the money.

She went out with it ten minutes later, and, the calls on her time being many, remained out so long that at half-past six she hadn't come back. At that hour, on the other hand, Scott Homer knocked at her door, where her maid, who opened it with a weak pretense of holding it firm, ventured to announce to him, as a lesson well learnt, that he hadn't been expected till seven. No lesson, none the less, could prevail against his native art. He pleaded fatigue, her, the maid's, dreadful depressing London, and the need to curl up somewhere. If she'd just leave him quiet half an hour that old sofa upstairs would do for it; of which he took quickly such effectual possession that when five minutes later she peeped, nervous for her broken vow, into the drawing-room, the faithless young woman found him extended at his length and peacefully asleep.

THE situation before Miss Cutter's return developed in other directions still, and when that event took place, at a few minutes past seven, these circumstances were, by the foot of the stair, between mistress and maid, the subject of some interrogative gasps and scared admissions. Lady Wantridge had arrived shortly after the interloper, and wishing, as she said, to wait, had gone straight up in spite of being told he was lying down.

"She distinctly understood he was there?"

"Oh yes ma'am; I thought it right to mention."

"And what did you call him?"

"Well, ma'am, I thought it unfair to *you* to call him anything but a gentleman."

Mamie took it all in, though there might well be more of it than one could quickly embrace. "But if she has had time," she flashed, "to find out he is n't one?"

"Oh ma'am, she had a quarter of an hour."

"Then she is n't with him still?"

"No ma'am; she came down again at last. She rang, and I saw her here, and she said she would n't wait longer."

Miss Cutter darkly mused. "Yet had already waited — ?"

"Quite a quarter."

"Mercy on us!" She began to mount. Before

reaching the top however she had reflected that quite a quarter was long if Lady Wantridge had only been shocked. On the other hand it was short if she had only been pleased. But how *could* she have been pleased? The very essence of their actual crisis was just that there was no pleasing her. Mamie had but to open the drawing-room door indeed to perceive that this was not true at least of Scott Homer, who was horribly cheerful.

Miss Cutter expressed to her brother without reserve her sense of the constitutional, the brutal selfishness that had determined his mistimed return. It had taken place, in violation of their agreement, exactly at the moment when it was most cruel to her that he should be there, and if she must now completely wash her hands of him he had only himself to thank. She had come in flushed with resentment and for a moment had been voluble; but it would have been striking that, though the way he received her might have seemed but to aggravate, it presently justified him by causing their relation really to take a stride. He had the art of confounding those who would quarrel with him by reducing them to the humiliation of a stirred curiosity.

"What *could* she have made of you?" Mamie demanded.

"My dear girl, she's not a woman who's eager to make too much of anything — anything, I mean, that will prevent her from doing as she likes, what she takes into her head. Of course," he continued to explain, "if it's something she does n't want to do, she'll make as much as Moses."

Mamie wondered if that was the way he talked to her visitor, but felt obliged to own to his acuteness. It was an exact description of Lady Wantridge, and she was conscious of tucking it away for future use in a corner of her miscellaneous little mind. She withheld however all present acknowledgement, only addressing him another question. "Did you really get on with her?"

"Have you still to learn, darling — I can't help again putting it to you — that I get on with everybody? That's just what I don't seem able to drive into you. Only see how I get on with *you*."

She almost stood corrected. "What I mean is of course whether —"

"Whether she made love to me? Shyly, yet — or because — shamefully? She would certainly have liked awfully to stay."

"Then why did n't she?"

"Because, on account of some other matter — and I could see it was true — she had n't time. Twenty minutes — she was here less — were all she came to give you. So don't be afraid I 've frightened her away. She 'll come back."

Mamie thought it over. "Yet you did n't go with her to the door?"

"She would n't let me, and I know when to do what I 'm told — quite as much as what I 'm not told. She wanted to find out about me. I mean from your little creature; a pearl of fidelity, by the way."

"But what on earth did she come up for?" Mamie again found herself appealing, and just by that fact showing her need of help.

"Because she always goes up." Then as, in the presence of this rapid generalisation, to say nothing of that of such a relative altogether, Miss Cutter could only show as comparatively blank: "I mean she knows when to go up and when to come down. She has instincts; she did n't know whom you might have up here. It's a kind of compliment to you anyway. Why Mamie," Scott pursued, "you don't know the curiosity we any of us inspire. You would n't believe what I 've seen. The bigger bugs they are the more they 're on the lookout."

Mamie still followed, but at a distance. "The lookout for what?"

"Why for anything that will help them to live. You 've been here all this time without making out then, about them, what I 've had to pick out as I can? They 're dead, don't you see? And *we 're* alive."

"You? Oh!" — Mamie almost laughed about it.

"Well, they 're a worn-out old lot anyhow; they 've used up their resources. They do look out; and I 'll do them the justice to say they 're not afraid — not even of me!" he continued as his sister again showed something of the same irony. "Lady Wantridge at any rate was n't; that 's what I mean by her having made love to me. She does what she likes. Mind it, you know." He was by this time fairly teaching her to read one of her best friends, and when, after it, he had come back to the great point of his lesson — that of her failure, through feminine inferiority, practically to grasp the truth that their being just as they were, he and she, was the real card for them to play — when he had renewed that reminder he left her absolutely in a state of dependence. Her impulse to press him on the subject of Lady Wantridge dropped; it was as if she had felt that, whatever had taken place, something would somehow come of it. She was to be in a manner disappointed but the impression helped to keep her over to the next morning, when, as Scott had foretold, his new acquaintance did reappear, explaining to Miss Cutter that she had acted the day before to gain time and that she even now sought to gain it by not waiting longer. What, she promptly intimated she had asked herself, could that friend be thinking of? She must show where she stood before things had gone too far. If she had brought her answer without more delay she wished to make it sharp. Mrs. Medwin? Never! "No, my dear — not I. *There* I stop."

Mamie had known it would be "collar-work," but somehow now, at the beginning, she felt her heart sink. It was not that she had expected to carry the position with a rush, but that, as always after an interval, her visitor's defences really loomed — and quite, as it were, to the material vision — too large. She was always planted with them, voluminous, in the very centre of the passage; was like a person accommodated with a chair in some unlawful place at the theatre. She would n't move and you could n't get round. Mamie's calculation indeed had not been on getting round; she was obliged to recognise that, too foolishly and fondly, she had dreamed of inducing a surrender. Her dream had been the fruit of her need; but, conscious that she was even yet unequipped for pressure, she felt, almost for the first

MRS. MEDWIN

time in her life, superficial and crude. She was to be
paid — but with what was she, to that end, to pay?
She had engaged to find an answer to this question,
but the answer had not, according to her promise,
"come." And Lady Wantridge meanwhile massed
herself, and there was no view of her that did n't show
her as verily, by some process too obscure to be traced,
the hard depository of the social law. She was no
younger, no fresher, no stronger, really, than any of
them; she was only, with a kind of haggard fineness,
a sharpened taste for life, and, with all sorts of things
behind and beneath her, more abysmal and more
immoral, more secure and more impertinent. The
points she made were two in number. One was that
she absolutely declined; the other was that she quite
doubted if Mamie herself had measured the job. The
thing could n't be done. But say it *could* be; was
Mamie quite the person to do it? To this Miss Cutter, with a sweet smile, replied that she quite understood how little she might seem so. "I 'm only one of
the persons to whom it has appeared that *you* are."

"Then who are the others?"

"Well, to begin with, Lady Edward, Lady Bellhouse and Mrs. Pouncer."

"Do you mean that they 'll come to meet her?"

"I 've seen them, and they 've promised."

"To come, of course," Lady Wantridge said, "if
I come."

Her hostess cast about. "Oh of course you could
prevent them. But I should take it as awfully kind
of you not to. *Won't* you do this for me?" Mamie
pleaded.

493

Her friend looked over the room very much as Scott had done. "Do they really understand what it's *for?*"

"Perfectly. So that she may call."

"And what good will that do her?"

Miss Cutter faltered, but she presently brought it out. "Naturally what one hopes is that you'll ask her."

"Ask her to call?"

"Ask her to dine. Ask her, if you'd be so *truly* sweet, for a Sunday, or something of that sort, and even if only in one of your *most* mixed parties, to Catchmore."

Miss Cutter felt the less hopeful after this effort in that her companion only showed a strange good nature. And it wasn't a satiric amiability, though it *was* amusement. "Take Mrs. Medwin into my family?"

"Some day when you're taking forty others."

"Ah but what I don't see is what it does for *you.* You're already so welcome among us that you can scarcely improve your position even by forming for us the most delightful relation."

"Well, I know how dear you are," Mamie Cutter replied; "but one has after all more than one side and more than one sympathy. I like her, you know." And even at this Lady Wantridge wasn't shocked; she showed that ease and blandness which were her way, unfortunately, of being most impossible. She remarked that *she* might listen to such things, because she was clever enough for them not to matter; only Mamie should take care how she went about saying

MRS. MEDWIN

them at large. When she became definite however, in a minute, on the subject of the public facts, Miss Cutter soon found herself ready to make her own concession. Of course she did n't dispute *them*: there they were; they were unfortunately on record, and nothing was to be done about them but to — Mamie found it in truth at this point a little difficult.

"Well, what? Pretend already to have forgotten them?"

"Why not, when you 've done it in so many other cases?"

"There *are* no other cases so bad. One meets them at any rate as they come. Some you can manage, others you can't. It 's no use, you must give them up. They 're past patching; there 's nothing to be done with them. There 's nothing accordingly to be done with Mrs. Medwin but to put her off." And Lady Wantridge rose to her height.

"Well, you know, I *do* do things," Mamie quavered with a smile so strained that it partook of exaltation.

"You help people? Oh yes, I 've known you to do wonders. But stick," said Lady Wantridge with strong and cheerful emphasis, "to your Americans!"

Miss Cutter, gazing, got up. "You don't do justice, Lady Wantridge, to your own compatriots. Some of them are really charming. Besides," said Mamie, "working for mine often strikes me, so far as the interest — the inspiration and excitement, don't you know? — go, as rather too easy. You all, as I constantly have occasion to say, like us so!"

Her companion frankly weighed it. "Yes; it takes

495

that to account for your position. I've always thought of you nevertheless as keeping for their benefit a regular working agency. They come to you, and you place them. There remains, I confess," her ladyship went on in the same free spirit, "the great wonder —"

"Of how I first placed my poor little self? Yes," Mamie bravely conceded, "when *I* began there was no agency. I just worked my passage. I did n't even come to *you*, did I? You never noticed me till, as Mrs. Short Stokes says, 'I was 'way, 'way up!' Mrs. Medwin," she threw in, "can't get over it." Then, as her friend looked vague: "Over my social situation."

"Well, it's no great flattery to you to say," Lady Wantridge good-humouredly returned, "that she certainly can't hope for one resembling it." Yet it really seemed to spread there before them. "You simply *made* Mrs. Short Stokes."

"In spite of her name!" Mamie smiled.

"Oh your 'names' —! In spite of everything."

"Ah I'm something of an artist." With which, and a relapse marked by her wistful eyes into the gravity of the matter, she supremely fixed her friend. She felt how little she minded betraying at last the extremity of her need, and it was out of this extremity that her appeal proceeded. "Have I really had your last word? It means so much to me."

Lady Wantridge came straight to the point. "You mean you depend on it?"

"Awfully!"

"Is it all you have?"

"All. Now."

"But Mrs. Short Stokes and the others — 'rolling,' are n't they? Don't they pay up?"

"Ah," sighed Mamie, "if it was n't for *them* —!"

Lady Wantridge perceived. "You 've had so much?"

"I could n't have gone on."

"Then what do you do with it all?"

"Oh most of it goes back to them. There are all sorts, and it 's all help. Some of them have nothing."

"Oh if you feed the hungry," Lady Wantridge laughed, "you 're indeed in a great way of business. Is Mrs. Medwin" — her transition was immediate — "really rich?"

"Really. He left her everything."

"So that if I do say 'yes' —"

"It will quite set me up."

"I see — and how much more responsible it makes one! But I 'd rather myself give you the money."

"Oh!" Mamie coldly murmured.

"You mean I may n't suspect your prices? Well, I dare say I don't! But I 'd rather give you ten pounds."

"Oh!" Mamie repeated in a tone that sufficiently covered her prices. The question was in every way larger. "Do you *never* forgive?" she reproachfully enquired. The door opened however at the moment she spoke and Scott Homer presented himself.

IV

Scott Homer wore exactly, to his sister's eyes, the aspect he had worn the day before, and it also formed to her sense the great feature of his impartial greeting. "How d' ye do, Mamie? How d' ye do, Lady Wantridge?"

"How d' ye do again?" Lady Wantridge replied with an equanimity striking to her hostess. It was as if Scott's own had been contagious; it was almost indeed as if she had seen him before. *Had* she ever so seen him — before the previous day? While Miss Cutter put to herself this question her visitor at all events met the one she had previously uttered. "Ever 'forgive'?" this personage echoed in a tone that made as little account as possible of the interruption. "Dear, yes! The people I *have* forgiven!" She laughed — perhaps a little nervously; and she was now looking at Scott. The way she looked at him was precisely what had already had its effect for his sister. "The people I can!"

"Can you forgive *me?*" asked Scott Homer.

She took it so easily. "But — what?"

Mamie interposed; she turned directly to her brother. "Don't try her. Leave it so." She had had an inspiration; it was the most extraordinary thing in the world. "Don't try *him*" — she had turned to their companion. She looked grave, sad, strange. "Leave it so." Yes, it was a distinct inspiration,

498

which she could n't have explained, but which had come, prompted by something she had caught — the extent of the recognition expressed — in Lady Wantridge's face. It had come absolutely of a sudden, straight out of the opposition of the two figures before her — quite as if a concussion had struck a light. The light was helped by her quickened sense that her friend's silence on the incident of the day before showed some sort of consciousness. She looked surprised. "Do you know my brother?"

"*Do* I know you?" Lady Wantridge asked of him.

"No, Lady Wantridge," Scott pleasantly confessed, "not one little mite!"

"Well then if you *must* go —!" and Mamie offered her a hand. "But I 'll go down with you. Not *you!*" she launched at her brother, who immediately effaced himself. His way of doing so — and he had already done so, as for Lady Wantridge, in respect to their previous encounter — struck her even at the moment as an instinctive if slightly blind tribute to her possession of an idea; and as such, in its celerity, made her so admire him, and their common wit, that she on the spot more than forgave him his queerness. He was right. He could be as queer as he liked! The queerer the better! It was at the foot of the stairs, when she had got her guest down, that what she had assured Mrs. Medwin would come did indeed come. "*Did* you meet him here yesterday?"

"Dear yes. Is n't he too funny?"

"Yes," said Mamie gloomily. "He *is* funny. But had you ever met him before?"

"Dear no!"

499

"Oh!"—and Mamie's tone might have meant many things.

Lady Wantridge however, after all, easily overlooked it. "I only knew he was one of your odd Americans. That's why, when I heard yesterday here that he was up there awaiting your return, I didn't let that prevent me. I thought he might be. He certainly," her ladyship laughed, "*is*."

"Yes, he's very American," Mamie went on in the same way.

"As you say, we *are* fond of you! Good-bye," said Lady Wantridge.

But Mamie had not half done with her. She felt more and more—or she hoped at least—that she looked strange. She *was*, no doubt, if it came to that, strange. "Lady Wantridge," she almost convulsively broke out, "I don't know whether you'll understand me, but I seem to feel that I must act with you—I don't know what to call it!—responsibly. He *is* my brother."

"Surely—and why not?" Lady Wantridge stared. "He's the image of you!"

"Thank you!"—and Mamie was stranger than ever.

"Oh he's good-looking. He's handsome, my dear. Oddly—but distinctly!" Her ladyship was for treating it much as a joke.

But Mamie, all sombre, would have none of this. She boldly gave him up. "I think he's awful."

"He is indeed—delightfully. And where *do* you get your ways of saying things? It isn't anything—and the things aren't anything. But it's so droll."

"Don't let yourself, all the same," Mamie consistently pursued, "be carried away by it. The thing can't be done — simply."

Lady Wantridge wondered. "'Done simply'?"

"Done at all."

"But what can't be?"

"Why, what you might think — from his pleasantness. What he spoke of your doing for him."

Lady Wantridge recalled. "Forgiving him?"

"He asked you if you could n't. But you can't. It 's too dreadful for me, as so near a relation, to have, loyally — loyally to *you* — to say it. But he 's impossible."

It was so portentously produced that her ladyship had somehow to meet it. "What 's the matter with him?"

"I don't know."

"Then what 's the matter with *you?*" Lady Wantridge enquired.

"It 's because I *won't* know," Mamie — not without dignity — explained.

"Then *I* won't either!"

"Precisely. Don't. It 's something," Mamie pursued, with some inconsequence, "that — somewhere or other, at some time or other — he appears to have done. Something that has made a difference in his life."

"'Something'?" Lady Wantridge echoed again. "What kind of thing?"

Mamie looked up at the light above the door, through which the London sky was doubly dim. "I have n't the least idea."

"Then what kind of difference?"

Mamie's gaze was still at the light. "The difference you see."

Lady Wantridge, rather obligingly, seemed to ask herself what she saw. "But I don't see any! It seems, at least," she added, "such an amusing one! And he has such nice eyes."

"Oh *dear* eyes!" Mamie conceded; but with too much sadness, for the moment, about the connexions of the subject, to say more.

It almost forced her companion after an instant to proceed. "Do you mean he can't go home?"

She weighed her responsibility. "I only make out — more's the pity! — that he does n't."

"Is it then something too terrible — ?"

She thought again. "I don't know what — for men — *is* too terrible."

"Well then as you don't know what 'is' for women either — good-bye!" her visitor laughed.

It practically wound up the interview; which, however, terminating thus on a considerable stir of the air, was to give Miss Cutter for several days the sense of being much blown about. The degree to which, to begin with, she had been drawn — or perhaps rather pushed — closer to Scott was marked in the brief colloquy that she on her friend's departure had with him. He had immediately said it. "You'll see if she does n't ask me down!"

"So soon?"

"Oh I've known them at places — at Cannes, at Pau, at Shanghai — do it sooner still. I always know when they will. You *can't* make out they don't love me!" He spoke almost plaintively, as if he wished she could.

"Then I don't see why it has n't done you more good."

"Why Mamie," he patiently reasoned, "what more good *could* it? As I tell you," he explained, "it has just been my life."

"Then why do you come to me for money?"

"Oh they don't give me *that!*" Scott returned.

"So that it only means then, after all, that I, at the best, must keep you up?"

He fixed on her the nice eyes Lady Wantridge admired. "Do you mean to tell me that already — at this very moment — I'm not distinctly keeping *you?*"

She gave him back his look. "Wait till she *has* asked you, and then," Mamie added, "decline."

Scott, not too grossly, wondered. "As acting for *you?*"

Mamie's next injunction was answer enough. "But *before* — yes — call."

He took it in. "Call — but decline. Good!"

"The rest," she said, "I leave to you." And she left it in fact with such confidence that for a couple of days she was not only conscious of no need to give Mrs. Medwin another turn of the screw, but positively evaded, in her fortitude, the reappearance of that lady. It was not till the fourth day that she waited upon her, finding her, as she had expected, tense.

"Lady Wantridge *will* — ?"

"Yes, though she says she won't."

"She says she won't? O — oh!" Mrs. Medwin moaned.

"Sit tight all the same. I *have* her!"

"But how?"

"Through Scott — whom she wants."

"Your bad brother!" Mrs. Medwin stared. "What does she want of him?"

"To amuse them at Catchmore. Anything for that. And he *would*. But he shan't!" Mamie declared. "He shan't go unless she comes. She must meet you first — you're my condition."

"O — o — oh!" Mrs. Medwin's tone was a wonder of hope and fear. "But does n't he want to go?"

"He wants what *I* want. She draws the line at *you*. I draw the line at *him*."

"But *she* — does n't she mind that he's bad?"

It was so artless that Mamie laughed. "No — it does n't touch her. Besides, perhaps he is n't. It is n't as for *you* — people seem not to know. He has settled everything, at all events, by going to see her. It's before her that he's the thing she'll have to have."

"Have to?"

"For Sundays in the country. A feature — *the* feature."

"So she has asked him?"

"Yes — and he has declined."

"For *me*?" Mrs. Medwin panted.

"For me," said Mamie on the door-step. "But I don't leave him for long." Her hansom had waited. "She'll come."

Lady Wantridge did come. She met in South Audley Street, on the fourteenth, at tea, the ladies whom Mamie had named to her, together with three or four others, and it was rather a master-stroke for Miss

Cutter that if Mrs. Medwin was modestly present Scott Homer was as markedly not. This occasion, however, is a medal that would take rare casting, as would also, for that matter, even the minor light and shade, the lower relief, of the pecuniary transaction that Mrs. Medwin's flushed gratitude scarce awaited the dispersal of the company munificently to complete. A new understanding indeed on the spot rebounded from it, the conception of which, in Mamie's mind, had promptly bloomed. "He shan't go *now* unless he takes you." Then, as her fancy always moved quicker for her client than her client's own — "Down with him to Catchmore! When he goes to amuse them *you*," she serenely developed, "shall amuse them too." Mrs. Medwin's response was again rather oddly divided, but she was sufficiently intelligible when it came to meeting the hint that this latter provision would represent success to the tune of a separate fee. "Say," Mamie had suggested, "the same."

"Very well; the same."

The knowledge that it was to be the same had perhaps something to do also with the obliging spirit in which Scott eventually went. It was all at the last rather hurried — a party rapidly got together for the Grand Duke, who was in England but for the hour, who had good-naturedly proposed himself, and who liked his parties small intimate and funny. This one was of the smallest and was finally judged to conform neither too little nor too much to the other conditions — after a brief whirlwind of wires and counterwires, and an iterated waiting of hansoms at various doors

MRS. MEDWIN

— to include Mrs. Medwin. It was from Catchmore itself that, snatching a moment on the wondrous Sunday afternoon, this lady had the harmonious thought of sending the new cheque. She was in bliss enough, but her scribble none the less intimated that it was Scott who amused them most. He *was* the feature.